A Murder of Crows

Sarah Yarwood-Lovett

First published in Great Britain in 2022 by

embla books

Bonnier Books UK Limited
4th Floor, Victoria House, Bloomsbury Square, London, WC1B 4DA
Owned by Bonnier Books
Sveavägen 56, Stockholm, Sweden

A CIP catalogue record for this book is available from the British Library.

ISBN: 9781471415333

This book is typeset using Atomik ePublisher

Printed and bound in Great Britain by Clays Ltd, Elcograf S.p.A.

Embla Books is an imprint of Bonnier Books UK
www.bonnierbooks.co.uk

MIX
Paper | Supporting
responsible forestry
FSC
www.fsc.org
FSC® C018072

For Sandra and Stuart Yarwood:
Mum and Dad.
For all the love, inspiration, unshakeable belief,
and the big streak of stubborn in our DNA.
And *then* . . .

Chapter 1

Wednesday 25th August – 4.30 p.m.

Sophie's hand trembled as she slid the key into the lock. She hated the dark. But she forced herself, and the key, to overcome the lock's resistance, gritting her teeth as ornate ironwork gouged her thumb and fingers. *Oh, come on, you absolute ...* A click. Relief. Then dread. Flexing her hand, she pushed the oak door that led from the old house into the tunnel, almost glad when it didn't budge.

But she had to go in. No avoiding it. Setting her shoulder against the door, Sophie shoved. The door creaked, then flew open, sending her stumbling down the steps, into darkness. As she fumbled for the light on her phone, the dank icy air cut through to her bones. It was like walking into a morgue.

Low battery. Damn. She'd better be quick. Then she'd search the car for a charger.

Something dragged through her long blonde hair. She ducked, swallowed a shriek, clawing at her hair. The dangling cobweb, dense with dust, stroked her cheek as the disturbed spider scurried across her neck. Desperate to flick it off her, Sophie swatted it, shaking herself. Imagining it creeping under her shirt, she shuddered, her flesh crawling.

She ached to run back. But she drew a breath. *Come on.* A distant creak from the house made her spin round. She peered into the dark tunnel, a blur of black after she'd been staring at bright light. *Maybe the draught had made the door swing.* She shivered. The itch crawled over her skin again.

Her light cut out. She stabbed the phone's screen, pressed the button. Nothing. *Great.*

In the dark, the walls closed in. She shrank down and crept towards the house. A sense of something – *someone?* – lanced her with fear.

The crunch of stones made her freeze. *That wasn't my footstep.* Her heart pounded.

'H … Hello?' She forced the sound out through dry lips and a tight grimace of dread. She sensed rather than saw the shadowy form. Her panic spiked. She stumbled towards the house, the sliver of light, *safety*.

Suddenly, a dazzling, bright white light blinded her. She held up her hands, squinting, shrinking.

A heavy blow smashed the side of Sophie's skull, flinging her against the wall. Pain exploded in her head, her stomach boiling with nausea. Lurching forwards, Sophie flinched from the sharp light, cradling her head with protective arms. She touched her temple, fear thudding as her fingertips grew warm, sticky.

A sharp metallic tang slammed the back of her nostrils.

She scrabbled, frantic, the iron taste of blood in her mouth, pounding behind her eyes.

She fell to her knees. Another strike.

Wednesday 25th August – 4.30 p.m.

Deep in the woods of Manor House Farm, Dr Nell Ward tore away the last decomposing leaves clinging to the wrought-iron gates of the tunnel, set in the embankment's slope, and staggered back, panting. The earthy odour of decay filled her mouth and nose as she flicked rancid leaves off her hands. She didn't care. *Found you. At last.*

It had taken nearly an hour to dig through decades of leaf litter to expose the gates. She wouldn't have known they were there but for the Edwardian map depicting the area as it was 400 years ago. That, and a slight dip in the bank. Her persistence had paid off.

Nell checked the map, showing the tunnel's 1,500-metre underground route from the cellar of the fifteenth-century house to the entrance before her. The tunnel snaked below the neglected formal garden and the habitats she'd surveyed earlier.

The meadow's haze of flowering plants and grasses had revealed chalk grassland so biodiverse it could be a nature reserve. Amongst buzzing invertebrates, she'd watched a rare red-shanked carder bee bumble up the spiral blooms of an autumn lady's tresses orchid.

The soaring oaks and beeches rang with the melodies of twenty-four bird species, plus one silent, solemn little owl who'd observed her working. It was a joy to survey near home for once. Especially when it meant exploring private, gloriously undisturbed ancient woodland, settled against the chalk downland hills that rolled across south-east England. She'd had a good day's work; caught the musky scent of fox, tracked down a badger sett and found proof of dormice. And now she could see if the tunnel was suitable for hibernating bats.

Grabbing the fedora from her rucksack, Nell took a selfie by the gate. She groaned at her pale face, flushed, spattered with skeletal leaves, a livid scratch across her forehead still bleeding from crawling through brambles earlier. But she sent the photo to Adam anyway, with the text:

Indiana Jones got nothing on me – found our Tunnel of Doom.

His reply was instant: NO WAY! 👍

Nell's eyes strayed to his profile picture: even in the tiny image, his wide, irreverent grin was apparent, the sleeves of his old hoodie pushed up strong forearms, a wave of dark hair fallen across shining eyes. Typing bubbles appeared. She waited for his text.

Love your authentic ecology look. What's your hedge count today? 😜

She felt a smile tug at her lips, a fizz in her stomach at the hint of flirting. *Don't be an idiot. Adam flirts with everyone.* Despite his mum's best efforts to encourage him to settle down with a nice Punjabi girl. Which would count her out. Even if she was interested. Once, while they'd been mid reptile survey, she'd heard him on the phone to his mum, beginning to agree to a date, side-eyeing her, then switching to Punjabi. Nell had been measuring an adder and prepared to tease him, a thirty-something man, being matchmade by his mum. But he hadn't seemed embarrassed. He just shot Nell *that grin* and said he couldn't possibly disappoint her. When Nell asked if he meant his mum, he laughed and said no, his prospective match. Nell rolled her eyes then, and realised she was doing it now. Even though she was in the same boat, with parents keen to see her safely paired up. Not just because of the whole inheritance thing. Ever since the … *incident*, there had been general *wariness*. Nell shuddered at the memory, sharp as the brambles she'd crawled through. She wasn't getting involved with anyone any time soon. Certainly not a colleague. Not when she took such pains to keep her private life firmly separate from work.

Nell put her phone away. Then took it out again and texted:

Crawled through about 20 hedges today. Plus, badger sett right in the sodding brambles.

It was almost 5 p.m., so she added:

Better get on. Lots to do before you get here tonight.

The rusted gates needed a firm shove, and then only parted just enough for her to squeeze through. She braced herself, knowing it would be like stepping into a fridge. Water dripped from the roof with doleful, echoing plips on pot-holed ground. Her site boots squelched in puddles, crunched over bricks. Reaching up to wiggle a lump of loose mortar in the gappy brick ceiling, Nell imagined hibernating, frost-speckled bats snuggled in the crevices, come the winter. *Perfect.*

She paced 400 metres into the tunnel, noting the temperature. Scanning the crumbling walls, she spotted some short, thin pellets: bat droppings. *Yes!* Carefully, she scraped as many as she could find into a sample pot, finished her notes, and shoved her kit in her bag.

As she turned to leave, the hairs on the back of her neck shivered to attention.

She froze.

It wasn't just a response to the deep-in-the-bones coldness. Or the dark. Or being alone. She was used to all that. Holding her breath, Nell listened, heart thumping.

A droplet of water splashed beside her, making her flinch. She turned off her torch and stared into the darkness, her senses tingling.

A dull clank echoed from the bowels of the tunnel.

Dark dread slithered down her spine. Stepping back, Nell winced at the quiet clink of one brick nudging another. A brick must have fallen from the ceiling, smashed on the floor.

Yet her skin prickled at *something*. A primal need to run streaked through her.

Resisting, she assessed. Listened. Droplets, like an irregular clock, urged her to *move*.

Alert as a cat, Nell crept with measured steps, flinching at the crunch under her boots. With shaking legs, she hurried, then dashed to the gates.

Squeezing out, she jerked back as her rucksack caught. Her body flashed with panic. She yanked, twisted, tugged her bag.

It pulled free. Nell shot forwards on her knees, gasping, sweat slicking down her back.

A rustle in the leaves made her spin round and leap to her feet. The blackbird, rummaging in the leaves Nell had dug through, clattered into the sky with a warning shriek.

Nell's deep exhale made her sag. Dusting mud off her hands, she wished she could brush off her unsettling uncertainty as easily. She got out her phone to call Adam, then pocketed it. She didn't want him, or anyone else in the office, to think she was an idiot, spooked at falling mortar, needing a hand hold to do her job.

In the bright summer sunshine, she felt ridiculous. *Stupid overactive imagination.*

Chapter 2

DS James Clark leaned out of the car window to press the video intercom on the gatepost. Unable to reach, he opened the car door and released his seatbelt, half-hanging out of the car and stretching his arm until he just … managed … to tap the button. Next to him, his DCI, Val Johnson, looked out of the window, as if she'd not noticed his misalignment of the car.

He couldn't tell what lay beyond the solid wood, seven-foot-high gates, but this wasn't where he'd expected their first person of interest to live: the exclusive end of Cookingdean village, where rambling gardens of tucked-away listed cottages met downland hills. Driving here, the winding leafy lane from Pendlebury had brought them through the narrow high street with Tudor houses sprinkled between family-owned shops. They'd turned at The Mill, a destination pub opposite the cricket green, gone past the quaint church and headed down a flowering high-banked, single-track lane, to these gates.

The intercom buzzed. 'Hello? Can I help you?' a woman's voice asked. Well-spoken, assertive, but clipped, as if her reception and the fortress-like entrance were designed to deter.

'We're looking for Dr Nell Ward. We're from the Major Crime Team at Pendlebury police station. I'm DS James Clark, with DCI Val Johnson.'

A pause, then, 'What's happened?'

James glanced at Val, then leaned towards the camera. 'We're making some enquiries. Can we come in? It's easier to talk face to face.'

'Sure. Look, I'm in the middle of something. But come in.' A buzz released the gates, which slid silently open. Inside, a stable block had been reimagined as a triple garage, and a long, squat flint barn seemed to have been converted into two semi-detached homes. The state-of-the-art security was inconspicuous unless you knew what you were looking for: burglar alarm flanked with infra-red security lights, and discreet cameras which tracked their car, and now them as they walked to the wide oak door set in a glass frame. A quick flash of movement accompanied the rattle of a security chain and the thunk of the door's deadlock. It opened a crack.

'Hi, may I check your badges?'

He and Val held their IDs up to the gap, one above the other. Neither expected their ID to be checked, nor to hear Dr Ward call 101 and ask for their descriptions. James wasn't sure if he was impressed or irritated by her unusual meticulousness, and he checked his watch, sighing. The early hours call-out to examine the murder victim in that dank, musty tunnel had kicked the team into gear. He itched to make progress. And, once they'd finished here, they could finally grab breakfast and coffee. *God, I need a coffee. This is going to be a long day.*

The image of the murdered woman in a pool of her own blood was burned into his mind: Sophie Crows' right temple, above eyes widened with shock, was battered, bloody, caved in. Bright white fragments of bone splintered across a lumpen soup of vermilion clotted blood. The stark, intimate sight of her brain matter, wormed from the safe enclosure of her skull, had made James heave. Even now, he bit the inside of his lip, swallowed hard.

A tinny voice came through Dr Ward's phone. 'DS James Clark, six foot, dark hair, blue eyes, mid-thirties. DCI Val Johnson, five-nine, grey bobbed hair. Wouldn't like to quote her age.'

Seeing Val pretend not to hear, James hid a grin. Val was a master of the inscrutable expression. It made her seem in control, unshockable. He'd tried to emulate it, with varied success. Like him, Val had had a series of late nights. Unlike him, her tailored grey suit was sharp, white shirt so crisp it looked starched, her appearance as organised as her mind. Her entrusting him to coordinate this case was huge. He had a lot to live up to.

When Dr Ward ended the call, the door closed while she rummaged with the chain. James's impatience was swept away when he saw her and found himself smiling into deep brown eyes, bright with amber flecks. They were sparky, lively, with a hint of mischief, despite the shadow of concern across her face. That was understandable; everyone worried when he and Val called. But it made Dr Ward's delicate features, emphasised with the cute pixie cut, quite fawn-like. He held her gaze one second too long.

The startling, almost-forgotten sensation of attraction stirred. It had been two years since he'd split up with his ex. Burying heartbreak and wounded pride in work had done James's career wonders. But his ex had been an idiot to imagine a detective couldn't spot that she was cheating on him; reading body language was second nature. So, when he noticed Dr Ward's eyes flick to his lips – the briefest of micro-expressions – it took effort to hide his tingle at what might be mutual attraction. Somehow, he forced a neutral, professional face in front of Val.

Nell handed back their ID. 'Thanks, DS Clark, DCI Johnson.'

'Please, call me Val.'

'James.' His smile was usually warm at this point, a deliberate tactic to invite first-name terms, nurturing familiarity to get under someone's guard. But today he didn't need to fake his keenness to build a rapport.

She smiled back. 'Call me Nell. I hope you don't mind me checking. I never have visitors, and it's quiet out here. What's this all about?' A white cotton glove, like the type you'd wear to handle ancient artefacts, dangled between her fingers. She wiggled her hand into it. The manoeuvre was awkward, as her other gloved hand held a bundle of tissue and a medical-looking pipette.

James stared at the tissue as it moved. 'Er … As I said, we're just making some enquiries.'

He followed Nell inside and tried not to let his jaw drop at an interior design that belonged in one of his collectors' copies of *Architectural Digest*. Beyond the hallway's coat cupboard, a vaulted ceiling arced over the living area. Past a reclaimed-wood dining table, his eye was led to glazed bifolding doors to a walled garden and downland views. A maddening aroma of rich coffee wafted from the statement kitchen, off to his left, where navy cupboards and wood countertops were crafted between the barn's chunky timbers, hung with gleaming copper pans. Antique rugs lent warmth to the patinaed flagstones, and stairs led to a glass landing and bedrooms over the kitchen and two other closed rooms. *Crikey, how much did ecologists get paid?*

He'd always imagined barn conversions, with all the wood and exposed rough walls, to be draughty or dusty, with spiders lurking in cobwebby corners. But this place was pleasingly immaculate. The flint faces in the wall practically sparkled. He made a point of wiping his shoes on the doormat, delighted to win a smile from Nell as she led them to the kitchen.

'Can you tell me what your enquiries are about?' asked Nell.

Knowing Val would make herself unobtrusive, to give him the chance to lead the conversation, James began. 'We understand you were at Manor House Farm two days ago.' As the colour drained from Nell's already pale face, concern warred with a shiver of instinct. *Jesus. She knows something.* 'We have a few questions about what you were doing there.'

'Is … Is this about Sophie Crows? Has something happened to her?'

Quite the conclusion to jump to. He watched her carefully. 'Why would you say that?'

'I …' Her cheeks flamed. 'I just had a feeling something was up. And when she didn't show up to our meeting …'

The coffee pot's beep made her jump. A Pavlovian response made James's stomach growl but he ignored it.

'Oh, I'm sorry. Can I get you a drink?'

James focused on Nell. 'Hang on. Sophie *didn't* meet you?' Nell's scheduled meeting with their murder victim was why she was the first – maybe only – potential witness on their list.

'No. Even though her car was there …'

James prodded his iPad into life, listing questions. How did she know it was Sophie's car if Sophie wasn't there? Where was it parked? His team had found it this morning in the locked garage. Unless the door had been locked since Nell's visit, she couldn't have seen in through the window without scaling a fence and climbing along it. And why on earth would she do that?

'If you had cause for concern,' he asked, 'did you call the police to mention it? Get an incident number?' His finger hovered, poised to note it so he could chase it up.

She shook her head, cheeks reddening even more. 'No. I … I thought I was being paranoid. It's not unusual for clients to skip meetings. Things crop up at the last minute.'

'But you thought something was wrong? You even asked if something had happened to Sophie as soon as we asked you about Manor House Farm.'

Nell shifted, looking uncomfortable.

James tried a different angle. 'So how long were you there, on Wednesday?'

'Um ... I got there about 11 a.m. and left about ten thirty.'

James noted the times, then frowned. 'Do you mean you left at 11.30 a.m?'

'No. My meeting with Sophie was at 6 p.m. And I left at about half-ten at night.'

They'd been informed the meeting between Nell and Sophie was earlier. *What the hell had she been doing there all that time?* 'We understood your meeting with Sophie was at 5 p.m.'

James's eyes flicked to Val. Her alert body language, still, leaning forward, eyes narrowed, meant he'd have to shift gears. He'd be selective about what he asked now, in case any questions would be better served in a more ... formal setting. He held in a sigh.

As his DCI appraised Nell, Val's eyes rested on the scratch across her forehead. Nell caught her gaze, rubbed it self-consciously with the back of her hand. Turning to James to answer his question, Nell shook her head. She wiggled her free hand out of her glove, looking at the bundle in her other hand, as if she'd forgotten about what she'd been doing. Tilting her hips, she winkled her phone from her pocket, unlocked it one-handed ... *just* – her thumb stretching across the screen. She flicked through her emails, then passed her phone to the detectives. 'Here are my emails with the project manager, Anna Maddison, arranging it for 6 p.m.'

The tissue in Nell's other hand twitched and a pink nose snuffled from the burrito-like wrapping. James took the excuse to lean in. 'What have you got there?'

'Sorry, I was mid-treatment when you arrived. He's an injured long-eared bat.' James's eyes widened, curious, and she looked surprised, pleased, at his interest. 'If he's a grey long-eared, he's one of the UK's rarest mammals. I need to measure him to check, but his bandit mask is a good indication. See? So I've called this one Zorro.'

James hid a shudder but stepped back. *Bloody bats.*

'He was attacked by a cat and at death's door. I've made him use energy he barely has to warm up so I can hand-feed him ...'

'Oh.' James took the hint. 'Well, feel free to carry on while we talk.'

'Thanks. Come on through.' She stood, nodding at the freshly brewed coffee. 'And if you'd like a drink and don't mind helping yourself, mugs are in there.'

'Thank you.' James sprang into action at the corner dedicated to coffee pot, kettle, toaster and espresso machine, taking care not to spill anything in a kitchen gleaming with surgical cleanliness. Val arched an eyebrow as she passed him the milk, pausing before she closed the copper – custom? – retro fridge. She, too, it seemed, felt the need to polish off her finger-marks.

The utility room was one of the closed rooms, where a wide counter accommodated the bat's vast mesh enclosure. An angled lamp lit a tray with mealworms and implements. Nell sat at the counter while James and Val stood in the doorway – him clutching his coffee, Val scanning Nell's emails.

As Val checked all the email folders, James knew it was up to him to keep Nell talking. Something he'd done a hundred times in other investigations. But now with her, it somehow felt awkward; he couldn't deny he found her attractive. Finally, he started to speak, but recoiled as Nell reached for the wiggling mealworms, placed ten in a row and decapitated them one by one with nail scissors. Picking up one wriggling, headless body she squeezed its custardy innards up to the neck, offering it to the bat, 'OK, poppet. Dinnertime.'

Averting his eyes, James asked, 'So you were at Manor House Farm for nearly twelve hours. What were you doing there all that time?'

'Ecology surveys.' The bat flinched from the squirming worm. 'Oh, come on, poppet.' She raised the worm to the bat's nose. The bat sniffed, then chomped the worm's golden body with tiny jaws. James's stomach turned. Catching Nell's face, he forced a smile. 'Protected species, aren't they? You work with the Bat Conservation Trust?'

'Volunteer. Around the day job.'

'BCT work with our Wildlife Crime Unit sometimes.'

It was no good: as she fed the bat another worm, he felt sick.

She dabbed a tiny spatula in a pot marked ANTIBIOTIC CREAM and painted it on the bat's back teeth, then offered water from the pipette. 'Here you go, poppet, this'll wash away the taste.' She explained,

'The cat injured Zorro's elbow joint and punctured a wing, so there's a risk of infection. If he was a feisty pipistrelle I wouldn't worry. But long-eareds are fragile. He barely drank yesterday. I can't let him die on my watch.' On cue, Zorro chewed another worm.

James had seen a cat flap in the thick oak door. 'Ah. Is your cat the culprit?' He moved closer and leaned against the counter.

Nell shook her head as she fed Zorro another worm. 'I keep Jezebel in at night, when she'd hunt most.'

'I'd have thought with all the wildlife they kill, cats would be the ecologist's enemy?' He didn't mean the words to sound so provocative, tried to add warmth with a smile.

'I can't help being a slave to my cat. She was dumped by the M25 when she was a few weeks old. I don't think even the most saintly ecologist could resist a kitten.' Zorro seized an offered mealworm. 'And I'm a pragmatist, not a purist.' She glanced up at him with a half-smile. 'So if you're expecting me to be a tree-hugging, evangelical vegan, I'll disappoint you.'

Her conspiratorial delivery, her dark-eyed gleam under darker lashes, flashed heat through him. *I wouldn't say I'm disappointed.* But then she squeezed out the guts of another mealworm for the sodding bat. For the second time that morning, James wanted to heave. He turned to Val, thumbing towards the door. 'I'll, er … while you're … I'll just …'

Val glanced up from Nell's phone and nodded. He could put the time to good use, investigating the intriguing Jekyll and Hyde living area. Fascinated, he drank everything in. This end of the room was normal: sofas around a low coffee table opposite the TV, tasteful nature prints on the wall, framed photos on the dresser. He scanned them for signs of Nell having a romantic partner, telling himself it was just standard background intel. The photos were mostly other couples or groups, all dressed up for fancy events, but none with her obviously paired up. One shot was vintage-style, cute, with her in a boilersuit beside a classic car, oil streaks on her face. An interest in cars was an improvement on bats. He hoped Val would ask Nell if she had a partner; he'd look too interested in her reply.

The other end of the room held an array of well-ordered oddities, inviting inspection; a microscope took up one side of the wide desk, in front of the window, with rows of Petri dishes and canisters of samples.

Beside them, a scalpel, syringe and metal pins from something that looked like a pathologist's dissection kit were set out.

Bookcases lined the far wall, bottom rows heaving with textbooks: *Genetics, Chemistry, Microbiology, Physiology,* upper shelves crammed with journals, articles, academic papers and artefacts. A tiny, perfectly woven bird's nest sat beside two white tubs labelled BADGER-BAITING PELLETS. He remembered a prosecution the Wildlife Crime Unit had made over badger baiting, digging badgers out of setts to fight dogs bred to kill. *Can't imagine Nell being involved. Unless … was she a saboteur?* Unease thudded. He hoped not. That was a brutal world.

An open box protruded from the shelf below, labelled HEAD COUNT in thick red pen, 13 written in pencil, over traces of erased numbers. James squatted, peering in to see creamy, domed skulls in various shapes and sizes. A noise made him leap up, his elbow knocking something. Turning, he saw thin brown pellets scattered across the desk.

In embarrassed haste, James swept the pellets into his hand, funnelled them back into the narrow canister, trying to catch any that dropped to the desk.

Nell approached. 'Zorro's eating well, so I can give you my full attention.' She took in what he'd been doing and irritation flashed. 'I'm sorry I kept you. But I don't appreciate strangers rifling through my home.' Her tone was tight with indignation, her breathing steady like she was striving to compose herself.

He never apologised for opportunistic searches, but clumsiness – and upsetting her – made him guilty. 'Sorry, I spilled your … your … what are these?' He raised the pot, labelled MHF.

'Droppings. I'm sending them off for DNA analysis.' Her face stretched in concern. 'Oh, for God's sake, have they gone everywhere?' She ran over, but the way she stopped short, scanning the floor before treading, reminded him of his SOCO colleagues assessing a crime scene to ensure they didn't trample on evidence.

'I only spilled them on the desk. And I scooped them all back up.' James let her check the canister's contents, then fix the lid firmly. 'It would be droppings.' He winced, dying to wash his hands. 'From what? No … I don't want to know. If I spill things in an ecologist's house, I deserve what I get.'

Washing his hands at the kitchen sink, James noted Val's grim face. She waited for him to dry his hands, then showed him a photo on Nell's phone. 'There are no emails moving the meeting from 6 p.m. to 5 p.m. Unless they've been permanently erased. But there's this.'

What's significant about a picture of Nell, grimacing and flushed, by some gaping entrance in a wood? He tapped the screen and the photo dropped back into the thread of texts. A friendly – *flirty?* – exchange between her and some guy called Adam. James prickled. *Are they a couple?* Then he saw it: Tunnel of Doom. *No ...* He froze, gaping. Stirring himself, he handed the phone back to Nell, thoughts racing.

Nell stared back, like a deer caught in headlights. 'What is it?' Looking at the screen, outrage stretched her face. 'What are you doing scrolling through my private messages?'

'You let us look at your communications a minute ago. And, under the circumstances, your *full* cooperation would be appreciated.' Val tilted her head, cueing James.

He took a deep breath. 'Dr Ward, the post-mortem results show Sophie Crows' murder occurred while you were at the property.' His words made her flinch, her breathing rapid, her shoulders tense. 'This makes your version of events that day very important. If you saw Sophie on Wednesday, you may have been the last person to see her alive.'

She shook her head. But then she bit her lip.

Instinct stirred again. She was hiding something. Val's unspoken expectation hung heavy. *Oh God.* He steeled himself, looked right into Nell's eyes. 'You'll need to come to the station today, to make a statement about your activities at Manor House Farm. And *exactly* what you were doing in this tunnel.'

Great. The first woman he'd been interested in for ages. Of course she'd be a suspect.

Chapter 3

James pulled up outside David Stephenson's place: the ground-floor flat of a wide, converted Georgian townhouse, to the south of Pendlebury's market town, near the Cookingdean road. Jumping out of the car, James squinted at the morning light glinting off the obnoxious gold paint job of the mid-eighties BMW, parked outside.

Beside him, DS Ashley Hollis gestured at the car. 'David's?' At James's nod, she said, 'Bold choice. There's an intriguing start to my psych assessment.'

James shot her a grin. His day always brightened when he got to work with Ashley. When they'd met at Bramshill College, she'd avoided the bravado of a new class, measuring up her cohort over her coffee. She used her unassuming appearance to her advantage; with her bright hazel eyes and her afro scooped into a high bun, she seemed younger than her thirty-five years. But her psychology background meant her insights were gold dust. And family liaison officers got closer to families; usually their primary suspects.

Muffled shouting made them now pause, then sprint to the wide sash window.

Inside, David stood with his back to them, holding his phone out. 'What the *hell* were you thinking? This'll ruin everything!' Wheeling round, he jumped at the sight of faces at the glass and threw the phone on the sofa. The red mottling on his face crept down his neck.

James raised his hand, an awkward hello, and pointed at the door. David deflated, clenched his jaw, exhaled. Then he nodded and went out to the hall.

As they walked to meet him, Ashley muttered, 'Half of all murdered women are killed by their partner, or their ex.' James recognised the mantra she recited every time she had to get close to a new family while keeping a professional distance and informing the investigation. As David opened the door, she switched on a kind, gentle smile.

David wore the same suit James had seen him in earlier, at about 1 a.m., after his panicked phone call had triggered the search team to examine Manor House Farm, then at 6 a.m. at the station to identify his wife. David had stumbled out of the mortuary, crumbled into one of the plastic seats lining the corridor, held his head in his hands and sobbed.

'Sorry.' A pinched smile flashed then faded from David's face. He gestured at the phone. 'I don't usually lose my temper like that. I … I haven't slept. And …'

'I'm so sorry for your loss, Mr Stephenson.' Ashley steered him inside. 'I'm Ashley Hollis, your family liaison officer during the investigation. Can I call you David?' As usual, she'd dropped her DS title in case it put him on guard and created a barrier. David nodded.

Inside the flat, James felt snow-blind. White and glass furniture within white walls. *A showroom had more personality.* David slammed his laptop shut and sat on an indentation on the leather sofa under the window. James imagined David had sat there all night.

'We couldn't help overhearing, though,' Ashley said. 'Everything OK?'

'Oh.' David shrugged. 'Work.' Another taut smile, a sheepish jut of his chin. 'I overreacted. I'm not thinking straight.' He rubbed a hand over his face, rasping on his stubble.

'Understandable.' Sitting down Ashley asked, 'What work do you do?'

'I'm a developer. Working with Soph on Manor House Farm. I handled the finances, planners and permissions. Sophie deals with the contractors … Dealt.' His face trembled.

'Must have made a good team.' A sympathetic nod. 'Why Manor House Farm?'

'We own it. A bequest.'

'Oh? To Sophie or to you?'

'To her.'

'Oh. So how will your work there be ruined?'

'Like I say, overreaction. My planner, Simon Mayhew, thought I'd want to defer the planning application.' He shook his head. 'Poor sod.

Only trying to be respectful. But I don't see any reason to delay. I need something to do.' His leg jittered. 'It's what Soph would've wanted.'

James sat. 'Did any contractors, interested parties, or locals know about the tunnel?'

'No one I can think of. My project manager, Anna Maddison, would know.'

'I'll ask. I've got her details.' Anna had confirmed Sophie's meeting with Nell.

Glancing at David's wedding ring, then the pictures on the mantelpiece, Ashley asked, 'Sophie Crows. She kept her family name?'

David's fingers curled into his palms. 'For her family's sake, I think.'

'Was she close to her family?' Ashley picked up the two framed photos, the only adornments in the plain room. A young Sophie on a horse with a rosette, beside beaming grandparents. A wonky shot of a Vegas chapel behind close-up faces, Sophie's half-covered with a cerise veil, David, laughing, sheened with sweat.

'Yes. Her parents died when she was young,' David said. 'No siblings. Her grandparents raised her. She adored them. Her grandmother, Marjorie Crows, is at Applewood Residential Care Home.' He gestured at the photos. 'That's why we eloped. My parents are divorced, sister's abroad. It seemed best. We ... well, I tried to turn it into an adventure. So the obvious absences wouldn't hurt so much.'

'Have you told Mrs Crows yet about ... Sophie?' Ashley asked.

'No. Ah, no. Not yet. I only called Applewood yesterday to ask the receptionist if Sophie was there. She wasn't.' David winced. 'I will call, but I'm dreading it.'

'Would you like me to break the news? I'll need to see her anyway.'

'Would you?' David's shoulders dropped.

'Of course. And while I'm here, may I look around? I may find something that helps us.'

'Uh ... sure.'

'Could I take Sophie's computer?' At his nod, Ashley added, 'And yours?'

'Mine?' David's frown was the foggy expression of someone exhausted and overwrought, trying to follow a conversation. 'Er ... Yeah, OK. But I'll need it for work.'

'We'll get it back to you as quickly as we can.'

His shrug was reluctant, but Ashley took it as a yes, deftly bagging the laptop and labelling it before he could protest. 'Thanks, David.'

As Ashley headed for the hall, James leaned forward, changing the subject and keeping him talking. 'Since I last saw you, we've confirmed Sophie's time of death was between 4 and 6 p.m. on Wednesday.'

'Wednesday.' David rubbed his face. 'She had a meeting, I think. Anna will know.'

'I know you've spoken to my colleagues, but if you can recall any of Sophie's activities on Wednesday, it would help.'

David nodded. 'I left early – before she got dressed. I had an important meeting to prepare for at the planning conference at Pendlebury Hotel. I was there from 8 a.m. Wednesday until 2 p.m. Thursday. I didn't even realise anything was wrong. I even went to the office before going home. I'd texted her and she answered some, but not all. Come to think of it, I didn't hear anything from her after Wednesday lunchtime. But I ... I wasn't worried.' His face contorted. 'She forgot to charge her phone all the time. It was often dead ...' He winced.

James tapped his iPad. SOCO had bagged Sophie's phone; it must have been on her person when they found her.

'I got home about 6 p.m. Sophie wasn't here. It got later, I got more and more worried. I drove to the manor, my office. Nothing. I rang Applewood, called her two best friends. No one had seen her. At about 11.15 p.m., I reported her missing. I wish ... I wish I'd ...' He screwed his eyes shut. 'I wish I'd never gone to that damn conference.'

'Was it busy?' James asked.

'Er, yeah. The hotel was fully booked with planners, consultants, developers.'

'Good. So you won't have any trouble giving us an alibi, then.'

Friday 27th August – 9.45 a.m.

After the visit from the detectives, Nell jangled with adrenaline. When they'd arrived, her first fear was for family, especially her mother; her political work made her a target, the worry of an attack always simmering under the surface. But they'd have asked for her by the family name she preferred not to use, if that was the case: Lady Eleanor

Ward-Beaumont. But that initial thought was swept away with the memory of the tunnel. It had prickled the back of her mind since the survey.

And James hadn't exactly stood on ceremony when he'd poked through her living room. *What a nerve!* But this was a murder case. And she had to go in and make a statement. Restless, Nell texted Percy:

Free for a chat?

Her best friend didn't disappoint. Immediately, Percy FaceTimed, her copper curls bouncing from being driven over a bumpy Highland track on her Scottish estate. 'I'm showing my new gillie the ropes. Ben, meet Nell.' For a second, the phone swung to a man in a flat cap, who raised his hand from the Land Rover's steering wheel, then back to Percy. 'I've got a sec. You OK?'

Nell summarised the exchange with the detectives. Percy was horrified at the murder, asked about Nell, what would happen next, what the procedure was. 'I have to go in and make a statement. But the detective sergeant has already poked around my place.'

'Well, they'll take any opportunity, won't they? Can't blame them for that. What if you're a hardened crim?' She flashed her typically glib grin, then leaned in. 'You said the DS was James, right? How old?'

'About our age.'

'Handsome?'

'Um …' Remembering his keen blue eyes gazing into hers, quiet confidence that didn't spill into arrogance, the hint of a hidden, sexy smile, Nell bit her lip.

'Busted! *That's* why you're so riled. Did you leave your comfy pants out?'

Oh, bollocks. Did I? At least he hadn't gone upstairs. 'Well, he had no reason to search! And no right, actually; I'm a witness, not a suspect.' She scrunched her nose. 'Although, to be fair, he did apologise. And he looked like he meant it.'

'So what's your problem? Give 'em a break, Nell. They're just trying to make the investigation as speedy as possible. Go and give your statement. Doesn't sound like a one-on-one with your dishy detective'll be that much of a hardship. Oh, gotta go. I'll text later.'

Percy's pragmatism and James's questions resurrected the guilt she'd felt about not acting on her instinct. Deep in her bones, she'd known something awful had happened. She'd been denying it. Hoping ... *Was what I heard ... Sophie's murder? Could I have stopped it? Or helped her?*

Well, James needed her cooperation now. It was the least she could do. Grabbing a USB, she saved the hundreds of timestamped photos, showing her progress across the property. She printed off emails and risk assessments, adding them and receipts to her folder of survey maps. Then she transcribed her phone calls, and her texts with Adam about his tyres. He had to wait until next month to replace them. Well, she could help with that, too.

Once she'd sent a quick text to her mechanic, she checked there was nothing she could add to her paperwork for the police. If they saw where she was, and knew she hadn't seen anything, maybe it would narrow down their areas of focus.

The phone call invaded her pensive silence. She hadn't expected her mechanic to reply today. 'Leave it with me, Nell. I'll deliver the tyres to Adam after the Bank Holiday.'

It was only fair: she could afford it more easily than Adam probably could. And she'd have been the one with shredded tyres if he hadn't covered that site so she could survey Manor House Farm. She'd tell Adam she got mates' rates. Which was sort of true. But then Adam might want to know how, and that would mean more questions which she'd have to deflect. *But it's a shame, because he might be interested in this project ...*

'You tested the bike yet?' It was like her mechanic read her mind.

'Yeah.' Despite the stress, she felt her smile stretch across her face. 'Great time on the track. You were right, the acceleration's *brutal* from the electric powertrain.'

'Yeah, well, be careful. Accelerate too hard and you could dislocate both your arms.'

Packing her bag, Nell's hands shook. It made her look guilty. Well, *guiltier*. She had to get the adrenaline out of her system before she got to the station.

Maybe the suggestion from her mechanic sent her to the hall cupboard. Pushing the coats aside, she reached for her leathers. Bank

Holiday weekend traffic would be a nightmare. She couldn't make detectives wait or hold up an investigation. This was the *responsible* choice.

In the garage, she slung her leg over the prototype electric superbike and eased into the suspended saddle, a matt black sculpture around the exposed chassis. Stretching over its body, she reached for the low handles and tiptoed out, punching the button to close the door behind her.

She held back past the cricket green and pub and through the high street but, as the sweeping country lane opened before her, she squeezed the throttle until the trees blurred, leaning deep into the bends, knee skimming the road. Senses sharpening, she scanned hedgerows and verges far ahead for movement in case an animal darted out. She felt like a liquid extension of the bike, conscious of every micro-adjustment of weight and steering as she carved racing lines down the empty road. The hard hit of acceleration surged through her veins, chasing out her fears.

Chapter 4

James listened to Ashley's assessment of David Stephenson on their way back to the station.

'I haven't seen the crime scene. But, if David's our murderer, he'd be a planner. His place was tidy, organised. He's above-average intelligence, controlled even under duress. He seems good at putting a good face on things. Not just the argument on the phone. But—'

'But also a striking car which looks expensive?' James suggested.

'Yeah. And a well-cut suit hiding how he's filling out. In his thirties, like us, but going by the creases on his belt from working his way down the notches, he's getting comfortable. Could be a sign of a contented relationship? Or of a man who knows his partner's not going anywhere – either out of devotion … or out of dependency.

'Then there's all the expensive, if minimalist, furniture in the lounge. When you get to the bedroom, it's all IKEA flatpack. He has all the storage space, laid out just so. Her stuff's crammed into a wardrobe. Like she'd shrunk to fit what space he'd permit her.'

'Apparently, they were only married eight months,' James said. 'That's not a long time to move in properly. Maybe she saw it as a temporary move, just making do until they moved into the manor?'

'Or maybe he's very territorial? Over his flat and her bequest? If that's a motive and he *is* our murderer, like I say, I think he'd be meticulous. He might've practised. He'd have taken whatever he needed with him and taken it away again afterwards. No messy unknowns.' She nodded towards the mortuary as James parked. 'Let me know how it fits with the PM and SOCO's results.'

James gave a mock salute as they headed to different ends of the station building.

The hollow chemical odour, pear drops and metal, hit James as he opened the path-lab door. The crime scene manager, Dr Saunders, led him to Sophie Crows, lying on the stainless-steel table, her face ghost-white above the green medical sheet.

'Cause of death, as you know, repeated blows to the head.' Dr Saunders' latexed finger circled Sophie's shattered temple. 'The parietal bone's fairly weak, this wouldn't have taken much force. From the angle of impact, the first strike was by a right-handed attacker facing her, who struck her twice more when she was on the ground.'

She held up a clear labelled bag: a bloodied brick, with long blonde strands stuck to it. 'The weapon. Yet to be compared to others from the tunnel, but it seems the killer improvised with what was to hand. From the marks on the brick and the ground, it was dropped or thrown afterwards.'

James sighed. An opportunistic, impulsive attack probably wouldn't fit David Stephenson. *We're looking for more of a risk-taker.*

Turning, Dr Saunders pointed at her computer screen, a close-up of red specks streaking across the tunnel wall's patchy brickwork. 'Our biologist confirmed the blood spatters had three different angles of impact, so the killer struck her at least twice when she was on the ground. From the blood patterns and her lividity, Sophie wasn't moved after death. There are no fingerprints on the tunnel door, except one smudged print. We'll check it against Sophie's since, in all probability, she walked in herself.'

She clicked again, opening a picture of a partial footprint.

James leaned in. 'Aha. Nice. Not complete, but good detail. Where was it?'

Another click brought up a diagram of the tunnel, divided into thirds. 'Let me set some context.' She drew a circle around the third of the tunnel nearest the house. 'SOCO found nothing here. The tunnel floor was bricked and dry, strewn with debris up to about a third of the way in, where Sophie was found.

'But, from the end near the wood,' she pointed at the third of the tunnel furthest from the house, 'we got partial prints like this one, walking towards Sophie. They dried up as the ground got more solid, in this middle section, so it's hard to say if the wearer walked in further than that. But if they didn't get further than the prints, they wouldn't have seen Sophie in torchlight. This partial print is the best we have.

Hiking boots. Small for a man, average for a woman. A specialist is taking measurements to cast a mould, work out the gait.'

She swivelled on her chair to face James. 'Before you ask, I know you want me to fast-track this. Your chief's already been on at me—'

James balked at Chief Constable Trent getting involved. 'What—'

'He's handling the press. He expects lots of interest, so he's making much of the scrutiny, the public, press, expeditious results.' She rolled her eyes but gave James a folder. 'Evidence photos for your board. And I've saved them to the case file, too. I'll keep you updated. But I'm up against it. I *would* say I'm down to a skeleton staff for your case, but …'

Her grin dissolved as James's gaze flicked to Sophie, then the floor. 'Yeah. Well, you get my point. Most of my lot's helping the road team with their burned-out car. The forensic recovery's painstaking. I'll do what I can for you. But you might want to break it to the chief that I'm not bloody Wonder Woman.'

Friday 27th August – 10.45 a.m.

By the time Nell locked her bike in the station car park, her jagged nerves had settled. The blistering ride had purged the jittery adrenaline, restored her faith in her control.

James and Val met her in reception. James's gaze flicked down to her leather trousers and rested on the outside of her knees. Self-conscious, Nell rubbed the scuff on her outer right knee, and fine dusty gravel showered the tiled floor.

Glancing between them, Val frowned, then directed them down the hall.

In the interview room, Nell hooked her leather jacket over the back of the chair, put her helmet on the table and sat down.

'You've come prepared.' Val nodded at the folder and USB Nell had pulled out from her messenger bag and set on the table. Her tone had a cynical edge. Nell's heart began to pound.

James flicked on the camera and stated their names. 'It's 11 a.m., Friday 27th August. Statement from Dr Nell Ward.'

Nell glanced at him, unsettled at the formal, unfamiliar process. She attempted a smile, her mouth dry, trying to get on friendly terms again. *Maybe James had just been trying to get me to lower my guard?*

Opening the form on his iPad, James said, 'You're not under arrest, you're free to go at any time. We've asked you for a detailed account of your activities at Manor House—'

'Sure,' Nell interrupted. 'I've saved everything to show what I did, and when. My emails with Anna Maddison to arrange the meeting, and with the local bat and badger groups for data to help plan my survey. I left home about 10.30 a.m. The risk assessment shows my route, twenty-four miles to Manor House Farm, I got petrol on the way, here's the receipt—'

James held up a hand, halting Nell's monologue. He passed her a picture of a blonde, smiling woman. 'Do you recognise her?'

The photo silenced Nell for a moment. 'No ... But ... God, she's *young*.' She glanced up. 'She must be in her twenties?' Guilt sliced through her gut again.

'Twenty-six,' James said.

Jesus. 'I ... I thought she was older. Since she was a client. And the homeowner.' *Inheritance? Poor woman, must have lost her family at a horribly young age. And now ... Sophie ... Sophie Crows ... Had she heard it before? Repetition must be making it familiar.*

'Fine. Carry on,' Val said.

As Nell reached for her folder to unfold a map, the sleeve of her top slid up her arm.

Val's eyes narrowed. 'How did you get those scratches on your arm? And your face?'

Nell tugged her sleeve down to her knuckles. 'Oh. Badger setts.' That was a full explanation in her world. But the detectives didn't look like they understood. 'I haven't found a sett yet that isn't right in the middle of brambles. I have to crawl through the thorns to survey them. It's just an occupational hazard.'

'Huh. I'd wear arm protection, or at least long sleeves.'

'Well, I do. Of course. Haven't found anything so far that can withstand the thorns.'

Val pursed her lips. 'Carry on.'

Nell had a sense of being given enough rope to hang herself. 'I arrived at 11 a.m.' As usual, she'd treated the satnav's ETA as a challenge and arrived ten minutes early. 'Or thereabouts. I parked at the lay-by near the wood, began the survey at the lake and river, then moved on to the grassland, woodland, working towards the house and grounds. These numbers on the map are photos I took, matching the timestamped photos on the USB. So you can see exactly where I was, and when.'

The detectives seemed unmoved. Nell continued, 'You see how huge the woodland is. The house is beyond the high bank.' She traced the map's topographical lines. 'For most of my survey, I wouldn't have seen the house, or anyone there, from the wood.'

Val leaned forward. 'And no one would have seen you? While you took six hours to wander around a wood.'

Nell felt her face flush at Val's scepticism. 'I wasn't wandering. I was conducting a detailed survey. Those codes on the plan are species I've recorded: trees, understorey, flora, grasses. I work out the woodland's age from ancient woodland indicator plants, like native bluebells, any veteran trees, relics of ancient hedgerows.

'Then I assess what protected species the habitat may support, and look for evidence. I listen for bird calls, look for rare plants, detect scents of species, like otter, which gives a hint of hay or jasmine tea. I comb every centimetre for the tiniest clue. Pawprints, disturbed vegetation, spraint, ground marks like scratches or snuffle-holes of badgers foraging for worms, feeding remains like owl pellets, a single hair caught on brambles or mammal paths going right through the thorns. Same again for the lake, river and grassland.'

Sensing the need to prove she did more than glance around the landscape, she took two hazelnuts from an envelope. 'See?'

James took the hazelnuts and studied them. 'What's so special about these?'

'Notice the different tooth-marks?' Nell had trained so many ecologists this year, she still couldn't help teaching. 'This one, with the vertical marks around the rim and surface?'

He squinted at the fine detail. 'Maybe?'

'Diagnostic pattern of a wood mouse. Whereas this one' – Nell pointed at the second nut – 'has a smooth rim, tooth-marks angled on the surface. Proof that the woodland supports hazel dormice, a protected species.' As she opened another envelope, he leaned in, bringing a faint, pleasant ocean-fresh scent of shower gel and aftershave.

Val held her hand up. 'Yes, OK, we can see the detail is quite … forensic. And this took you until six? When you claim your meeting with Sophie had been arranged?'

'Yes.' Nell frowned. 'And you've checked my emails from Anna Maddison, scheduling the meeting. They're the only mails I've got. I returned to the car at ten to six and drove to the manor. Even though the place seemed deserted, I knocked on the front door. Sophie wasn't there, so I left her a voicemail.' Another tidal wave of guilt. Nell swallowed. 'I emailed Anna at about six fifteen to say Sophie hadn't arrived but I'd do what I could.'

'So how long did you stay?' James asked.

'Until ten thirty.'

'Wait – at six, no one was at Manor House Farm to meet you?' Val's tone was dangerously smooth. 'Yet you stayed for a further four and a half hours. Why?'

'I could complete my survey outside, even if Sophie Crows couldn't make it.' Nell realised she was twisting her hands in her lap and clasped them. 'Clients often don't turn up. They like the idea of being around while you survey, but it can be tedious for them. They're busy juggling meetings with several surveyors, so things often crop up. Or they're held up.'

Or …

'Didn't you have to leave if the client wasn't present?' Val asked.

'No. I had permission to be there. And clients prefer me to do what I can, rather than cancel or postpone, because a return visit adds to their costs. So, I got on with it. But the survey was tricky because Adam – um – my colleague Dr Adam Kashyap, couldn't make it, either. I expected him between seven and seven thirty, but he had car trouble. He texted at seven to let me know.' Nell showed her phone to James, hanging on to it this time. He took in Adam's contact details on the screen, as Nell passed him the transcript.

James read it out. '*Sorry, Nell, was heading over but all 4 tyres flat. Rough site this morning. Booking an Uber but I'll be late for survey, sorry.* And your reply: *Don't worry. I can manage here on my own. Do you need the site car?*' He checked the message on the screen Nell held up, nodding.

Val pursed her lips. 'Unfortunate.'

'So, you were there alone,' James said. 'For the whole time? Until ten thirty? Surveying in the dark? Exactly what type of survey can you do in the dark, Dr Ward?'

She looked up, surprised at his tone. 'A bat survey, detective.'

'A bat survey. Huh.'

'Yes. Bats come out at night. So that's when we do the surveys.'

Val's mouth quirked with a swiftly hidden smile.

'That, er … explains it,' he said, nodding towards Nell's chest.

'What?' Following his gaze down to her long-sleeved T-shirt, she read the upside-down slogan that Adam had printed for a joke birthday present: ECOLOGISTS DO IT IN THE DARK. *Great*.

Val cleared her throat. 'Was that feasible? For one person to do two people's work?'

'I had to adapt it. Sophie had wanted to be present for the inspection of the house and garage, which helps because I can go inside and check loft spaces.' At their curious looks, she unfolded an architect's plan of the house. 'Inside, I look for evidence like droppings or feeding remains. Outside, I record possible access points, which can be any gap, about two centimetres or more, in pointing, tiles, soffits, fascias. Then my team and I observe those points in nocturnal bat surveys.

'Bat survey times are linked to sunset, which was 8.20 p.m. on Wednesday, so the survey began at 7.50 p.m. and ended at 10.20 p.m. I stayed until 10.30 p.m. because I'd seen some long-eared bats, and they emerge late. I waited to make sure I hadn't missed any. I counted about twenty, so I know it's a maternity roost. Zorro's probably just been weaned. And if he *does* turn out to be a rare grey, then a new maternity roost is a major find.'

James still frowned at Nell's plan, riddled with codes. She deciphered it.

'I stood here' – she pointed at the corner of the manor – 'to watch these two sides of the house. I wore headphones plugged into a bat detector to make bat calls audible. The marks on the roof are where I saw bats emerging, and these loops are their flight lines. This form has the times and species of every call. The timed sound recordings are also on the USB.'

'Did you go inside the house at any point? Or the garage?' Val asked.

'No, without Sophie turning up, both were locked. I surveyed outside and looked through windows. To see into the garage, I climbed up on the fence and shimmied along.'

'That's quite a high fence. Not an easy task,' James noted.

Val's assessing gaze travelled over Nell. 'But then, you look quite athletic. And strong.' She stared at Nell's site boots, bulky with metal insoles and steel toecaps, before meeting her eyes again. 'Even so, you do go to a lot of effort. For your bats. Did you see anything in there?'

Nell refused to shrink from Val's appraisal. 'Adam and I are certified in climbing trees and aerial rescues for bat surveys, so a fence wasn't a big deal. I didn't see much. A red Citroën DS. Personalised number plate, SMC 2000. I assumed those were Sophie's initials.'

James glanced up. 'Very precise observation.'

Growing wary, Nell crossed her arms. 'Well, I'm trained to observe. And I like cars. It's nice to spot signs that someone's attached to their car, like a number plate or tuning.'

'An ecologist who likes cats, cars and bikes. Is that allowed?' He mirrored her, folding his arms. But she glimpsed the hint of a smile, almost breaking through his professional demeanour.

Nell opened her mouth, then closed it. The electric bike experiment was just one of her projects to address her guilty pleasure's carbon footprint. At least they hadn't clocked what else was in her garage.

Val ignored the diversion. 'What happened after the survey?'

'I didn't go straight away. Zorro was attacked. I got him away from the cat and gave him some water and a quick check before heading off. Then I drove to Adam's so he could drop me home and keep the work Volvo, while his car's out of action.'

'Adam's address is in Pendlebury. Which route did you take?' Val asked.

'The country road.'

'Why not the dual carriageway?'

Nell shrugged. 'It's a nice drive, takes about the same time.'

'And there are no speed cameras on the country route.'

Nell looked up sharply. *Was he making the point that she couldn't corroborate it?* But his very blue eyes fixed her with a knowing gaze, which sent an unexpected shiver of electricity through her. She had to look away.

Val leafed through Nell's maps. 'I haven't found a plan yet that shows the tunnel's woodland entrance. How did you come to know about it?'

'The map at the bottom of that pile is Edwardian. It's the only map I've seen it on.'

Val pulled out the plan, thick from multiple folds. 'Where did you find this?'

'On a historical map website.' She clamped her lips, regretting how glib she sounded.

'Is it usual to look up historical maps? I can't see its relevance to an ecology survey.'

'Sometimes older houses like these have tunnels, ice houses, follies, cellars. They can make good hibernacula, so I usually check when I prepare for surveys.'

'How thorough of you.' Val's eyebrow arched.

'Thanks. I am thorough.' Nell tried to smile but her cheeks burned.

'We saw that you uncovered the entrance,' James said. 'Did you go in?'

'Yes, to see if it would be suitable for overwintering bats.' Nell squeezed her clasped hands. Her fingertips turned red with pooling blood as her knuckles whitened. She let go.

'What did that involve?' His gaze flicked down to Nell's fidgeting hands.

'Just a quick check. It took longer to dig the gates free. Inside, I took the temperature, did a quick inspection. I didn't walk the whole tunnel, just enough to see if it was suitable.'

The two detectives waited, a wall of silent patience.

'Bats go into torpor to hibernate, so they need stable, cold conditions. Confirming winter roosts out of season is tricky – all you can do is record the temperature. Field signs, like droppings, get lost in the debris on the floor. But some had stuck to the wall, proving its use. So I took a sample, then left.' She shuddered recalling the sound in the frigid darkness, her muscles screaming *flight*.

But Val studied Nell's map, frowning at a rust-coloured stain in the corner. She took a clear evidence bag from her pocket, labelled it, folded the map and placed it in the bag.

Nell watched her with growing alarm. 'What's the issue with the map?'

'Just something for forensics to check. I assume you won't object to giving fingerprints and DNA? You can wait here when we've finished and an officer can take those before you go.'

The scientist in Nell saw the necessity but warred with her need for privacy, especially of her personal data. Her Conservative-MP mother could testify (off the record, at least) how easy it was for government databases to lose information or be hacked. 'Only if it's unavoidable.'

'It is.' Val sent a text then looked at Nell. 'Do you and Adam work together often?'

'Yes.' Nell leaned back in her seat, her eyes fixed on Val's.

'For how long?'

'About three months.'

'Not long.'

'No. But in survey season, we work ninety- to a hundred-hour weeks, round the clock. You get to know your team mates pretty well.' *Oh God. Adam couldn't say the same about her. Even if he thought he could.*

'Does he often miss surveys? Or cancel at the last minute?'

'No.'

'What a dream colleague.'

What the hell was that supposed to mean? Nell's cheeks flamed at Adam's character being impugned.

Tilting her head, Val asked, 'How would you describe your relationship with Adam Kashyap?'

James's head whipped up from his notes, studying her as she answered, 'Colleagues.'

'That all?' Val pressed.

'Yes.'

'Four punctures, by accident rather than design, seems a bit … unlikely,' Val said.

Nell's stomach throbbed. 'Sorry, what exactly are you suggesting?'

'I'm not suggesting anything. We're gathering information. About a murder. Of a young woman. In a tunnel very few people knew about.'

Nell stared at her, torn between laughing at the absurdity of the unspoken accusation, or throwing up in horror. *I'm here to help, to give information … Aren't I …?* 'Look, I can see my being there, for so long, is … unfortunate. But surely all this corroborates my story.' The laden word toppled into silence, held by the detectives.

'Did you see or hear anything else? However small?' Val asked.

YES! Nell's palms went clammy. *But they'll ask why I didn't do something. Or help.* Her face burned. *But I didn't know for sure it was anything … significant. It was probably – most likely – a falling brick. Like hundreds of others that'd fallen.*

Chewing her cheeks, barely able to look at them, she shook her head. *Coward.*

Val stood. 'For the foreseeable, Manor House Farm is a crime scene and can't be disturbed. Make sure your colleagues know they can't access the area until further notice.'

'If you think of something which may help' – James offered his card, again looking right into her eyes – 'here's my number. Call me. Any time.' At Val's cough, he stood to leave.

Nell reeled. *It can't be over. They hadn't agreed I had nothing to do with it yet.* 'Wait! You could check with another ecologist! You'll see how long the surveys take, how accurate my notes are, and cross me off your list of suspects.' *Jesus … I'm a suspect.*

The detectives glanced at each other, then at Nell.

'What you've shown us,' said DCI Johnson, 'is that you were there. Alone. No witnesses. No alibi. At the time of the murder. Don't go far, Dr Ward. We'll need to talk to you again.'

Chapter 5

Chewing his sandwich, James stood back from the evidence board. Even Val had to be pleased with their progress: a large map covered half the board, locating Manor House Farm at thirty minutes' drive east of Cookingdean, as Dr Ward had said. Judging by her scuffed leathers, she's fast on that bike of hers – and probably in a car, too – so it wouldn't have taken her that long. The manor was also around thirty minutes from Pendlebury via country lanes; the dual carriageway was quicker, except at rush hour when the road ground to a halt and the route also took about half an hour. And, at the moment, the town's never-ending roadworks added even more time to both routes.

A sketch of the tunnel from the manor's north wing had been marked up with the locations of Sophie's body and the woodland entrance.

The photos Dr Saunders had given him showed SOCO's progress. Others showed the grounds, the woodland entrance to the tunnel masked by leaf litter, the heavy door from the utility room with the ornate iron key in the lock. A chip of red plastic about two millimetres in diameter, coated with dust was labelled, BESIDE KITCHEN DOORMAT. Headshots of Nell and David from their LinkedIn profiles: Nell before the pixie cut with artfully messy hair and long descriptions of her experience and linked articles; David's brief profile included a photo of him standing at a distance at a conference. They'd had to blow the picture up and his image was grainy. A note confirmed neither Nell nor David had any other online presence.

By contrast, Sophie's two friends – Isobel Wright and Katie Miller, who David had contacted when Sophie was missing – had every social-media account going. Ashley had pinned up the clearest headshots, angled towards the camera, cheeks sucked in, lips pouting. They seemed very image-conscious, but then they did run an online dating site together.

Val brought over coffees. 'Chief's in a bad mood. He said this would attract a lot of press and he was right. He's just gone through the wringer with local news. He's not looking forward to speaking with the nationals tonight.'

'Ah. So he doesn't think I'm up to dealing with the statements.' James hid his disappointment with a sip of coffee.

'You and me both, if so.' She sighed. 'Not a great endorsement of my application to the Strategic Command Course.'

James fixed his eyes on the board. He hadn't known Val was gunning for promotion to assistant chief constable. But it made sense. *Who'd replace her as his DCI?*

'He reckoned *appropriate* gravitas was needed,' Val continued. 'He's cancelled his leave. Except for tomorrow, when he's taking his wife to Nye Hall Hotel. Even he couldn't work on his ruby anniversary. All that trouble for the sake of the chief's old-school ego.'

James shot her a sidelong glance, waiting for the old-boy-network soapbox rant. Chief Constable Trent was such an anachronism that James had never heard anyone use his first name, Tony. He was Chief or Trent. Maybe sir, to his friends.

'Why the bloody hell has he got a team if he doesn't trust us?' Val huffed a frustrated sigh. 'And, speaking of teams, I need to discuss something delicate.'

'Oh?'

'Look, James, with the scrutiny this case will get, we can't afford for it to get messy.'

James prickled with anticipated embarrassment. 'What—?'

'I don't want to make you feel awkward, but I sense you've taken a shine to our prime suspect. Do me a favour; let me know if it's a problem. If it'll affect your judgement, we can reassign you. Reassigning isn't a big deal. Cocking up a major case *is*.'

Trying to ignore the heat in his face, James answered, 'Yes, ma'am.' The pride he'd felt at Val asking him to lead this major case corroded a little.

'Good. Because although she's very self-controlled, I'd say she's taken a liking to you.' Val paused and James knew she was appraising his response. He tried not to look pleased. 'You're about the same age, you could build a good rapport. If we can get her to open up a bit, we'll make faster progress. On this case. That you're still leading.'

Her words bolstered him, but now he felt the weight of responsibility, not just the pleasure at being trusted. 'You really see her as a prime suspect?' He felt his face flush again and groped for logic. 'Seemed more the caring, nurturing type with that bat.'

'I don't think the mealworms would agree with you.'

James grimaced at the memory.

'Even if her survey gave her a valid reason to be in the tunnel, it's a perfect excuse to cover her tracks. Given all we have to follow up on, yes, she's currently my prime suspect.'

James racked his brains. *What had he missed?*

'She's a scientist. You said she'd been working on her own projects, examining samples under her microscope, using dissection tools. She's not squeamish. But how many people do you know who keep bottles of chloroform in their fridge?'

James hid a groan. When Val had paused before closing Nell's fridge, all he'd spotted was an unusual amount of ready meals for someone with so much fancy cooking equipment.

'Can you find out if chloroform was used on Sophie? And give Saunders the historical map Nell used to find the tunnel. It looks like there's a smear of blood on the corner, I'd like to know if it's Sophie's. The scratches on Dr Ward's arms and face may account for the blood on the map, but I want to compare her DNA to any skin cells we might find under Sophie's nails.'

'Yes. I'll get on to it.' Relief surged at the chance to redeem himself.

'And let's start background checks and get onto her phone network,' Val said. 'See who she's calling and texting, and keep tabs on her location. I get the sense she's hiding something. She's as forthcoming as we could hope for over anything work-related. We can't shut her up. But ask about relationships or something personal and she shuts down to curt answers, closed body language.'

With Val's challenging expression, he had to offer something. 'Our resident psych expert says we're looking for an opportunistic risk-taker. David's a planner, organised. But Nell—'

'God, Nell even more so, with her surgical order and meticulous notes—'

'She's a risk-taker on her motorbike. From the state of her leathers, she takes some serious racing corners.'

Val's eyes narrowed and James felt her assess if that was all he'd been checking out. 'OK.' She pointed at the board. 'One picture here really bothers me.' She sipped her coffee.

James knew a test when one was thrown at him. He scoured the board, but inspiration deserted him. His stomach sank. Then he focused on a photo, leaned closer, frowning. 'Hang on ... That photo. Of the tunnel entrance in the wood? When did SOCO take it?'

'This morning.' Val's tone warmed a little.

'So that was ... that was afterwards?'

'Exactly. Nell, by her own admission and evidence, dug those gates free, went into the tunnel, allegedly to find bats. But then she buried the gates again. By hand. Until they – and her route into the tunnel – were totally invisible.'

Friday 27th August – 12.30 p.m.

Adam paused mid pull-up, his face above the high bar in his hallway, giving him a view of the street through the semicircular glass at the top of his front door – and of the woman loitering by his Subaru Forester. What the hell was she doing? She held her phone up – taking a photo? A bead of sweat trickled down his forehead as he held the position, abs tight. She seemed to be typing. She was bending down now. Was she *poking* his tyre? He dropped to the floor, grabbed his keys and sprinted outside.

'Hey! You all right? Can I help you?'

The woman sprang up, her grey bobbed hair swaying, framing an owlish face. She straightened her jacket.

Adam noticed she wore blue latex gloves and frowned. 'What's going on?'

'Are you Dr Adam Kashyap?' At his nod, she said, 'I'm DCI Val Johnson. Val.' She smiled, peeled off her gloves and showed her badge. 'I should have spoken to you first. But as I passed the car I thought I'd take a quick look.'

'I know they're all flat. But she's road legal—'

'Yes, I see that.' Val pointed at Adam's door. 'Can we chat inside?'

'What's the problem?' Adam folded his arms, then realised the position emphasised his biceps, probably making him look more combative than intended. Instead, he offered a handshake. 'What's this about?'

'It's about a murder. Of a young woman. At a site I believe you intended to visit. Manor House Farm.'

Air vacuumed out of Adam's lungs. 'W ... what?' He stared at her. 'Who? When?'

'It happened between four and six o'clock, on Wednesday evening. Two days ago.'

Adam pushed his hand through his hair. That was when Nell had been there. He had to literally tell his brain he'd seen her since. He heaved a breath, like his lungs were holey bellows, taking effort to fill.

'The young woman was Sophie Crows.' Val gently tugged him along the pavement. 'A news bulletin's going out today, appealing for witnesses.'

Adam fumbled with the key to open his door. *At four, Nell would have been wandering around the ... woods? Then the tunnel. Then house. Had it happened at the house?*

Inside, he swiped a tangle of headtorches from the sofa to a foldaway table doubling as a sideboard, and gestured for her to take a seat. He shoved aside an airer spread with clothes and perched on the mismatched chair.

'Can you tell me why you were working at Manor House Farm?'

'I was supposed to join my colleague, Nell, for a bat survey. She spent most of the day there doing the rest of the work. Surveying the lake and stream, and woodland with records of badgers. She wanted to find the sett. And she'd found out about an old tunnel. Wanted to see if it would be a bat hibernaculum.' He found the photo Nell had sent and passed his phone to Val. 'Here. She didn't know if she'd be able to find it. Or get in.'

'Yes. The entrance seems to have been buried. Can't have been a nice job ...'

'Wouldn't put Nell off. She isn't squeamish.' As Val's eyes narrowed, Adam qualified, 'She's thorough. Determined. Wouldn't think twice about digging into a tunnel.' He noticed Val scrolling through more of his texts. It didn't stop her questions.

'Do you think she'd do the same on any other project? At any other place?'

'Oh yeah. She has done. She found a forgotten grotto at one site. Totally overgrown. Needed a machete to hack her way in. Hence the Indiana Jones joke in that text. But we see all sorts on site. You can't be precious about getting your hands dirty. Or be easily put off. We've been shot at by angry tenant farmers, threatened with knives and dogs.' He shrugged. 'Not everyone is happy to have an ecologist poking around their land, especially if they're not expecting it because the communication's got mangled.'

'Does that happen often?'

'No. Just memorable when it does.' Adam grinned. Val didn't.

'Sounds stressful. What does Nell do in those sorts of situations?'

'Same as most people, I guess. Tries to defuse things. Talking, listening, explaining what we're doing, offering to leave.' He shrugged again. 'If all else fails, running.' This smile wasn't returned by the detective, either. Nebulous guilt crawled over him.

'Is she good at keeping calm under pressure, or stress?'

'I guess,' Adam said. 'Yeah, she's pretty composed.'

'And how would you describe her mood when she saw you on Wednesday night?'

'Er ... Normal. Worried, maybe.' At the narrowing of Val's eyes, he added, 'About the injured bat. She thought it could be a rare species, so she was excited about finding the roost, but worried he'd die on her watch.'

'Have you and Nell worked together long?'

'No.' *Where are all these questions going?* 'Around three months. But it seems longer. We've done so many surveys. You get close quickly when you're out at all hours.'

'Close?' Val held his gaze. 'In the colleague, friend or relationship sense?'

'Good question,' he said. 'Definitely the first two. Jury's out on the third.' Val had reached the texts from his mother. He could do without a detective seeing his mum trying to organise his love life. He nodded at the phone. 'You all done there?'

Passing it back, she said, 'I see your mother addresses you as Aravindan …?'

'Oh. Yeah, Aravindan's my given name. Adam – well, Adam seemed easier at school and it's just stuck. Socially and at work.' He raked his hair, sweaty from his workout, then realised he was probably making it stick up in crazy thick waves while he tried to look serious.

'What's your workplace like? Open plan? Do you hot desk? Use your own laptops or PCs, or do you share?'

'It's all open plan. But we have our own desks and computers. Most of us use a PC in the office and a laptop at home.'

'Do you lock your PCs when you're in the office? Practice any security protocols?'

'Not really. We all have confidential projects, but then we all work on each other's projects in one way or another – surveying, mapping, reporting.'

'Could you or anyone else read Nell's emails? Reply on her behalf? Change plans?'

'Well, theoretically.' Adam stared at the detective. 'But why would anyone want to?'

'What if you needed to swap a survey? How do you appoint who does what?'

'Those managing the project see who's free with the right skills, schedule it in, send emails to organise. Then juggle all the last-minute requests that mess up all that planning.'

'Was Manor House Farm one of those?'

'It was, actually. I was free but Nell asked me to cover her site so she could survey the manor. It was fine by me. Easier site.' He felt Val's eyes burn into him. Clearly this was damning news, so he added, ultra-casual, 'It's nothing unusual. It needed someone who could survey for all the species anticipated. To make sure we didn't miss anything. She was best for the job.'

'So where did that put you? On Wednesday? At the time of Sophie's death.'

'Uh …' *Jesus. Am I under suspicion?* Blinking, he focused. 'Like I say, I covered Nell's site. Quince Meadows. By 4 p.m., I was driving back on the M25. I got a pasty and a coffee at some services so I could have a quick turnaround at home and head straight out for Nell's bat survey.' He rifled in his rucksack by the sofa, producing a screwed-up receipt. 'Here you go. My gourmet dinner.'

She glanced at it. 'But you didn't actually go to Manor House Farm. You sent a text, claiming these punctures prevented you. Yet you'd driven to a site and back again with no problems?'

Adam wasn't riled by her persistence. She reminded him of his mum, using the backing-him-into-a-corner tactic, when she tried to convince him to date her friend's sister's daughter. 'I must have got some slow punctures on site. It's a pretty rough spot. Glass and rubbish everywhere. By the time I got home, recharged my phone and grabbed a jumper, the tyres were flat. I tried booking an Uber, but the roadworks added a half-hour delay. I'd have missed the start of the survey. But Nell texted to say she could manage. Then she drove to mine afterwards so I could take her home and keep the work car.'

Photographing the receipt, Val typed on her phone on the table, and texted it to DC Hesha Patel, along with a request for CCTV footage of the services when Adam was there, and ANPR check of road cameras between Quince Meadows and Adam's flat. She scrolled to the photo she'd taken of his car's number plate, and sent that, too. Adam knew he was supposed to see.

She handed the receipt back. 'If your lot are anything like my lot, you need proof of every penny for expenses. But I don't think you can expense your tyres, if you were going to try. I doubt they're flat from punctures at your site.' She flicked to her photos of his tyres, zoomed in, pointed. 'All four tyres are punctured on the sidewall with clean, elongated holes. I'd say they've been slashed. I'll have to impound your car for forensics.'

What the ...? 'How long will that take? I need to replace the tyres so I can use it next week. I can't monopolise the work car forever.' At least no one else needed the ancient Volvo while he had reptile traps to check during the Bank Holiday.

'A few weeks, I'm afraid.' She didn't look afraid. 'Someone went to some lengths to stop you meeting Nell at Manor House Farm. Perhaps to make sure she was there on her own.' A shrug. 'Or maybe you did it yourself, to give the impression you couldn't have been there.' As Adam stood up, protesting, she mused, 'Or maybe Nell did. To ensure she'd be there alone.'

Chapter 6

James was dropped off in front of the blue-and-white police tape fluttering across the gates of Manor House Farm and waved at the uniformed officer on duty. A line of cars of the SOCO team told him he'd find a hive of activity, so he signed in, ducked under the barrier and strode up the wide, tree-lined driveway. Beyond the row of copper beeches, the formal garden was a tangle of neglect, grading into grassland and swallowed up by woodland. Gravel crunched under his boots as birdsong echoed around him in energetic bursts.

The house loomed into view. A contrast to last night, when the mansion had been all imposing architecture and ominous shadows, shifting in the torchlight of the search team, now it glowed in the noon sun. Honey stone, graceful arching mullioned windows, ornate chimneys, and a hodge-podge of extensions from its fifteenth-century origins made it both grand and cosy. *You'd never guess a SOCO team was inside, examining a murder scene.*

He paused at the corner where Nell had stood for her survey, imagining her watching the south and east elevations. In total darkness. Alone. For bats. He shivered. She must visit as many creepy places as him. *They possibly kept similar hours …* He stopped his mind wandering and spotted DC Ed Baker by the front door, typing slowly with one finger on his iPad. Ed scratched at his balding head, sighed, then prodded the screen.

'You all right, Ed? I thought you were on house-to-house?' James said.

Ed looked up. 'Yep. There's only one neighbour so I've brought my team to join forces with the search team. They're on drains and bins now. Dr Saunders said our murderer would've got blood on their clothes so they'd've had to clean up, dump or destroy them.'

James nodded. 'OK. How was the neighbour?'

'Mr Gilpin. Farmer.' Ed unfolded a map and refolded it into one large paw. 'His farm backs onto Manor House Farm, here.' He ran a finger across the woodland, then looked at James. 'Made me wonder if our murderer might've cut across the farm to avoid using roads but the other side's cut off by the railway.' He traced the line around the woods beyond the gardens and lake. 'It's an active line, and fenced off, so there's no access that way. And Mr Gilpin says he saw nothing suspicious.'

'Did he know about the plans to develop Manor House Farm?'

'He knew it was on the cards. But he didn't know any details.'

James wondered if that was true. Val had mentioned Adam's site encounters. Had there been a dispute? If so, had it turned violent …? He fired off a note. Ed watched in awe.

'We've started ANPR, CCTV and PCN checks in case it gives us something on cars.'

'Let's hope.' James pulled on his plastic suit and booties. 'We've impounded Sophie's car, but we couldn't find any record of her movements. So she must have stuck to back roads. We're still looking. And we're checking all our suspects' cars, too. For now, I'll see how SOCO are doing.'

The empty house held the thickened atmosphere of history. The hall flagstones were worn with seven hundred years of footsteps. The stone arch into the farmhouse kitchen was polished at waist height where every hand since medieval times had caressed it in passing. The wide kitchen was dominated by a stone-mantled fireplace enclosing ancient bread ovens.

James paused on the steps into the cellar. The tunnel was washed with ice-white light from the SOCO-assembled floodlights, crouching bodies busy measuring, photographing, dusting. He called to Dr Saunders, overseeing the team. 'OK to come through, doc?'

The identikit officers continued their work as Saunders tutted at him. 'I said I'd fill you in. But come in if you must. Keep on the plates.'

Like a macabre game of hopscotch, James tiptoed across the steel squares, laid to preserve the scene, the air musty and dank.

Saunders turned off her headtorch and folded her arms. 'We're on a roll here.'

'I know. Don't mean to interrupt. It just helps me to keep the crime scene in mind.'

Huffing, Saunders snapped off her gloves and took her phone out of her pocket. 'Fine, let me fill you in on today's headlines. That red chip of plastic by the doormat of the kitchen door into the utility room? Nothing. Inert, standard grade plastic. Coated with dust because there was honey on it. But, you know, we found it in the kitchen and we've no idea how long it was there for.'

James shrugged. 'Fair enough.'

'But I do have something from tech. They've got hold of Sophie's emails. Saving to the server as we speak. Here.'

She handed James her phone and he read the recent messages. Mostly from Anna Maddison to Sophie, professional in tone. He lingered on one dated Tuesday 24th. Anna asked to move Sophie's meeting with Nell from 6 p.m. to 5 p.m. *Nell had been copied in.* He returned the phone, his stomach churning. 'That's, er … that's great. Just great.'

'Good.' Dr Saunders smiled sweetly. 'And now will you kindly sod off?'

Ducking under the police tape, James admitted to himself that Val was right; he had to remain impartial. *There's no good reason why Nell would lie about the meeting.* Glum, he returned the wave of the uniformed officer, who inclined his head across the road at a new yellow Porsche Boxster, its roof down, a woman in the driving seat.

James walked over. 'Hello, can I help you?'

'I'm Anna Maddison. I spoke—'

'To me.' He smiled at David Stephenson's project manager. 'DS James Clark. But this is a crime scene. You can't go in.'

'I know.' She nodded, the highlights in her mahogany bob glinting as she clamped cerise lips together. 'It just seemed so … unreal. I had to come out and see it for myself.' She pulled a handbag onto her lap and fished out a tissue.

The bag's thick supple fuchsia leather looked expensive; and its interlocking Chanel Cs proved it was. As she dabbed her eyes, James took stock of her. Late thirties. Immaculate make-up, tightly tailored jade dress, which looked designer.

'Anyone at home who can look after you a bit, Anna? Spouse? Partner?' A perfectly normal question he hadn't been able to ask Nell.

The shake of Anna's head set off alarm bells. *How much was she making as a project manager for a small-time developer? Not enough to afford all this, surely.*

'Well, try and take it easy. This is always a shock for everyone involved. Especially since you worked closely with Sophie. And David.'

Her cheeks trembled. 'To think he was at that conference when poor Sophie …' She dabbed her eyes again.

'Did you go to any of the conference? Or see David during that time?'

'No. I kept things running back in the office. I didn't see David again until Thursday, after the conference finished.'

'Can I ask where you were on Wednesday afternoon?' As Anna turned an alarmed face to him, he added, 'It's just procedure.'

'Oh. Well. I finished work early and went to Nye Hall Hotel.'

'Oh, very nice. Did you go with anyone?'

Anna shrugged. 'If you want to verify I was there, surely the hotel staff can do that.'

James didn't argue. Staff would also say who she was with. 'You must be kept busy, arranging contractors and surveyors for this place. Do any of them know about the tunnel?'

'Not many. The structural engineer found it, and told the architect about it. It wasn't relevant to anyone else and it's not on any maps I know of.'

'Well, can you tell your contractors they can't access the place for the foreseeable?' James spotted Ashley leaning on her car, checking her watch. He straightened up.

As Anna nodded and drove away, James made another note:

Verify if Anna was at Nye Hall and who with. Run financial investigation. Did she tell Sophie/Nell different meeting times to get Sophie alone? Is she having an affair? With David? Or Sophie?

Friday 27th August – 1.30 p.m.

Alone, at home, Nell couldn't shake the image of Sophie's photo. *What exactly happened to her? While I'd been right there.* Guilt rose up again, until she was hugging the loo, retching up coffee and bile.

Being categorised as a suspect rather than a helpful citizen had also unnerved her. *Will the police track my phone?* She'd felt so paranoid about that, so exposed, that she hadn't turned it on after the police interview. But she had to tell her team that Manor House Farm was out of bounds. She fired off a brief email and ten missed calls loaded on the screen. All from Adam.

A thrill shivered at the idea that he cared. Unless … did he need something for site? She went to call him back but several Twitter notifications appeared. She scanned them as she put the kettle on.

All the posts were Sylvia's, in marketing-manager overdrive. The first, a captioned photo of her glamorous pose in front of EcoLogical Consultants' stand at the conference:

EcoLogical Consultants at Pendlebury Regional Planning Conference – always here to help if you need ecology surveys for your development!

The next post was Sylvia in typical Hunting Mr Right mode, having unerringly sifted the gathering for the most eligible bachelor, smiling at the bar with the handsome man she'd met:

Meeting new friends at the Pendlebury Regional Planning Conference!

God, it seemed like a lifetime ago, yet it was only yesterday Sylvia had returned to their office from the conference, excited about her new conquest. *Was his name Troy?* Fair-haired, handsome, muscular, mid-thirties. Sylvia made herself timeless enough that it was impossible to say if her preferred age range of men was just five years younger than her, or fifteen.

Over the photo, a text from Sylvia popped up:

Can you fact-check a blog for me? I'd like to post it ASAP.

Grateful for the distraction, Nell replied.

Sure. You're a bit keen on a long weekend?

Sylvia usually spent Bank Holidays in Biarritz or at exclusive art exhibitions, not hunched over a laptop.

> Baiting a man trap, darling. Still can't find Troy's details so I'm squeezing any social-media-worthy item I can from that conference in the hope it'll tickle his alerts and he'll get in touch. I've emailed you the blog.

Nell made a cup of tea that she wasn't sure she wanted, and perched at the table, reading Sylvia's article. She had nothing to add to the witty take on ecology's role in the planning process, sent Sylvia a reply and – at last – brought up Adam's number again.

Before she could call, her phone rang. Not Adam, but her father. 'Nell, have you got a minute?'

'Yes. Of course.' She swallowed her frustration.

'How do I get my photos from my camera to my iPad? I've persuaded your mother to go to Paris for a week. She needs a break. But I've run out of room on the card.'

Ugh. This wasn't going to take a minute. Nell prepared for a long conversation and checked the kitchen cupboard; despite her nausea, this was a biscuit situation.

'Remember what we did last time? Have you opened the app? And signed in? You'll need your password.' She unwrapped a packet of chocolate-chip cookies, waiting for her dad to follow the procedure, get something wrong, do it again, then admit he'd lost his password. In the silence punctuated by her dad's tuts, she opened the secure app where she stored her passwords. And her parents'.

While she talked her dad through each step, several times, two more calls from Adam beeped, increasing her impatience. As she began to text him, her father cheered. 'Aha! We have lift-off. Thank you, dear. We're off tomorrow, back next Friday. Bon voyage, eh?' He hung up.

'Yeah. Bon voyage. Great.' Nell went to bite the cookie but the sweet smell was too much. She shoved it back into the packet and, finally, called Adam.

'Nell? Are you OK?' From the background hum of traffic, Adam was driving. 'The police saw me about my car. And why I couldn't get to Manor House Farm. God, when they said a woman had been murdered, I …' His ragged breathing crackled. 'I knew you were OK but, well … I was worried.'

'I'm … I'm OK.' Was she? After the unsettling police interview, Adam's heartfelt words gave a warm glow of comfort.

'Look, I'm on my way to check traps at Birchby Copse,' said Adam. 'But let me bring you a takeaway for dinner. And my dazzling company.'

She felt too sick to eat. And after James nosing around her house, she wasn't ready to lower the battlements just yet. 'It's kind of you, but I really can't.'

'I've got some supplies for Zorro, too.'

Nell hesitated. She was low on mealworms. But still …

'If you really don't want company, I can leave them at the gate?'

'Sorry, I don't mean to sound ungrateful. It's been a strange day. And honestly, I'd prefer to get out of the house.'

'Ah. Then I know just the thing.'

Chapter 7

Friday 27th August – 2.30 p.m.

James was lost in emails as Ashley pulled up at Applewood Residential Care Home.

'Look lively.' She yanked on the handbrake and jumped out. 'We're running late.'

Scrambling out, he hurried after her as she pointed and clicked the car key over her shoulder. Dashing into reception, he just caught up with her as she accosted the receptionist.

'Hi, we're here to see Mrs Marjorie Crows.' Ashley showed her badge.

'Ah.' The receptionist, already flushed and with hair escaping a bun, looked worried.

'I'm sorry we're late. I know we said we'd be here at about 2 p.m.' Ashley grimaced at the hall's grandfather clock, as it struck the half-hour.

'It's not that …'

The receptionist's voice drowned under the swelling wail of an approaching siren. She ran out from behind the desk to jam the doors open.

As a pair of paramedics sprinted from the ambulance, James and Ashley flattened themselves against the hall wall, keeping out of their path.

'Mrs Crows,' one of them said.

'Room 12, follow me.'

James and Ashley rushed after them. The room at the end of the ground-floor hallway had its door propped open. Running in, James saw the carer by her bed spring back, making room for the medics. Mrs Crows seemed to be asleep, her frail frame barely indenting the pristine sheets and pillowcase, the grey curls framing her sallow face slicked with sweat.

'She's non-responsive. I found her like this ten minutes ago.'

One paramedic assembled the stretcher as another sat at the bed. 'Mrs Crows? Mrs Crows, can you hear me?' He checked airway, breathing, pulse; lifted one eyelid and shone a torch in her eye, then checked the other.

Ever suspecting foul play, James glanced at the door's lock. A Yale, which automatically locked once the door was closed. The carer's retractable key-fob was clipped to her belt. The bay windows were ajar, but still locked. On an outside wall he noticed an alarm, its A1 logo slashed with a lightning bolt. This place took security seriously.

'She's in a coma.' The paramedic stood up. 'We need to get her to Pend fast.'

The carer turned – and clapped eyes on Ashley and James. She held out a blocking hand. 'Who are you? What are you doing in here?'

'Police.' Ashley held up her badge. The carer frowned but stepped back.

While his colleague slid the stretcher beside Mrs Crows, the paramedic tapped the carer's arm. 'Can I have that copy of her medications and what she's been given today?'

'Oh, yes. I got it ready.' The carer handed him a box. 'This is all her medication. Just blood pressure tablets. With a copy of her dose record for this week.'

'How's she been in the past few days?' he asked. 'Have you noticed anything?'

The carer bit her lip. 'No. Nothing. I've checked her notes. She's been fine.'

Ashley shot James a look. He raised his eyebrows in agreement and turned to the paramedic. 'We came here to tell Mrs Crows that her granddaughter was tragically murdered two days ago. So Mrs Crows may well be in danger.'

'*Sophie?*' the carer asked, shocked. 'Sophie's dead?'

'I'm afraid so,' said James.

The medic nodded as he and his colleague carried Mrs Crows out. 'She'll be in A&E at Pendlebury Hospital. I'll ask if they can put her in a private room so it's easier to keep an eye on her.'

Ashley passed James the car keys as she spoke to the paramedic's back. 'I'm the family liaison officer. Can I ride along? Save you reporting back.'

'If you're quick.'

As the paramedics sped Mrs Crows to the car park, James turned to the receptionist and carer. 'Can I see where you keep the medication?'

The receptionist frowned, eyeing the carer. 'You don't think …?'

James attempted a reassuring smile. 'We just need to be thorough, since Mrs Crows' condition coincides with her granddaughter's death.'

'Sure.' She beckoned him down the opposite corridor to Mrs Crows' room. A waft of meat and cabbage, and the distant clatter of cutlery and chinaware suggested staff were clearing after lunch. His stomach growled. *Did I have lunch?*

'Here you go.' The receptionist passed the staff room and stopped at the office. Stretching the key cable, she unlocked the door and pushed it open.

A wide desk took up the far wall, a window on the wall facing the door flooded the room with light. The nearest wall was devoted to storage. The carer went to the desk and took out a key, then unlocked one of the cupboards. James peered in.

Pill-dispensing trays were stacked on the desk shelf next to a sign-in/out book and a locked box marked MORPHINE. Below it, sat the square black drug case that carers carried around to dispense the medication. Containers with residents' names were lined along the higher shelves, arranged in alphabetical order, a gap between Mrs Brock and Mr Cruikshank.

'You said Mrs Crows only took blood pressure pills? High or low?'

'For high blood pressure,' the carer answered. 'That's all. Apart from poor eyesight, she's in excellent health for someone her age. And, like I said, she's been fine until today.'

'Anything different about her medication? A change of brand or dose?'

'No, according to her, it's been the same for years.'

'And this cabinet's always locked, with the key in that desk, and the door locked?'

'Always. It's not just drugs in here. There's confidential information. We're careful.'

'Could the drugs get mixed up when they're taken round to residents?'

'Not for Mrs Crows. She only has these, so they're not transferred into a dispensing tray like we'd do for residents with several pills at different times of the day. We just take her bottle in the case on the morning round, and give Mrs Crows her tablet straight from there.'

'Anyone else have keys? Like visiting relatives?'

'Oh no. All staff have masters. But guests don't have keys. Or borrow them.'

He turned to the receptionist. 'So are guests escorted? Accompanied?'

'Accompanied to a resident's room or directed if the resident's in the lounge, day room or garden. All guests sign in at the front desk. I'll show you if you're done here?'

At James's nod, the carer locked the cupboard and returned the key. As they returned to reception, the office door slammed shut, locked, behind them.

'Here's the sign-in book.' She slid the ledger to him. He scanned the 'Visiting' column, struck by the sight of Sophie's round handwriting and how frequently it appeared. She'd seen her grandmother most days. David Stephenson's name was conspicuously absent.

'Who's this?' He pointed at the scrawl of a guest of Mrs Crows, 2 p.m. Wednesday 25th August. Signed out the same time as Sophie, 3.30 p.m. The day she was killed.

'Um.' She leaned in to read it. 'That's Andrew Arden. Mrs Crows' solicitor.'

Friday 27th August – 7 p.m.

Nell hugged the warm paper packets, tangy with the scent of hot salt and vinegar, fresh from The Codfather (with its stylised sign of a fish in a tux) as she walked along Cookingdean's higgledy-piggledy high street. She wove around the timber-framed, uneven Tudor houses overhanging the narrow path between shops, and past the vast, high wall of Cookingdean Hall, its ancient bricks weathered to a soft pink. Reaching The Mill gastropub (with still-working mill wheel), and the farm shop supplied by local organic farmers, she crossed the road to the village green. Settling on the bench under the horse chestnut tree by the cricket pavilion, she scanned the few people dotted around the green. Adam's unmistakeable languid walk brought him into view from the opposite direction, suggesting he'd parked at the village hall. As she waved, a football whacked her ankles.

'Here, miss! Over here!' The hopeful kid waved.

Fumbling with the precious parcels, Nell stood, angled herself behind the ball. Her awkward kick sent the ball curving away from the child, past his parents. It skittered across the path of a couple who jumped apart from holding hands as they strolled along the river, and headed straight for a sleeping female mallard, head tucked peacefully under one wing. As ball hit duck, she leaped, wings outstretched, quacks rising in indignation, making her companions along the riverbank flutter in a ripple of disturbance.

When Nell glanced back at Adam, he was silently laughing at her, shaking his head, phone jammed under his chin. As he approached, he mouthed, 'My mum.' He spoke in rapid Punjabi, letting his mother vent before ending the call. 'Sorry about that. Family drama.'

He sat beside Nell and nodded towards the little boy creeping up on the flock to rescue his ball. 'I see you barely dabble in football, but surely even you know that's a fowl.'

Nell groaned, then grinned. 'She should have been Peking. Then she could have ducked.'

'Argh. Terrible. And you don't sound very repentant for an ecologist who just attacked an innocent, sleeping *Anas platyrhynchos*.'

Passing Adam one parcel, she nodded at the bird fastidiously preening her feathers, one eye on the little boy. 'I think she'll live.'

As Adam unfolded the paper, the intense vinegary hit made Nell's stomach growl, her appetite returning. She unwrapped her meal, armed with the tiny wooden fork.

Adam peered at her small serving. 'What? No chips? Who goes to a chippie and doesn't get chips?'

'I didn't feel hungry. Then.'

'Yep. I see serious chip regret.' Adam regarded a fine example, and popped it in his mouth, whole. He reached inside his rucksack and passed Nell a takeaway box. Its contents writhed. 'Could turn to these, if you get desperate.'

'Couldn't eat mealworms without the matched wine. It'd be a waste.' She stared towards the river. 'Look! Kingfisher!'

As Adam squinted through the willows, she nabbed a chip.

'Argh! That's a low move!' Adam looked delighted. He moved his chips an inch away so Nell would have to reach further if she tried it again.

The buzz of Nell's phone interrupted the companionable moment. Percy's name flashed. Adam looked away, eating another chip.

Nell checked the text.

Has your dishy detective seen more than your comfy pants yet?

She squeezed the side button, blacking out the screen, and shoved the phone away.

'Everything OK?' Adam asked.

'Fine. It's nothing. Just a friend.' She pointed at his phone. 'How's your family?'

'Ah, it's chip distraction tactics now?' At Nell's cheerful nod, he shrugged. 'Aanya's driving Mum mad.' He pretended not to notice Nell's blatant chip-theft. 'I'm to give her a pep talk at the family BBQ on Monday, about how our more conservative relatives expect us to behave when we go out for Marla's wedding. My big sis is marrying into a very reserved family. Which'll suit her. She's a shy, quiet one. Aanya, however, is not.'

'Oh?' Nell had been about to steal another chip but stopped short. *Had he mentioned it?* 'How long are you going for?'

'Going next month, the celebrations go on for weeks in Delhi. Aanya will be trouble. But she's a teenager, and she's always got away with murder—' He winced. 'God, sorry …'

'I might need some of her luck, then.' Nell mustered a smile.

He studied her face, his brown eyes full of concern. 'I relent. Have all my chips. They may not serve any in prison. Your chip days could be numbered.'

'Thanks for the vote of confidence.' Nell took a chip anyway.

'You're the one who said you're a prime suspect. Two choices, then: one – work out your prison survival strategy or two – implement the great escape plan.'

'Or three – prove my innocence?'

'Sure, but never hurts to have a back-up plan. Just get a false passport, get to France …'

'Where's my false passport coming from? You got contacts?'

'Fair point. OK. Can you canoe across the channel?'

Nell frowned as she chewed. 'That's likely to get me drowned in the North Sea. Less escape plan, more elaborate suicide mission.'

'Motorboat to Monaco?'

She tried to shrug. That was, actually, entirely feasible. 'Stick to supplying chips.'

'I could also help with some distraction this weekend?' He shot her a tentative sideways glance.

She held his gaze, butterflies fluttering. 'Oh?'

'Why don't you ask Erin over to show her Zorro? She won't have seen a grey long-eared bat before. I hadn't. It'd be valuable training. And Sylvia, too. She'll see what's involved in bat care, take some photos, write an article.'

Nell's thud of disappointment drowned under instinctive resistance. 'They might not be free—'

'I happen to know they're both free tomorrow morning. Erin needs training.'

Nell silenced him for a second with a wry glance. As the team's newly graduated field assistant, Erin was proving a handful. Full of enthusiasm, yes, but convinced her Master's meant she had nothing left to learn – unless Adam was teaching.

'Do it for Sylv, then. She's desperate for anything she can make a blog out of at the moment.'

Nell opened her mouth but hesitated.

'I've overstepped. I'm sorry. It's just not every day we find a grey long-eared bat. It's special. I was going to invite myself along, too. I wanted to see how the fella's doing.' He shot her *that grin*, and Nell shook her head, unable to suppress her own smile.

'*Fine.*'

'Great. I'll tell them.' Adam tugged his phone from his pocket and sent a single joint text: 👍 , then turned to her. 'Everyone's been dying to see your place, too. No one's ever got beyond the big gate. We've all Google Mapped you, so we know it looks pretty cool.'

'What?'

'Oh, what do you expect? It's standard practice before we see any site.' Adam chewed, his expression growing philosophical. 'You're so mysterious about everything – perhaps that's why the police are so interested?'

Nell ached to deny it. But maybe Adam had a point.

'So, how *did* you leave things with the police?'

'I'm serious about being a suspect. I was there, with no alibi. They don't seem very convinced by my explanations.' The detectives' obvious disbelief – the grubby, indelible stain of suspicion – rose up like a swelling tide.

'Surely they're just eliminating you?' At Nell's unhappy shrug, Adam looked outraged. 'As if you'd harm anyone! And you've no connection to the place! You can't even have a motive. It's crazy.' His protective outburst sparked hope in Nell. Then he stared at her. 'Do you know anything? Like where it happened?'

Nell nodded, bit her lip. 'The tunnel.'

He put his chips aside and turned towards her.

'When I went in, right after I sent you that picture, while I was in there, I …' Once the words were out, there was no taking them back. He'd think she was an idiot. Or a coward.

He waited.

'I think I heard it happen. I heard something. Like a brick falling. And, you know, the ceiling was full of gaps from fallen bricks. And damp. So I've been trying to pass it off as just that. But I got that … that *feeling*. That something-wrong, hackles-up feeling.'

'Did you hear anything else?'

Nell shook her head. 'No.'

'Any idea of how far you were from it?'

Nell bit a trembling lip. 'Hard to tell. But it seemed to come from the far end. Near …' Her voice fell to a whisper. 'Near the house.'

'Jesus. What did the detectives say?'

'I … I didn't tell them. Well … it sounds pathetic, doesn't it? I heard something like a brick fall in a tunnel where literally hundreds have fallen, strewn all over the floor as proof.'

'It might. Until you factor in a murder.' Nell, they'll take it seriously. It'll help, surely. They'll be able to narrow down their timeframe.'

'Yeah, to exactly when I was there.'

'Doesn't matter, does it?'

'They already think I'm a suspect, Adam. Hardly anyone knows about the tunnel, it seems. They asked how I found out about it, why I went in. No, *dug* my way in.'

'But you had legitimate reas—'

'And if I tell them, what are they going to say? Why didn't I get help? And why didn't I?' She dropped her eyes, stared at her lap. 'And … and then Sophie didn't show up for her meeting. And *still* I didn't raise the alarm. I mean, if the detectives don't already think I'm dodgy as all hell, they will when they know that.'

And James would no doubt think she was pathetic for not having the wherewithal to even make an emergency call. *Not that I should care what he thought …*

'What if I could've made a difference? What if me calling someone or … or … intervening in the tunnel—'

'OK, hold up. How could you have known, Nell? You're speaking from hindsight. But you had no way of knowing something had happened.'

'But I *did*.'

'OK, fine, your instinct kicked in. But you know better than I do how often we override our instincts. You're the one telling our new recruits that they should never stay at a site if they feel uneasy, even if they can't work out why, so they don't feel bad about acting on it. You wouldn't need to say that if it was as natural as it should be to follow our primal warning system. You can't feel bad for that.'

'But she's dead, Adam. And maybe I could have prevented it.'

'*Please* don't suggest you could have intervened because you could have got yourself killed, too, and *that* thought makes me …' He clamped his lips together and reached for her. She stared down at his hand gripping hers fiercely. She didn't want him to let go.

Adam misunderstood and released her hand. 'Sorry. Look, Nell, you might have seen something. You may not even realise it yet. What if you remember something? What if the murderer knows you were there? Or saw you? Or thinks *you* saw *them*?' His voice cracked. 'Jesus, Nell … You could be in serious danger.'

Chapter 8

Saturday 28th August – 8 a.m.

James walked down Pendlebury's Georgian high street, scanning its buildings for 31A, or a plaque bearing Andrew Arden's name. The solicitor's office was in one of the symmetrical townhouses at the Farrow and Ball end of town, clustered with designer boutiques and exquisitely expensive homewares.

The high street already bustled with shoppers. By lunchtime, the Old Coach Inn overlooking the river would be crammed with contented patrons enjoying a local ale with chef's recommendations. And by mid-afternoon, the tea room by the honey-coloured castle ruins would buzz with customers coveting artisanal pastries. The town sprawled westwards as houses shrank, and shops and pubs dominated – where most of James's weekend call-outs came from.

What would Nell notice, if she was here? Would she just enjoy the view of the river flowing alongside the high street, willows shading swans as they glided past spear-like yellow flowers, or need to grub around in the undergrowth to find some special species? She'd undoubtedly tell him all these graceful old buildings he loved were full of bats.

Ahead of him, Val pressed a brass doorbell. The smart blue door clicked open and they followed gold-lettered signs up the wide stairs to the office. Andrew waited for them on the landing, casting a long, thin shadow over the banisters. He had such an agitated air that James checked to see if Andrew's foot was tapping. It wasn't. But his eyes darted between them and his office door, and, as they reached him, he led them in without allowing James's friendly introductions to break their stride.

In the office, lined with law tomes and framed legal qualifications, Val sat in one of the leather armchairs. 'Thanks for agreeing to see us.' She nodded at the photos of Andrew's wife and children, on the desk beside his open diary. 'Especially on a weekend.'

But Andrew was weighing up two files he'd taken from the stack on his desk, as if unsure which to give them first. 'I expect you want to see Sophie Crows' will.' He handed a file to Val. 'But I also want you to see this.' He passed James the other file and sat down.

Before James could open his file, Val had scanned hers and frowned. 'Sophie changed her will – on the day she was murdered?'

'Yes. *Exactly*. And I don't think it was a coincidence.' As Andrew clasped his hands, James noticed they were shaking.

Val turned the pages. 'Sophie named Pendlebury Horse Sanctuary as her beneficiary?' She passed the file to James who checked the date.

Jesus. Val was right. Three days ago. He leafed to the end of the will, saw the witness's name: Henrietta Lambert. From her slanted, copperplate handwriting, he guessed Henrietta's age. 'Sophie signed this at Applewood Residential Care Home?'

Andrew's tense features rippled with surprise. 'Yes. As it happens. We met at 2 p.m. Sophie had phoned beforehand, on August 16th, wanting to change her will. I drew up the papers, she only had to sign them with a witness.'

'I assume the witness is also a resident at Applewood?' James shot a glance at the diary on Andrew's desk, open on August 16th. He'd got all his facts together in preparation for their meeting.

'Yes. Mrs Lambert is a good friend of Marjorie Crows. Hence meeting at Applewood to sign the documents.'

Interesting that Sophie turned to her grandmother and Henrietta Lambert, rather than her own friends. 'What did the original will say?' James asked.

'Well, Sophie planned to leave her estate which, in the natural order of things, would have been her family home, Manor House Farm, to her husband, David Stephenson. But she changed her mind. And it's not only that new will that prevents him from inheriting ...' Andrew nodded at the file in James's hands.

James opened the folder and sat back, surprised. 'Petition for divorce?'

'*Exactly*. When Sophie rang on August 16th, she asked me to draft these papers for her. I sent them to David Stephenson's solicitors a few days ago. If they acted promptly, David would have known Sophie intended to divorce him before she was mur …' He pressed his lips together and sank back into his chair.

James slid a sidelong glance at Val. David had given no inkling of any issues in his marriage. He turned back to Andrew. 'What was Sophie's reason?'

'She cited unreasonable behaviour.'

'Oh?' Val leaned forward. 'In what way?'

Andrew stared at his hands. 'David had been deceiving Sophie. It made her wonder if the whole marriage had been a sham. Especially when she looked back at how he'd gradually taken control of all her finances.' He looked up at Val, anguish etched into his face. 'And, when she finally found the courage to respond, look what happened to her.'

James fought to keep his expression neutral. The solicitors he'd worked with were usually jaded cynics – yet Andrew could barely contain his emotions. Such a mild-looking man, with sensitive features making him look older than his age, which James guessed was mid-thirties. He'd had solicitors place documents before him while pointedly pursing lips and raising eyebrows to infer a motive lay within. He'd never seen anything approaching an accusation.

'How did he deceive her?' Val asked.

'David was dishonest about his plans to develop Manor House Farm. Sophie wanted to convert her family home into an equestrian centre. It was a lifelong dream. Let me explain.' Walking to the wall by the sash window, Andrew unhooked a framed sepia photo and passed it to James: two men in suits outside a familiar, splendid country house.

'This is my grandfather and Sophie's great-grandfather at Manor House Farm. Our law firm only got started when Sophie's great-grandfather retained my grandfather, then my father, as their family solicitors and referred clients. Our two families were always close.'

He took a deep breath. 'When she was a child, Sophie's parents were killed in a car accident. The Crows are her paternal grandparents and they became her guardians, and she moved in with them at the manor when she was still very little. The trauma she'd suffered made her very withdrawn, and I know Mrs Crows was terribly worried about her. Sophie didn't make friends easily, despite them trying to help her integrate with other children, and she had awful nightmares.

'I'm about ten years older than Sophie,' he explained. 'I remember how shocked we all were at the accident. Mrs Crows drew Sophie out of her shell by getting her interested in horses. Over the years, she transformed. Her skills as a talented horsewoman grew. She gained confidence. It was wonderful to see. She's still mad about them. Was ...' Andrew turned to look out of the window, taking a breath before continuing.

'She'd always wanted to run an equestrian centre. I think, because of her experiences, she believed in the benefits of equine therapy. She wanted to share that with others. David supported the plan. In fact, he was so supportive, not just of her ideas, but of her in general, that she married him and persuaded her grandmother to bequeath the manor in trust when she moved into Applewood so Sophie could start the conversion.'

Andrew's face hardened along with his voice. 'Then, everything changed. On August 16th, Sophie found proof David had plans for a different development.

'On the same day, not knowing she'd found this out, he gave her paperwork to transfer the manor from her name into the ownership of his company. He justified this because of how he'd suggested they split the tasks: she oversaw the design – of a centre she now knew he'd never intended to build – while he handled planning and funding – of a different plan altogether. He'd reasoned the manor had to be in his company's name to raise the necessary capital.'

'What was this different plan of David's?' James asked.

'I don't know. I couldn't get much sense out of Sophie when she talked about it. She was so angry. So upset. I just focused on helping get her affairs in order.'

'Did you manage to dissuade her from signing the manor over to David?' Val asked.

'I didn't need to,' he said. 'Neither Sophie nor Mrs Crows would do that.'

'Ah. Mrs Crows didn't want the manor to be in David's name, either?' Val asked.

'Correct – and that was true even before Sophie's discovery of David's ulterior plans. Rather than transferring the manor from Mrs Crows to Sophie, we arranged for the manor to be in both Sophie's and Mrs Crows' names, as joint tenants with rights of survivorship.'

Val glanced over the property deed that Andrew passed to her. 'So the estate would pass to the survivor and then, upon *their* death, to whoever they'd left the estate to.'

'Exactly. Under the joint tenancy, Sophie understood she wouldn't inherit the manor outright until the death of her grandmother. And Sophie changed her will so in the event of her own death, the estate would go to the local horse sanctuary. For two reasons: firstly, she wanted her centre to work with the horse sanctuary and provide stabling, and we'd drawn up a contract of how the two entities would co-exist; and, secondly, a bequest to a charity makes it difficult to contest a will.' A hint of fire flashed in Andrew's grey eyes. 'Just in case.'

James absorbed the implications. *Sophie expected David to challenge the will.* 'Did Sophie have any reason to think she was in danger?'

Meeting James's gaze, Andrew said, 'I don't know. But she *was* m … murdered.' He swallowed. 'So she *was* in danger. As soon as she protected her assets.'

'Did David know about the deeds?' Val asked. 'Or of Sophie's changes to her will?'

Andrew shook his head with reluctance. 'Honestly, I don't think so. The fact he'd drafted paperwork to transfer the deeds from Sophie to his company suggests he didn't. But I *do* think he knew about the divorce. I think *that* was the … catalyst.'

He slid a business card across the desk towards James. 'These are David's solicitor's details. I've written my home address and phone number on the back in case you need to reach me.'

Ringing David's solicitors as they walked back to the car, James wasn't surprised to hear the office answerphone. He glanced at Val. 'We're back to the spouse, then.'

'Yes.' Val gestured in the direction of Pendlebury Hotel. 'If I drop you off, you can check David's alibi. I'd better get back to the station.'

As they walked along the river in pensive silence, under the draping willows, James noticed Val frowning. 'Penny for them?'

'I can't put my finger on it. Something about that conversation …'

'The inheritance?' James asked.

'Ah, yes.' Val snapped her fingers. 'He used an odd phrase – *Sophie understood she wouldn't inherit the manor outright until the death of her grandmother*.'

'That's not odd, is it? She'd have inherited it in entirety if Mrs Crows had died first.'

Val shook her head. 'No, that's not what he said. He said it's what Sophie *understood* to be the case. They're not the same thing.'

James kicked himself for missing the nuance. 'We can't ask Mrs Crows anything at the moment. The hospital reported no change this morning. Do you think this Mrs Lambert, the friend she trusted enough to be her witness for her confidential affairs, could be persuaded to talk?'

'Apply tea. And cake. And patience.'

Saturday 28th August – 9 a.m.

Adam reached through the car window to press the buzzer. As the solid wooden gate began to slide open, he felt oddly trepidatious. He'd only ever picked Nell up or dropped her off outside her house. Beside him, Sylvia held up the local paper so their colleague, Erin, could read the article from the back seat. He distanced himself from their hushed tones – 'Ooh, I can't believe this happened on one of our sites. Poor Nell. Imagine! She was there!' – and focused his curiosity on Nell's habitat.

They were only thirty minutes from his place in Pendlebury, but the contrast of Nell's home in this sleepy, picturesque village nestled in the emerald embrace of the downs, to his shared flat in the lively town centre was marked. Having grown up in London, he liked the vibrancy, the convenience of town. But he had to admit, the endless view was amazing, and the *peace* – only birdsong and the rustle of leaves – somehow instantly calmed.

As he pulled into the drive, he noticed the garage; *triple? Bit excessive for her Smart car. Unless she shares it with her neighbour?* Its green roof overspilled with candyfloss swathes of white stonecrop, golden rudbeckia and herb-scented oregano, humming with bees. Solar panels on the flint barn's roof pitched towards the late-summer sun, raised up so bats roosting under roof tiles still had access.

They'd talked in the park last night until dusk, when the cooling temperature and midges had made Nell decide to go home. Throughout the evening, her worries hadn't lessened, and his had grown. But Nell still kept her guard up. She only let people get close to her gradually; he sensed she was worth the wait.

Nell greeted her colleagues with a bright smile, which hid the fact she'd barely slept (due to checking the locks and alarm a million times, jumping at every creak – and barns creaked a *lot*), plus her usual turmoil at this breach of her borders. But she'd invited them as her guests, and wanted them to feel welcome. And Adam had been kind to try to distract her last night. She'd tidied her already pristine home, changed clothes twice and spritzed perfume liberally.

Erin – about a decade younger than her and Adam and typically full of energy – bounded in and along the hall runner, leaving a trail of dry mud. Adam had said that mentoring her at work was like trying to train a wayward, over-excited puppy. Now, Nell tried to hide her annoyance, but Sylvia must have noticed. She began to slip her heels off, revealing matching scarlet toenails.

'Don't worry about shoes, Sylv.' Nell greeted her with a hug. Though she barely looked a decade older than her and Adam, Sylvia's coyness about her age suggested she might be more than that. Permanently glamorous, and in her element schmoozing as the team's marketing manager, she wore a leopard-print sheath dress, looking like she was about to host a talk show. A lifetime in PR made her a stark contrast to the ecologists, wearing combats and hoodies in camouflage tones of greys and khakis. You could never accuse Sylvia of blending in.

'Darling!' Sylvia bestowed fragrant air kisses, then cast her shrewd eye around the space. 'What stylish country living! You *must* give me the name of your designer.'

'Yeah, it's all … a bit … *original*, isn't it?' Erin wrinkled her nose at the Chinese apothecary dresser standing next to three tobacco-coloured Chesterfields, which were arranged around the carved Indian coffee table.

Adam whistled. 'Nice gaff.' His cheeky smile dropped. 'Bloody hell, your TV's bigger than my bedroom. We should have the team movie night here, not at my place. You don't have housemates to placate, either.'

'You only have housemates because you want to live in town.' Nell prodded him towards the kitchen. 'I know my coffee won't be hipster enough for you, but can I get you one anyway?'

'You *have* to tell us all about Manor House Farm. Did you see the killer?' Erin followed, tying her long jet-black hair in a messy bun.

Nell inhaled sharply and glanced at Adam. 'No.' She forced her tense jaw into a smile. 'But I did see a few bats. Including Zorro.'

Erin tugged the newspaper from Sylvia. 'We read about it. I can't believe you were *right there.*'

Nell's look at Adam was harder this time. He gave a slight shake of his head. *So he hadn't said anything.* She took the paper and scanned the article.

Local heiress murdered at her family home

Sophie Crows was killed at Manor House Farm, near Pendlebury, on Wednesday 25th August. Sophie, 26, was working on a development at her family estate with her husband David Stephenson, where she was found bludgeoned to death after David reported her missing.

In a statement, Sophie's husband said: 'I'm very grateful to Chief Constable Trent and his team for their quick response. I just want justice for my beautiful wife.'

Police are appealing for any information that may help their investigation into Sophie's last moments when she failed to turn up to a meeting at Manor House Farm.

Police have identified key suspects and are following up lines of enquiry.

Chapter 9

Nell's hand flew to her mouth. 'Oh God.' *I'm a key suspect.*

'That's your meeting they've mentioned, isn't it?' Erin asked.

Nodding, Nell felt the blood drain from her face. Val's words – *Don't go far, we'll need to talk to you again* – rang in her ears.

'Only going to be a matter of time before the journos find out and track you down. They'll be camping out here for an interview with you.'

The sick feeling churned. *Oh God. Oh God …*

'Yes, it's awful, isn't it?' Sylvia said. 'Poor girl, only twenty-six. Newlywed, apparently. And that amazing house. So much potential.'

Erin snorted. Nell and Sylvia swung round to look at her. Erin blushed. 'Well, yeah, her being killed is awful. But she wasn't exactly the type to roll up her sleeves, was she? She didn't even arrange the meeting with you, Nell – her project manager did it for her. And she wasn't painstakingly renovating her *family estate* – excuse me while I vomit. No, she was selling it off for a housing scheme! Typical toffs. Have everything they could wish for, with no financial worries. And do they appreciate it? No. Are they satisfied? Even with some idyllic mansion? No. They want to make even more millions. While most of *my* generation will never have a hope of owning our own homes. And they don't even do a day's work for all that money and privilege. It's *disgusting*.'

This wasn't the first time Erin had sounded off about social injustice, usually triggered by anything to do with home ownership, but Nell still felt her face burn. She couldn't count how many times she'd been accused of the same thing: fellow college students had insisted that, in her position, she didn't need to study and could stay out drinking – oh, *and* pick up their tab. She'd even overheard her family's estate manager complain about having to babysit the airhead aristo (*nice*) when Nell had hoped to work-shadow and learn from him. Even her doctorate hadn't convinced him she wasn't hobby-horsing when she'd started the rewilding scheme across the estate, because, as she'd heard him say, the likes of her could afford what she wanted, and got degrees through donations rather than achievement anyway.

'You don't actually know any of that, Erin.' Nell heard her starchy tone and tried to take the edge off. 'You're making assumptions which could be totally unfair—'

Erin opened her mouth to retort but Nell ploughed on.

'The only thing we *do* know about her, Erin, is that someone killed her.'

As Nell tried to calm her breathing, Adam reached out to take the paper from her, his eyebrows raised in silent enquiry. Nell gave a slight nod. 'How about that coffee?'

'That would be lovely. And I'm looking forward to seeing your little bat,' Sylvia said. 'I've got a fab article planned.' She eyed Nell's coffee machine. 'Ooh, those are rather good. Espresso, please, darling.' She perched on a stool at the breakfast bar.

'Can I have an Americano, please?' Adam asked. Nell nodded, flicking buttons on the machine.

'Macchiato for me.' Erin heaved herself onto the counter, legs swinging, the heel of her boot thumping against a cupboard door.

As the aroma of fresh-roasted coffee filled the air, Nell saw her guests gaze around the room. Adam checked out the Sonos speaker behind herbs on the window-ledge, while Sylvia stared at the block of Japanese chef knives. 'Keen foodie, Nell?' she asked.

'God, no. Not unless someone else is cooking.' Nell handed the drinks around. 'Right, let me introduce you to my guest of honour.'

Adam let Erin and Sylvia investigate Zorro's large mesh enclosure first. It was draped with tea towels, a small shape moving below one of the cloths. Adam gaped. 'He's hanging up?'

'Yes, since last night. Good sign, isn't it?' Nell pulled on a pair of white gloves and handed a pair to Erin. 'I measured his thumb, forearm and tragus to confirm he's a grey rather than a brown long-eared; juveniles look so similar.'

'So that's a brand-new record of a rare maternity roost for the county.' Adam beamed. 'Amazing!'

Erin broke their shared delight, waving her gloved hands at Adam. 'I feel like I should start miming.'

Sylvia fished her phone out of her scarlet Birkin as Nell plucked the bat from the safe folds, unpinning each tiny claw from the material. His bright eyes blinked up at them. Nell flicked on the lamp and deftly half-wrapped Zorro in a tissue. 'His injury's healing, but you should still be able to see why he was unable to fly.' Nell opened his wing.

'Oh, because of the tears in the wing. Of course.' Erin nodded.

'No. They wouldn't usually stop a bat from flying. Take a closer look.' Nell held the bat up to the lamp. The light shone through his wing, like a living X-ray. Erin shrugged.

'See the inflammation in his elbow?' Nell prompted. 'The swelling and redness have gone down a lot but the injury's still visible. How old would you say he is?'

Erin peered at Zorro's knuckles. 'Less than five? Not sure beyond that?'

'He's not yet one. Take a good look at the gaps, like windows, in his joints. They'll calcify and close up as he gets older. These are a useful size to memorise – so wide, they show he's only a few months. Born this summer and just weaned, probably just taking his first flights independent of his mum.'

'And then he got swiped?' Sylvia sounded stricken.

'Yes. I put him on antibiotics to prevent infection. And now he's putting on weight, he's building up fat pads on his shoulders, here.' She moved Erin's index finger to Zorro's shoulders 'Still a bit bony, they should feel well-padded under his velvet fur. He's got a little way to go before he's back to fighting weight. Before I release him, I need to give him some test-flights so I know he can fend for himself in the wild.'

As Sylvia took photos, Nell said, 'I'm not sure if he'll fly today so don't expect too much. He may be weak and his injury may be painful. But we can see. He'll let us know.' She smiled at Erin. 'Do you want to be his launch-pad?'

'All right.' Erin held her hands out.

Nell transferred the bat with great care. 'Cup him in your hands – long-eareds need to be very warm before they fly. He'll wiggle firmly when he's ready.'

'OK. Oh, no – he's … he's going for my sleeve. What do I do?'

'Just keep calm, hold him firmly so he doesn't wander about. Then open your hands slowly, and take your top hand away.'

Sylvia began filming. Zorro twitched his long, elegant, alert ears in different directions as he chattered inaudibly, his echolocations bouncing off the walls around him. But he didn't take off. Erin looked at Nell uncertainly.

'He's probably too low in energy,' Nell said. 'And his flight muscles are rusty.'

'Will it prevent him from being released?' Sylvia asked.

'No,' Nell said. 'Medication, feeding and flying practice, and he'll get there.'

'How do you know when he's ready to release into the wild?' Sylvia asked.

'When he can fly with good stamina and accurate agility.' Nell placed Zorro in his enclosure. He seized one of Adam's wriggling mealworms with tiny white teeth and scurried up the wall to hang behind the tea towel.

'Hey, his appetite has improved,' Adam said, moving close to see. 'You must have hand-fed Zorro for hours to get him used to mealworms.' The hairs on Adam's broad forearms tickled Nell's arm. She caught his woodsy, green, clean scent.

'Well, Zorro's clearly in good hands,' Sylvia announced. 'You know, I'm sure I could tap up some contacts and score a cover with *BBC Wildlife* magazine. An ecologist saving one of our rarest species, discovering a significant new roost. It's a captivating story in the right hands.' She flourished her manicured hands. '*Comme moi*. And you'd make a gorgeous cover photo, Nell.' She pursed her lips. '*If* we could get you out of your drab site gear.'

'Oh, not me,' said Nell. 'Adam helped out. He supplied mealworms when I ran out, so he could have his five minutes of fame. Or any of my trainers. I can ask at the bat AGM next we—'

'Oh God, Nell. You poor thing.' Erin laughed. 'Sounds like your social life totally revolves around bats.' She nudged Adam. 'Trust Ads to come to the rescue, though.'

Nell had never heard anyone call Adam Ads. *Are they closer than I thought?* She'd seen them flirting at work lately. But the sick punch in the stomach surprised her. Well, Erin was cute. If annoying. But Adam wasn't likely to notice her irritating ways. For a split second she thought about hanging on to the present she'd made for Erin, then decided she was being petty. It was a professional gift. Erin – and Adam for that matter – were colleagues.

Reaching into the cupboard, Nell drew out a bat-dropping reference library in a wide, flat plastic case. She'd got up early to painstakingly put it together. Not an obvious gift for anyone other than an ecologist, but it was a valuable tool, and it was unusual to get a full set of all eighteen native UK species, which she'd listed neatly down the left-hand side from the tiny *Pipistrellus pygmaeus* to the largest, *Nyctalus noctula*. A precise row of droppings was aligned next to each name, grading in size according to species. It had taken almost two years to put her own together. But thanks to Zorro's contributions she was able to make a set for Erin right at the start of her training. She could even have the Ferrero Rocher chocolates from the flat Perspex box Nell had repurposed as the specimen case. 'This is for you, Erin.'

'Oh, fantastic!' Adam bent over it, examining the exhibit.

Erin frowned at it as Sylvia peered at it. 'Is that what I think it is?' Sylvia asked. 'You're giving droppings – *droppings* – as a gift?'

'Not just any droppings. *This* is the elusive, complete reference library.' Adam grinned at Erin. 'You're properly inaugurated now. No escape. I'm envious.'

Nell handed him a small pot. 'To add to yours.'

Adam beamed but caught Erin and Sylvia still looking puzzled and explained. 'When we survey a roost for bats, we'd take a sample of droppings for DNA analysis to accurately identify the bat species. But a good library is incredibly useful for visual comparisons to narrow down the options for initial assessments. Once you've done the squidge test.'

He reached into Zorro's cage to demonstrate. 'Bats eat insects. Their elytra make bat droppings sparkly and crumbly. But if the dropping was mice or rats', they, erm, squidge.'

'Ugh, you ecologists with your unhealthy scatological interests.' Sylvia's lip curled in exaggerated disgust.

Adam shot Nell a conspiratorial grin, then bit his lip. *Instant butterflies.*

Erin put the case on the counter. 'Yeah, I'm not sure I'm cut out for bats. Takes too many years to get a licence. I'll do newts and reptiles.' She shot Nell a look. 'You're not a fan of snakes, are you, Nell? Adam does the training for that.' She nudged Adam's arm with hers, glancing up at him. 'And I already know you're a really great teacher.' With a dazzling smile she turned back to Nell. 'Ads is teaching me to climb.'

'Oh.' Nell fought back any betrayal of her surprise. It looked like Adam was doing the same, until he managed an uncertain smile. 'But if you're not going to survey bats, you won't need to do tree climbing surveys so—'

Erin rolled her eyes. '*Nell!* Not everything is about the bats. This is just for fun. Or haven't you heard of that?'

Saturday 28th August – 9.15 a.m.

James walked across Pendlebury Hotel's car park, spotting the CCTV camera covering the narrow strip of parking behind the low brick wall which separated it from the street. The hotel looked tired, its whitewash having seen better days and the sign missing an E, but it was well positioned for business. Ripe for a Travelodge takeover.

Inside, a young receptionist was dealing with an irate guest. James hung back and waited, badge at the ready. He wanted their CCTV footage, and he didn't want to have to wait to get a search warrant. He flashed the receptionist a sympathetic smile.

The guy leaned over the counter, stabbing the desk with a fat finger as he emphasised his points. 'I arranged the conference here, with enough delegates to keep you fully booked for a couple of days. These extra two nights with my family were supposed to be *free.*'

'I'm sorry, sir, I don't see a note on your booking. Let me check with the manager.'

'Good. Tell Damo it's Simon. Simon Mayhew.'

James noted the familiar name. *So this is David's planning consultant.*

As the receptionist scurried off, Simon turned with a grunt and shook his head at James. 'Couldn't organise a proverbial in a whatnot.'

Knowing his smile was unconvincing, James introduced himself and held up his badge. 'Once you've sorted your bill, can I ask you a few questions about the conference? For our enquiries—'

'Oh, yes. Sophie Crows. Nasty business. Of course.' He checked for the still-absent receptionist. 'This was supposed to be a treat for the wife. Nice getaway for a day or two.'

James took in Simon's Rolex, his well-fitted suit, that he held the latest smartphone, then glanced around at the well-worn reception of the tired hotel. 'Allow me to recommend Nye Hall. It's got a great spa.'

'No sense in paying for that when the missus is a member of the leisure centre down the road. Ah.' He smiled at the arrival of the manager. 'Damo. There's an error on my bill.'

Damo smiled tightly, tapped the computer and nodded. 'All sorted. And thanks again for the conference. Everyone seemed happy. Perhaps it'll become a regular event?'

As the men shook hands, the lift doors opened and a weary woman exited, dragging an overstuffed suitcase on failing wheels, two small boys clinging to her drapey cardigan. 'Si, we're all packed. I'll take this out to the car. Then you can look after the boys while I have a swim.' At the words, she smiled, her exhausted expression chased away like storm clouds.

'Sorry, love. Duty calls,' said Simon. 'You'll have to watch the kids now. I need to help the detective sergeant here with his enquiries. You go along, I'll meet you in the café at lunchtime.'

Her face fell, but Simon had already turned back to James. 'Bar?' He led the way without waiting for James's answer and sat at a table in the corner. 'How can I help?'

'What can you tell me about David Stephenson's development plans?'

'Ah.' Simon drew his laptop from its bag. He fired it up and turned the screen towards James. A map loaded onto the screen. 'Guy's a genius. I've been trying to sort out the local masterplan here for years. We've got pockets of land dotted across the county, but nothing contiguous. And that's the key. David was smart enough to realise that.'

He leaned in and pointed at two fields beside Manor House Farm. 'Perfect example. The farmer who owns these is Mr Gilpin. He's been trying to flog these for as long as I can remember. But developers can't do anything with them, because they're inaccessible. Hemmed in by the railway, the rest of Gilpin's farmland – which he can't sell any more of or reconfigure – and Manor House Farm.' He looked at James with an expectant expression.

'But include Manor House Farm, and you've got access. And more land to develop.'

'Bingo.' Simon tapped the mousepad and another map loaded of the proposed development. Rows of houses bristled across fields, and the grounds of Manor House Farm.

'You haven't retained the manor house in the plan? Isn't it listed?'

'By some miracle, no. All those extensions over the years meant it got overlooked. Huge footprint, wasted as one dwelling.' He sat back, a smug smile playing on his lips.

James took in the hundreds of houses. 'Looks very profitable. But what did Sophie think about her family home being destroyed?'

'David said she was a realist, but also pretty sentimental about it, so I was under instructions not to bring it up in front of her. Didn't want to rub her nose in it. And David submitted a back-up plan, in case the council didn't go for this masterplan scheme.'

'Let me guess. Converting Manor House Farm into an equestrian centre.'

'Precisely. Although we both knew the council would go for the housing scheme. We're crying out for houses. Desirable area. Commuter-belt. Like I say, been trying to crack it for years. David's idea, plus my know-how, makes a winning combination. It took just six months to get this plan together. We finalised it a couple of weeks ago and submitted it in my name. You know, to grease the wheels.'

James fixed his eyes on the screen. *Clever. So if Sophie looked up David's name on the council's planning site, she'd have only found the renovation, not this. So how* did *she find out? Ah ...* 'Did the council put up the notice of planning application on the Manor's premises?'

'Yes. But, predictably, the nimbys must have taken it down.' Simon shrugged. 'I never saw it. But I did get the architects to send a paper copy to David. Lots of developers like to wallpaper their office walls with their major wins.'

Ah.

'But now the council have gone into overdrive, asking for every kind of survey going. Apparently, one letter from the public has been uploaded on the planning portal and you can bet others will follow. Bloody nimbys. So the council are keen to dot every bleeding i.'

'If the surveys are needed, wouldn't you do them anyway?'

Simon fixed James with a condescending look. 'Oh, detective. You must know in your line of work, there are ways to get things done, and then there are the long-winded ways you're forced to do things for the sake of appearances. Or bureaucracy. I like results, not rules.'

James eyed him. 'Sounds risky.' *He's exactly the type to pursue a complaint if he fell foul of this investigation but police procedure hadn't been followed to the letter.*

'Just prudent with budgets,' said Simon. 'The extra surveys will ultimately cost David hundreds of thousands.'

'How did he feel about that?'

Simon snorted. 'He wasn't happy. Raising extra capital before breaking ground is tricky. He'll increase his loans. It'll just dent his profit. But I get his frustration. You want to spend on things that matter. Like architects and planners, not poxy trees and fluffy bunnies.'

'Was he angry with you? For not warning him that he might need these surveys?'

Simon shrugged. 'He tried to pass the buck. But it's water off a duck's back. You have to roll with the punches in this game. Especially with the chance of getting a major scheme off the ground. David had a bit of a rant but that was just the old greed monster coming out. He'll still turn a sizeable profit.'

'And was David here on Wednesday, between 4 p.m. and 6 p.m.?'

'Oh yes, he was here.'

'You were with him?'

'Um. Well, we met a couple of planning officials. There.' He pointed at a table in the opposite corner. 'Trying to reduce those damn surveys. No dice. That was after lunch, about 2 p.m. until about 3 p.m. David said he'd get some air and go to his room.'

'Oh?' James prickled with anticipation. *Convenient.* 'How long was he in there for?'

'He said he'd eat in his room, rather than joining the meal in the restaurant at 7 p.m. Couldn't blame him. Licking his wounds after the councillors were so stubborn, no doubt. By the time we'd eaten and came back in here at 8 p.m., he was sat here, drinking a brandy.'

'Did you see him at all between 3.30 and 7 p.m.?'

Simon shook his head.

After James had emailed in Simon's statement, he watched Simon leave for the leisure centre's café and then turned to the receptionist.

She'd been rolling her eyes at Simon's departing back and blushed that James had caught her. He grinned. 'I think I'm going to be another demanding customer.' He showed her his badge. 'I need to know what David Stephenson did here from 3 p.m. to 8 p.m. on Wednesday. Apparently, he got room service?'

'That would have been Elena.' She picked up the phone and asked Elena to pop to reception to talk to a detective. 'Anything else?'

'May I see your CCTV? Of the car park? And anywhere else you might have it?'

'There's a camera at the back of the hotel. It doesn't work, but I'll make a copy of the recording from the camera in the car park. Just within that time?'

'Give half an hour each way. And thanks.' He turned to see a willowy teenager approach, wearing the hotel uniform, chewing gum.

'I'm Elena.' She had a deep eastern European accent and looked uneasy. 'What is the problem?'

'There's no problem, Elena. I'm asking about a guest. David Stephenson. On Wednesday, during the planning conference, you took a room service meal to him. He was in room …' He turned hopefully to the receptionist who was tapping on the computer.

She scanned the screen. 'Room 27. He had the Ahi tuna, according to the bill. He called the kitchen at 5 p.m.'

'Oh. Yes. While we were preparing for the formal dinner for all the guests. We were short-staffed so I help in kitchen. I had to run with tray, to get back in time to set the tables. I took to his room about five thirty.'

'Did you see him? Or just leave it by the door?'

'Of course I take it in. Put it on table, set it out nicely.'

'And he was there? Did you see him?' James grasped at the straw.

'Yes. Said thank you. Gave me very nice tip. I rush back. Later, I collect empty tray from outside his room. About six thirty. Before we start serving in the restaurant.'

Fishing his phone from his pocket, James found David's picture. 'This was him?'

Elena peered at the screen. 'Yes. Anything else? I have to collect breakfast trays.'

As she dashed off, James turned back to the receptionist. 'Could

I send our SOCO team over, to check the room? Just in case we unearth anything useful.'

'Well, he checked out on Thursday. It's been cleaned and someone else is in there …'

'Anything you can do to help would be appreciated.' James knew he could push it, but warrants took longer than charm.

'I'll help the guest move tonight, when they're back, and I'll make sure no one else goes in. OK for your team to come tomorrow?'

'Perfect.' James smiled.

She pushed a USB across the counter. 'Here's your copy of the CCTV. And Mr Stephenson made a phone call at 4 p.m. It lasted one hour.'

James frowned. 'An hour? Could the phone have been left off the hook?'

The receptionist shook her head. 'No. If the receiver's knocked off, it sets off an alarm. It's very loud. We'd have heard it. And the call's to an international number.'

James looked at her in surprise. 'Oh?' *Who used landlines these days? Especially for international calls. You'd Skype or FaceTime.* A lightbulb. *Unless you wanted it to be logged.* 'Can you give me the number?'

She glanced at the office. 'I don't know. It's not the best time to ask the boss. He's not happy. He offered Simon a free room, but he's just been strong-armed into paying his huge bar bill. And he's cagey about things like phone numbers at the best of times. CCTV is one thing – it's the hotel's, we can hand it over at our discretion, especially as anyone can see people coming and going. But private phone numbers are another thing altogether.'

'This *is* a formal murder inquiry,' James reminded her.

'In which case, it won't be hard to get a warrant, will it?'

James left the hotel with a sense of frustration. *I probably don't even need a warrant.* David needed twenty minutes to get across town at rush hour, plus the extra thirty minutes the roadworks added to journeys this month, plus another twenty-five minutes to reach Manor House Farm, whether by country lanes or jammed main roads. That was two and a half hours. Plus time for … the attack. And for clearing up.

David just didn't have time.

Chapter 10

'James?' On the other end of the call, Ashley's voice sounded urgent. 'Mrs Crows had a stroke, which led to a coma. She still hasn't come round. The doctors say these types of comas can last weeks. Or even years. So they're monitoring her.'

'What could have caused it?'

Her exhale crackled down the phone. 'I know what you're thinking. At her age it could be natural causes. She's eighty-eight, with high blood pressure so she has been on this medication for years. She has a history of angina and TIAs. It might *not* be suspicious.'

Dread uncurled in James's stomach. *It had to be suspicious. It was too coincidental.* 'Let's not take any chances. Get uniform on the ward and in place before you leave. Ask them to get a move on, I'd like you to meet me at Applewood in about an hour, if you can. Ask the hospital to monitor her closely and run every kind of test to see if anything contributed to her stroke. See if it could have been induced.'

Saturday 28th August – 10.15 a.m.

Sensing rising tension from Nell – probably at being invaded en masse for over an hour and Erin's … *Erin-ness* – Adam suggested they head home. He dropped Erin off first, but not before she'd insisted he take her climbing later. His phone buzzed with a text and he asked Sylvia to check it.

Shifting unhappily on the Volvo's grubby seat, Sylvia took the phone. 'It's Erin, giving you more dates she's free to go climbing.' Another buzz. 'Hmm. She's "gonna climb Adam like a tree". Sylvia pursed her lips. 'And I thought *I* was direct. That rather removes any ambiguity, doesn't it?'

Adam shrugged, hoping Sylvia couldn't tell he burned with embarrassment. 'She's only human.'

Three quick buzzes. 'She's "blushing". Says that was meant for a friend. "L-O-L".' Sylvia's eyes narrowed, as if unconvinced. 'If Erin's confident enough to tell her friends you're a sure thing, you'll have to let her down gently, you know.'

'What do you mean?'

'Oh, come on. I've seen you in the office. It's obvious your affections lie elsewhere. One doesn't give the last chocolate Hobnob to just anyone. If your heart was any more on your sleeve, you'd need to have it surgically removed.'

Adam couldn't help laughing. 'And I thought I was being so enigmatic.'

'Yet you haven't made a move because you don't know if Nell will turn you down and you're not used to being knocked back. It doesn't mean you should lead Erin on.'

'It's just flirting, Sylv. Didn't think you – of all people – would be down on that.'

'Don't give me that. *Ads.*' Sylvia was clearly gratified by his sheepish look. 'We both know it's delicious fun – *if* both parties have the same expectations. But if they don't …'

He must have looked crestfallen, because she relented. 'If you really want my two-pennyworth, I'd say Nell feels the same. After all, you've got inside her inner sanctum.' She chuckled at her innuendo. 'In, what? Four months? I've not managed that in four years. And, I have to say, it's not what I expected.'

Adam's hopes soared, but he wrenched his thoughts from Sylvia's first sentence. 'What do you mean?'

'Well. It's all a bit luxe, isn't it? Yet Nell doesn't exactly dress like she's got money. Hangs around in combats, jeans and T-shirts. No designers. Not even brands.'

'Well, yes, practical, for site work. But … you think she likes me?'

Sylvia sighed. 'I despair of the younger generation. Yes. Nell likes you. But more to the point, what's your theory on her? Orphan of wealthy parents? Con artist? Murdered a millionaire ex-husband? Discerning kleptomaniac?'

Buoyed by Sylvia's affirmation, Adam joined in her game. 'I'm thinking spy.'

'Hmm.' Sylvia gave an approving nod. 'As in, industrial espionage or as in, all this ecology lark is a front for a life of international subterfuge and danger?'

'Oh, the latter,' Adam said. 'Most definitely. And when she's not surveying, I bet she's got a few trench coats in her wardrobe.'

His cheeks instantly burned and Sylvia's head snapped round to look at him with a mischievous grin. 'Aha! So a spy fantasy peppers your pickle.' She gave another gleeful chuckle.

Adam shook his head, trying to own his unguarded remark. 'What's not to like? Bit of danger, bit of glamour, fast cars. You, of course, would be the villainess …'

'Oh yes, in the slinky dress at the casino, dripping with diamonds,' Sylvia agreed.

'… who meets a grisly end in the finale,' Adam deadpanned.

'Live fast, die young. That's my mantra, anyway.' Sylvia's gaze slid towards Adam. '*Don't* say it, sweetie. Being young at heart is what matters.'

They shared a contemplative silence until Sylvia said, 'Nell is a bit of an enigma, though. I've known her years yet I can't always read her, and reading people is my forte. She always seems to be … holding something back. If I was interviewing her for an article, I'd feel infuriated with her not sharing what my journo's fevered imagination would decide were all the juicy bits. And then I'd do my best to wheedle them out of her.'

Adam laughed at Sylvia's honesty. 'Same here – it's natural curiosity, isn't it? We ecologists spend all our days looking for evidence in the field, trying to piece together species' activities from the most minuscule field signs, playing detectives. So, when things don't quite add up, it's …' He groped for the right word.

'Disconcerting?' Sylvia offered.

'Intriguing.'

Sylvia cackled. 'Get away with you.'

As Nell's guests left, Erin and Sylvia's laughter at some remark Adam had made echoed across the drive before the gate glided shut behind them. Alone again, Nell sighed at the mud and leaf fragments that were now ground into the antique hall runner from Erin's boots, despite the large inset doormat she could have wiped them on. *Bloody Erin*. Nell brushed the dried mud out, then hoovered, scrubbed Erin's boot marks off her kitchen cupboard door, cleaned up Zorro's equipment, and gathered up the coffee cups.

Erin had chipped her cup. Nell stared at the gouged rim. Erin hadn't even mentioned it, let alone apologised. She'd left the reference library behind, too. Well, that was fine. Nell could take it into the office for other people on the team to use.

As Nell loaded the dishwasher, her irritation grew. So much for Erin's proclamation about valuing and appreciating things. Bloody hypocrite. Dishing out judgements based on assumptions and presenting them as facts while not living up to the same standards. She'd seen it again and again. This was exactly why she liked to keep her distance. She should have said no to Adam's suggestion to have them round. Erin had probably only agreed as a way to spend time with him. If only Nell had refused, Erin could have gone climbing with Adam instead, and at least she wouldn't have had to watch them flirting. Ugh. She imagined Erin tumbling artfully off a bouldering wall, holding her hands out for Adam to pull her to her feet, his muscles flexing, Erin staggering against him, him bending to kiss her. Ugh.

She slammed the dishwasher door. The silence was deafening. Even Jezebel was out exploring. For the first time, her house felt … empty.

It was fine for her colleagues: they socialised, shared their lives like normal people. It hadn't been difficult. Until Adam. A black hole of emptiness swelled in her chest. She squashed it down. She couldn't expect to have everything. And she'd chosen to guard her privacy at all costs. So she was used to silence, to keeping herself busy.

Her fingers twitched towards her phone. She texted her mum:

Time to chat before you leave for Paris?

The reply was quick and crisp:

Love to. But your father's been looking after the passports. (= Lost). Hunting high and low … 💀

The local paper had been left on the kitchen counter. Nell stared at Sophie's sunny smile. Erin was right about one thing, the media would be keen to report on the case. It had been awful seeing her own name in print before. The thought of it appearing in relation to a murder sent a shiver of dread up her spine. If the police had finished with her, she didn't exactly want to push her luck.

But the word leaped out at her. *Bludgeoned*. Sophie had been bludgeoned. And she'd heard it happening. She'd have to tell James. There was no denying it anymore.

Chapter 11

Having relinquished the car so Val could drive to the station, James got out of the Uber at the driveway entrance, beside the sign – APPLEWOOD RESIDENTIAL CARE HOME – and waited for Ashley. Henrietta Lambert would almost certainly know about Sophie's murder, either from seeing it on the news, or in the local paper today. He just hoped she wouldn't be too upset to help with enquiries.

James assessed the care home as he considered his approach. Even from this distance, it was obvious the Tudor mansion had been adapted for frailty. Aside from the high-tech security system, each entrance was flanked by handholds and rails, every set of steps paired with ramps. The ground-floor French windows had grab-rail-enclosed slopes leading to private gardens, which were carved from the undulating grounds and levelled with paths wide enough for wheelchairs. A landscape of fragility. He'd need to be gentle.

He turned at the sound of a car and waved at Ashley. She parked and they walked up together. 'If this Mrs Lambert is anything like my gran, I'm preparing myself for a bit dithery but sharp as a tack underneath,' she said.

'Let's hope.' James was willing to be patient if it meant information.

Inside, a flushed receptionist – a different one to last time – helped an elderly guest sign in while also assisting a waiting resident. The phone rang, then her pager buzzed.

She greeted the detectives with a pleading expression. 'Could you wait a moment while I deal with all this?'

'Of course,' Ashley said.

The receptionist let the answerphone take the phone call while she helped the resident, then showed the visitor the way to the day room.

A few minutes later, James saw her race down the corridor in response to the call on her pager, so he reached for the sign-in book, flicking back to the day of Sophie's murder.

'Andrew Arden came here on Wednesday. To meet Sophie and Henrietta Lambert, and Mrs Crows?' He scanned the list of names. 'Ah, yes, here he is.'

Ashley looked over his shoulder. As James flicked back through the dates, she said, 'There he is again, Monday 23rd August.'

James glanced down the column. 'No, that's someone from the alarm company.'

Ashley shook her head. 'Not that one, the one below it.'

'Ah, yes.' James flicked all the way to the first page. 'Looks like that was it. But this book only goes back to the start of July.'

'OK, well, our chaperone approaches,' Ashley warned. He replaced the book on the desk, open on the right day, picked up a pen and signed them in.

'Sorry to keep you,' the receptionist gasped as she ran back. 'Now, how can I help?'

James turned on his best smile as they showed their badges. 'I'm hoping you can help us with two things. One's easy, we'd like to speak to Henrietta Lambert. But the second is trickier. We'd like to take a look in Mrs Crows' room. And, no, I don't have a warrant. But time is against us, given that she's in a coma a few days after her granddaughter was murdered. If we can find out anything that could help our enquiries …'

The receptionist bit her lip. 'I can't really argue with that. Mrs Crows adored her granddaughter. I'm sure she'd want to help. Look, I'm acting manager this weekend but I'm sure the boss would agree. Just don't take any paperwork until either I can get the boss to confirm it's OK, or you have a warrant.' She gave James a spare key. 'Here. Have you signed in?'

'Yes.' James pointed at their names in the book. 'I noticed that Sophie came here most days to visit her grandmother. Did her husband, David Stephenson, ever come?'

'No. We all thought that was odd. I overheard Mrs Crows asking her about him. Sophie always said he was busy with work but sent his love. And when she showed us her snaps from their wedding in Las Vegas, she said it was easiest because David's relatives were a bit scattered.' She gave a sad shrug. 'Some people just aren't very family minded. We have some lovely residents who only see their loved ones at Christmas. But you never know, with families. There can be all sorts of reasons for estrangements.'

'Do you remember how Sophie was when she came here on Wednesday 25th? She signed in at 11 a.m.'

'Oh, I remember. Because, of course, that was the last time I saw her. I've replayed that again and again, wondering if I could have changed what happened.' She chewed her lip. 'Sophie seemed … agitated. Upset. She stayed for lunch. Which is always lovely. Most of the residents know her and had something to say when they saw her in the dining room. After lunch, Mr Arden joined them in Mrs Crows' room. And soon after that, Sophie left.'

James held the brief silence as the receptionist gathered herself.

'Anyway, Mrs Crows' room is number 12, on the ground floor along there. And you'll find Mrs Lambert in the day room, that way, doing the crossword.'

'Thanks.' James steered Ashley quickly away from the desk, then whispered, 'Mrs Crows' room first. In case she changes her mind.'

Her room looked startlingly different to their last visit. Elegant but empty, silent, the scent of floral talc and lavender polish cloying in the overheated space. An uncluttered red leather-topped desk stood in the bay window, giving its user a downland view. The desk was orderly: a pen stand held two silver fountain pens, a blotter bore ghosts of letters past, and a collection of business cards were tucked into the leather surround.

Photos of Sophie at various ages were up on the mantelpiece, always with a horse and some huge rosette. The most recent picture showed Sophie beside a sign. James could only make out the letters RHSU. In another, a younger Sophie had her arm around a formidable-looking elderly woman: short silver hair shaped around her head like a helmet, her stern face softened with coral lipstick and blusher, immaculate in tweed skirt and cream blouse. The woman's steel-blue eyes crinkled with her confident smile as she looked directly at the camera.

'This is our Mrs Crows, then,' Ashley said, snapping on latex gloves. 'Smart, organised. The type who gets things done, I imagine.' She took a photo of the picture, then looked around the room, checking drawers and inside wardrobes. She felt under the mattress before going into the en suite where James heard the quiet click of the bathroom cupboard.

With gloved fingers, James opened a large envelope and whistled. 'I've found the paperwork Andrew Arden mentioned, which would transfer the deeds of Manor House Farm from Sophie's name to David's company. It's dated 16th August, so Sophie must have brought this with her. If David had gone to the trouble of drawing this up, he couldn't have known how Sophie and her grandmother had handled the inheritance of the manor. It's unsigned, which bears out what Andrew Arden said.'

He laid out the pages on the desk blotter to take pictures. Checking the photos, he saw his close-up shots had caught three of the business cards tucked into the blotter's border: Andrew Arden; Dave Dixon LLP; George Humby, Handyman. He smiled. His dad hung on to every card he was given, too. Only his all ended up forgotten in his useful drawer.

'Nothing to report,' Ashley said as she walked back into the bedroom.

James opened the desk drawers. Most contained stationery, shopping lists in a spiky hand, and more photos of Sophie and horses with dates on the back. In the top drawer, he found a letter. He read it and laughed. 'Looks like Mrs Crows did a thorough job of petitioning the council to force David to carry out every type of survey going for his housing development.'

But looking at it again, the fluid copperplate wasn't Mrs Crows' writing, or Sophie's. *So who'd written this?*

Saturday 28th August – 12.15 p.m.

The vibrating hum of her phone pierced the silence and made Nell jump. It was disturbingly loud, only growing louder as she prised it from her tight trouser pocket. It was Adam. Nell winced as she answered, shrinking back into the bushes.

'Nell? I'm sorry about this morning.' Adam's voice and the background sound of driving seemed to boom through the phone speaker. She clicked down the volume.

'What? It's fine,' she whispered, as she squinted at the uniformed police guard standing on the other side of the blue-and-white police tape. The legal side. Where she should be. He turned and looked in her direction. *Had he heard?* She shuffled back an inch.

'No, it's not fine. I don't know what Erin was going on about with her training. I'm sorry I talked you into having her over and she didn't appreciate your efforts.'

It was clear what Erin did appreciate.

'It's fine, Adam. It's not a big deal. A murder case is at least good for putting things in perspective.'

'Yeah, I imagine. Are you OK about … all that?'

'Yes. Fine.'

'You … you don't sound very fine. Why are you whispering?'

'Well, I've just been to the police. To tell them what I heard in the tunnel—'

'You did?' An exhale puffed down the line. 'I'm so relieved you told them. So now they'll realise you may be in danger. Offer some protection instead of treating you like a—'

'Yeah, that's not exactly how it went down. Oh … bollocks …' Nell crouched low as the guard walked along the cordon towards her. She had hoped to speak to James; even if he thought she was pathetic, at least he seemed inclined to believe her. But, instead, it was Val who received Nell's update with the sceptical remark that, now she was a person of interest, how handy she could suddenly remember more details. The cynicism had pushed Nell to take a more … *proactive* approach.

'What are you doing?'

'I can't really speak now.'

The silence at the end of the line convinced Nell that he had gone and it wouldn't be rude to hang up. But as her thumb reached the button, Adam swore through the phone.

'Nell, I can see where you are. You're still sharing your location with me from doing the survey. What the bloody hell are you doing?'

Saturday 28th August – 12.15 p.m.

Applewood's receptionist beckoned James and Ashley as they approached. She nodded towards a woman in a burgundy coat, handbag on her knee, reading a paper over the top of her gold-rimmed spectacles. Her tight grey curls formed a sculptural sea of waves, which didn't move as she shook her head at the article, blinking rapidly.

'That's Mrs Lambert. She's just asked me to book a taxi to go to the police station. I thought I'd wait for you to see her, and then book one if she still wanted to go.'

James nodded, and Ashley approached like a stalking cat, as if trying not to alarm her. 'Mrs Lambert?' she enunciated. 'I'm DS Ashley Hollis. This is DS James Clark. Can we help?'

Mrs Lambert looked up, her eyes bright in her plump face. 'I'm not deaf, dear. And it might be private that I want to speak to the police. I don't like my private affairs bellowed all over reception.'

Ashley looked instantly contrite. 'Sorry. But can we help? Or would you rather go to the station?'

'Well, that depends. Are you investigating Sophie Crows' murder?' She patted the front page of the Pendlebury *Herald*. Under her stern tone, her face trembled.

'Yes.' James stepped forward. 'And I was hoping to speak with you, Mrs Lambert.'

'Good.' Mrs Lambert heaved herself up on her polished black walking stick. 'May I have some tea and cake for my guests in the day room?'

James and Ashley both shook her heads. 'Oh, none for—'

Mrs Lambert tapped James's ankle with her stick, firmly enough to shut him up but not enough to hurt, and he saw sense. 'Do you know what, I'd love some tea and cake. Thank you.'

Mrs Lambert turned an innocent smile to the receptionist, who folded her arms. 'Righto. I'll call the kitchen and someone will bring you a tray.'

Mrs Lambert led James and Ashley down the corridor. 'Come along.'

They passed Applewood's immaculately laid dining room and came to a bright Victorian-style conservatory, where morning sunlight flooded through the windows. Two elderly men played cards. One raised beetling eyebrows at them as they passed. James bit back a smile at the pile of cash at stake. A cookery programme absorbed three women, each criticising the chef's methods.

When Mrs Lambert gestured at some seats, James set down the

photo albums they'd been permitted to take from Mrs Crows' room and offered to help with her coat.

'Thank you, dear.' She patted a spare chair and he folded the coat carefully over it as she fussed with her navy cardigan. Her seat commanded a view of the grounds. A large cedar shaded the lawn and the generous borders along the driveway were planted with colourful flowers and mature shrubs. The side table next to her had a copy of yesterday's *Times*, a stopwatch stopped at eight minutes and twenty-one seconds, and the cryptic crossword completed in strangely familiar copperplate writing. *Ah.*

'Right.' Mrs Lambert adjusted her glasses and searched her handbag. She pulled out a sheet of carefully folded paper, then peered at it. 'You want to know about Sophie's visits, I expect. And I see you've searched Midge's – Marjorie's – room.' She nodded at the photo albums. 'Which means you probably want to know about the wills. And the development.'

'Wills?' James asked. 'Plural? Both Sophie and Mrs Crows changed their wills?'

'Yes, dear. That's the point.'

'Sorry, what's the point?'

'Sophie changed her will. And she's been …' Mrs Lambert waved her hand over the paper, shaking her head, trying to form the words. 'And Midge changed hers, and look – two days later, she's taken to hospital. I very much hope that looks suspicious to you, detectives.'

'Yes. It does. But can you tell us why Mrs Crows changed her will?'

'Yes. Ah, here comes tea.' Mrs Lambert nodded at the carer bearing a tray with a huge pot of tea, three teacups on saucers and a slice of lemon drizzle cake. 'Thank you, dear,' she said as the carer left them to their conversation, then nodded at James. 'You can be mother. Now. Where was I? Oh yes. It started with Sophie.' For a second, her lip tremored. 'Poor darling Sophie.' She took a sharp inhale and squinted at her note as it wavered in her hand.

James poured the tea, using the opportunity to glance at the note.

Chicken supreme = Monday, croquet = 16th.

'Sophie visited on Monday the 16th. Poor girl was in a dreadful state. She arrived after we'd finished our game of croquet and were in here having tea, so it must have been about half-past three. Her husband dropped her off, his car stopped about where yours did.'

James shifted in his seat, unnerved at her unexpected observation. He tried to hide it by pulling the plate of lemon drizzle towards him. It did look delicious. But Mrs Lambert shot him a wounded, indignant glare. Hastily, he pushed the plate back. When he pushed it all the way across the table to her, Mrs Lambert rewarded him with a small smile.

'Thank you, dear. I'm only allowed one slice a day, unless a kind visitor orders on my behalf. And I do have to keep my strength up, you know. As I was saying, Sophie walked up the drive. Odd, I thought. What young man doesn't take his young lady right to the door? She waved him off. And as soon as he'd driven away, she just … sagged. Like the stuffing had been knocked out of her. She took a large envelope out of her bag and made a telephone call. She came inside but, about thirty minutes later, she was back out there, pacing while she was on the telephone again. That's when Midge came down and told me all about it.'

Mrs Lambert paused to sip her tea, snick off a corner of cake with a silver cake fork and eat thoughtfully.

'What did Mrs Crows tell you?' Ashley asked.

'Sophie had found out that her husband didn't intend to develop her home, Manor House Farm, into a riding school, as they'd agreed. It's a beautiful home. Probably needs some work now but plenty of potential. Sophie will … *would* have made a wonderful job of it.'

She fished a lace-edged handkerchief from her sleeve and dabbed her eyes.

'But, as it turned out,' she continued, 'her husband had very different plans. *He* wanted to build a large housing estate. The plans arrived through the post from the architects. Sophie worked out his return could be several million. Well, you see, he and Sophie had not been married long. She feared he had only married her to get his hands on the manor. She seemed to think the house was the key to his development idea.'

Mrs Lambert took another forkful of lemon cake and finished her tea. 'Well, of course, we put our heads together to come up with ways to scupper his plans. The first thing was to make sure he couldn't get his hands on the family home. That's where the wills came in. Oh, and did you know Sophie had begun divorce proceedings? That was the second step. The third was to take him to the cleaners. *Before* he realised he couldn't get the land.'

James fought to keep his face straight, then realised she'd be gratified by seeing his reaction, and let out a shocked chuckle. *Don't mess with the old guard.*

'Of course, Midge's connections helped no end. The mayor used to scrump in her orchard. And she knows several councillors. They all played their part to get the planning officials to act quickly. We'd sent them copies of our letter, asking the council to require the full set of surveys for this development that Sophie's husband had planned on the sly. Sophie had appointed an architect to design her riding school. He'd advised her about doing surveys before she could start work so Sophie got her fancy telephone out and looked up all the other types of surveys one should do for a large development.'

Mrs Lambert held up her hand and checked the surveys off on her fingers. 'Archaeology, endangered wildlife, protected trees, landscape, increases in traffic, noise, hydrology. Sophie's architect had told her about all the policies and legislation the council had to uphold, so she looked all those up and we cited those in our letter. I wrote out the copies, of course, Midge's eyesight not being what it was. I've got a spare you can have. Unless you took Midge's copy from her room, too?' She sat back, looking weary. 'Any more in that pot, young man?'

James poured her another cup.

'So did Sophie think the letter and the surveys would stop David?' Ashley asked.

Mrs Lambert sipped the tea James gave her. 'Oh no, dear. She just wanted to hit him where it hurt: his wallet. She estimated those surveys could cost forty to fifty thousand pounds, based on the advice her architect had given her. It sounds a lot but, in the grand scheme of things, it wasn't; Sophie said he'd already have needed to raise over two million pounds through considerable loans and a punishing repayment schedule just to get started. So he'd probably meet the building costs through partnerships with construction companies. Bearing in mind his return could be multiple millions, Sophie didn't think these extra – relatively minor – costs would stop him. But …' She pointed a finger to emphasise her words, and then took a sip of tea.

Ashley leaned forward. 'Yes?'

'Sophie realised his loan repayments would be carefully calculated, and any change to the repayment period would make a significant difference to the overall amount. It wasn't the *cost* of these extra surveys. It was the *time* they would take and how they extended the repayment period that would be financially catastrophic. She estimated that for every two months of delayed work, an extra hundred thousand pounds could be added to his costs. Plus, any delays would put his partnership with the construction companies under strain. And *then* he'd find out it was all for nothing! Because he wouldn't be able to use the land anyway! Sophie signed the letter. She wanted him and his planners to know it was from her.'

She sat back. 'You know, she was always such a gentle, quiet girl. Quite different to Midge, who was always quite the sergeant major. But that afternoon, it was nice to see a bit of her steel in dear little Sophie.' Her face trembled. 'I hope that wasn't why ...'

Tutting, Mrs Lambert shook her head. 'No good thinking like that. I wanted to tell you something else, but it's gone out of my head. Memory's not as sharp as it was. It will come to me, I'm sure.'

'And Mrs Crows' will. Do you know what the amendment was?' James asked.

'Ah, yes. Well, Midge had made herself and Sophie joint tenant owners of Manor House Farm. Normally the set-up would be that, when Midge dies, her half would go to Sophie, and then, if anything should happen to Sophie, it would all pass to the husband. But now, of course, Sophie and Midge wanted to make sure that wouldn't happen.

'Midge was quicker on the uptake than Sophie. Once she learned about the husband's plans, Midge got the solicitor over here to change her will on –' she glanced at her note '– oh, yes, Monday. The 23rd. Sophie changed her will a couple of days later on Wednesday 25th. Which of course was the same day ...' She twisted her hanky in her hands.

'So, you see, detectives, Midge changes her will right after we put a spoke in the wheel of the husband's plans, and then she falls mysteriously ill. It's too coincidental. I was at Bletchley, my dear. I'm trained to see beyond coincidences. Midge is my dearest friend. And Sophie is ... *was* a like a granddaughter to me, too. I want to know you're going to catch the ... the *bastard* who did this.'

James met her eyes. 'I promise you, we're doing our best with our enquiries. Ashley here stayed with Mrs Crows all night until we could put her under police guard.'

Mrs Lambert gave them a watery smile, patting Ashley's hand. 'Thank you, dear.'

'But can you tell us who Mrs Crows named as her new beneficiary?' James asked.

'Oh. Yes. Midge didn't tell Sophie what she did. She believes she was protecting Sophie's interests. Midge left half the estate to Sophie. And the other half to her solicitor. Andrew Arden.'

Chapter 12

The police officer strode around the perimeter of the cordon, towards Nell. Her heart pounded so loudly she was sure he could hear it. Adam was still berating her through the phone. With a pang of guilt, she hung up. Holding her breath, she crept back until sharp branches speared her back, so she folded her body as low to the ground as she could. *God. I should do more yoga.* The officer strode towards her.

Damn. Had he heard her phone call? God, of course she'd get a call at the worst possible moment. Bloody Adam. Kind, lovely Adam. She pressed herself low into the spiky brambles as the officer walked right past her, his boots crunching on the loose stones of the country lane skirting around the boundary of Manor House Farm.

A phone rang. *Oh bollocks. Not again.* Nell stared at her phone's blank screen, then realised the officer was taking a call. Her exhale ruffled the leaves near her face, but he turned, paced back to his spot at the bottom of the drive. Nell grabbed her rucksack, scanned the grounds through the undergrowth and crept off in the opposite direction.

Her mouth was dry. She couldn't afford to get caught. This was definitely an arrestable offence. But she had to try. Val's and James's unconvinced expressions were scorched into her mind. If her information so far hadn't proved her innocence, she'd have to find something that pointed at someone else's guilt.

Startled at a rustle of leaves, Nell slammed herself against a broad, rough oak, twitchy as a deer. *God, never mind the officers, what if the murderer returned to cover their tracks? No, you're being irrational ...* Yet, when a thrush emerged from a bush in a ruffle of feathers, a worm dangling from its beak, Nell's legs threatened to wobble underneath her.

Dear God, come on. She was the only one who'd looked around these woods in such intimate detail right before Sophie's murder. If something was different, if there was some minute clue, she could well be the only person who'd notice. *Get on with it.*

The midday sunlight, at odds with her feeling of unease, filtered through the dark, leafy boughs of towering oaks, hemmed with hazel hedgerows. Around her, chirruping wood warblers and nuthatches declared their territories.

Nell picked up a nibbled hazelnut, with dormouse tooth-marks, below tendrils of traveller's joy threaded through the hazel like a dormouse highway. She followed the winding vine like she had before. A few paces on, the plant was ripped, strands straggling in the hazel.

She frowned, sure the traveller's joy had been perfectly intact before. She checked her photos, scrolling on her phone until she found the picture of the hedge. There was no doubt. When she'd last been here, the plant hadn't been torn like this. The strands dangled, flung around the hazel trees, as if flayed inwards by something bulky ploughing between the trees, from the road. And here the trees were most widely spaced, almost two metres apart. Examining the branches, she found a twig had snapped inwards, almost invisible amongst the dense leaves. Bulkier than an animal or a human. Just about the height and width of a car. The broken twig could be the height of a wing mirror. She snapped some quick photos.

Ducking under the police tape, she checked the officer wasn't walking along the lane, then viewed the plants from the road: perfectly intact. Back inside, she scouted for tyre tracks, but the baked ground resisted helpful markings. This wasn't a track or bridleway. Anyone who squeezed their car through the trees to off-road would have to wind between the dense bushes and scrub. No one would take this to be a turning into the manor. *Unless ...*

Nell stood, unease spiking through her. The wood echoed with staccato shouts of blackbirds, punctuated with the hammerings of a woodpecker that almost matched her pulse.

If the murder happened while she'd been inside the tunnel, Nell knew for certain the murderer hadn't accessed the tunnel the way she had, from the wood. And they'd taken this route to get to the house. Looking for signs had been one thing; *finding* them was another. She was walking in the footsteps of a killer.

A sharp warning screech of a blackbird made her swing around, her gaze darting everywhere for signs of police, or the murderer intent on silencing her.

Adam's words – that Sophie's killer knew she'd been at the scene of the crime – looped in her head as the rhythmic sound of crunching footsteps approached, slow, careful, as if trying to be quiet. Nell crouched, then lay on the ground and elbowed herself under the boughs of a rhododendron. Her breathing grew shallow as fear cycloned in her chest.

Her view was obscured by the broad leaves, but she saw jean-clad legs walk past. They angled this way then the other as the person turned, obviously scanning the area.

Heat slicked over Nell's body. She grappled for her keys, gripping them in her fist, metal tines poking out between her fingers. Her steel-toe-capped site boots were good for kicking. She knew from practice that she could kick a six-foot-tall man in the head if she had to. And not all the plum places for damage required that much balance.

In front of her, through the branches, the legs stopped.

Saturday 28th August – 12.30 p.m.

James put the call on speaker so Ashley, driving, could hear. 'Go ahead, Hesha.'

'We've got some financials on Anna Maddison. She's had four payments transferred into her bank account over the past two months. Ten thousand pounds each. But I can't trace them. They're from a Swiss numbered account.'

'So someone's paying her a lot of money, and going to a lot of trouble to cover their tracks. Blackmail? Knows something she needs encouragement to keep quiet about? Can you extend the search, see if she's had any earlier payments. And look at other accounts. Try David Stephenson, Sophie Crows, Simon Mayhew, Nell Ward. See if anyone has any corresponding outgoings.'

As Hesha signed off, James glanced at Ashley. 'Can we reroute? Try David's office. If Anna's not there, we'll call on her at home.'

Thirty minutes later, Ashley parked beside Anna's Porsche. 'Lucky first time,' she said. Her phone beeped and she sighed. 'Can I catch up on my millions of emails while you speak to her?'

'Sure.' James got out of the car and approached the building.

Inside, he heard Anna's voice. He tapped on the inner door and opened it a crack. Anna jolted with surprise, then looked relieved and beckoned him in, waving at a chair. '… I apologise for any inconvenience. I'll let you know when the manor is accessible again. Thanks for your understanding.' She rang off. 'I hate answerphones, but at least it's efficient.' She crossed out a task on a short, neatly written list.

It was amazing she could find a pen, the pen-holder on her metal-and-glass desk seemed to only contain cuticle sticks and nail files. Her seat blocked the window, wasting the view of the river. Behind the uncomfortable chair that James perched on, a pair of white plasticky sofas flanked a glass coffee table, on which architecture magazines were scattered, even though David didn't seem to have put any design principles to good use here. The high corniced ceiling allowed light to flood the room, but the hard white walls drained any warmth. James couldn't help wondering what Nell would do with a space like this.

The open double doors into David's office showed the room was empty. Even though he was absent and their project had ground to a halt, Anna was doing a convincing job of looking busy. Files were spread across the desk, while email alerts bleeped on her computer.

'I wouldn't normally be in on a Saturday, I've just come in to tell the surveyors they can't access Manor House Farm. And to email the planning officers to tell them the development is on pause.' She smoothed her sleek bobbed hair.

'You didn't prefer to call or email from home? Save the trouble of coming in?'

Anna shrugged. 'I came in just in case David turned up. It can't be nice to be home alone …' She chewed a fuchsia-glossed lip. 'To be honest, he's barely spoken to me since …'

James nodded. 'Of course. Who appointed the surveyors originally?'

'I sent out for quotes and reviewed them, summarised their pros and cons for David.' She selected a folder from the pile on the desk. 'They're in here if you want to look at them.'

James took the file and glanced through the detailed quotes.

'The archaeology and hydrology surveys were starting on Tuesday. They're the ones I cancelled today. The ecology survey began the same day that Sophie …' She grimaced.

James turned to the three ecology quotes and leafed through them.

Anna pointed at the top one. 'EcoLogical Consultants weren't the cheapest but they could do the work quickest. And they were the only consultancy to mention surveying the tunnel between the house and the wood. The ecologist found the tunnel on an old map. Edwardian, I think she said. It gave me the impression they were thorough and wouldn't miss anything that would cause us future problems. I'm sick of expensive consultants doing that to us.' She pursed her lips. 'I recommended them to David on that basis.'

He flicked through EcoLogical's quote, pausing at Nell's photo in the 'Project Team' section – a striking shot of her making notes among the cobalt-and-ruby haze of a wildflower meadow. Her bearing was so upright it gave her a somewhat haughty air. But her smile lit up her face, her eyes startlingly bright, like they were gazing right at him. Her defensive clipboard barrier hinted at guarded vulnerability. Realising he was staring, he turned the page.

Dr Nell Ward's PhD research in environmental economics and policy contributed to a white paper by NGOs in mitigating impacts of development on natural ecosystems.

Moving to ecological consultancy, Dr Ward expanded her botanical and protected species survey skills. With survey licences for great crested newts, barn owls, dormice and bats, her portfolio of work includes producing ecological appraisals and writing Ecology Chapters for Environmental Impact Assessments for high-profile developments.

The habitat survey and bat assessment of the house at Manor House Farm would be undertaken by Dr Nell Ward. The evening bat surveys would be carried out by Dr Nell Ward and Dr Adam Kashyap, both Senior Ecologists, licensed to survey bats.

In his picture, Dr Adam Kashyap managed to be irritatingly handsome even in chest-waders and wielding a pond net. He was tall with unkempt dark wavy hair and a wide, infectious grin. *God, they'd make an annoyingly great-looking couple.* He could imagine himself with Nell, at swanky events like the police balls, sophisticated and elegant.

But with Adam, it would be all exhilarating adventures: casually abseiling down cliffs and knowledgeably exploring rainforests, all while rescuing rare species. He held in a sigh and read on.

Dr Adam Kashyap's research doctorate (*Pesticide Effects on Brain Development of Pollinators*) has informed governmental strategies and national management models.

As an ecological consultant, Dr Kashyap specialises in invertebrates, advising on brownfield development and living-roof design. His broader skills include protected species surveys, including reptiles and badgers, with licences to survey bats and great crested newts.

Four more pages detailed the survey methodology and itemised costs, with a standard contract in small print. 'May I take this?' At her nod, James asked, 'Why did you choose them if they weren't the cheapest?'

'Because they could deliver the work the quickest, which kept the overall expenses down. Since we had to accommodate delays and costs, completing the surveys as soon as possible was essential to minimise expenditure.'

'And how did David feel about having to do these surveys?'

'Like anyone would who'd just had the rug pulled from under them, to the tune of a few hundred thousand.'

James said nothing. He waited.

Anna sighed. 'He was in this position because of Simon. His planning consultant.' Her jaw tensed. 'Consultant my arse. The man's a fool. And David told him so. I nearly cheered when I heard him tearing a strip off Simon. It was long overdue.'

'They had words, then?'

'Yes. Firm words.' Anna turned to her screen, tapped the mouse with a manicured finger. 'On Friday the 20th.'

'Did he think Simon could have warned him, then?'

Anna sat back in her ergonomic chair. 'Yes! Of course! That was his *job*. These are, it turns out, standard surveys for a development this size. Simon's an experienced planner. He couldn't *not* have known. And David was paying him handsomely for his advice.'

'So why *didn't* he warn David earlier?' James asked.

'Good question. Simon claimed he'd been negotiating with the council to eliminate the need for the surveys. But that's a load of rubbish, if you ask me. If that *was* what he'd been doing, he'd have told David earlier and got the credit for trying to save him money.'

'Do you think Simon was just lazy? Or careless with someone else's money?'

'*I* think Simon was under pressure to get a big development through. This area is notoriously difficult to get any housing schemes permitted. And every year the housing target is missed, so the council's budget for the following year is reduced. And that diminishing budget hurt Simon. It reduced the pool of developers who could afford to invest in a major scheme. And no major projects meant no annual bonus. And, very possibly, no job at all.'

She glanced at the door, leaned across the desk and lowered her voice. 'There were redundancies at Simon's company recently. David's scheme wouldn't only be a coup for Simon, it would probably save his career. *I* think he needed David to get to the point of no return before these surveys were raised. And, given David went to Simon with a career-saving idea, look how Simon repaid him. With negligence. Withholding information he thought would be unwelcome from his client, burying his head in the sand, allowing David's problems to grow down the line. Simon's an incompetent, irresponsible, spineless fool.'

'Would these surveys put a stop to the development?'

'I hope not, for obvious reasons. It's not easy to find schemes like this. That's why David had to impress upon Simon how serious this was. He told Simon they both needed this to work out but if it kept haemorrhaging money, there'd be no deal. For either of them. He said he'd have no choice but to sack Simon and appoint a different planner. Unless Simon could soften up the council, keep the costs down and keep the development on track.'

'Did Simon manage to sort anything out with the council?'

'That's what the conference was for. Simon pulled strings to arrange it as David's perfect chance to, I quote, "describe the local socioeconomic benefits of the proposed housing development over an encouraging scotch". Anna shot James an arch look.

'And, if it didn't work, were you worried you'd lose your job here? If David needed to make cutbacks?'

The corner of Anna's mouth twitched in amusement. 'Oh no. I'm irreplaceable to David. I make sure of that.'

James glanced at her PC. 'I'll need to ask our forensic team to take a look at that. Just procedure. May I have your permission to take it today, or would you prefer I get a warrant?'

Anna flourished her manicured hands. 'Be my guest. I'll tell David that I'll have to take enforced leave.' She slid a key off her keyring. 'Here's the spare key. Lock up and post the key through the letterbox when you're done.'

She glanced at her watch. Cartier. The diamonds on the face glittered under the stark lighting. 'I'll leave you to it.' Anna slid her iPhone into her fuchsia Chanel handbag. 'I'm having lunch at Fevrier.'

'Very nice. It's got a Michelin star, hasn't it? I recommend the truffles,' James said, with heavy irony, as they walked outside. As he dialled the forensic team, he noted how she'd shut down the conversation when the focus was about to turn to her. He wasn't worried. He'd check Anna's story. And her financials. Then he'd return.

Saturday 28th August – 12.35 p.m.

As Nell watched the legs through the branches, still standing stock-still right in front of her, she imagined how she'd tackle an attack. If this person saw or heard her, he'd have to plough through the branches to reach her. That would give her a chance to land a solid kick somewhere tender. Buy her time to run. Not easy in tight leathers and heavy boots, with a rucksack. And a police officer to avoid.

She took a deep breath. Her nose filled with the earthy scent of woodland. And something else. Another woodsy, green scent, but warmer. Familiar. The tension melted out of her. *What's he doing here?* She sent a text.

I'm behind you.

A second later, the legs turned.

'Nell?' She'd expected the whisper to be Adam's, but hearing it was still a surprise. A strange fizz of annoyance (at not being left to get on with it) and delight (that he'd go to stupid, risky, illegal lengths to help her) swept through her.

She reached out and yanked Adam through the branches, the huge shrub enclosing them both in its green canopy.

'What are you doing?' he hissed. 'There's a bloody police guard.'

Nell held her hands up with an incredulous face to convey, *yes that's why we're hiding.* 'You should go. The police aren't interested in you. I'm the one on their radar.'

'I'll go when you go.' Adam folded his arms, his whisper firm.

'Don't be a pain in the arse. I've found something. I want to look around some more. And two of us will be more visible than one.' She eyed his red T-shirt, pointedly. He zipped up his green hoodie as high as it would go and folded his arms again. His eyes ran over her outfit, eyebrows flashing up at the leather trousers.

Oh, this wasn't the time for difficult questions. 'Fine, come on, then.'

She showed Adam the ripped traveller's joy and the photos of the same plant during her survey. 'If a car's been driven in, they can only get so far – look, the scrub and brambles get too dense. The car could have been left here, hidden by bushes, with just enough room to turn so they can drive out again.' She gestured at the clearing before the undergrowth encroached. 'But from here onwards, the murderer would have gone on foot.'

As they walked, Adam pointed at the ground. 'I see the clues to the badger sett.' A wide, low mammal path, cleared of the leaf litter and debris that otherwise covered the ground, crossed their route. The hard clay surface had been polished to a sheen by numerous low-slung badger bellies.

'I laid some sand outside the sett entrances to see if I'd get any paw prints. You reckon we might be lucky and the murderer could have walked that way and left a print of their own?' She raised a hopeful eyebrow and darted off.

As Adam caught up, she showed him the patch on the ground. 'Here's where I put out some bait.' Nothing remained of her house speciality: Crunchy Nut Cornflakes with honey, laced with coloured, inert pellets which would show up in the badgers' latrines to reveal the boundary of their territory. From the disturbed debris around the bait, the badgers had eaten it all, probably as soon as they'd emerged to forage. About the time she'd been engrossed in the bat survey of the house.

Squinting through the trees, Adam whispered, 'Wow, it's quite the place.'

Nell checked the sett: the eight entrances each had a wide apron of golden sand strewn out before them, showing a muddle of claw- and drag-marks. Obvious activity, but no clear print – of badgers or humans. 'Nothing.'

Returning to where they started, Adam asked, 'Why don't you think the murderer used the drive? Why bother off-roading?'

'Well, we're not the only people working on the project. Anyone could turn up.'

'So the murderer would have to know about the development. And know the property pretty well. Or have the chance to scope out where they could hide their car.'

'Yes. Which narrows it down to Sophie's husband, Anna Maddison, and any planners or contractors working on it.' She winced. 'Like an ecologist.'

They fell silent as they walked towards the house, then halted at the thinner bushes lining the top of the driveway. The signs of disturbance since she'd last been there painted a clear picture. From the grooves and ruts in the gravel, Nell imagined vehicles transporting the search team, detectives, pathologists, Sophie's body ... The long grass of the overgrown, untidy garden trampled by searchers' footsteps. Some large leaves unnaturally folded, where a searching stick had overturned plants to look for signs of Sophie. Or her killer.

Would they have noticed the torn traveller's joy, so well disguised, draped in the hazel trees? It was the only sign someone had driven into the wood. And she'd only noticed it because of the plant's importance to link trees for dormice. Even she could appreciate her view of the wood was pretty niche.

Someone dressed in a protective suit emerged from the house carrying a case. Nell and Adam squashed together in the hedge.

'Have you seen enough now?' Adam's whisper was hot against her ear, and she could practically feel the pulse in his neck. A smidge faster than hers. She resisted giving a flirtatious reply: *not nearly enough.* But another officer came out of the house and Adam dragged her away. 'Come on, Cookingdean's Most Wanted. We're pushing our luck.'

Chapter 13

Saturday 28th August – 2.15 p.m.

James's sense of doom increased as he hurried along the bleached corridor, dodging knots of slow-walking families, following Ashley to the hospital desk. The uniformed officer on guard had texted to say that Mrs Crows had visitors: Sophie's two friends, Isobel Wright and Katie Miller. James wanted to get there quickly to take statements.

'Hi, I'm back again to see Mrs Crows. Any news on those toxicity tests?' Ashley asked the nurse behind the desk.

'What tests were those?' The nurse frowned at the screen. 'Ah.' She clicked the mouse, then turned to check a whiteboard on the wall. 'No. Not yet.'

'Do you think you could … You know.' Ashley wound circles in the air. 'Speed up proceedings a bit. Given that the lab will also take some time.'

'We only decided to do them a few hours ago. And we do have other patients.'

'Any other patients involved in a murder investigation?' Ashley asked.

The nurse folded her arms.

'These are urgent. Not only for our inquiry, but possibly Mrs Crows' life. Could you get someone to do them in the next ten minutes, while we're here? Then fast-track the lab?'

'I'll do what I can.' As they walked away to Mrs Crows' room, the nurse muttered, 'If anyone can empathise with overwork and under-resourcing, it should be the poxy police.'

James flinched but Ashley shrugged, then knocked on Mrs Crows' door. Inside, three faces turned to look at them. The officer by the bedside cabinet nodded as they entered.

The two younger visitors sat beside the bed. James introduced himself and Ashley, then asked, 'How's Mrs Crows? Anything to report?' He gazed at the frail woman in the bed. Her hand rested on her chest, a cannula dripping solution into her ridged, green veins.

'No change,' the officer said. 'And just these two visitors.'

'Hello, Mrs Crows.' Ashley's smile made her tone warm. 'Nice to have two of Sophie's friends come to see you.' She turned to the young women, inviting introductions.

'I'm Isobel,' the dark-haired girl said. A small bunch of flowers had started to wilt in her clenched hand. James noted the FLOWERS NOT PERMITTED sign, and her disappointment.

'I'm Katie.' The other girl brushed auburn hair back from her pale face. They both had immaculate, selfie-ready make-up which looked startling to James, in real life.

'I can't believe what happened to Sophie,' Isobel said, her eyes wide. 'It's just so ...'

'... Awful.' Katie stared at her lap. 'I feel like it was my fault. I ... I, like, didn't even reply to David when he texted me to say she was missing.' Sounds of cars outside filtered through the window as James waited for Katie to fill the conversational gap. 'What if I had? What if I, like, could've told him where to look?'

'Where would you have suggested, if you had replied?' James asked.

'Oh, I don't know. Her grandmother's? The manor?' She shrugged.

'They were checked straight away,' James said. 'But you can help with something. I need to know more about Sophie. Can we get a drink in the café and take your statements?'

A harassed nurse bustled in and asked them to leave so she could take Mrs Crows' tests. Ashley flashed her eyebrows at James. But, pleased though he was at seeing progress with the tests, James didn't share Ashley's optimism.

Minutes later, he put two almond-milk skinny lattes on the Formica table for Sophie's friends, gave Ashley a large Americano and sipped his own flat white. 'How did you meet Sophie?'

'So, it was like, we were all thrown together at uni,' Katie said. 'Housemates on day one. We, like, totally clicked. Soph preferred a small group of friends. We got close quickly.'

'Who else was in her small group of friends?' James asked.

'Only us, really,' Isobel said. 'She didn't like talking about her family. It brought up the accident. And the fact that she lived in this manor house. Some people at uni had, like, wealthy backgrounds. They were there for the ride, not the degree. Sophie wanted to be a serious businesswoman. She had big plans for her place and wanted to make a proper go of it. For her grandparents, I think. If anyone found out about her home, they were either jealous or took the piss when she tried to study. So she was very private.'

Katie nodded in agreement. 'She didn't even hook up until she met David.'

'What did you think of him?' James asked.

The young women looked briefly lost for words, until Isobel shrugged. 'Barely knew him. They met at the end of uni, so we'd never gone out with him as a group. No mutual friends.'

'Did you keep in touch after graduation?'

Guilt flickered on Isobel's face. 'At first, but not so much recently. Apart from the occasional WhatsApp. Katie and I started our business. And it's a beast. *So* much to do – increasing our client base, growing networks and presence. Keeping in touch sort of … slipped. You don't notice the time. You come up for air and a year's gone by.' Her words rang with regret.

'We met for drinks when we first graduated,' Katie said. 'Soph came to London a few times and we hit some bars. But it happened less and less. She stopped suggesting dates, and we did, too.'

'Did David ever join her, in those visits?' James asked.

'Never,' Isobel said. 'She said it was her girls' weekend escape.'

Coercive relationship? James leaned back and drank so Ashley could take over.

'Was it difficult for Sophie to join you?' Ashley's tone was light. She added sugar, which James knew she didn't take, to her coffee to avoid any confrontational eye contact.

'I did wonder if D didn't like it,' Katie said. 'When she was with us, he messaged her all the time. She'd sometimes get pissed off with the things he texted. She tried to hide it, but I watch loads of YouTube body language stuff. So it was, like, totally obvious to me.'

Ashley smiled. 'Very perceptive. Do you know what his texts said?'

'She never showed us. We never asked,' Isobel said.

'Do you think he had anything to do with her visits tailing off?' Val asked.

'Maybe.' Isobel shot a wary glance at Katie. 'But we were busy. She could have been, too.' Her miserable shrug looked more like a slump. 'We'll never know now.'

'You said they got together towards the end of uni,' Ashley said. 'When was that?'

'At her grad ball,' Katie said. 'She, like, literally couldn't have left it any later. Wasn't for want of us trying. We're *matchmaking queens*.'

Ashley looked quizzical at the emphasis. 'Oh?'

'We created a dating app. It's, like, supercoool.' Katie's vocal fry lengthened the word. 'We matched up our friends. We were good at seeing how people would, like, fit.' A suggestive smile flickered. 'To start with, we kept track for fun. When we realised how many people we'd set up, our database became an algorithm. By the end of uni, we had a start-up. Now, we run events for clients our app has matched, but *they* don't know who they're matched *with*.' She leaned in and murmured, 'Imagine: dark, sexy bar, throbbing music, and one of the select gathering is your perfect match. It's electric – like sexy human soup. We called it Singularities.' She eyed James as if expecting to explain the name.

'I get it,' James said, annoyed she assumed he wouldn't.

Katie didn't look convinced. 'Because it, like, combines singles with—'

'Yes. The big bang,' James interjected. 'I get it.'

Katie twirled a strand of hair around her finger. 'I don't think you do. It's a pun. Big bang. Like, the start of a whole new universe and—'

'Yes,' James interrupted, wanting to get back to Sophie. 'Monumental sex. I get it.'

Katie's lips twitched. 'Well, if you get monumental sex, you won't need our app!'

Ashley smirked at James over her coffee cup. James groaned at himself, then laughed.

Isobel didn't laugh. James noticed concealer caked in hollows under her eyes. Heavily defined eyebrows twitched, failing to rise or crease her forehead.

Isobel showed them a YouTube clip. 'This is what we were doing while ... Sophie ... While it happened.' In a moodily lit bar, Isobel and Katie mixed with clients then retreated to the background in selective edits of laughter, conversation and lingering eye contact.

James saw the name of the bar on a drinks menu. *Cerberus.* 'What time was this?'

'It started at six,' Isobel said. 'Midweek mixers are early for the straight-from-work crowd. We arrived about three, set up, sorted the lighting, arranged seating so people could get cosy without being overheard. We briefed bar staff on keeping the mood going, to help with small talk if people were nervous. Had a bite to eat, got glammed up. The evening flew. Some people started leaving at nine, but a few stayed to the end, at eleven.'

Katie showed James their Uber trip details on her phone. 'After we cleared up, we got the Uber at eleven thirty. Arrived home at, like, ten to twelve.'

'The next day we did the follow-up, in the office,' Isobel said. 'Personalised info for each client, let them know if they'd found their match or not, curated the clips for social media, checked in with the venue. Knackering. We zoned out for the night. Movie and pizza. I didn't even notice David's text. Which is just …'

'Yes, me neither,' Katie said. 'It's, like …'

'Awful,' Sophie's only two friends said in unison.

Saturday 28th August – 3.30 p.m.

James hefted the morning's yield of Mrs Crows' photo albums, David's solicitor's details, and the ecology quote onto his desk, then loaded Pendlebury Hotel's USB. He threw Ashley her sandwich, unwrapped his own and ran the CCTV video of Pendlebury Hotel, picking up the card to call David's solicitors again while he watched the screen.

As Ashley peeled cellophane off sweaty bread, she mumbled, 'I need whatever Anna's got. Give me a Michelin star over a petrol station sarnie any day.'

'Umm.' James ended the call as the solicitor's answerphone clicked, already engrossed with the grainy video footage, noting David's stationary gold BMW in its parking space at 14.30. He fast-forwarded until he saw activity. At 15.14, a tall blond man in a blue suit walked down the hotel steps, into the car park. *David.*

'Yeess.' James leaned forward. The man walked out of the camera's range and James held his breath. Six minutes later, he walked back up the steps and into the hotel. With a groan, James pushed his sandwich aside, but kept hopeful eyes on the screen. After a few more minutes of no activity, he hit fast-forward. Nothing. The time ticked by in the bottom right corner. He got to 20.00, then 20.30 and the recording stopped.

'Damn it!' He shoved his chair back, nearly colliding with Hesha bearing coffees.

'Whoa!' Veering away, she saved the valuable caffeine. 'What's going on?'

'I was sure I'd find David slinking off on the hotel CCTV. But he just had a walk around the car park, which Simon Mayhew mentioned. Cooling off after a chat with planning officials didn't go his way.' He tossed the solicitor's card aside, too. It didn't matter if David knew if Sophie had filed for divorce, if his alibi was solid.

'Ah. I'm deep in CCTV-duty, too.' Hesha cracked her neck. 'Trying to find Anna Maddison in hours of footage from Nye Hall Hotel. She checked in at about four thirty. Booked a double room in her name, for two, but her companion didn't join her until eleven.'

'Who was that?'

'The receptionist said he checked in as Mr Smith. Tall and fair-haired and *he* was married. Tan line where a wedding ring would be. The staff run a sweepstake on how many affairs they check in each month. Highest at Christmas, if you're wondering.' The cynicism was incongruous in Hesha's cheerful, youthful voice. *Give it a few years, she'll be as tough as Val.*

'Was the man David Stephenson?'

'Not sure. I'm checking the CCTV. Haven't got a good view of his face yet.'

'So what did Anna do, all alone, until eleven that night?' James asked.

'That's what I'm working on. I know from the hotel docket that she had dinner at 7 p.m. Until then, she'd taken herself for a walk in the grounds. Luckily for me, that's just about fifty acres, with barely any camera cover. So I need to check all the cameras' footage at all the times, until I pick her up again. It's a right pain.' Hesha rubbed her neck.

'No helpful hotel staff saw her around the time of the murder?' James asked.

'I wish. But no. She may have been enjoying an innocent evening constitutional, or she may have been somewhere else entirely.'

'Ugh.' James sympathised with Hesha's painstaking task, then leafed through the ecology quote and took out Nell's photo, adding it to the board.

Ashley joined him. 'Very pretty.'

'Just more up to date. With the haircut.'

'Uh huh.'

James tried not to look flustered under Ashley's sharp eyes, glad of the interruption by a junior officer darting in, holding the door for Val, then waving a sheaf of computer printouts. 'Results of recent car searches on the PNC and ANPR data for DC Hesha Patel.'

'Aha! Brilliant, thanks.' Hesha scanned the pages as she gulped her coffee.

'Is this a good moment for a catch-up?' Val asked James, who nodded, turning back to the incident board.

'We can take Isobel Wright and Katie Miller off the list of suspects.' He crossed them off the board. 'The bar owner corroborates their account of running a filmed event in London at the time, and both women appear throughout the video.'

'But they did allude to tension in Sophie and David's relationship,' Ashley said. 'Possibly coercive, if he made it hard for Sophie to spend time away from him. And, since she'd lost most of her family, she wouldn't be hard to isolate. Something to bear in mind.'

Hesha summarised her printouts. 'Hot off the press, here's the vehicle info. We know Sophie's car ended up in the garage at Manor House Farm. Her vehicle was recorded near her and David's flat in the morning but there's no more coverage after about 10.30 a.m. when she drove towards Applewood. To get to the manor, her route would have taken her along some country roads with no camera coverage. So we can't verify what time she arrived.' She huffed in frustration and looked at the next printed sheet.

'David drove to the conference, parked up for the duration of it and didn't move the car, then drove back to the office and home, exactly as he said.' She turned the page. 'Nell Ward used a company car.' She frowned. 'Her records are patchy due to using country lanes. But road cameras verify her stop for petrol, so what we *can* check of her journey seems to be as she described it.'

She turned the page. 'Adam – or Aravindan – Kashyap was recorded by several cameras on a motorway, matching the journey he gave us between Quince Meadows and Pendlebury. His stop at a service station matches the break he said he took. He has access to the same work car Nell used, and he's been driving it since his tyres were slashed.

'Anna Maddison left the office a little earlier than she says, but she must have used country roads because her route isn't verified.'

Hesha frowned. 'I don't recognise this. Anyone request ANPR for a car reg Five-Tango-Four-Lima-Lima-One-Zero-November – red Audi TT? Owned by Paul Dunn.' At the blank faces, she read out, 'Brief stop at Tesco on the dual carriageway to Pendlebury – ring any bells?'

'Oh, red TT?' Val said. 'Yes, it's the burned-out car from the industrial estate. Joyride gone wrong, they think. Someone in the roads team must have asked for a reg check and it's got picked up with our set.' Val paused. 'Stopped at Tesco? For alcohol, maybe?' She shook her head. 'Can you send it to them, sharpish, Hesha? They'll need it.'

Val shot a piercing gaze at James. 'That's a timely reminder that a lot of our team are helping the roads team with their enquiries. Chief said he'd get some extra hands on deck if we need them. Do we?'

James scanned the board. Progress seemed good. 'I think we're OK. Thanks, ma'am.'

'Fine. So, are we any nearer making an arrest? Or have we just got one main suspect with a solid motive but an equally solid alibi, and another main suspect with no alibi but no clear motive?'

James added a picture of Andrew Arden to the board. 'Let's keep in mind our friendly solicitor is due to become the proud owner of Manor House Farm, should Mrs Crows die. So he has a hefty motive.'

Hesha stretched after scouring CCTV footage. 'Maybe David's alibi is so watertight, with the phone call from the hotel room – I mean, who does that these days? – because he knew he'd need one. Maybe he had an accomplice?'

Val folded her arms, letting James take the lead. He got the hint. 'Like?' he asked.

'Anna?' Hesha suggested. 'Whose precise location will probably be impossible to verify. Maybe that's what the payments were about? Maybe she and David were having an affair?'

'Otherwise, someone who depended on the development?' Ashley added. 'Like Mr Gilpin? He didn't tell DC Ed Baker in his house-to-house that David had bought his fields, did he? So he's keeping pretty tight-lipped about his connections.'

James shrugged. 'I can imagine someone wouldn't divulge selling their land—'

'Yeah, but Mr Gilpin's land was tied up in a development that Sophie was sabotaging. It also gives Simon Mayhew a motive, since this was such a key scheme.'

James nodded. 'True. But Simon's also got a watertight alibi. He was at the conference.'

'Maybe Simon had the accomplice?' Ashley suggested. 'Working with Anna? Or a surveyor who knew the site? If a major development is important for one consultant, it could be equally significant for another. Guaranteed work, high local profile, reputation ...'

'How many consultants had been commissioned?' Val asked.

'Ecology, archaeology and hydrology,' James answered. 'Anna cancelled the archaeology and hydrology surveys this morning.' He tried not to squirm at the unfortunate fact: 'Only the ecologist had been to the site.'

'And it sounds like David approved the surveys,' Ashley said. 'So he'd know Nell would be there, and when. What if she was his accomplice?'

'Somehow, all roads of this investigation lead us back to Nell Ward, don't they?' Val looked at James. He sighed, his heart sinking. But he couldn't disagree.

Chapter 14

Nell put her bike away and closed the garage. She and Adam had crept out of the wood, avoided the police guard and snuck back to Adam's car – and Nell dreaded him asking how she was getting home. She still didn't know where to start with explaining all the things he didn't know about her background. But then Erin had texted. And Adam had dashed off. Of course. *Bloody Erin.* At least the summons meant Adam hadn't seen her bike, and bought her some time.

But she couldn't talk herself out of the pang of regret. *Maybe it would have been a good way to start that discussion?* He'd turned up at the manor, he'd breached a crime scene, put himself at risk to help her. *Had there been a fizz of chemistry?* Nell opened the front door, typed the code into the alarm, pulled her boots off. She sensed she could trust Adam. But it wasn't just trusting *him*, it was trusting her own judgement. It was hard to make that leap when you'd believed someone to be trustworthy before – but been so badly, utterly wrong. *And when Erin had snapped her fingers, he'd gone running, hadn't he?*

Why was she turning this into a big deal? Adam was just concerned for her safety. They were colleagues, friends. *He's kind-hearted. He'd have checked up on anyone.*

Inside, Jezebel met her with a hopeful purr and rubbed against her legs, nudging Nell towards the cupboard of cat food. 'Nice try; it's too early for dinner.' Nell scooped up her fluffy cat and rummaged, one-handed, for a tape measure. She'd still got something out of today that could distract her. And might just help with the case.

Gripping the end of the tape measure with a sock-clad toe, Nell measured up to her shoulder, which matched the height of the torn traveller's joy in the woods. It took three attempts with Jezebel batting the tape but eventually Nell measured 1,350 mm. She scoured the website on her laptop, showing dimensions of every car model. Any

Ferrari or Lamborghini could have limbo-danced under the vine without tearing it. But most cars, which were that height or taller, would have torn it. The murderer's vehicle could be anything from a Mini to a van. No help at all.

Jezebel looked stricken as Nell retracted her new toy. Nell shared her disappointment. She'd hoped her unique view of the wood would glean some clever, major insight, so she could offer the investigation some dazzling solution and redirect their investigation firmly away from her. No such luck. She wasn't just out of ideas, she feared the detectives had reached the same impasse: a dead end, with only one person in the frame: her.

A buzz in her pocket broke the gloom. Adam.

Sorry about dashing off. Hope you're OK? You didn't hang about, getting home! 😜

Her phone buzzed again. Erin. A selfie. *Since when did Erin send me photos? Ah. She's at the sodding climbing gym, that's why. Poured her twenty-something, yep – as I thought, cellulite-free – body into improbably flattering Lycra. She even looks sort-of OK in a climbing harness.* Nell huffed, staring out of the window. *She's just playing games, don't get wound up.*

Another message from Erin beeped:

In good hands! 💪

Ugh!

When the phone buzzed again, she nearly flung it across the room. But it was Percy. The beam across her freckled face didn't falter at Nell's grumpy hello.

'Oh, you sound happy. I'd've thought any day you're out of clink is a win.'

'At least in prison you can be left in solitary confinement.'

'I'm not sure that's an *option*, exactly. What's the problem? Are you coming under too much fire from your handsome detective?' She waggled her eyebrows. 'Resigned to ending up in handcuffs one way or another?'

'No. I am Off Men.'

'I know. Since forever. Well, since—'

'Yeah, OK, don't dredge up ancient history.'

'But I had high hopes! First time you've sounded interested in anyone for ages.'

Distracted by Jezebel jumping onto her lap, making her move her computer, Nell asked, 'Who?'

Percy's eyebrows shot up. 'There's more than one?'

'There's none. Very much none.' Nell lifted the phone up and leaned back as Jezebel circled her lap, her fluffy plume of a tail tickling Nell's chin.

'Not buying it. And you know I won't let it go now. You may as well tell me everything.'

'I thought there might be something with a guy at work.' Jezebel finally curled up and raised her chin, eyes squeezed shut, awaiting fuss.

'Ah. Adam. Ecological action man with bulging biceps and irreverent sense of humour.'

'What? How …?' As Nell stared at Percy, the break in attention was remedied by a pointed head nudge from Jezebel.

'Mentionitis. You've talked about him before. Just a bit. So what happened there?'

'He flirts with everyone. I misjudged things.'

'Don't strike him off for being a flirt. Doesn't mean he's not into you.'

'I'm pretty sure he's into someone else. And, you know, he's a colleague. I don't want things at work to get complicated.'

'So, what about the handsome James?'

Feeling herself blush, Nell had to admit, 'Yeah, there's definitely something about him. He's … intriguing. Seems completely professional. But, every so often, I get a hint that he might be interested. But it's hard to tell, you know, underneath all the questioning for murder.'

Percy nodded gravely. 'And, of course, in his position, he'd have to remember the Midsomer Rule.'

'What's that?'

'Whenever any detective on TV fancies a suspect, they're always the one who dunnit.'

Saturday 28th August – 5 p.m.

James hung up. He wanted to hurl his phone across the incident room but he placed it on his desk, took a deep breath.

'Free therapy with your coffee?' Ashley put a refilled mug on his desk.

'Deal. I'm chasing down Andrew Arden's alibi. He was with a client. He emailed a copy of his diary with his client's contact info. But I think the client in question has gone abroad for the Bank Holiday. I'm getting a foreign ringtone and they're not answering. Not even texts.'

'They'll be back tomorrow. Tuesday latest. Probably. End of the week, for sure.'

'Oh, you're no help. We're on a crunch. Val's getting it in the neck from the chief. He needs to see something decisive. And I don't like where the investigation is going.'

He reacted to Ashley's raised eyebrows before even she had a chance to fully elevate them. 'I know. I'm clutching at straws. I just want to cover every alternative before …'

Ashley levelled a long look at him. 'Before your favouritism shows?'

'Before we lose the opportunity to cover all bases. I'm just being thorough, Ash.'

'Yeah. Of course you are.'

He huffed a long sigh. *Tonight was not going to be fun.*

Chapter 15

Nell stirred her homemade Bolognese sauce as it bubbled on the hob. She was making an effort to eat properly, even though she didn't really feel like it. Nor was she a great cook. The rich, herby aroma filled the kitchen. It looked quite good, actually.

Feeling scratchy from the afternoon creeping around Manor House Farm, Adam rushing to see Erin, then Erin's goady texts, Nell had spent the afternoon trying to occupy her brain with something useful. Curling up with a coffee, and Jezebel purring on her lap, she reviewed the rewilding update for her family's estate. She'd been there for the arrival of the old English longhorns the previous week and shared the exhilaration as the huge cattle became acquainted with their new grazing land, yanking branches with their curved horns to strip – and pollard – the saplings. Baseline surveys had been taken, with more scheduled to show increasing biodiversity as time went on. Nell felt a spark of excitement at the positive start, and the impact this would have. At least she could make a difference to *something*.

Zorro's evening test flight had been successful, in marked contrast to the morning, but he'd been impossible to catch. Hence her late dinner. But it was a good sign. Plus, his weight approached normal levels, his injuries were healing, and she'd given him his penultimate dose of antibiotics. At this rate, he'd be ready to return to the wild soon. It was great progress. But she still felt unsettled.

Her thoughts kept sliding back to the woodland around the manor. She'd been so certain she'd find *something*, give James some major breakthrough to solve the case, put her in the clear, and get the whole thing over and done with. *But then, what?* He'd have no reason to see her. Unless he asked her out. Or she asked him … Her mind wandered to an imagined date, and what he'd be like outside of a murder investigation. The crinkles around his eyes suggested he laughed a lot, and she had a hunch he was insightful, and kind ... *But then, I can't always trust my judgement, can I?*

Her gate intercom rang. Nell sighed, turned off the hob and strode to the display screen. It was him. James. The sight of his tentative expression made a smile spread across her face as her heart thumped. She buzzed him in, checked the mirror, ruffled her hair ... *Oh God ... What if he's here because he knows I've been back to the manor ...?* Too late now, he was coming in. She heard the car door slam. Then a second door. Her stomach dropped. *Oh God ...*

Offering tea or coffee, she led James and Val to the kitchen and shoved the pans containing her abandoned meal to the back of the stove. Typical that the one time her cooking hadn't been a disaster, it would spoil anyway.

'Sorry to interrupt your dinner, Dr Ward.' Val gestured at the hob.

'It's fine.' *Well, it had to be, didn't it?* The impassive detectives gave nothing away. Nell's unease rose. She poured coffees, then they walked into the living room together. The stern-faced detectives sat on one sofa while Nell took the one opposite. She sat upright, ankles clamped together, back straight, hands resting in her lap. She made no attempt to fill the awkward silence. James seemed absorbed with something on his iPad, yet to make eye contact with her. Nell prickled with apprehension, disappointment hollowing out her chest.

Val began. 'We have some more questions regarding Sophie Crows' murder.'

'OK.'

'Do you know a Simon Mayhew? From PTP planning consultants?' Val asked.

Nell grappled with the unexpected name. 'Yes ... Ah. Is he the planner involved with Manor House Farm? I'm sure Anna Maddison mentioned him, if I remember correctly?'

'Have you worked with him on any other projects?' Val asked.

'Yes, a few,' Nell said.

'What's your working relationship like?' James's suspicious tone made Nell's heart plummet.

'Distant.' Nell's mind was racing. Between James's demeanour and the mention of Simon Mayhew, she wondered what about the development had caught the detectives' focus.

'Did you like working with him? Do you get on?' James probed.

Nell hoped frankness would make them cut to the chase. 'No. To be brutally honest, seeing his name on a project always makes my heart sink. He cuts corners. It creates problems for specialists like us, advising clients of surveys they need, because he'd already given the impression there'd be no need for any. It usually makes clients quite … frustrated.'

'What happens when he tries to make you cut corners?' Val asked.

'Nothing,' Nell said.

'So you go along with it?'

'No, I mean I *don't*. I talk to the client, even when Simon makes that difficult. My issue is that it's planners who control when specialists like us are brought on board. If we can talk to a client before a scheme is fixed, we can design out a lot of expensive surveys and mitigation measures. But if we're commissioned last minute, which is Simon's approach, then there's no scope for that. When options are limited, everything's more expensive. And our surveys are seasonal, so a lack of forward planning creates delays and adds extra costs.'

'What's the advantage to Simon's approach, then?' James asked. 'It can't make his clients happy?'

Nell shrugged. 'I think he hopes he'll get away with excluding the surveys. Hopes the council wouldn't realise surveys are needed. There's not always thorough regulation, so maybe it works sometimes.'

'You're saying councils don't check?' James asked.

'Not always,' Nell said. 'But that doesn't make the need for surveys disappear. It usually just gives them room to grow into a problem which is more difficult and expensive to manage. And it also gives people opposing developments ammunition because they can check the council's website to see if the right surveys have been done.' Nell shrugged again. 'Simon's methods have never made any sense to me.'

James frowned. 'So how does all this fit with your ecological values, then? Careless councils, ruthless planners – who you work alongside. This housing development would see acres of woodland buried under concrete. Don't you care about that?'

'Yes, *of course* I care about that. But if I'm the ecologist on the scheme, I at least have a shot at making a difference. Like advising how retaining habitats benefit not only the environment, but also the developer.'

'OK, so what would you have recommended for Manor House Farm?' James asked.

'I could explain how it's impossible to replace ancient woodland, and that the costs of addressing impacts of the destruction on protected habitats and species would be considerable. But, conversely, research has proven that green space provides wellbeing benefits for future residents, which could be reflected in housing prices – so financial value, as well as environmental value, is achieved by retaining the wood. And there's lower-value habitat at the manor that offers developable land, without the impact. If they only built on that, even though the area is smaller, it would generate a similar profit once the overall costs and added value are taken into account. There would also be a lot of positive publicity and goodwill to be gained by retaining such important habitat. But in reality, it comes down to money.'

Val leaned forward. 'Ah. Money. So, be honest: you and Simon are both consultants. If schemes don't happen, that puts you both out of work, doesn't it? So you have a common aim. Has Simon ever persuaded you into doing something … let's say less than above board?'

Indignation rocketed through Nell's chest. 'Absolutely *not*.'

'He didn't have anything over you?' James asked.

'No.' Nell folded her arms.

'What was it you told us when we first met you?' Val asked. She made a show of consulting notes on her iPad. 'Ah, yes. That you're not a tree-hugger or a purist. But more of a pragmatist. It'd be pretty pragmatic to accept back-handers for developments which will probably happen anyway. And you do have a pretty nice place here.'

'You may call taking back-handers pragmatic. I'd call it corrupt.'

'So are you saying you're corrupt, now?'

Nell fought the provocation. 'No, *obviously* not. I'm saying I wouldn't engage in that. In any way. With anyone. For any reason.'

Val leaned forward. 'Allow me to summarise where we are. You were due to meet the murder victim at the time of her death. You're one of the few people who know about the tunnel, and you went in. You have a working relationship with Simon Mayhew and his tactics to put pressure on developments. In all our current lines of enquiry, there you are. Popping up as a consistent link. Not forgetting, of course, you're the *only* person we can place at the scene – at the *exact* time of the murder.'

A short, shocked laugh escaped Nell as she stared at Val, stunned at her tone. 'I've never disputed I was there. I've shown you why, and what I was doing, and exactly where I was on the estate, for the whole time. I've given you copies of the photos I took, which are timestamped. I've given you receipts.'

The detectives looked unmoved. She blotted clammy hands on her jeans.

'I know I don't have an alibi.' She swallowed hard, her mouth dry, at the laden word. 'But surely all this amounts to something?'

Val sat back and James leaned forward to take up the questions.

'Yes, you gave us a lot of information. We've taken some time to look through it. But the fact is, Nell, it's very easy to alter the date and timestamp of a photograph. None of your information is sufficient in the absence of an alibi. All it does is confirm you were there before, during and after the time of the murder.'

So even he didn't believe her now. Fear slithered in her stomach. *Oh God. Oh God.* 'Look.' Nell held up her hand protectively, the natural authority instilled by her upbringing breaking through her rising fear. 'Your questioning seems to be getting serious. I won't continue without legal advice.'

Standing, Nell halted the conversation, registering a flicker of surprise on James's face as she walked to the door. She gripped the handle to steady herself. Her legs threatened to give way, but she fought to appear calm as she stood, waiting for them to leave.

Val raised her eyebrows but neither she nor James stood up. 'That is, of course, your right,' she said. 'In which case, we'll need to continue this conversation at the station. Do you require legal aid or for us to call out the duty solicitor?'

Nell's heart pounded. *They were going to drag her to the station now?* She swallowed down her nausea and looked the DCI in the eye. 'Thank you, I have legal representation. I'll take a moment to make a call.'

The detectives began to stand.

'Stay here, please,' Nell said. 'I'll make the call in the kitchen.'

Leaning against the kitchen cupboards, Nell scrolled through her contacts until she found Charles Barrington. Her finger hovered over his name. A hot wave of shame-filled dizziness swept over her as she recalled the last time she'd needed him. She rested her cheek against the cool, painted wood and squeezed her eyes shut. As awful as it had been, Charles's effectiveness had been devastating. Her sword and shield. Which was lucky, since she didn't have a choice in the matter.

She tapped his number, took a deep breath, listened to the dialling tone. It was 8.15 p.m., but not too late for her to call him.

'Nell?' Charles's baritone instantly reassured.

'Charles, I'm sorry to call. I …' Nell's façade evaporated at the sound of his voice. 'I think I'm in real trouble.' Her bewilderment was audible, even to her. 'I'm being questioned in relation to a murder. The police seem to think I'm a suspect. They want to take me in for questioning.'

'Are you under arrest?'

'No. But it's … it's getting serious. I've said I can't discuss it further without you. They want to take me to the station now. Is there any possibility you can help?'

'Which station?'

'Pendlebury.'

'Give me a moment …' There was a brief pause, then, 'Right, you're about ninety minutes away …'

Nell's heart sank. 'You're in London? Working?'

'Yes,' Charles replied.

Nell's mind raced to find a way to minimise Charles's disruption. 'I think Conor's in London. If he can give you a lift to Pendlebury Station, could you work in the car?'

'Of course. If that suits him, it works for me.'

'Thanks, Charles. I'll call him straight away.'

'Before you go, Nell, some instructions. It's important you don't say any more to the police until we've spoken. I'm sure you'll have been very cooperative so far, but from now on you'll have to be more circumspect. Speak to absolutely no one until I get there. When I arrive, I'll go through disclosure with the officers to see what evidence they have so far. Then I'll talk to you. Until then, you'll be put in an interview room. It will be a long wait, and you might believe some officers are only being conversational. But *no talking*. Right?'

'Right.'

'Good. Next, they will want to search your home.'

Nell's stomach lurched.

'Do *not* consent, ask them to get a warrant. It will give me time to get there and assess the situation. OK?'

'OK. Thank you, Charles. One other thing, though. My parents are off to Paris. I'm glad they'll be away. I don't want them to know about this.'

'My dear, I may be your family's solicitor but what we discuss is confidential. Even so, don't rule out what support you may need at this stage.' Charles ended the call.

Nell scrolled to Conor Kennedy and dialled. He answered within two rings.

'Good evening, Nell.' Nell unclenched a little at Conor's warm, Irish brogue.

'Evening, Conor. Are you still in London by any chance?'

'No. Your parents took an earlier train so I'm nearly back at Finchmere.'

'Oh …' Nell bit back the involuntary note of disappointment.

'Everything OK?'

'Yes. Well, no.' She sighed. 'Not really.' At Conor's patient silence, Nell found herself explaining. 'I hoped you could give Charles a lift over. I … I'm being interviewed by the police in relation to a murder—'

'Charles Barrington?' Conor sounded worried. 'And you're at which station?'

Nell heard the squeal of car tyres. Relief and gratitude flooded through her. 'Pendlebury. I'm sorry to—'

'Tell Charles I'll be there in under two hours. And at the station before midnight.' The line went dead.

She texted Charles with Conor's ETA. His reply was instantaneous.

Thanks. Gives me time to get organised.

Nell took a deep breath. She was fortunate to have their support. But their immediate, sober responses increased her worry. She tried to ignore her churning stomach and be practical as the detectives spoke in low murmurs in the living room. She transferred her congealing dinner to the fridge, made a flask of coffee and grabbed some biscuits and a chocolate bar, tucking them into her messenger bag. The latest, unread copies of *New Scientist* and *Forbes* sat on the counter and she added those, too.

Zorro! And Jezebel! Oh God. She dashed to the utility room and filled a bowl of food for Jezebel. Not knowing how long this would all take, Nell gave her a generous portion. Like magic, her cat slinked up, even though it wasn't dinnertime yet. Nell placed the food and water bowls in the bathroom to keep cat firmly separate from bat, in her absence, and locked the cat flap. For Zorro, she put extra dishes of food and two additional bowls of water in his cage, then closed the utility-room door so Jezebel couldn't get in.

Back in the living room, Nell nodded at the detectives. 'Thanks for your patience. My lawyer can get to Pendlebury Station at about midnight. Would you like me to meet you there, then?'

'You're not formally charged with anything at the moment,' Val said. 'But it's best you come with us to the station now.'

Dread crawled over her, but she'd expected this answer and nodded.

As if wanting to make the most of her compliance, as they walked to the door James asked, 'We'll need to search your home. Do you consent to us proceeding?'

Nell hid the burn of betrayal at his request by shrugging on her jacket, slinging her bag over her shoulder. She raised her chin. 'No, I absolutely do not consent to a search. If you need to search my home, you will need to obtain a warrant.'

She ushered them both outside, set the alarm and locked the door behind them.

Saturday 28th August – 11.45 p.m.

James read his interview notes one last time. Technically, he was ready to question Nell when her solicitor arrived. But it didn't feel good. He took his coffee and wandered down the silent corridor to drink it staring out of the window at the drizzle hazing in the lights from the lamps around the station's entrance. It was the nature of the job to do things you didn't always like. While he didn't have any conviction in questioning Nell, he couldn't defend her and seem impartial – Val and Ashley would be only too quick to point that out. He wished he had another plausible suspect. But he'd failed there, too.

Even Hesha seemed to have Nell in her sights. She'd finished checking the CCTV footage and launched straight into Nell's phone records with surprising enthusiasm for someone faced with an Excel sheet of numbers at nearly midnight.

Over the muted chime of the station's clock tower striking 11.45 p.m. he heard the low rumble of a refined, powerful car as a burgundy-and-silver Bentley Mulsanne swept up to the entrance. A fine mist of rain dazzled in the headlights and beaded on the damson wings, reflecting the lamplight.

Driver stopping to make a call? Or a wrong turn? But the driver got out, opened the rear passenger door, extracted an umbrella from the door's recess, opened and held it up, ramrod straight, as he surveyed his surroundings. A second man, tall and smoothing his thinning flint hair, emerged from the car. He buttoned his jacket and straightened his yellow silk tie, then spoke to the driver, took the umbrella and marched to the door like a brigadier about to discipline his brigade.

'Er ... ma'am?' James called along the corridor to Val.

The door opened and the man entered, just as she joined James in the corridor.

Val approached the visitor. 'Can I help you, sir?' she said. 'I'm DCI Val Johnson. And this is DS James Clark.'

'Good evening.' The man shook their hands, grey gimlet eyes boring into them. 'Charles Barrington, of Barrington and Co.' He handed Val his thick, hand-pressed business card.

James smoothed his shiny high-street suit, self-conscious and uncomfortable, not just because the stranger wore Savile Row's made-to-measure finest, but because his whole demeanour was so formidable, polished. Even Val looked dishevelled beside this guy.

'I'm here to represent Lady Eleanor Ward-Beaumont. Also known as Dr Nell Ward.'

James started at the revelation, spilling hot coffee on his shirt. 'Bollocks.' Nell had made no mention of this, and their searches hadn't uncovered an alternate identity. He held the hot, stained patch away from his chest. 'Sorry, ma'am.' He turned to Val, pained that he'd revealed they were on the back foot. A man like Charles would use that to his advantage. *Great.*

Val remained as impassive as ever, though her jaw clenched at his reaction. 'We'll take you through disclosure,' she told Charles. Eyeing James's stained shirt, she added, 'Or perhaps I will, while DS Clark gets cleaned up.' As she walked down the corridor with the lawyer, Val glared at James over her shoulder. He understood; he'd use the time to do some digging.

Returning to the incident room, he stared at the board of assembled evidence. Nell was peerage? *Explained the flash house. But if she had money, she definitely didn't need a job that involved hanging around in odd places at night. Why would she do that?*

Hesha wandered over. 'Hope you're having more luck than me. Seems our Nell Ward mostly calls de-listed numbers. Which is mighty strange, and very inconvenient. Why do I always get the awkward jobs?' Her eyes widened at the state of him. 'Oh God, what happened? Not wasting coffee! That's our life force!'

When he didn't respond she waved a hand in front of his face. 'Earth to James? Any signs of life?'

James turned to her. 'Sorry. Can you do me a favour and look up Lady Eleanor Ward-Beaumont, please?'

'Er, yes. Now?' She raised her eyebrows in surprise. 'Sure.'

As Hesha tapped on the computer, James rummaged in his bottom drawer for a spare shirt and changed.

'Nothing on file,' she called across the office. 'But a general search finds plenty.'

James dashed to her desk and peered at the screen. Hesha scrolled through lists of press articles. Various charitable events hosted by the Earl of Finchmere, Lord Beaumont and his wife, Imelda Beaumont, MP (not using either Lady or Countess) with daughter Eleanor. An interview with Lord Beaumont about the future of classic motor racing at Finchmere and Eleanor's fledgling idea to launch a class for classic cars that had undergone electric conversions. A piece on Finchmere's sustainable agenda, led by Eleanor, turning their organic farms into rewilded land. Images of Eleanor – Nell – in gowns at balls, in boilersuits racing classic cars, and in a Barbour and wellies leaning against a wooden gate.

'Bloody hell.' James stared at the photos.

'Explains her odd phone records, though. Probably family, taking security precautions.' Hesha began an advanced search of the police's computer for privileged information that couldn't be publicly accessed. 'Ho ... ly crap.'

James leaned closer. Old tabloid articles lifted from social-media archives showed Nell in a series of grainy photo-stills from a phone video.

'Tabloid journos never fail to disappoint, do they?' Hesha pointed at the unimaginative headline, THE LADY IS A TRAMP, blazing above the pictures. Nell cavorted in a luxurious hotel room with a rakish, good-looking young man. She wore a skimpy red devil costume and devil horns, then lingerie and devil horns, then just devil horns, in poses extolling the myriad benefits of yoga.

With a flash of heat, James undid the collar he'd just buttoned. 'Wow. Well ...' He averted his eyes.

'They wouldn't get away with a headline like that now,' Hesha said, scrolling on. 'And wouldn't it be great if, for once, it was a more accurate, PRIVILEGED WHITE MALE PIG SELLS OUT; TRIES TO MAKE PRESS COMPLICIT IN CRIME, and the pictures of Nell were redacted, leaving just him looking like a right ... Oh, *no*. The lowlife only went and released the *video*.'

James dropped in a chair. 'Bloody hell,' he said again. He felt dazed. 'Doesn't really fit with her arm's length image, does it?'

'Maybe that's exactly why she *is* so distant? Once burned, and all that. You know as well as I do, revenge porn is a horrible business. What a cheap, cowardly pig.'

Scanning the search results, her curled lip relaxed, then she gave a jubilant laugh. 'Ha! Looks like she got her own back. You don't often see tabloids back-pedalling this hard. She must have absolutely *hammered* them in court. Hence why you can't find these on the internet. She got a super-injunction slapped on them.' She squinted at the screen. 'Some hotshot lawyer – Barrington somebody? – got them every which way possible.'

Oh God. James rubbed his face. 'That same hotshot lawyer is going through disclosure with Val. As we speak. And then I'll be sitting opposite him while we question Ne ... *Lady Eleanor* Ward-Beaumont.'

'Oh no!' Hesha shot a sympathetic glance at James, then frowned. 'I'm pleased she fought back over those pictures. But it does suggest she's not the type to let things go.'

James nodded slowly. Val was right. Again. He hadn't been impartial enough. He'd seen what he wanted to see, and barely knew the first thing about her. He glanced at Hesha's screen again. 'Oh, bloody *hell*.'

Hesha looked at James in alarm. 'What ... what is it?'

Wincing, James pointed at a photo captioned: *House of Commons debates prison reform.*

'What about it?'

'That's Imelda Beaumont, MP, shaking hands with our chief constable, Tony Trent. Supporting his pet project. And I've just rushed through a search warrant and turned over her daughter's house.'

Chapter 16

Saturday 28th August – midnight

Nell watched the second hand of the interview room's clock tick towards midnight. She'd been here for almost four hours. With the sugar rush from biscuits and chocolate, and buzzing from the coffee, she'd read her magazines from cover to cover under the harsh halogen lights. Various officers had offered drinks but she'd declined each time to avoid conversation. She rolled her shoulders and stretched her back, stiff from the uncomfortable plastic chair. The guilt of revisiting the crime scene weighed heavy. *What if they've found out? They'll be even more convinced I'm hiding something.*

The door opened again and Nell braced herself to resist discussion or deny accusations.

To her huge relief, Charles walked in.

'Charles.' She stood up and kissed his cheek. His stern expression crinkled into his more familiar genial face.

'Hello, my dear.' He sat down, opened a folder, took out a legal pad and removed the cap from his fountain pen. 'Let's get started.'

As Nell set out her version of events, Charles made notes, then pondered in silence.

'This is how I see it.' He leaned forward. 'It doesn't sound like the police have much evidence against you. If we look at means, motive and opportunity, the means is there – Sophie Crows was struck on the head with a brick from within the tunnel—'

'Oh, no.' Nell winced. *So … planned or opportunistic? Or planned to look opportunistic?*

'They don't have any motive for you – as yet—'

'No, of course not.' Nell brimmed with indignation. 'How could I have one, when I didn't know Sophie?'

Charles steepled his fingers. 'But you had ample opportunity – you were there when the murder occurred. They haven't been able to place anyone else there at the time. I believe they've focused on you to count you in or out of their enquiries.' He cast a knowing look at Nell. 'The investigative power is supposed to be with the officers. You've probably overwhelmed them with cooperation.'

Nell squirmed. 'Just trying to help. And show I was too busy to, you know, kill anyone.'

'Well, your helpfulness has alerted suspicion. So, to business. Their questioning will be planned and strategised. You must be circumspect in your answers. You can, of course, answer "No comment", though the police will simply reframe their questions to get answers. Straightforward answers will expedite the process. I'll intercede if necessary.'

Nell felt the blood drain from her face. As Charles looked at her, his face softened.

'This won't escalate to arrest. It'll be over soon. And if the police persist on this tenuous basis, I'll raise it with my good friend Chief Constable Trent over a round of golf next week.'

Ouch. A less-than-subtle hint to make more use of her position rather than suffer the meritocratic chip on her shoulder. *But I'm a hypocrite. As soon as it all gets a bit real, I fall straight back into the arms of privilege.* She was lucky to be able to call on someone like Charles, and that he'd drop everything for her. But, equally, the police were wasting time on her. Time they needed, urgently, to redirect to finding the killer.

'Are we ready to proceed?'

Nell took a deep breath. 'Let's get this over with.'

James jumped up at Val's summons. He felt treacherous at having seen the video stills of Nell – her not knowing only worsened the violation. But he couldn't disagree that Nell had adeptly hidden significant facts. Her entire *life*, for God's sake. They had ammunition – and he'd have to use it.

'Folder,' Val hissed from the doorway.

James trudged back to the desk for the interview plan. At her glare, he squared his shoulders. *Professional face.* They joined Nell and Charles in the interview room, started the recording and stated their names.

Across the table from Nell, James felt flustered. He kept his eyes on his notes, trying to focus on the questions.

'Could you please give your full name?' Val asked Nell.

When James finally looked up, he was surprised to catch Nell grimacing. 'I am Lady Eleanor Ward-Beaumont. My mother kept her name, Ward, and double-barrelled it when she married. But people forget and just call her Lady Beaumont, which aggravates her no end. So I've taken her name, too. Solidarity.' She attempted a smile. 'But no one ever calls me that. I don't use my formal name for anything and even, on the rare occasion I see anyone out and about who knows me from Finchmere, if they know me well enough to recognise me by sight, they'd call me Nell. I use Dr Nell Ward professionally, and you were introduced to me like that because I was at Manor House Farm in a professional capacity. But I prefer to be called Nell.'

Charles introduced himself, adding, 'I'd like to make clear that, one – my client has not been arrested, two – she's fully cooperating with this request for questioning, and three – this cooperation is typical of her conduct throughout this investigation thus far.'

'Thank you,' Val said. 'For the benefit of the recording, we're investigating the murder of Sophie Crows. DS James Clark is showing you a photo. Can you confirm if you knew her?'

Nell studied the photo again. 'No. As I confirmed before. I've never met her.'

'Do you know her husband, David Stephenson?' Val asked.

Nell shook her head. 'No, I don't know him either.'

James took a deep breath. He met Nell's gaze and said, 'By your own admission you were at Manor House Farm – the location of Sophie Crows' murder – when she was killed. For the recording, can you specify the times you were there?'

Nell went through the times and dates again.

'Did your arrangements with Ms Maddison include accessing the tunnel?' Val asked.

'Of course,' Nell said. 'I wouldn't access private property without permission.'

'How did you access the tunnel?' James asked.

'Via the entrance in the woodland.'

James nodded. 'Can you describe it?'

Nell frowned. 'Well, it was almost impossible to see. The leaves had covered the entire entrance and if you weren't looking for it – with a rough idea of where it should be – it would be easy to miss. It looked like it hadn't been disturbed for years.'

'It looked like it hadn't been disturbed for years.' James echoed her words as he typed. Then he studied her. 'But you disturbed the leaves, didn't you?'

Charles cleared his throat. 'No need for implications when an interviewee is being cooperative.'

James paraphrased, trying to keep the questioning on track. 'All right, you've confirmed you moved the leaves. Can't have been very easy.' Imagining the task, James grimaced. 'Deep piles of mouldy, slimy leaves. Must have taken a while?'

'Yes, ages.' Her level gaze met his.

James managed to maintain eye contact. 'So, can you explain why, if you had permission to access the tunnel, and since you'd planned to meet Sophie Crows at the house, you didn't use the door from the kitchen? You intended to meet her at 6 p.m., yet you didn't start the bat survey until 7.50 p.m. Why didn't you look at the tunnel then?'

'I wouldn't have had time. The external inspection of the house – looking for access points bats could use – was very detailed. You must have seen the state the house is in. Every gap in the pointing and roof tiles had to be mapped. It took at least an hour. Had Sophie been there, next I'd have checked the roof void, which would've taken about forty minutes. I wouldn't have had time to do the inspection *and* access the tunnel, so I decided to use the woodland entrance. And I suppose I naturally gravitated there because that's where bats would get in. Inspecting access points is a key part of a survey.'

'How would bats get into the tunnel in the first place? Since the woodland entrance was completely covered?'

'Because, over the years, the leaf litter has piled up against the iron gates. But the semicircular roof of the tunnel makes a gap above those gates. It's small, almost imperceptible, but big enough for bats to detect. But the entrance would have been clear when bats first used it. And since bats return to their hibernation sites every year, now the local population will know of it.'

'You're saying bats remember where they go each year, and then, what, communicate between generations?' He almost laughed.

Nell nodded. 'Exactly. Bats live for up to thirty years. And different species, of all ages, cluster before returning to the same hibernation sites. Year after year.'

'OK. Fine. And let's say we accept that you had good reasons to *not* access the tunnel through the house, and instead chose – *chose* – to dig your way in, with your bare hands, through a completely leaf-covered entrance in the wood, we're still left with a real quandary.'

Nell looked at James. He couldn't tell if her expression meant unease or guilt.

'Because *after* you'd accessed the tunnel, you re-covered the entrance with leaves. No small task. And, again, unpleasant. Can you explain why?'

'Oh.' Nell expelled a long breath. 'Of course. Since bats *were* using the tunnel, it was important I didn't change the conditions. I had to leave it exactly as I found it.'

'Ah, of course. For the bats,' James said. 'Forgive me if I'm a bit jaded from my line of work, but when someone goes to so much effort to hide where they've been, I don't imagine they're looking after some elusive species. I tend to think it's because they don't want anyone else to know they've been there.' He leaned forward. 'Are you sure that's not the real reason you took such great lengths to cover up the fact you were in the tunnel?'

'No.' Nell stared at James. Her large eyes widened, giving her that fawn-like look again. He looked away, studying his notes, focusing on the facts Nell had concealed, so that he could continue.

'Even though prints matching your boots led to Sophie Crows' body?'

Nell gaped and Charles interrupted, 'Provocation. No comment.'

'Some coincidence, you have to admit, though,' James said, as if thinking aloud.

'No comment,' Charles repeated.

Val regarded Charles, then addressed Nell. 'We have some undeniable and damning points: one – you were there, alone; two – your own footprints led to Sophie's murdered body; three – you endured some disgusting, strenuous work to cover up the fact you were there.'

'I haven't denied I was there. And I'm not great at covering up if I'm telling you what I did myself, am I?' Her voice sounded high, tight. But then she frowned, stared into the middle distance. 'Hold on … Hold on a sec.' She leaned forward, finger up as if an idea germinated. 'If the murder happened in the tunnel, have you considered the fact there could be unusual DNA profiles on the killer's shoes?'

James saw her eyes gleam. Inspiration? Or deflection?

'Nell …' Charles held up his hand.

'Yes, I *know* the same DNA would be on my boots. But someone, in addition to me, could also have DNA on theirs, with a profile which matches the tunnel. A hibernation site is one of the few places you get different species of bats together. And most hibernacula are, by their nature, unused, undisturbed, pretty inaccessible to humans. You couldn't pick that material up just anywhere.'

She looked at James. 'The data I gave you includes a spreadsheet of species from the local bat group with local hibernation sites and the list of species at each one. If the murderer happened to step on a few droppings, and had traces of them on their soles, you could get the particles analysed.' She squinted as if concentrating. 'You'd need to make sure a lab could do a qPCR analysis to look for multiple species from a small sample. It's a long sho—'

Charles held up a hand. 'Enough, Nell.'

Val cleared her throat. 'We were discussing how you covered up any sign of being in the tunnel. Covering tracks is usually useful for delaying discovery of a crime. Once a body is found and there's evidence of a person being within close proximity of a murdered body, it's not unusual for our suspects to produce perfectly valid explanations – both for being there, and for covering up the fact.'

'And I've already explained I wasn't covering anything up,' Nell insisted. 'It's my job to make sure the conditions in the tunnel were maintained.'

Val arched an eyebrow. 'You make much of those conditions being suitable for bats. But you're a biologist, *Dr* Ward. You'd know those exact conditions provide an ideal environment to hide a dead body.'

Charles shot a daggered look at Val, then James. 'And you're no longer asking questions, you're merely presenting theories. So we will terminate this interview.' He tucked his notes into his file and stood up.

Before Nell could stand, a knock on the door interrupted them. Val got up and murmured with the officer hovering in the doorway. She looked through the folder being offered, then looked over at Nell, her lips set into a firm line. She thanked the officer, strode back and dropped the folder onto the table with a thud. Nell flinched.

'Nell Ward, we have evidence which indicates you've been lying to us,' Val said. 'We're placing you under arrest on suspicion of the murder of Ms Sophie Crows. You do not have to say anything. But it may harm your defence if you do not mention when questioned something which you later rely on in court. Anything you do say may be given in evidence.'

Nell stared at James in shocked disbelief. He swallowed and looked away. Her panicked gaze swung to Charles, whose lips were set in a tight, grim line, a vein throbbing at his temple, his grey eyes dark with controlled fury. He stood beside Nell and squeezed her hand. 'Don't worry, my dear. I assure you this will only be for a short while. I will,' he emphasised his words, '*deal* with this.'

A female officer herded Nell down a narrow corridor. Behind her, Charles said, 'I'll need to see your evidence. But for the moment, please excuse me while I call Tony.'

Through the double doors, Nell found herself propelled into the clinical custody suite. An overwhelming, hot wave of disinfectant and sharp, sour sweat and possibly vomit assaulted her nostrils. Nell's confusion made her clumsy and uncoordinated. She stumbled. She got her right and left confused when turning for photos. At least they already had her DNA and fingerprints. She fumbled with her belt and laces, apologising to the wiry officer who manoeuvred her through the various procedures with surprising strength and deftness.

'You must be in favour, love,' the officer said, dryly. 'No internal exam required.'

Nell's stomach lurched. *That* hadn't even occurred to her.

Another officer checked a computer behind the desk. 'Put her in Cell 4.'

'You've got the penthouse suite.' The officer led Nell to the cells. As she passed the doors with their name plates, sobs leaked from one cell. From another, someone shouted, 'Shuuuud uuuppp!' A thump on a door as Nell passed it made her jump. One cell was open. The occupant of the cell opposite sang, off-key and with impressive volume, 'I AIN'T SORRRRRRRYYYYYYYYYY.'

The annoying cacophony jarred Nell out of her bewilderment.

'King-size double with luxurious Egyptian cotton bedding.' The officer pointed at the narrow concrete slab with thin mattress and sparse blanket. 'State-of-the-art bathroom.' She gestured to the stainless-steel sluice in the corner. 'And full room service. You've missed dinner. Breakfast is in six hours.'

The door slammed shut before Nell could respond. A squeak of marker pen on her nameplate whiteboard, then fading footsteps.

She paced around the cell, recoiling from the stained mattress. She eyed the camera in the corner, then the sluice, with distaste, determined to not use the facilities.

Her neighbour's tuneless yelling persisted. They still weren't sorry. The other neighbour answered it by banging on their own cell door. Further away, the sobbing continued. Nell closed her eyes. She tried to block out the noise and think.

She trusted Charles. He'd said it would only be a short while before he got her out of here. How long before the police would have more questions? Minutes? Hours? *Days?*

She stared at the cell door in disbelief. Surely, any moment now, someone would arrive and apologise for the mistake. What on earth did the police think they'd found to warrant her arrest? There wasn't anything incriminating to find! How could she even *be* in this position? Did they really think she was lying? Even James? *I'm an idiot. He was just playing good cop, wasn't he?*

Nell attempted to herd her scattered thoughts, trying to use this time to work out what the police could be thinking.

What had the police disbelieved or disputed? They'd been surprised at the email Anna Maddison had sent about the time to meet Sophie. They'd asked if she'd received another email, changing the time. She definitely hadn't—

Realisation struck: the police must have seen an email to her from Anna, changing the time. Which meant someone at Anna's end had faked it, so she didn't receive it. Or, someone at her end had deleted it. Someone with access to her computer. God, in her office, that could be anyone.

Then the real penny dropped. *I was in the tunnel at nearly 5 p.m. when Sophie ... so if Anna had changed the meeting to 5 p.m., that's when Sophie expected to meet me. That's why she was there ...*

Her hands flew over her mouth as bile rose in her throat. So her meeting had definitely been used by the murderer. And so had the fact that she would have gone in the tunnel at some point. *God, that was a risk.*

And it meant the murderer knew her.

Chapter 17

Sunday 29th August – 1 a.m.

Nell tried to squash the panic. She had to think – clear her mind and sift through the jumbling thoughts. Yet, still, a voice told her she was being ridiculous.

I'm not being paranoid. I've been arrested. For murder. And someone's very possibly framed me. The familiar sick feeling settled in her stomach as she reviewed her colleagues – *friends* – through a veil of suspicion. Surely no one she knew could be capable? Taking a breath, battling to stay calm, she replayed the days before the murder in as much detail as she could remember, searching for any clue of anyone, anywhere, doing anything out of the ordinary.

It had been six days ago, Monday 23rd August, when Anna Maddison had first contacted her about surveying Manor House Farm. According to Anna's email, the surveys were urgent. They always were, so Nell had begun the quote straight away while, from the next desk, Sylvia regaled her with tales from her weekend date at Glyndebourne opera house (incredible performance, fabulous picnic hamper, lacklustre male company).

With every arriving ecologist, the chatter, laughter at jokes from site and constant sound of the kettle boiling for rounds of tea, had grown, along with the stack of survey equipment. Rolls of roofing-felt for reptile traps and clean pond nets had been stacked against whitewashed wall. Rows of wellies and waders had been scrubbed, ready for redeployment.

Staggering through the door, Adam had heaved two large backpacks next to the pile of equipment, then he'd made a beeline for her. 'Nell! Are you a sight for sore eyes!'

'Adam! How did you get on at Ambledown?'

'Oh, you know. Long hours, zero sleep while I took a roof apart tile by tile. Better than a marathon session at the gym!' As he'd flomped into the springy office chair and scooted to Nell, steering with his toes, he scrolled through his phone then held it out to her. 'Check out the new bat roost we built.'

Before Nell could lean in, Erin had bounded over, thrusting a pair of combat trousers between them. 'Here's your trousers back, Adam.'

Nell eyed them. They were unlaundered, folded, the legs rolled up.

'Oh, er, thanks.' Adam had shoved them onto his desk before glancing at Nell. 'Erin borrowed my spare pair after she fell in Little Smitington Pond last week.'

Irritation had flickered across Erin's face at the explanation, then she'd nudged Adam's arm. 'Let's see your photos.'

Across Nell's computer, Sylvia had winked at Nell, whispering, 'She's been trying to get into his trousers for ages.'

'Impressive.' Erin was gushing over Adam's pictures, while Sylvia bit back a grin.

Adam had looked at Nell for her reaction to the photos, then registered all the maps and aerial photos open on her screen, along with a schedule of works and proposed plans. He'd whistled. 'Major housing scheme. Manor House Farm, eh? Looks interesting to survey. Who's the client?'

'Anna Maddison from DMS Development, LLC.'

'Oh?' Sylvia frowned. 'New client but it rings a bell. Hang on.' She'd studied her screen as her manicured finger scrolled the mouse. 'Ah. Someone from there will be at that Pendlebury Regional Planning Conference on Wednesday. I shall schmooze.'

'We should let you get on, Nell.' Erin had walked towards the kitchen, looking back for Adam to follow. But he'd hesitated.

'I've got time to look at your photos, Adam,' Nell had said. 'I'd love to see.'

Beaming, Adam then showed her the new roost – a replacement for one that, after the roosting features were taken apart by hand to make sure no bats were killed, had to be demolished.

'It went pretty well. Most of the brown long-eared bats found their new roost. But this one' – he'd showed her a close-up of a furry face, two beady eyes peeping from under a roof tile – 'had to be personally escorted to their new home. It's smarter than my flat – top-notch carpentry, neat access gaps under the shingles, a hibernaculum on the north side for winter.'

Nell remembered how conscious she'd been of Adam's closeness, his warm scent of fresh sweat and sawdust. But his mention of a hibernaculum had sparked an idea: she'd check the historical map website before she emailed the quote.

After Adam had disappeared home to collect some survey equipment, Nell found the fateful tunnel on an archaic map. She'd printed a copy of it and included an access request for the tunnel and the cost for surveying it in her quote. Anna had accepted it within the hour.

As she'd added the surveys to the calendar, Nell fielded more emails from Anna: yes, she could fit the survey of Manor House Farm in on the afternoon of Wednesday 25th August; yes, she could survey Mr Gilpin's land the following week, once its purchase and access had been finalised; yes, she agreed not to encroach on the manor house and garden for the bat inspection until 6 p.m., when she'd meet the homeowner; and yes, after the inspection she'd start the bat survey. Nell emailed Adam, asking if he'd cover her survey at Quince Meadows on Wednesday, then join her at Manor House Farm for the evening bat survey.

She'd only just fired off fast-tracked requests for records of flora and fauna (county records, bats, badgers, dormice, birds and herpetofauna) for Manor House Farm and two kilometres around its ten acres when Sylvia had nudged her. 'Lunch?'

Alone in her cell now, Nell sagged against the wall. *I didn't lock my computer.* It had never even occurred to her. No one in the office did. Projects were confidential but workload was always shared and discussed within the team. But had that given someone the opportunity to read the email Anna may have sent, which she'd never received?

No one in her office would use her computer, surely? Perhaps a colleague looking for something urgent may have deleted or moved the email by accident? Or …? Slow, seeping dread iced Nell's veins. *Who?*

By the time Adam had returned on Monday afternoon, Nell had moved on to a report. 'So you're palming off the salubrious Quince Meadows to me while you play lady of the manor, eh?'

Ouch. 'Is that OK?'

'For my usual fee, a pre-dawn survey and a packet of Hobnobs.'

'Done. So, while you cover Quince Meadows, I'll get to Manor House Farm about 11 a.m. to do the habitat survey and inspect the house ahead of our bat survey that evening. The homeowner's meeting me at 6 p.m. so I can inspect the roof void, too, which'll help.'

'Very good, ma'am.' Adam had given her a mock salute.

'Good. Can you arrive about 7.30 p.m. so we have time to get organised?'

Adam had checked Google Maps. 'Oh yes, ma'am. Of course, ma'am. If it's no trouble, ma'am, I'll stop for a pasty for dinner on the way.' He'd pretended to tug his forelock.

Nell had thrown the cuddly toy bat she'd got in the work Secret Santa at him, and Adam caught it, one-handed, with a grin.

An email flashing on Nell's screen had caught her eye. 'Aha, badger group records for Manor House Farm.' She'd opened the spreadsheets. 'There are badgers in the area but no one's located a sett. What's the betting it's in the manor's private woodland?'

'If you find it, will you bait-mark it?'

She nodded. 'I've got some pellets at home. If there's a sett, we'll need to know their territory boundary at some point, so I may as well get a head start.'

'You'll be busy. Think I got off lightly with Quince Meadows.'

Nell had returned Adam's grin. She loved it when his eyes lit up like that. 'And I found this.' Nell had unfolded the Edwardian map. The unwieldy A0 sheet swamped her desk.

'What's that, Nell?' Sylvia had moved closer to see.

'A tunnel, attached to Manor House Farm's fifteenth-century house.'

Erin had joined them, with a tea for herself and a coffee for Adam, as Nell traced the faded map's features. 'See, it leads out to the wood. Could be an escape route for a priest hole?'

'Oh, it'll be for affairs,' Adam had asserted. 'Isn't it a rule that every stately home has a route to smuggle in consorts? And tunnels are *obviously* the easiest way to do that. Typical decision by people who don't have to do the work. No danger the toffs'll pick up a shovel and dig it themselves.'

Nell had hidden a wince. 'Liaisons aside, it could make a perfect bat hibernaculum. The local bat group gave me lists of bats hibernating in an ice house nearby, which includes some rare species. Pipistrelles and brown long-eareds. But also barbastelle and Bechstein's bats – amazing – and grey long-eareds – *incredible*.'

'You should *so* survey it,' Erin had said.

Nell had caught a hint of sarcasm, but Sylvia had nodded. 'Do, and if you find anything interesting, remember I want a blog, please.'

'I'll try. The client's just emailed to permit access, so who knows what I'll find.'

'Well, Indy, after you'd machete'd your way through the undergrowth to find that grotto, maybe in this Tunnel of Doom you'll find your holy-*grey-l*-long-eared bat.' Adam had grinned as Sylvia and Nell groaned. 'Come on, that's genius punnage.'

'Terrible.' Nell had shaken her head.

'Oh, I expect better retorts from you! What happened to being Traders of the Last Snark?'

Nell had held her head in mock despair. As she'd glanced up, laughing, Adam lobbed the cuddly bat back – but, as it flew past Erin, it made her jump and fling tea from her cup all over Nell's jeans, just as the bat walloped Nell in the head.

Gasping, Nell had tugged the scalding material away from her legs and crotch.

'Oops!' Erin's grimace hadn't quite concealed her amusement.

'God, I'm so sorry, Nell.' Adam had looked mortified. As Nell had dabbed herself with ineffectual tissues, he'd held his hands out, offering something. 'Want some spare trousers?'

Tuesday had been an uneventful day of ploughing through reports, the highlight being when Adam had made a tea round and given her a chocolate Hobnob with a wink, leaning close to whisper, 'That's the last one. Don't tell a soul.'

That remembered delight turned to a shiver as she thought about the next day. Wednesday. The day of the fateful survey.

Had anyone acted oddly in the office the next day? On Thursday, almost everyone had been out on site. The peace had been shattered when Sylvia whirled into the office that afternoon. 'I need some muscles, please.' When three junior ecologists had flexed ironically at her, Sylvia pushed her sunglasses into her blonde waves and beamed. 'You fine specimens. Come with me.'

Moments later, Sylvia's assistants had staggered back into the office, lugging display screens, boxes of leaflets, easels and long, unwieldy canisters of rolled-up banners.

'Put them in the storage room. Phew, I'm exhausted.' She'd sunk into a chair beside Nell and slipped off red stilettos, wiggling ruby-manicured toes. 'I must look a sight.'

'Yes, horrific,' Nell had agreed. In tailored palazzo pants, leopard-print blouse and immaculate, sun-kissed make-up, Sylvia looked like she'd flown in from Saint-Tropez.

'Oh, darling,' Sylvia had feigned affront.

Ignoring Sylvia's pout, Nell had asked, 'How was the conference?'

'Forget the conference. It's all about meeting *people*. Ask me about the *people*.' Sylvia had settled back into her seat, beaming in expectation.

'OK, who did you meet?'

'Oh.' Closing her eyes, Sylvia had sighed in wonderment. 'Darling, I think I have at last met The One.' She paused. 'Troy …'

Nell had spluttered at the name. 'His name is Troy? Seriously?'

'Troy,' Sylvia had continued archly, 'is simply the most perfect man. Charming. Handsome. Funny. And, remarkably enough, one of the few men who doesn't have an ego bigger than his,' she stage-whispered, 'shoe size.' She'd given her trademark wicked laugh. 'I met him in the bar after the day of presentations. We talked about all sorts. He's never been married. He's younger, but not indecently young. We both like photography. And he's been a model. We're both into fitness. In fact, he's a personal trainer.'

Nell had been puzzled. 'He's not a planner, then? Or works on developments? Why was he at a planning conference? I thought the hotel had been booked out for the event?'

'Huh.' Sylvia had chewed her lip, then shrugged. 'I don't know why he was there. He didn't mention any involvement with developments, either. And his interest was personal, not professional, when I gave him my card. I'll put it down to fate.'

'So, are you seeing any more of him?' Nell had asked.

Sylvia had given another wicked chuckle. 'Oh, darling, I've seen all of him already.'

Nell had prodded her and Sylvia relented. 'I hope so. He wrote his number down for me on the back of one of my business cards but I've only gone and lost it. I'm so *cross* with myself. I gave him a card, so it's down to him. But I'm certain he'll be in touch. We had a real connection. Oh, wait, I've got a picture of him.' Sylvia had produced her iPhone from her scarlet Birkin.

Noting Sylvia's glowing face, Nell had realised she'd not seen her look so happy in ages. She'd leaned in as Sylvia scrolled to the photo of herself and a handsome man at the hotel bar. Recognition had flickered, but Nell couldn't place it. Another picture caught Troy's expression of delight as he gazed at Sylvia. 'He looks quite smitten in that photo.'

'Yes. And this week would be the perfect opportunity to spend more time together.'

'Oh, yes, you'll be down in Wales, won't you?'

Adam had handed Nell her coffee from his tray of drinks. 'Hi, Sylvia. Good conference? Did you meet our new client?'

Sylvia had shaken her head. 'No. I was inundated with people asking lots of questions. But I didn't worry about it since Nell's already won the work.'

Looking up from the photo, Nell had seen Adam looking at the picture, then her, his smile faltering. Sylvia had reclaimed her phone. 'Don't worry, Adam. He's all mine.'

Nell had felt she'd missed something but, before she could ask, Erin called Adam over and Nell watched him give Erin her herbal tea as he laughed at a joke. Erin had leaned towards him, her hand on his arm as she gazed up at him.

Sylvia had regarded Nell. 'When, exactly, are you going to put that gorgeous young man out of his misery?'

Brushing off Sylvia's scrutiny, she'd whispered, 'He's interested in Erin. And anyone can see she's into him. He's not exactly discouraging her, so he must like her.'

Sylvia shot her a wry look. 'Darling, *you* read the landscape, *I* read the manscape.'

A world away, in the cell, Nell relived her flash of embarrassment at Sylvia's words. But, while they'd been joking in the office, Sophie's body lay cold in the tunnel, waiting to be found. And someone wanted it to look like she had killed her.

The stark danger sharpened Nell's mind: at work, only Sylvia, Adam and Erin knew she'd be going into the tunnel. They all had a chance to intercept Anna's email. But Nell couldn't imagine any of them would harm someone and frame her. Even Erin. She was a pain, but she wasn't a murderer.

It must have been someone from Anna's side. Her? Or David? Or Simon, perhaps?

Simon's strategy of cutting corners was a strange one. *Does he do it out of desperation? To meet targets? Would that desperation stretch to murder?*

Anna was an unknown quantity. Nell was sure she hadn't met her. David's name wasn't familiar either. And, when she'd logged the job, their system confirmed DMS Development, LLC was a new client. Nell paced, running out of inspiration.

Did something in my flat incriminate me? As she mentally reviewed her home, Nell's stomach dropped. While she was imprisoned, Zorro and Jezebel weren't being fed. She'd added extra rations, but not enough for more than a day. Cats adapted to feast or famine. But Zorro wouldn't. He couldn't take a backwards step so close to release! She hated keeping a bat captive for longer than needed – and grimaced at the irony.

If she could get in touch with Adam, he'd keep Zorro fed. Maybe he could be her one phone call? Nell sighed. Erin had been right. Her life really did revolve around bats. But when she'd called at Adam's after the survey so he could drop her home and keep the work car, he'd been excited to see a grey long-eared, too. She was glad he'd shared Zorro's rescue. And it would never have happened if his tyres hadn't been flat.

Adam's car.

Nell sat up straight. *Punctures. In all four tyres. How often did that happen?* She couldn't count the number of rough sites she'd been to over the years where she'd been sure a slow puncture on the drive home would be inevitable. And even then, it didn't always happen. But she'd never had punctures in every tyre. Her heart thudded.

Adam's tyres must have been slashed.

If the murderer wanted to prevent Adam getting to site to be an alibi for me, is Adam in danger, too?

Chapter 18

Sunday 29th August – 1.30 a.m.

James pinned up the photos documenting the search of Nell's home as Val studied them. Her fingers tapping against her thighs was the only giveaway of her restlessness. He glanced at the clock: 1.30 a.m. *How much longer will we have to wait?*

'Sorry about rushing through the warrant.' He'd been so keen to prove he could make a tough decision over Nell; not expecting them to find anything, it seemed a safe way to indicate objectivity. Now they'd not only uncovered her true identity, they'd found evidence she'd lied about the investigation. And his professionalism would probably be called into question. *Again.* His stomach knotted. Trent would give him a bollocking.

Val shook her head. 'It was the right call with the information we had. And you don't need to be sorry, it's my responsibility.'

Along the silent corridor, a door slammed. James jumped and shot Val a wary glance. She did a double-take at James's face. He must look like a rabbit in headlights. Unexpectedly, she winked. 'Come on, detective sergeant. Have some faith in yourself.' The surprise encouragement unravelled his tension and he followed her to Trent's office. They waited outside, hearing murmurs of conversation between Trent and Barrington.

After an age, Barrington strode out. He pointed to the interview room along the corridor. 'I'll wait in there, collating my notes.'

'DCI Johnson! DS Clark!' Trent bellowed.

Great. Titles. Plus bellowing. Oh, and Trent in dress uniform. Meaning he'd detoured home from his anniversary celebrations at Nye Hall Hotel. He's impressing his status on someone. Barrington? Or me and Val? Probably all of us. Great.

Trent's ring-fenced anniversary was the reason Val had called another chief constable to sign off the warrant. From his thunderous face, James guessed Trent felt undermined. That, and Trent's wife probably hadn't been too happy when Barrington summoned him away from their hotel. Their chief was simmering with a good dollop of affronted professional pride and a pinch of marital disharmony. *Perfect.*

James cast a sidelong glance at Val, wondering how she'd tackle this mess. He also wondered – with new insight – if this was why she never discussed what she did with her time off from work. Whenever she was called in from leave, she never carried baggage. If Trent had done the same, he would have been part of this decision, instead of them having to ask the superintendent to sign off Nell's search warrant.

Val opened her file and looked at Trent. 'If I may, sir, I'd firstly like to apologise for this … infringement on your celebration—'

He cut Val off. 'The less said about that, the better. As you can appreciate, this places me in a very difficult position. I need to understand what led to your decision.'

'Of course, sir. We've uncovered evidence showing Dr Ward—'

'Lady Eleanor Ward-Beaumont,' Trent corrected her.

'Lady Eleanor Ward-Beaumont was introduced to us as Dr Ward because she was at the manor in a professional capacity. And she's asked us to use that title, or call her Nell.'

Trent pursed his lips, clearly pained at the idea of first-name levels of informality.

Val got the hint. 'Dr Ward's identity is just one way she's been deliberately deceptive during our enquiries. And while I'm sure her family connections will vouch for her good character, she is now nevertheless a person of interest.' Val paused, then added, 'Wealthy people can and do commit crimes. I can cite cases—'

'Yes, all right, don't remind me.' Trent sighed. 'However, there are two key issues which show a failure of due process here. The first issue is that your team failed to discover your suspect's identity. That's an embarrassing indication of investigative carelessness.'

'I apologise, sir,' Val replied. 'However, all police conduct operates a strict non-discrimination policy, which applies across the board. So, while we didn't appreciate our suspect's background, arguably we should have treated her no differently had we done.'

Grimacing, Trent said, 'Nice try. But Charles has pointed out that if we didn't look into Lady Eleanor Ward-Beaumont properly then there's every chance we've been equally remiss with other suspects. He has the means to halt this investigation with immediate effect due to basic incompetence. It's inexcusable, Val.'

Val nodded, a pained expression on her face. James felt disappointed that his chief constable didn't acknowledge how unusual mistakes were on Val's team. He noticed Val's application form to the Strategic Command Course sat pointedly in the centre of Trent's desk. Beside him, James sensed Val brace herself as she continued.

'Our *suspect* has no criminal record, so there's nothing on our database. When we checked her credentials more widely, she has an entire professional identity around the name Dr Nell Ward. We spoke to her manager at work, checked her LinkedIn profile, did a general web search. Everything used her professional name. Even her car registration. Though we've now found she is insured on a collection of cars registered in her father's name. Which gives us quite a list of vehicles to now exclude from the investigation. But, crucially, nothing linked Nell Ward with Lady Eleanor Ward-Beaumont. She's obviously been very deliberate about that. And we initiated all background checks, including phone records, as soon as she was a known suspect. It's a shame that our team is under fire for being more proactive on this investigation – by finding evidence that warranted further searches – than our various records offices.'

'It might be understandable if it was the only issue,' Trent said. 'But it isn't. The second issue is the rushed search warrant. For one thing, it required my signature – and I am less than impressed with my jurisdiction being bypassed. For another, it could have – *should* have – waited until morning and gone through the proper channels.'

'Sir, if I may, up until this point, this person of interest had cooperated on their own terms. Our questioning strategy was intended to regain control. We had an opportunity to expedite a search of their home before they'd have further opportunity to remove any potential evidence. I concede it was rushed, however, it cannot be denied that we uncovered new evidence which points to motive and gained useful and timely information. Sir.'

'Motive?' Trent's eyebrow arched.

'We think so,' Val said. 'Something that's come to light from a search of her property.' She put her file on the desk. 'It's outlined in here for your review, sir.'

Glancing through it, Trent frowned then gave Val a curt nod. He shoved his chair back and paced to the window. 'Charles's argument is Lady Eleanor Ward-Beaumont posed no risk. The rush wasn't justified. Again, he's emphasised that a failure to observe appropriate protocols in our most basic procedures suggests a failure of any and all other investigative processes.'

Val nodded. 'I appreciate your position, sir.'

'I hope you do. It's only because Charles and I are long-standing friends that I've been able to defuse this situation. Charles has a ruthless reputation in ending careers where process isn't observed.' He paused, allowing the threat to hang.

He stared out of the rain-drizzled window, onto the dimly-lit car park. 'Charles has – *kindly* – agreed to you proceeding with your questions but *only* because it will deal with the matter as quickly as possible for Lady Eleanor Ward-Beaumont, and *only* if we conduct these as a regular interview, not under arrest conditions. Charles is of the opinion that Lady Eleanor would prefer to get this over and done with now rather than return tomorrow, which is understandable since she's unlikely to have a restful night. Fortunately, Charles is as keen to be discreet about this situation as we are, so we won't suffer repercussions with the press *if* we resolve this quickly. God knows, I'm having difficulty enough keeping the journalists happy.' Trent sighed. 'Move Lady Eleanor from her cell to an interview room while you prepare your questioning strategy. You'll have about thirty minutes to interview her.'

'Understood, sir. However, it doesn't negate the evidence we have to indicate motive and to demonstrate that she has already lied in our enquiries so far.'

'Yes, I do realise that.' Now it was Trent's turn to look pained. He paced back to his desk. 'But this agreement would not prevent a re-arrest *if* evidence – and due process – are followed.' Trent's eyes bored into Val. 'So you'd better ensure this next stage of questioning is bullet-proof. Understood?'

'Yes, sir.'

'Good. Then please proceed.'

Val nodded. 'Thank you, sir.'

'And I'll observe.'

James hid his wince by standing and turning to tuck his chair in. Val maintained her neutral expression as she said, 'Thank you, sir.'

James closed the door behind them and raised his eyebrows at Val.

'I've already prepared the interview questions, ma'am.' He held up a folder.

'Good. I'll review them, then let's get started.' Val read as she walked. 'And you'd better be on form.'

'Why?' James followed.

'Because – even though the lawyer has our heads on the block, and Trent is observing – I asked you to lead this case, and I'm not demoting you. I still expect you to lead the questioning.'

James stopped in his tracks and stared at her. Emotions turmoiled: gratitude of her faith in him, fear of cocking it up, having to ask Nell *those questions*, before the most merciless audience …

'Come on, DS Clark. You can't cut teeth without chewing on a challenge.'

Chapter 19

Nell resumed her seat beside Charles, opposite Val and James in the interview room. She was bursting to ask the question – but she had to wait for James to start the camera, state their names, and the date, and the time. Then he began, 'Right—'

'Wait. I need to ask you something. I'm worried about Adam …'

James sighed, shoulders sagging, and glanced sideways at Val.

Nell ploughed on. 'He couldn't join my survey in the evening because his tyres were punctured. All four of them. How often does that happen?' She looked at James, then Val. 'I think they were slashed. I'm sure you do, too. But that means someone's followed him, either to site or work or,' she shivered, 'his *home*. Doesn't it?' The detectives didn't respond. Desperation bubbled up from her chest. '*Please* – can you make sure he's safe? And do you have any way of finding out who did it? Because whoever—'

'Thank you.' Val held up a hand. 'Noted. Now, let's focus on your questions, please.' She nodded at James to continue.

James cleared his throat and consulted his notes. 'You've repeatedly claimed you don't know Sophie Crows or her husband David Stephenson—'

'I don't,' Nell interrupted.

'Are you sure? We have evidence that shows you knew both David and Sophie.'

Nell frowned at Charles in confusion.

James continued, 'Pictures of you at an event with them were found in your home during our search.'

'What?' The room spun. *How could there be pictures? What the hell did they mean?*

James produced two evidence bags, each containing a photograph, and laid them before Nell. A photo of a formal ball showed Nell with friends. One man had his arm around Nell's shoulders, clearly her partner for the ball. Another showed Nell wearing the same dress, beaming with a dark-haired young woman, also in formal wear, at a crowded bar. The same man stood behind them.

Nell studied the pictures, keeping her hands in her lap. As her brain made sense of the images, she recognised their faces and she leaned back with a sigh of relief. 'Oh, no, there's been a mistake. That's Dave. Dave *Dixon*, not David Stephenson.'

James shook his head. 'This man is David Stephenson. In this photograph, he appears to be your boyfriend.' His tone was even but, as he studied Nell, his eyebrows drew together.

'No, you're wrong. He's Dave Dixon.' She dropped her gaze and shifted in discomfort. 'And he was just my flatmate's brother. She invited him along so I wouldn't be a total gooseberry.'

'OK, for the sake of argument, let's call him Dave Dixon. Tell us about him.'

'They're photos of a graduation ball. After I got my doctorate. You don't usually go to a ball after a PhD but Lou, um, Louise Dixon, my flatmate' – Nell pointed at the dark-haired girl in the photo – 'had done a Master's and was excited about the funfair theme and persuaded me to go. It was our last hurrah, if you like, before she headed off to Europe. Lou dragged Dave along because she was going with her boyfriend, and I'd met Dave once or twice when he'd visited.'

'We're not interested in this woman' – James pointed at Louise – 'but this one.' He tapped the corner of the picture. A blonde girl in a silver dress stood in the background. 'Sophie Crows.'

What? Overcoming her aversion to the photos, Nell picked up the picture and squinted at the slightly unfocused image. Her skin prickled as realisation dawned. It *was* Sophie. She looked about twenty-one, celebrating her first graduation.

'This picture shows her as part of your group.'

'It may look like that, but she wasn't. I've never met her.'

'Photos we took from Sophie's home show her and David as a couple on that same evening. Looks like your date, Dave *Dixon* … whatever he may have called himself, left you for her during your own graduation ball.'

Nell laughed, incredulous. *How could they believe this?*

Without looking up, Charles emphatically paused his writing to warn James. 'Questions, not postulations, DS Clark.' He resumed his notes with the air of one who expects obedience.

James shot a look at Val, then at the camera. 'OK, Nell, be honest with us. Did David leave you for Sophie in the middle of celebrating an important night?'

Nell tried to stay calm. 'Look, all this focus on Dave – or David – and Sophie is ridiculous. Dave and I weren't a couple. We'd just been paired up for the evening.' She grimaced. 'Nothing else. No big romance. He didn't even see me home after the ball. When I was ready to leave, he said he'd met some friends and wanted to stay on. And that was fine, because, like I say, we weren't a couple. He may well have got together with Sophie after I left. It's not improbable, to be honest—'

James interrupted. 'But it's a special occasion, isn't it, a graduation ball? You wouldn't ask just anyone to be your date. You'd ask someone … special.' James studied her face. 'Wouldn't you?'

Nell felt her face burn but fought the urge to look away. 'I didn't have anyone special. My background … complicates things. It's hard enough to make genuine friends, let alone have a meaningful relationship. I don't want to see someone without being honest but it's a roll of the dice: some love the idea more than the reality, some are put off, some resent the privilege, some … some get close to you to use you. It's easier if people don't know. To forgo relationships altogether. So, Dave was … convenient.'

'Convenient?' James's lips turned down. 'Interesting description.'

Nell winced. 'On the couple of occasions I'd met him, he'd never once asked anything about me. He was one of those guys, always too busy saying how great *he* was, what *he'd* done, what *he* thought. I couldn't have got a word in if I'd wanted to. So the problem of having to sidestep talking about my life never arose. He went to a lot of effort to give the impression of being wealthy and successful. He drove a gold BMW, of all things. Certain it was a future classic. To be fair, it probably was. So, since Lou wanted to go as a foursome, I knew he at least wouldn't ask any awkward questions. There was nothing else to it. And these photos were, what, buried in a box under my bed? Hardly framed and cherished.'

'You still kept them. With what looked like other sentimental keepsakes,' Val said. *Oh God. Even James didn't look convinced.*

'Well, yes. Because it was our last night out, before Lou and I went our separate ways. We were good friends …'

'Are you still in touch?' James asked.

Nell shook her head. 'No, Lou got a high-flying job in Basel. Over time, contact just … well, fizzled out.'

'You considered her a good friend,' he pushed. 'But even she didn't really know you.'

Nell chewed her lip then forced the words out, like an owl heaving up a pellet of skeletons. 'I keep my family life separate because … some people … have betrayed confidences in the past. It's caused … a lot of hurt. To me and my family.' She took a gulp of water. 'It's turned into a tendency to keep people at … a bit of a distance.'

She gazed at the photos. Groups of girls laughing with the easy abandon of unguarded friendship. But her own smile didn't reach her watchful eyes. Nell now recognised the standoffishness that others saw, even commented on. The hollow, lonely feeling expanded through her chest.

Her mother had warned her she was making life more difficult for herself, recommended she repair her social connections. But the scandal her college ex, Julius, had caused prodded her old bruise. From that point, a fierce fortress of privacy seemed to be her only option. It was only now she felt the gulf it created. Her face flushed as James spoke.

'So, *you* didn't consider David to be your boyfriend,' James said. His eyes fixed on Nell's face, no doubt reading something else into her blush. *Brilliant.* 'But did *he*?'

'No. Well, he might have flirted. But it was never going to become a relationship.'

Nell paused and squinted at the images from the ball. A champagne-hazed memory of Dave crystallised: his arm around a blonde girl in a silver dress. She peered at Sophie in the corner of the photo. Same silver dress. Nell's stomach dropped.

'Oh my God,' she whispered, realisation dawning. 'He *was* with Sophie that night.'

Val noted Nell's reaction. 'So you *had* met her?' she said.

'No.' Nell bit back her impatience. 'Like I said, we might have been at the same ball. Along with several hundred others. But I've never met her, or spoken to her.'

'Yet *now* you recall where David met her. When he was supposedly on a date – a special night – with you,' James confirmed.

'Yes, I think I recall him meeting her now.' Nell shrugged. 'But, *as I keep saying*, there was no special relationship. It was a night out with Lou and our friends.'

'When was the last time you had any type of communication with David?'

'Since then, only once. Lou had asked where I'd moved to, I'd said near Pendlebury, and Dave … David … called when he was in the area. Asked if I was free for a coffee while he was passing through. But I was working … and we'd not spoken in ages. I didn't think there was much point meeting up.'

'So he's got your contact details? And he knows where you live? Which happens to be right where his development is? That's … well, that's quite the set of coincidences.'

'Not really. No more than Sophie living in the area, too. Which is presumably the reason he was in the neighbourhood.'

'You're right, that's another coincidence.'

Charles coughed.

'I haven't changed my phone number since uni. So yes, he had my number. It doesn't change the fact we haven't been in touch for years.'

'It *is* quite incredible, though.' James sat back. 'Out of all the ecologists, in all the country, *you're* the one commissioned to do David's survey, at the home of him and his wife. The woman he left you for during your graduation ball. Not only that, but you had reason to meet Sophie there – conveniently alone. That presents quite the opportunity, doesn't it?'

Nell fought to steady her breathing and moderate her tone. 'I didn't know these surveys were for someone I knew. I didn't know Dave was a developer or that he is apparently David Stephenson. All my communication was with Anna Maddison, and David Stephenson's name was never mentioned. You can easily verify that with Anna and by checking my emails. Again.'

'Were you aware Sophie's family owned Manor House Farm?' James asked.

'No,' Nell said.

James shifted in his seat. 'You mentioned your past relationships have hurt your family.'

Nell's head snapped up to stare at him, taut as a snake tagged on a target. 'Yes.'

'Is that because – honestly – you're a bit too red-blooded for platonic relationships?' James slid the grainy printed article across the table. He sat back, as if expecting an explosion.

But the reaction came from Charles. 'That story has a super-injunction against it. This material was illegally obtained. Circulating it, printing it, is also an offence. Not to mention the undue distress you've caused my *innocent* client. Allow me to do you a favour, *detective sergeant*, before I request the court draw up a warrant for arrest. For *you.*' He leaned across the table and tore the pages into neat strips, as if about to lay a fire. The uppermost strip unfortunately framed Nell's naked breasts.

Nell's embarrassment was molten. Her head pounded with a surge of blood, her face lava-hot. The room rocked as clamped-down memories propelled to the surface.

The volcanic reaction of her parents when she had had to discuss the details with them, then Charles and his legal team, blazed in her brain. Sheer mortification. No eighteen-year-old needed to dissect the specifics of a drunken fumble, let alone have each new position corroborated with paused, zoomed-in checks, with an audience of grim-faced men in dark suits and parents pulsating with disappointment.

Nell had never felt so acutely that she'd let down the people she loved. Their faith in her, in her judgement, seemed damaged beyond repair. Shame gnawed like a parasite.

'How dare you,' she heard herself saying. Her voice, low, tremulous, seemed to come from somewhere else. 'I've been nothing – *nothing* – but cooperative with you, despite the arrest, despite the inferences that I could somehow be guilty of something so … so …' She swallowed. Gasped for breath. Raised her voice. 'You're not only wasting your time questioning me while a killer's still out there, now you're spending valuable investigative time dredging up an irrelevant scandal?'

Charles rested a warning hand on her arm.

Nell shrugged him off, leaping up. 'What possible connection does a stupid mistake I made over *fifteen years* ago have with Sophie's death? I was a victim of a horrible crime. I hope you're not trying to infer that I was somehow to blame for someone selling me out? Or that I'm morally dubious?' She stared at James, then Val, knowing her face was burning, hating the fact she couldn't style it out. It was all she could do to not cry in sheer frustration that despite Charles's best work, this reminder of one single slip still dogged her.

The pain of her family aside, it had been utter social death. The ripples damaged their estate business – especially for hosting weddings – which struggled for a few years until the episode subsided and they rebuilt their reputation. Nell had learned how fickle her circle was. Only Percy had weathered the eruption with her, resolutely repeating that the shame wasn't Nell's. She'd cheered Nell on when she screwed up the courage to battle Julius in court, only lamenting that Nell could have raised a criminal case, rather than just a civil one. But Nell knew she'd hit Julius where it hurt most, especially when she donated the substantial damages to Women's Aid.

'Lady Eleanor,' Charles drew her back to the situation at hand. 'I merely require your instruction. I advise we terminate this interview – which, I remind the company, *you* graciously granted. Subject to your approval, I further recommend we file a police misconduct complaint with the Independent Office for Police Conduct.' Charles closed his briefcase and stood, shoulder-to-shoulder with Nell, facing the detectives.

Nell looked at Val, then stared James down, fury and betrayal burning through her eyes, until his gaze dropped to the floor. She shook but her control was iron, forged from practice. She nodded once. 'Do it.' She turned, opened the door and walked into the corridor, with Charles close behind.

A man about Charles's age barrelled out of a side room into the corridor, stopping in front of them.

'Bad job, Tony,' Charles castigated. 'I'll be in touch. Grounds for malicious prosecution and misconduct in public office at the very least, I should think.'

Tony caught Charles's arm. 'Charles, let's discuss this—'

Charles stared down at Tony's hand, then raised his gaze. 'You've already sat me down in your office and negotiated – and *this* was how your team chose to use their time? No. We'll deal with this *my* way now.'

He turned Nell into the narrow corridor, his arm around her, crushing her against the thick fabric of his suit. The sensation reminded Nell of when the story hit the evening papers. She'd been out at a club with friends. Paparazzi, hoping for a gratuitous reaction, had hunted her down. One bouncer bundled her out of the club, while another was a human shield between her and the photographers. Her evasion made things worse, taken as a flashing, neon declaration of guilt. In the follow-up articles, the press ripped her apart like a cackle of hyenas falling on carrion.

As Charles steered her towards the exit, she heard the low rumble of her parents' Mulsanne. Panic punched her in the guts. This case already had press crawling all over it. It only took one or two reporters to have heard of an arrest and be out there. If her past scandal had hurt her family, she couldn't imagine what they'd say if her picture was splashed all over tabloids declaring her arrest for murder. She imagined the headlines: SEX-TAPE HEIRESS ARRESTED FOR MURDER OF EX-LOVER'S WIFE.

Her mouth slicked with salt. She was going to be sick.

Outside the doorway, a light flickered, like photo flashes. Nell recoiled. Heat prickled all over her body. She tugged at Charles.

'Can we find another way out? Please?' she asked. Her voice sounded thin, breathy.

Charles half-turned. 'It's fine, Nell. There's only Conor out there, waiting in the car.'

'But …'

'It's half-three in the morning, Nell. Trust me, no one's out there.'

Nell burned with shame that he understood her reluctance.

Charles squeezed her hand, and opened the police station door.

Trent glared at Val, then James in the corridor. He jerked his head towards the interview room. 'Get back in there,' he growled.

Val and James shuffled backwards into the small room and sat down. Trent paced, then stabbed the 'off' button on the recorder and swung round. 'What the *hell* was that?' His jawbone pulsed under his skin.

Val took a deep breath. 'It was a legitimate approach to questioning, sir. I appreciate we'll have the complaint to answer but we can defen—'

'Have you quite lost your mind?' Trent looked incredulous. 'Yes, complaints aren't unusual. But I don't think you heard me earlier. A disgruntled suspect who doesn't know the process and gets bored with the paperwork is one thing. *Charles Barrington* is quite another. He knows what he's doing. He shuts down investigations. He *ends careers*.' Trent paced. 'I'd already had to persuade him to comply with the interview.' He grabbed the strips of paper from the desk and shook them at his detectives. 'What the hell were you thinking, raking this up?'

Val took a breath. 'We had a person of interest, who frequently commandeered our questioning. Having found out she'd lied, and then uncovered her connections to the victim, this was our approach – which I approved – to rattle her. To see what we could uncover when she didn't feel in control of the questioning.'

'This wasn't just rattling, this was an ambush! When you'd already been granted special dispensation.'

'Sir, if I may.' Val turned her palms up. 'Her lawyer had negotiated to reduce our questioning time. Smart move, I admit. But it meant we possibly only had this single, limited opportunity to really get below the surface. What if her lawyer blocked us again? When *could* we have got under her skin?'

'When you've got some *real* bloody evidence.' Trent glared at them. He shook his head in disbelief and stormed out, slamming the door.

Sunday 29th August – 3.30 a.m.

Conor held the door open for Nell. She sank into the back seat of the Bentley and closed her eyes as Conor sat in the driver's seat and drove off.

'I arranged a housekeeping service for your place,' Conor said, looking at her through the rear-view mirror. 'Didn't want you returning to chaos. They'll work overnight so I've booked rooms for us all at Nye Hall Hotel. It's big enough to be anonymous and serves food all night via room service if you're hungry. And you've a late check-out, if you want it.'

'Thanks, Conor.' She tried to smile, but she hadn't thought through the impacts of invasion. Images of officers searching through her home – rifling through her personal possessions, private notes, ugh, *underwear* – piled on top of Nell's humiliation. Their violation – and James's brutal questioning – festered like black rot in her stomach.

How could he use that against her? *He must have looked through every frame. God, had he seen the video? What a ... God, when will I learn? Every time I start feeling something for someone, it comes back to bite me.*

Even Adam had just been setting up a climbing date with Erin, under the guise of coming over for training. God, I'm a total fool.

She bit the insides of her cheeks until she tasted blood. Even so, as she leaned back against the seat, hot tears leaked down her face.

'Right.' Charles fastened his seatbelt beside her. 'I'll get to work on the complaint. I'll take time to make it iron-clad, so I'll file it at the end of the week.'

He glanced at Nell, as she wiped her face and looked at him. His face flustered with shock. 'Oh, no. There's no time for sentiment. A lot is on the line, here, Nell. We need focus, please, not feelings. The press injunction still stands, but social media remains a risk. I'll get a team onto it, but we must strategise damage limitation for your estate's business, for your profile. Not to mention the possibility of your re-arrest.'

Nell squashed her inconvenient emotions. It was second nature. Besides, she had another worry on her mind. She forced herself to ask, 'Just how close did my footprints get to Sophie's body?'

'Difficult to say. They dried up about a third of the way in from the wood. After which police couldn't discern how much further you'd walked. Sophie was found a third in from the house. So at most, you were a third of the tunnel away.'

Nell shuddered. 'I just know I didn't see her. In a way, I wish ...'

'*I* wish it didn't look so incriminating. And now they've searched your house, we can at least assume they've examined everything. But then, there's your car. And a forensic exam of your computer. The problem is, they believe they've found a motive, so they'll continue investigating.'

Nell shook her head. 'What? That I'm jealous because Dave went off with Sophie at the grad ball?'

Charles nodded. 'And you killed Sophie Crows to regain David's affections.'

'But … it's so ridiculous!'

'Yes, in your opinion. But plenty of people have killed for exactly that reason.' Charles glanced at her. 'The police have a second theory. That you and David had an affair and planned to kill Sophie together.'

Nell gaped. Then shut her mouth. Her brain churned. 'Of course … *David* would be a suspect …'

Charles shot her a sharp stare. 'Oh, no. Stop thinking like that. This is dangerous, Nell. If you dig, you'll provoke a murderer. Don't you dare do anything precipitous. Being called out to represent you at the station, I don't mind. Being called out to identify your body in the morgue, I would mind. Very much.'

Chapter 20

Sunday 29th August – 5 a.m.

James made himself a strong coffee. He felt vile. He'd never forget Nell's stricken face, that furious look. Not that she'd been slow to retaliate, threatening his bloody *job*. He glanced at Hesha, whose head drooped over the stack of reading on her desk, and poured her a cup. He nudged her awake, wafting the steam under her nose.

'What?' Hesha jumped, then smiled and rubbed her face. 'Sorry. Must've dozed off.'

'Not surprising. You going home for some proper shut-eye?'

Hugging the coffee cup, Hesha glanced at the clock on the wall. She shook her head. 'No point now. I'll push through. We're gunning for a fast result and I've got some things to follow up once it's a reasonable time to call people. You?'

'I daren't. Val's putting her neck on the line for me. I've got ground to make up.'

Hesha gave a wry nod. 'We heard.'

They looked up as the door opened. Ashley walked in. About three hours earlier than expected. She shrugged at James. 'The station grapevine's buzzing. I thought you'd pull an all-nighter.' Drawing up a chair beside them, she took a stack of foil-wrapped parcels from her rucksack. 'Bacon sarnies to keep us going, while you fill me in. At least my brain's had some sleep.' She poured a coffee from her flask and turned an expectant smile to James.

James gazed in disbelief as Ashley tossed him a sandwich. He caught it with a grateful smile.

'So, your sweet ecologist's not so sweet,' Ashley observed. 'Not what she seemed at all, for that matter.'

James couldn't respond. The wretched feeling churned so much he had difficulty taking a bite of the sandwich, until hunger and appreciation of crispy bacon between soft bread oozing with butter took over.

Taking a sarnie, Hesha filled in the awkward silence. 'I've been going through Marjorie Crows' photo albums.' She nodded at the open book. 'A catalogue of Sophie riding horses. Winning rosettes for one thing or another.' She sipped her coffee.

James wiped his fingers on one of the paper napkins Ashley had brought and flipped the thick pages.

In between horse pictures were vignettes of Sophie with her grandparents. Young Sophie was shy, peeping around someone, or hiding behind her long blonde hair. On a horse, though, she shone – sitting tall, smiling with confidence – as if her focus on the animal made her forget to be self-conscious. Marjorie Crows had been a handsome woman, with an air of tenderness around Sophie and, while her grandfather had a sterner demeanour, with Sophie he seemed enchanted, even playful. James imagined them dealing with the loss of their son and daughter-in-law while adopting Sophie. Their lives must have changed seismically overnight.

Ashley seemed to read his mind. 'Look like a nice family, don't they? Like they were making the best of the awful situation.'

James nodded and turned the page. He stared at a picture. The grandparents and a teenage Sophie stood in a familiar dark space, toasting with a glass of wine. Two other people – a young guy and an older man – were in the picture, also holding up glasses of wine.

'The infamous tunnel,' James said. 'There were wine racks in there. Looks like they uncorked something for a special occasion.'

Ashley studied the image and nodded, then grimaced. 'Sophie looks so happy there. And they're all so horribly close to where …' She shivered.

James studied the picture. 'Hang on … I think the young guy is Andrew Arden, and I imagine that's his father with him? There's a strong resemblance. Andrew said they'd been the family's solicitors, and friends, for years.'

Hesha leaned in. 'From the way Andrew's looking at Sophie, I'd say he wants to be more than friends.'

In the picture, Andrew stood beside Sophie. She was laughing, holding her glass up, hair tumbling over her shoulders. Her sunny nature radiated from the image, a leap in confidence from her younger self. From the shadows, Andrew gazed at her, his face intense and brooding.

James nodded. 'It does, doesn't it? I never even considered he might be one of the few people who'd know about the tunnel.'

Hesha stared at him. 'Did Andrew say if he and Sophie had ever had a relationship?'

'No. No suggestion from him. We didn't ask.'

'What if he did? And he still had feelings for her?' Hesha examined the photo, her brow creasing.

James shrugged. 'He's married with kids. There's every indication he's moved on.'

'Yeah, but when you went to see him, he was working at the weekend, wasn't he?' Hesha pointed out. 'On a Bank Holiday. Does that mean money trouble? Or trouble at home?'

James pursed his lips. 'Perhaps ...'

'Or ...' Hesha stood up and paced, working through an idea. She turned to face James. 'What if they never had a relationship, but he's always had feelings for her. *Then* he not only finds out that she was unhappily married, but that she was also planning to divorce? What if he followed her to Manor House Farm after they'd met at Applewood and tried to convince her to – I don't know – run off with him? And she said no, or they argued, and he lashed out?'

James nodded. He stood up. 'Time to pay Andrew Arden another visit.' He checked his watch, groaned and sat down. 'In about four hours.'

Val walked in and dropped an armful of files on the nearest table. 'Oh God, has someone brought bacon sandwiches?'

Ashley held up a wrapped package.

'Thanks, Ash.' Val took a bite, closing her eyes as she chewed. 'Please take note, this is the real path to promotion.' She raised her eyebrows at James. 'I've given Trent my statement. Next, we'll trawl back through what evidence we've amassed.'

'Is Nell discounted from enquiries now?' Hesha asked.

'Not yet,' said Val. 'Her economy with the truth and potential incriminating pieces of evidence mean we can't discount her. But we need to tread carefully.' She sighed. 'I hoped we'd get further when we questioned her. For now, she's still a suspect.'

James bit back his frustration. He'd hoped that awful interview would have ruled Nell out once and for all. The thought of a re-match … *Ugh.* He steeled himself, remembering her complaint, that his professionalism was under scrutiny.

Val lowered her voice. 'As I say, we have to be careful with Nell. Trent's hot and bothered because his old chum has waged war. But raising something in a police interview is *not* the same as circulating illegal material. So let's hope Barrington'll have the sense to not tie us up in red tape when we should be investigating. To answer your question, we've followed due process, and we'll continue to do so. And if it takes us back to Nell, so be it.'

James wanted to ask if all this – her defence of mainly his actions – had damaged her chance of promotion, but now wasn't the moment. She didn't even mention it. A deadweight of guilt made his shoulders droop.

The door was elbowed open by a junior officer carrying two white tubs, each bearing evidence labels. He set them on the table in front of James. 'Thought I should bring these straight over. These are from Dr Ward's house search.'

The team peered at the containers. The handwritten label on the lids said, *BADGER-BAITING PELLETS.* James recalled seeing them on the shelves by Nell's desk.

With latex-gloved hands, the officer opened both tubs, one filled with green pellets, the second with blue. He held one up. A small plastic chip, about two millimetres in diameter. 'Look familiar?'

'Exactly like the red one we found in the kitchen,' James noted.

Val checked the incident board. 'Found in the manor house kitchen, near the door to the tunnel.'

'We didn't find any red ones in her house. But I'll leave these with you. We're cataloguing the rest,' the officer said, as he departed.

'Is this grounds for re-arrest?' James asked, his mind racing. *What the hell does that mean? Nell got inside the house?*

'Not necessarily,' Val said. 'But it does mean we have more questions. We'll just have to choose our timing, and our approach. We've clearly touched a nerve. Nell may be more volatile than she seems. Everything in life has probably been easy for her. Money and influence breeds entitlement. Maybe David meant more to her than she admits? Especially if having a relationship with him after being so firmly bitten with the sex tape was a big deal. Might make it harder for her to trust. And likely to lash out if that trust is betrayed.'

James winced. He'd used their mutual attraction to try to gain her trust. Which hadn't yielded anything useful for the investigation. And had backfired. Spectacularly. Yet he knew first-hand what it was like to have that trust broken: having an ex cheat hadn't just been a betrayal, it had been a burning humiliation. But at least he hadn't had to face anything more public than friends and family finding out. No wonder Nell was kicking him where it hurt. He forced himself to assess her and considered another potential motive. 'I guess it's still possible Nell could have been David's accomplice. Maybe he can extend his loans, because now he's got the chance to get his hands on real money?'

Ashley picked up David's file. 'Interesting, isn't it, that he managed to charm two wealthy women? And he also changed his name?'

'Seems like everyone in this case has an identity crisis.' Val pursed her lips, then looked at the team. 'So, we'll follow up with other suspects. But we will continue to dig around Nell's motive. And, if we uncover anything else, we *will* re-arrest her.'

Chapter 21

Sunday 29th August – 7.45 a.m.

Nell woke, disorientated and with a sense of panic, tangled in the hotel sheets. Her sleep had been fitful. Her eyeballs felt like they'd been rolled through a desert. As she remembered where she was, the black weight of realisation unfolded across her chest. The arrest, the story coming out again, the search of her home, having to weather it all over again with the added risk of a murder – and a murderer – hanging over her. Nell tugged the duvet over her head and cocooned herself in the soft, co-ordinated white-and-duck-egg-blue bed linen. But she couldn't stay still for long. She needed to act. Or, at least, take charge of what she could.

She got up and opened the gold damask curtains. The hazy morning sunlight infused her with purpose. Charles would address the press and the complaint. Social media would always be a ticking bomb, even if Charles did everything possible. But, if the press got hold of her name in connection with the murder, her careful separation of background and career would be over. Her colleagues, Adam – they'd all find out about the story. They'd probably search for pictures. Nausea churned in her belly. And the scandal was still only part of the reason why she kept her background discrete. Once that died down, then would come the assumptions that her connections had bolstered any achievement she'd ever had.

The key thing was keeping a low profile now. No connection with the investigation, no attention from the press. She'd been lucky so far. But how long would her luck last? She wouldn't be safe until she was discounted from the investigation. And that wouldn't happen until the murderer was caught.

Charles had texted:

We'll have breakfast at 7.30 if you want to join, heading off at 8.30.

It was nearly 8 a.m. Nell's stomach growled with the gnawing hunger that usually followed back-to-back dusk and dawn bat surveys, with no time to sleep in between. The craving for caffeine and carbs. But first she needed to scrub the grimy cell, the seedy sense of suspicion, off her.

In the bathroom, she ran a bath, tipping in all the miniature bottles of bath oil she could find. Waiting for the bath to fill, she replied to Charles:

I'll see you in reception at 8.30 a.m., but I'll Uber home.

Sweet jasmine and vanilla wafted up through the steam. *Slight improvement on Cell 4.* Lowering herself into the scalding water, Nell scrubbed her skin until it was raw.

Thirty minutes later, she headed to the gift shop next to reception in the lobby, emerging with two bags just as Conor, then Charles, appeared.

'Did you sleep OK, Nell?' Conor asked in his soothing Irish brogue.

'Yes, thanks,' she lied. 'You?'

Conor nodded.

Nell noted a hesitation, as if he wanted to say more. She filled in the silence for him. 'I'm sorry for making you come out overnight at short notice, Conor. Thank you for all you've done, and for arranging extra things to help. I really appreciate it.'

Conor turned to face Nell. His shoulders were stiff, his hazel eyes serious in his craggy, tanned face. 'It's the least I could do. The very least. And if you ever need anything, or end up ...' He clenched a defined jaw under trimmed stubble. 'Well, you can be certain of my help.' His fists balled at his sides, his muscles visible inside his jacket sleeves.

Nell flushed at Conor's unexpected show of emotion and balked at the realisation that he may be talking about darker deeds than chauffeuring. She knew he was ex-SAS, privately assigned to protect her mother ever since her prison reform work had attracted death threats. The tension hung between them. Nell broke it, offering him one of the two gift bags she held.

'I found a decent bottle of whisky in the gift shop. Just a small thank you for the unexpected inconvenience.' Nell smiled, noticing his shoulders relax. 'And for all your training. I'm lucky to have someone like you in my corner.'

Conor's face softened, then he grinned back with the familiarity born of intense physical training sessions. 'Aye, well at least I know you can land a punch, handle a weapon and drive like a bat out of hell. You have been taught by the best, after all.' He thumbed his chest. 'Just keep up with the running. Your stamina's shite and you might have to count on it one day.'

The friendly insult was strangely reassuring. And, to be fair, it was true. 'I will.' But, recalling her thoughts in the cell, that she must have been framed, that Adam might be in danger, she shivered. *He might be right.*

'Good. You can't keep depending on being young and thin now that you're in your thirties. You have to work at it now. Keep in condition.'

'Yeah, OK, Conor. I've got the point.' She gave a theatrical sigh just as Charles joined them. 'Good timing, Charles, I think Conor was about to make me run laps of the hotel—'

'Now there's an idea.' Conor's face brightened.

Nell rolled her eyes and said goodbye to Charles. 'I'll Uber home, so I don't add to your journey. And here's a little something. Some decent whisky for you and a fancy tin of the hotel's homemade biscuits for Geraldine and Jasper. An apology for hauling you away from family without notice. And – thank you, Charles.'

'You can't win me over with aged single malts, Nell. Although I won't stop you trying.' A hint of a smile met his eyes. 'Just keep out of trouble.'

Nell watched them leave, then found the elegant breakfast room. Two cafetières of aromatic coffee and a pile of buttery toast later, she felt more human. She checked out at reception, then dropped into one of the wallowy armchairs and texted Adam:

I'm worried about your 4 punctures. Seems odd. Were they slashed? Please be careful.

Hitting 'send', Nell fretted she sounded like an idiot. Too late now. And if someone *had* slashed them, Adam should know. She shivered, and tapped the icon for an Uber.

'Nell?' Sylvia's voice carried delighted surprise. 'What are you doing here?'

Nell stood up and turned to be swept into an embrace of air kisses. Suddenly overcome, she held Sylvia in a hug, fighting down a sob threatening to erupt.

Sylvia hugged her for a long moment, then gazed at her. 'What's wrong, sweetie?'

Nell shook her head. 'I've ... It's ... It's just nice to see you.'

Sylvia's eyes narrowed, then she squeezed Nell's hand. 'I was on my way to the spa, for my facial, mani-pedi and hair appointment before I head off to Wales. But I'm early. *As per.* Time for a quick cuppa?'

They walked to the spa café and each had a green tea. Nell would have preferred another coffee, but no such toxins were listed on Purity Spa's menu. The spa café was a cocoon of nurturing: soft earth tones, delicate plinky music mimicking the stream trickling over the rounded stones of the water feature, lush with emerald ferns, the air heavy with scented oils.

'I'm putting in the prep just in case Troy finds me,' Sylvia said to Nell through the fragrant steam of her tea. 'Then I'll hit the road, get to Wales this evening and have a whole B&B to myself. Well, I will once the last guests have left tomorrow morning and my parents set off after lunch for their holiday. They're getting too old to manage it all, really. I'm pleased they'll at least allow me to give them a break.'

Nell was grateful for Sylvia's undemanding chatter. The normality of it, the encouragement to think about something else, helped.

'I remember the team weekend we had there,' Nell said. 'It's such a beautiful place.'

'Oh, yes, of course,' Sylvia exclaimed. 'Gosh, that was about three years ago! When my parents were just getting the B&B business started, before they'd renovated the guest rooms and it was still a camping ground.'

'It was great for botany and birding, I remember,' Nell said. 'So peaceful.'

'It's still like that. Completely unspoiled. Now, they've got an organic smallholding, so they grow the food they serve for meals, collect freshly laid hens' eggs every morning, and make their own honey from their beehives. It's idyllic. This year they've included retreats – yoga, art, writing. It's fabulous.'

Nell rotated her tense shoulders. 'You have *no* idea how great that sounds right now.' A retreat – or even just the chance to hermit herself away in a cave – sounded perfect.

'I'll send you the link. I've redone their website. It's very stylish.' Sylvia quoted, '*Unplug and unwind at our digital detox retreat in the heart of the Welsh countryside.*'

'Sounds like they've found a niche.' Nell cradled her mug, relaxing with the warmth.

'Partly out of necessity. It's a phone signal blackspot and they're a pair of technophobes. Not even Wi-Fi. Just a landline, diverting to answerphone so I don't mess up their prehistoric booking system' – she rolled her eyes – 'and an ancient computer plugged into the internet for emails, which I'll have to hack into to check my social media.'

'Oh. Tricky?'

'Not really. Their password's on a Post-it note stuck to the monitor. It's just that the computer's so old, it almost needs a starting handle to crank it up. But, if Troy does track me down, we'll have a few uninterrupted days before my parents return on Friday.'

Nell shot Sylvia a wry look. 'How are you expecting Troy to find you?'

Sylvia answered with a knowing smile. 'A girl has to have a way to lay some clues if she wants to be found. Haven't I spelled it out? I'm enlisting Facebook. And Twitter. And Instagram. He's got all my social-media details on my card. I'll just add the clickbait.'

Sunday 29th August – 8.30 a.m.

James and Ashley's round of visits began at the hospital, hoping for an update on Mrs Crows' test results. As they approached the desk, an alarm summoned the duty nurse away, seconds before they reached her.

Dread rose as James realised she was running towards Mrs Crows' room.

He and Ashley started sprinting after her, but running footsteps from all directions warned them to keep out of the way. Four nurses ran to Mrs Crows' room, followed by a porter wheeling a defibrillator, and two doctors hurrying in his wake.

Against the ominous monotone of the heart monitor, a nurse called out stats and numbers while the defibrillator crackled as it charged. Urgent muffled voices spoke in hospital code. Outside, powerless, James sent a silent prayer to a God he didn't believe in as Ashley grabbed hold of his hand. *Who knew she had such a crushing grip?*

Inside the room, a doctor called, 'Clear!' The high-pitched whine of the defibrillators and a dull thud cut through the heart monitor's moan. An expectant silence hung heavier than the fug of disinfectant, then the droning monotone revived the room's activity. 'Again. Clear!' Another whine, another muffled thud. Silence. That single note on the monitor again.

Two nurses in the doorway murmured unhappily as the doctor said, 'One more try. Clear!' But the monotone prevailed.

'Thank you, everyone for your efforts. Mrs Crows' time of death is 8.35 a.m.'

A doctor left the room while nurses and another doctor went in. Noticing James and Ashley, he came over.

'Are you family? Friends?'

James shook his head, extracting his hand from Ashley's and flexing it to bring it back to life. 'Police officers. We're monitoring Mrs Crows' condition in relation to a murder investigation.'

The doctor looked surprised. 'Oh, is that what the tests were all about?'

'Yes,' Ashley said. 'We still haven't been given the results.'

'Let me see if they're through.' The doctor walked to the desk and peered at the computer. 'Ah, looks like they came in a few minutes ago.'

Ashley's face turned thunderous.

'The toxicity tests showed her liver test results were abnormal.' His brow creased. 'Which is unusual for someone on tablets to control high blood pressure.'

Frowning, he turned to unlock a cabinet and ran his finger down the shelves until he reached a bottle. Taking it out, he shook a few pills into his palm, then studied them under a light. As he tilted the pills, his frown deepened, his mouth dropped open, his shoulders sagged. 'Oh, Jesus Christ.'

'What? What is it?' Ashley demanded.

James looked at her in concern. He knew Ashley felt protective towards Mrs Crows.

The doctor looked worried. 'Mrs Crows had been prescribed a thiazide diuretic, Hygroton. But these pills aren't Hygroton. These are midodrine.'

'And the significance of that is?' James could see Ashley was trying to curb her frustration.

'Midodrine is used to treat chronic low blood pressure. The tablets look almost identical to Hygroton. But if you give midodrine to someone with high blood pressure, it can trigger a stroke. And, in some cases, cause a stroke-induced coma. As it did for Mrs Crows.'

'If those tests had been done sooner, could you have done anything to reverse that?' Ashley asked, practically through gritted teeth.

'I don't honestly know. It's especially hard to gauge in elderly patients.'

Ashley looked furious. She turned away from the doctor.

'Could the tablets have been swapped here?' James asked.

The doctor gestured to the secure cabinet behind him. 'No, it's all kept under lock and key and only medical professionals give out the medication. And these tablets came with her from her care home. Applewood, was it?'

'So if they were tampered with, it would have happened there?'

'I ... I suppose. Or a mix-up at the pharmacy, perhaps. The address and phone number are on the bottle – here.'

Ashley got out her phone and took a photo of the chemists' contact details, then walked over to the reception desk to call them, while the doctor spoke to James.

'I'd think it highly unusual that a pharmacist would make a mistake like that. It's more likely something happened at the care home. But again, medication is dispensed carefully and kept secure.'

A nurse interrupted them, with forms for the doctor to sign. Seeing Ashley was still on the phone to the pharmacy, James took out his mobile, called Applewood's number, and asked to speak to the manager. The receptionist reminded him, 'Yes, I'm acting manager this weekend.'

After breaking the news about Mrs Crows, James asked, 'Is there any way Mrs Crows' medication could have been mixed up with someone else's?'

'I'll find out.' The receptionist put James on hold while she got a carer to check, and to examine Marjorie Crows' medical notes.

Ashley had finished her phone call and joined him.

'What did they say?' James asked.

'No possibility of a mix-up. They have very rigorous systems in place to only deal with one type of medication at a time. Very well-practised at adhering to those procedures and then checking and double-checking. The woman I spoke to was adamant that there was no room for error.' Ashley's expression was still grim, so James jerked his head towards the corridor. As they walked out, he put the call on speakerphone so Ashley could hear.

'Hi there,' the receptionist said. 'Sorry to keep you. I wanted to check really carefully. But there's no way Mrs Crows' medication could have got mixed up with someone else's.'

'How can you be so certain?' James asked.

'Because no one here is on medication for low blood pressure. So she couldn't have been given the wrong medication. It's impossible.'

Ashley looked at James as he put his phone away. 'So, someone tampered with her medication,' she said. 'Mrs Crows was murdered.'

Chapter 22

At the station, James updated the team. The sombre mood lasted a few minutes until the ribbing for Trent's admonishment started. Hesha joshed half-heartedly, knackered from lack of sleep, hugging coffee and reading emails. Ashley didn't join in, though her knowing gaze was worse than any wry comment. But Ed Baker was on form and looked about as gleeful as James had ever seen his gruff colleague.

Letting his computer screen shield him from the teasing, James read his emails until Ed relented and dropped a folder on James's desk. 'Here's something to keep you out of trouble. Forensics brought their reports up.'

James longed to sink into a deep sleep; let someone else plough through all this until they found a spark of hope. But if he showed signs of fatigue, Ed's heckling would only start up again. 'And what have you been doing, Ed? Got anything for us?'

'Yep. I've been busy. Checked out all the contractors working at the manor. One self-employed architect, who'd swanned off to Paris at the time of the murder. His car's on ANPR cameras and he's recorded at passport control at the Eurostar. And one structural engineer who works in a small team with three colleagues, who all had a client meeting at the Old Coach Inn, where the landlord vouched for them.'

He gestured at the board where James had written *Other contractors?* and he'd added their details, then crossed them out.

'And I went back to Mr Gilpin to see why he'd been so tight-lipped about his land. Turns out the purchase of his land wasn't finalised at the time of Sophie Crows' death. There was still a day or so to go before the completion date.'

James sat up. 'So he really did have a motive, if he knew Sophie was behind sabotaging the development?' He shook off the sluggish fog, hopeful of a new avenue.

'Don't get excited, he was at Pendlebury Hospital at the time of the murder with his son, visiting his wife who was recovering from an operation. And SOCO finally got to search David's room at the hotel. It had been cleaned, and another guest had stayed there, so caveat, caveat. But they found this.' He held up a clear, labelled bag. 'The cleaners missed it because it was stuck to the inside leg of the bed.'

James couldn't see anything in it, so walked over and took it from Ed. A single, tiny red pellet. 'Huh.' Like the one in the kitchen. Like the ones in Nell's house. What did that mean? Were they working together somehow? Swimmy from lack of sleep, the idea was nightmarish.

Returning to his desk, he sat heavily, sighing and checked his emails. 'I've had some updates, too. An email explaining why Nell had chloroform in her house. It's to do with her bat-rehabilitation work and it's all above board. She's licensed to work with bats and licensed to use chloroform, which is apparently used, albeit unusually, to euthanise bats with no chance of recovery. The Bat Conservation Trust and a local bat hospital – which really do exist, don't tell me you don't get to see all walks of life as a copper – all attest to her training.'

Ed grunted. 'Doesn't rule out the possibility she might've used it on something – or someone – else?'

James held up the folder. 'No, *that* doesn't, but forensics have. No smell of chloroform at the scene, no stains or blisters on the skin, no injection marks.' He scanned the next page. 'The blood on Nell's map was her own blood. And they followed up on the scratches she had up her arms, and checked Sophie's fingernails. But they found no skin cells. Not from Nell, or anyone else. No defensive marks on Sophie's hands or arms, suggesting she was surprised—'

'Or attacked by someone she knew?' Hesha said.

James nodded. 'The brick used as the murder weapon had no DNA on it other than Sophie's. Forensics matched it to the other bricks inside the tunnel. Which is what we expected. It just confirms that anyone with the opportunity and motive had the means.'

Holding up a picture of a boot print, he added, 'And, lastly, forensics have matched the boot-print cast with the unique wear pattern of Nell's boot.'

James let out a long exhale. 'A decent tranche of work, very kindly fast-tracked. And it gets us precisely nowhere.'

'Well, I've got something.' Hesha pinned a printed still from camera footage on the board. 'From the hours of CCTV footage from Nye Hall Hotel, I got a clear picture of the man who checked in with Anna Maddison. I spoke to Anna this morning and, after a *lot* of persuading, she gave his name: Sven Jorgssen. I've not spoken to him yet, but he checks out in a general search. Mid-fifties and married, hence her reluctance to tell us, especially when she realised we'd speak to him. It seems she's content as a mistress. And Sven seems to lavish plenty of expensive gifts on her and takes her on spontaneous weekends away.'

'Is he the source of those payments, then?' James asked.

'Maybe. Now I've got his name, I've asked the financial team to check his accounts. But again, don't get excited – I found Anna eventually in all those hours of footage. At Nye Hall, right in the middle of the timeframe of Sophie's murder.'

'Great.'

'Are we crossing her off?'

'Well, perhaps.' Hesha glanced at James. 'But …?'

'Go on,' James urged.

'Anna's intelligent, persuasive, and getting a load of money from her rich boyfriend. How easy would it be for her to slip some hotel security guard a chunk of cash to fudge Nye Hall's CCTV?'

'Well, it's possible,' James said.

Hesha nodded. 'I've been wondering ever since the tech team came back with results on David and Anna's computers this morning. Nothing incriminating on David's, so they've returned it. But Anna's …'

'Yes?'

'When they checked her deleted internet history, they found a strange order of a baseball cap and polo shirt, with A1 on it.' She glanced at James. 'I can't see her wearing something like that, can you? And no one in her family or friend circle, either, from what I can gather.'

'OK …' James frowned.

'But then tech also traced that email to her PC. The one to Sophie, changing the time of the meeting.'

James's eyes widened. 'Great.'

'Yes, but Anna claims she'd already left work that day, before the email was sent. She said David was still in the office with access to her computer. We'll keep hold of her PC, keep running checks, see if we pick up anything else.'

'Good,' James said. 'But who's lying? Her or David?'

Hesha shrugged. 'You know, it was interesting. At this point, Anna started to look upset. Almost fearful. She asked if she could go and stay with some friends, in another town. But she made a point of saying she'd keep us informed of her whereabouts and make herself available. There didn't seem to be an issue of her leaving the country, but I did take her passport – given Sven's address – even though she said she could hardly turn up at his marital home. It looked to me like she genuinely believed David may have been responsible for Sophie's murder. She looked … *frightened.*'

James's eyes narrowed. 'You're sure it wasn't a good cover so she could remove herself from the investigation while placing suspicion on David?'

'Maybe. She could be a very good actress …'

James scratched his chin. 'It's not far from Nye Hall to Manor House Farm, is it? A fast car, like a Porsche, could make the journey pretty quickly. I'll check it out.'

He made a note on his iPad, and spotted a memo he hadn't crossed out.

Warrant for Pendlebury Hotel for phone number of call made from David's room.

Groaning inwardly, James dreaded having to find Trent and ask him to sign one off. But at least it would show him they were following up all leads; he couldn't complain at that.

Sunday 29th August – 10.30 a.m.

When Nell got home, she rushed to check Zorro and Jezebel, worried that the police search and the clean-up afterwards had disturbed them, or worse, someone had unzipped the cage to check it, and Zorro had got hurt or escaped. Or met Jezebel. *Please don't let me find my cat eating my rare bat.*

Jezebel rubbed Nell's legs as she walked in, hinting at breakfast. 'Well, if you're hungry, that's a good sign.' Nell fed Jezebel, so her cat would be occupied while she tended to Zorro.

Phew. Zorro's enclosure on the counter was zipped shut. Closing the utility-room door behind her, Nell still checked the walls and floor as she approached the cage. She'd had enough escapees to have a practised drill.

Opening the cage, she saw that every scrap of food had been eaten. Even the extra rations. The tea towel fidgeted. Nell carefully drew it back and Zorro raised his head to chatter at her. He looked almost indignant. Nell replenished his food and Zorro fluttered down, devouring the squirming mealworms as if he were ravenous. He was undeterred from feeding as Nell cleaned the cage around him, refreshed his water and prepared to give him his final dose of medicine.

When he'd finished feeding, Nell scooped Zorro up. She checked his wing. No signs of inflammation or swelling remained. Fat pads had filled out his shoulders. She painted the antibiotic cream on his back teeth for the last time and rinsed the taste away with water. Zorro made his displeasure known as he chewed the end of the pipette. Nell grinned at his feistiness and warmed him in her hands for a test flight.

Within seconds, Zorro prised her hands apart, chattering boldly. With a firm wingbeat, he took off and swooped up to the ceiling, swerving around the light fitting, hovering and fluttering with great stamina. Judging by his agility, she'd be waiting for some time before she could catch him. He was ready to go home.

Nell had spent an hour trying various stealthy approaches, standing on the counter, flattened against the wall, leaning out as far as she dared without toppling, only for Zorro to flutter out of reach each time, as if they were in a comedy sketch. Finally, Nell gave up hunting and tried reverse psychology. As Zorro circled, she checked the evening's weather. Warm and dry, ideal insect-hunting conditions for Zorro to re-orientate himself.

She hesitated, then texted Adam noting he hadn't replied about his tyres.

I'll release Zorro tonight. Want to join me?

It didn't matter if he was interested in Erin. He'd been part of Zorro's rescue, he should have a chance to see his release. They could be friends, couldn't they?

His reply was instantaneous:

YESSSSS! 😊 Hurray! See you tonight!

With Nell no longer in pursuit, Zorro landed, panting, just within reach on the blinds. She gathered him up, unpicking each tiny claw from the fabric, and tucked him into the cage.

Looking around the rest of her immaculate house, Nell noticed the care taken to restore, no, *improve* order. Her clothes were rearranged by garment type, then colour, her books were alphabetised. She had only to reorganise some paperwork and ornaments. She felt another sting of guilt that she had this advantage to fall back on. Someone else would have come home after the gruelling night to chaos. At least she didn't have to relive the invasion as she put everything away. She felt grateful. And guilty.

A large bouquet of flowers had been arranged in a tall vase on her coffee table with a note from Charles.

Chin up and don't kill anyone.

Hilarious! Nell dropped the note in the bin. She checked her phone and made some tea, then checked her phone again. Another text from Adam:

How are you? Hope you haven't been arrested yet! 😊

'Ha-bloody-ha,' Nell said to the screen. She realised she ached for company.

As the kettle boiled, she texted back:

If you can run the risk of dinner with a criminal mastermind, we could get a takeaway tonight?

Instantly, her phone rang. Nell jumped, then shook herself and answered. 'Hi, Adam.'

'How're you doing?'

'I … I've been better, to be honest.' Nell tried to make her words sound light.

'What do you mean?'

'I … well, let's just say you hit the nail on the head with your text.'

'*What?*' Adam's voice rose an octave. 'Please tell me you're joking?'

'I wish I could.' Nell drowned a teabag with boiling water and set down the kettle. 'But if you don't mind associating with a suspected killer, honestly, I would love to see you.' As she said the words, her stomach tightened with apprehension.

'Yeah, I'll take my chances.' His voice was warm with affectionate humour. 'I'm on site until late-ish this afternoon. I'll grab some food on the way over. What do you fancy?'

'Ah,' Nell sighed as she plopped her teabag into the compost bin and stirred her tea. 'Do you know what, I could murder—'

'Jesus, Nell!' Adam laughed. 'You'll have to be a bit more circumspect now you're a wanted crim! I'll bring a curry. You just stay out of trouble.'

Sunday 29th August – 12 p.m.

James picked Ashley up from Applewood, her chin just higher than the stack of sign-in ledgers she clutched.

'I've been through them while I waited, but I want the pages photographed and logged,' she panted as she placed them on the back seat. 'And I'm certain, Nell, Anna, Simon or David haven't visited Applewood. But Andrew Arden has. At least twice.'

As they drove, James mulled over his approach. Maybe Andrew was doing well for himself, with a successful legal practice. Maybe he did have a happy family life. *Maybe.*

The satnav led them to a modest semi-detached house with an unkempt front garden on the outskirts of Pendlebury. He and Ashley dodged the bushes and grasses overhanging the path and rang the bell.

Behind the door, Andrew's voice called out, 'Can you get that?'

A harassed-looking woman opened the door, a plate in her hand. James and Ashley showed her their badges.

'We're looking for Andrew Arden,' James said.

'Oh? I'm his wife. Liv Arden. What's this about?'

'I'm DS James Clark, this is DS Ashley Hollis. Sorry to disturb you at the weekend. Your husband's been helping us with our enquiries about Sophie Crows' murder. We have a few more questions.'

Liv stood aside. 'Andrew?' She called up the stairs as she walked to the kitchen. Two little boys played at the edge of the breakfast table. One drove a truck at the stegosaurus his brother wielded. They crashed together, knocking over a plastic beaker of juice.

'Oh, for God's sake.' She grabbed the beaker and mopped up the mess. 'If you've finished, will you go and play in the garden? Not at the table.'

The boys raced through the open French windows down to the trampoline, jumping on it with bubbling laughter.

'They'll make themselves sick now,' Liv muttered. She cleared up the messy table: a chewed banana beside its skin, half-empty yoghurt pots, mucky plates and bowls and beakers, blobs of mysterious, gelatinous food stuck to the plastic tablecloth. Her sigh was weary as she dumped the crockery haphazardly into the dishwasher.

'What was it?' Andrew said as he walked into the kitchen. He caught sight of the detectives. 'Oh, hello.' He hesitated, mid-stride. 'How can I help?'

'Morning, Andrew,' James said. 'We have a few more questions about Sophie.'

'Oh, fine. How's the investigation going? Can I get you a coffee?'

'No, thank you,' James said. 'We'll just be a few minutes.'

Andrew gestured to a chair. 'Please take a seat.'

'I think it might be better to talk in private,' Ashley said. 'How about the garden?'

James noted Liv's reaction, swinging round to glare at her husband.

Glancing at his wife, Andrew shook his head. 'No, Livvie can hear anything we have to say.'

'Fine.' The detectives smiled and sat. Andrew sat opposite, his gaze darting between them.

James began. 'I'm not sure if we mentioned before that Sophie's body was found in the tunnel at Manor House Farm. Were you aware of the tunnel?'

'The tunnel? Yes. Well. Yes, I did know about it.' Andrew looked flustered.

James nodded. 'Good.' He slid the photo of him standing in the tunnel towards him. 'Can you tell us who the people are in this photo?'

Andrew looked surprised and peered at the picture. 'Yes. That's Mr and Mrs Crows. My father and me. And … Sophie.'

'You said your families were very close,' James said. 'In fact, more specifically, you and Sophie were very close.'

'Well …' Andrew sounded hesitant, but still affronted. He glanced at his wife. She folded her arms and leaned back against the sink.

'Did you and Sophie ever have a relationship?' James asked.

'No.' Andrew's tone was sharp. 'That—'

'Really?' Ashley interrupted. 'Two young adults, growing up so close, in these idyllic surroundings. No flush of romance?'

'Not at all,' Andrew protested.

'Did you want a relationship with Sophie?' Ashley asked. 'Had she spurned your advances? Rejected your affection?'

'Oh, really.' Andrew held his hands up. 'If you carry on like this, I'll have to get my own solicitor. But I'll say this. Sophie and I were close. And I did love her, in a way. A brotherly way. We all took her under our collective wing. We all wanted to get her through the ordeal she'd had. She was a sweet girl, but she was so obviously suffering. Mr and Mrs Crows wanted so much to create a happy home for her, but they were grieving themselves. In their circle, I was closest in age to her. I became a bit of a confidant. And I suppose I was flattered that she trusted me.'

'So, naturally,' James said, 'when Sophie needed to make a change to her will and start divorce proceedings, she turned to you. Not only as her solicitor. But as her trusted confidant.' Checking Liv's response, he saw her watching her husband with widened eyes.

'Yes, of course,' Andrew said. His neck blotched with crimson. His gaze darted between the detectives and his wife.

'Did it stir up anything else?' Ashley asked. 'Develop your fond feelings into something more?'

James marvelled at how Ashley was ignoring Liv's rigid body language: a glacier of hostility.

Andrew shook his head. 'No.'

'You didn't follow her to Manor House Farm? Perhaps talk to her?' Ashley asked. 'Or argue?'

Liv glared at them across the table and Andrew got to his feet. 'I've answered your questions about my feelings towards Sophie. Repeating them won't change the answer. What you really want to know is, do I have an alibi? And I've given you one. So you're clearly wasting time here.'

'Yes, I've tried to contact the client you said you were with,' James said. 'But I can't reach them.'

'Oh.' Andrew sank in his chair again. 'Yes. Harry's gone away for the long weekend. He's back on Monday. He's very, let's say, old school. So he probably turned off his phone to avoid roaming charges. But you can easily check with him tomorrow.'

'OK. One more day won't make much difference,' James conceded.

'Knowing Mrs Crows as well as you do,' Ashley said, 'what do you know about her health?'

'Well, I know she's in a coma and in hospital at the moment. Applewood called to tell me. But until then, I thought her in good health.' He frowned. 'I can't recall her complaining about anything except her eyesight. But she sometimes joked about being careful of her high blood pressure.'

'Have you visited her while she's been in hospital?' Ashley asked. His eyes flicked towards his wife. He nodded. She gaped.

'Have you heard from the hospital today?' Ashley asked.

'No ... why?' At Ashley's sombre expression, Andrew's face crumpled.

Ashley confirmed what he'd guessed. 'I'm sorry to tell you that Mrs Crows died this morning.'

'Oh God.' He leaned his head into his hands, looking shocked. 'I could see she was in a bad way when I visited yesterday evening. But you see, she's always been such a formidable woman, I just expected her to pull through somehow.' A silence drew out.

In the garden, the children shrieked. James watched their heads bob above the trampoline side-screen, their faces snapshots of excitement. Taken in isolation, their expressions could read as horror, mischief, shock, mirth.

One of the children yelled, then wailed. Liv's shoulders dropped. 'Oh, what *now*?'

'Mummy, Mummy, Barnaby hurted his toe,' the brotherly messenger yelled as he ran up the garden.

'Tell him he's got nine more,' Liv called back. 'And if he can't play anymore, he can always tidy his room.'

The messenger didn't break pace and swooped back round back to the trampoline. Within seconds, their game resumed.

Taking a deep breath, Andrew asked, 'Was it ... quick? Did she just pass away in her sleep?'

'Cardiac arrest,' James said. 'But her stroke was brought on by someone who'd tampered with her medication when they visited her at Applewood. And, so far, you're the only suspect we can place there—'

'*Suspect?*' Andrew and Liv repeated the word in horror.

'But what possible motive could he have?' Liv demanded.

'Oh.' Ashley pulled an *oops* face. 'You don't know?'

James studied Andrew as his head drooped into his hands.

'Now, with both Sophie *and* Mrs Crows dead, Andrew becomes the sole inheritor of Manor House Farm.'

'What?' Liv looked stunned.

James and Ashley exchanged looks. Sensing a marital row was about to blow up, James said, 'We'll leave you to it, for now. But we'll be in touch.'

As the front door closed behind them, James and Ashley lingered on the doorstep in silence. Ashley's eyebrows rose with the voices behind the door.

'When the *hell* were you going to tell me?'

'I never thought it would come to pass. I thought Sophie would inherit, and she'd bequeathed it to the horse sanctuary.'

'But you *did* know! You knew as soon as Sophie was killed that she couldn't inherit and it would all come to you. That special childhood place from that family you love so much. Well, nicely played, Andrew. And they hit a nerve, didn't they?'

'What?'

'I wouldn't be surprised if you had tried it on with Sophie.'

'God, you really don't think any of that holds weight, do you?'

'Well, you tell me,' Liv yelled. 'The woman's dead. Yet *still* she's inveigling herself into our relationship. You didn't even tell me she was getting *divorced.*'

'It's *confidential.*'

'Oh, come on. She wasn't just any client, was she? She was your special friend, who happened to be young and beautiful. *And* she owned a bloody manor house. You'd have had it *made!*'

'Oh, for God's sake, Livvie, this is all in your head—'

'Yeah. Mine,' Liv retorted, 'and now those bloody *detectives*'!'

Chapter 23

James squared his shoulders and knocked on David Stephenson's door, who answered, dressed in jeans and shirt; clean-shaven but with dark circles under his eyes.

'Any news?' David asked as they sat down.

'We're making progress. But I just wanted to ask you a couple of questions. I understand you recently changed your name to Stephenson?'

The police search had found the trail of David using that name dated back to about five years ago, ostensibly for his work.

'Oh.' David shook his head. 'Yeah, I changed my name because of my parents divorcing.'

'Huh. Interesting. Because your parents only divorced four years ago. How did you manage to predict it?'

'Mum confided in me that she wanted a divorce before she went through with it. And when I understood her reasons and what she'd been going through, I wanted to distance myself from my father. And his name. And I thought taking hers might give her some self-belief.' He pressed his hands against his jeans.

'So why doesn't your sister know about your change of name?' James checked his notes from his earlier phone call with Louise Dixon. 'That strikes me as odd.'

'Does it?' David shrugged. 'Well, I guess, lots of reasons. I don't know if Mum has confided in her, and it's not my business to mention it. Since Lou moved to Basel, we obviously see a lot less of each other. And we don't speak on the phone as often as I suppose siblings should.'

James had the question of the phone call David had made from his hotel room on the tip of his tongue. But something in his gut told him he'd be better off getting that information from the hotel. Instead, he nodded, allowed an understanding smile to spread across his face. 'Sure, I relate to that. I think I last spoke to my brother at Christmas.

Things take over. He's got three kids. Work's busy.' He paused. 'How's your own work going?'

'What?'

'Well, last time I was here, your planner wanted to delay things out of respect for Sophie, but you wanted to keep busy. But with the house being a crime scene, I guess progress is stopped for the moment?'

'Yes. It's true that I wanted a distraction. I think it was shock, the news not really sinking in. Now I don't care about the plans. I just want Sophie's killer caught.'

'Did you have to ask any of the surveyors to stop work?'

'No, Anna dealt with that.'

'But had you appointed them in the first place?'

'No. That was Anna.'

'Did you even check any quotes?'

'Nope. Anna.' David huffed. 'Does any of this matter?'

'Well, I wondered if you knew that you'd crossed paths with one of your surveyors before.'

'Oh?' David's chest started to rise and fall rapidly. 'Who?'

'Do you remember Dr Nell Ward?'

David leaned back in his seat. 'Nell?' His mouth twitched. 'Yes, I remember Nell. We went out when she was at uni. My little sister's housemate.'

'You were a couple?'

David nodded. 'Yeah. Well, she wanted a relationship. But I was fine with us being friends. I didn't want to make things messy if we had a bad break-up, since she lived with my sister.'

'So you rebuffed Nell's advances?' James had to bite his cheeks to stop his disbelief showing on his face. Looking at the man now, with his early-onset middle-aged spread, not to mention the ego Nell had referred to, James seriously doubted Val's theory of Nell being fixated with David.

'Yeah.' David shrugged. 'I guess to a student, a businessman like me looks like a good bet.'

James kept his eyes on his notes.

'And I was wary of Nell. She could have a bit of a jealous streak. You know, I'd get it in the ear if I flirted with a waitress. She could be a bit ... volatile.'

James recalled Nell's interview. *Definitely provoked. And vindictive enough to go for the jugular by instructing Charles to go after me and Val with that official complaint ... But she had been cornered. And their insistence of her infatuation with this guy had been the least of it ...*

'Did Nell have any reason to be jealous of Sophie?'

'No idea. She might have heard we were a couple. She might have chased the work on the manor specifically if so ...' He paused, staring at James, open-mouthed. 'You don't think ...?'

Sunday 29th August – 8 p.m.

Nell's spirits were buoyed by the promise of Adam's company as she uncorked a bottle of wine so it could breathe. The ping on her phone alerted her to an email from Sylvia.

> Darling,
>   As promised, here's the link about those retreats at the B&B:
>   Bryniau Tawel Farmhouse.
>   I'm leaving shortly and looking forward to the peace and quiet. I've left some hints for Troy to find me, so if he's looking, who knows, I may have a riotous time after all!
>   Much love, Sylvia x

Nell followed the link. The picturesque farmhouse she remembered appeared with its name plate above the front door: BRYNIAU TAWEL, BRECON BEACONS.

> Disconnect from your devices and reconnect with nature. With no mobile signal or Wi-Fi, Bryniau Tawel offers a temptation-free digital detox experience, liberating you from the stresses of modern life. Immerse yourself in tranquil Welsh countryside. Nourish yourself with zero-miles fruit, vegetables, eggs and honey from our organic smallholding. Nurture yourself at one of our wellbeing retreats. And leave here refreshed, re-invigorated, and welcome to return.

Nell opened the 'Retreats' link and read the offerings for yoga, art, writing, meditation, photography. An escape into the peace of the Welsh mountains, where no one could find her. *Exactly what I need.*

The email linked to Sylvia's Twitter feed, and Nell read her latest tweets. Above her photos from the Pendlebury Regional Planning Conference sat a screenshot of Bryniau Tawel farmhouse, from its website, captioned, *Blissful week of peace! Just me and the chickens here until Friday!*

Nell smiled to herself. *Very subtle, Sylvia.* If Troy was trying to track her down, just a search of the conference should do it.

And she should do her own research, too. With a surge of determination, Nell opened her laptop. She searched for David Dixon, then David Stephenson. A long list of various people loaded. Nell narrowed the search by local area. She clicked through the Facebook and LinkedIn offerings, finding David Stephenson, CEO of DMS Development, LLC, but his picture – him standing at a conference rather than a portrait – was minuscule and impossible to recognise him from. So she tried Louise's social media, to see if there was any link to him through that.

The buzz of her intercom interrupted the investigation. Adam was on the screen, waving from the car. She let him in and opened the front door.

'Oh, wow, something smells amazing,' Nell said as Adam set the large bag of food on the kitchen counter.

'Thanks.' Adam looked delighted.

'Yeah, not you. The food.' Nell laughed and thumped him on the arm. 'Oh God, I'm so glad to see you …' She choked as her throat closed up. She turned to hide it and took some plates from the cupboard in a welcome clatter.

Adam grinned and looked at his feet. 'Yeah?'

'It's been horrible. It's so good to see a friend instead of some heartless police officer.' Nell's voice tremored as the ordeal of the past day, not least the stab in the back from James, caught up with her.

'Oh?' Adam's grin faded into concern. 'Do you want to talk about it?'

'Let's eat, I'll fill you in.' Nell reached for her wallet.

'No, it's on me this time,' Adam said. He unpacked the food as Nell passed the plates and dished up a little of everything for them both.

He paused by the table with his plate, cutlery and wine but Nell nudged him towards the sofa. They curled up at opposite ends of the low Chesterfield, half-facing each other. As they ate, Nell recounted a select edition of the events around her arrest, omitting Charles, Conor and her additional appellations.

'Jesus, Nell!' Adam looked more and more worried as her story unfolded. 'What – so the client for Manor House Farm is someone you *dated*?' At Nell's grimace, he corrected himself, 'Sorry, OK, *an acquaintance*. And it was *his wife* who was murdered in the tunnel?'

Nell shivered. 'That's about it, yeah.'

Adam stared at her. He tried to change the subject. 'OK, you look like you've had enough of talking about it for the moment. So how's … Oh. Oh no.' He put his plate on the coffee table. 'We forgot about Zorro.'

Nell groaned. 'God. Talking about all this, I forgot …' She eyed their half-eaten food and barely touched wine. 'Look, let's go. By the time we get there, it'll be dark enough to release him. Then we can come back and reheat the curry.'

As Adam drove past the Manor House Farm's driveway, attracting the watchful gaze of the police guard, Nell shuddered. Around the corner, Adam pulled up in the lay-by. 'You really can't stay away from this place, can you?'

'Oh, don't.' She grappled with Zorro inside his travelling box and cuddled him in her gloved hands. 'I'll warm him up in here, though. Then we can just step outside to release him.'

Lights beamed around the bend and a Land Rover Discovery started to turn into the lay-by, braking sharply as the driver saw them and swerved. Manoeuvring, the driver pulled up alongside them. It was James.

'Oh God,' Nell muttered.

'What?' Adam asked.

'Police. One of the detectives. DS James Clark.'

'Was he the one who …?' Adam slammed his wrists together, miming being handcuffed.

Nell nodded, as James lowered his window, gesturing to Adam to do the same. Adam pretended not to notice, instead turning to Nell. 'Looks like he wants to speak to you. Do you want to?'

Sighing, Nell nodded and Adam pressed a button to open the window.

'Dr Ward. And ... Dr Kashyap, I presume? What brings you out here?' He didn't actually say 'to a crime scene', but he gestured at the tape, and Nell knew she'd have to justify herself.

But her tone was frosty. 'You wouldn't believe me if I told you, detective sergeant.'

It was the first time in a long time that someone she interacted with – outside of family and Percy – *knew* about her sex tape. James would never mention it. But the fact that someone knew, in a social situation, in front of *Adam*, made heat flash over her body like a rash. Beside her, Adam's body was nearly as tense as hers.

'Try me,' James said.

Nell sighed again and held up her hands. Zorro's delicate ears poked out through her white-gloved fingers. 'The bats, of course. I'm here for the bats.'

He gave her a hint of a smile. 'If only your bats could give you an alibi, eh? Would've made life simpler for both of us.'

'And if only you'd believe them if they could. You haven't exactly been convinced so far by anything I've said, have you?'

'Go on, then. Educate me.'

He had some nerve, sounding so bloody intrigued and ... *warm*, after the brutal interrogation he'd put her through. Yet relief coursed through her. Flustered, she dropped her gaze to Zorro, who squirmed in her hands, his face peeping out between her fingers, his eyes bright as he chattered.

'Looks ready to go,' Adam said as Zorro pushed against her hand. Looking up, she caught James's fascinated gaze.

'Yes, he's ready,' she said, and Adam jumped out of the car to open her door.

'Mind if I tag along?' James sounded genuinely interested. She nodded. She couldn't exactly say no, could she?

As the three of them walked along the lane, she felt the need to fill the silence. 'This woodland leads up to the house. So Zorro can use this for foraging and as a familiar landscape to find his roost.'

As she opened her hand, Zorro lifted his head, unfurling long ears, tilting them as he chattered. 'See him echolocating? Getting his bearings?' His ears pricked up and he crept up the slope of Nell's hand.

'He knows he's in familiar territory,' Adam said as Zorro bobbed his head, intelligent eyes darting left and right, pink nose snuffling at the evening air.

'He looks so fragile,' James said.

On the precipice of Nell's hand, Zorro stretched out his wings, on the brink of reclaiming his freedom.

'Oh, magic.' Adam locked his gaze with Nell's.

Zorro fluttered his wings, testing them. Then he swooped into the air.

'Whoaaah!' James stepped back, amazed.

Zorro circled around Nell twice. She beamed. She regarded it as the bat's victory lap, a thanks for the care and safe release home. Adam smiled in delight as Zorro looped around him, then flew higher, lost in the darkness.

'He's gone.' James sounded bereft. 'So quick. Just melted into the night.'

'But he's well and healthy,' Nell said. 'And back where he belongs.'

'Well, nice to see what you bat-botherers get up to first-hand.'

'I'm just relieved he made it. It's unusual for this species to recover.' She glanced at James. 'Lucky he didn't starve while I was incarcerated, eh?' The joke sounded like a dig and she cringed.

James's expression darkened and his tone grew serious, almost pompous. '*My* priority happens to be solving this murder. Are there any more bats under your tender care at the moment?'

'No.' Nell bristled. He didn't deserve her efforts to be civil, after what he and Val had put her through.

'Good,' James said. 'So, if we need to speak to you again, at least I won't have a starving bat on my conscience.' He got into his Land Rover and drove away.

Adam walked to Nell's side. 'Jeez, that was a bit ... OTT. You OK?'

Their arms touched, and neither of them pulled away.

'I'm fine. I'm glad at least something good happened today.'

Adam nudged her shoulder. '*Two* good things. Zorro's liberty. And yours.' He fixed her with a knowing gaze as they got in the car. 'What are you going to do with yours, now?' His mouth twitched. 'My guess is research, for starters ...?'

Nell's heart sped up. He'd read her mind.

Turning over the ignition, the ancient Volvo faltered. Adam tried again. The engine spluttered, then started. Driving to Nell's, he said, 'I reckon that DS Clark only gave you a hard time because he likes you. I mean, it can't be easy to be unbiased with you as a prime suspect.'

She batted the compliment away before it could land; Adam was wrong. She'd been deluding herself that James was interested in her. Adam was just flirting. Like usual. 'James—'

'Oh, James, is it?'

'Well, yes, that's his name. He's not interested in me. He's just being professional. Horribly professional, actually.'

'Oh?' Adam frowned.

'Well, he snooped around my house himself, for any clues that would make me look guilty. And I presume it was him who ordered the forensic search.'

'Oh.' Adam sounded less ebullient, more unimpressed now.

'And he's raked over my background.' Her face flamed and she looked out of the window. 'So I don't get the impression I've had any special treatment.'

Adam didn't comment. He stared ahead, focused on the road.

Guilt prickled Nell. She'd set a serious complaint in motion. James had every right to be unforgiving. He probably managed some semblance of affability in case it squeezed more details out of her. She'd been right to keep her guard up. 'I guess he doesn't want me to think I'm off the hook. I'm still a suspect because I knew David. My motive's passionate jealousy. Apparently.'

'Uh-huh.' Adam's lips set in a line.

'Which is utter bollocks.'

Adam glanced at her. 'I get it. Easy for people to get the wrong idea. I had to have quite an awkward chat with Erin about … misunderstandings. Didn't want to lead her on.'

Oh. Tentative hope bubbled as they drew up to the gate. She tried to sound casual. 'The code's 1947.'

'Bloody hell.' Adam turned a stunned expression to her. 'That's like getting the keys to the castle.' He looked touched, like he was about to add something sentimental, but instead, he leaned out to tap the keypad.

'Still up for dinner?'

'Are you kidding? Cookingdean's finest biryani is in there!'

Nell unlocked the door. 'You didn't reply to my text about your tyres.'

'Yeah ...' Adam ploughed his hand through his hair. 'I know.' He gave a long sigh. 'You're bang on the money. The police said they looked like they'd been slashed when they checked them.'

Nell turned towards him. 'Bloody hell, Adam. And you didn't think to mention it?'

'And ...' Adam looked like he needed to get the entire confession out. 'They impounded it. For forensics.'

'What the ...?' Nell stopped in the hall to stare at him. 'And, again, you didn't say anything?'

'No, well, I hoped it wouldn't be related. Could've been some local idiots. I didn't want to worry you.'

'Oh, nice way to be patronising.' Nell stomped into the kitchen to heat their food up.

'Yes, all right, I'm sorry. I just thought you had enough on your plate with the police questions and everything.'

'Yeah, well, for the record, I'd prefer to know.' Nell bit her sentence off. She could hardly demand that. Her face prickled. Then she recalled her ruminations in the cell. 'I was worried someone had followed you to damage your car, so I'd be at the manor alone. Sounds like the police think the same.'

'Oh, that's a little dramatic, isn't it?' Adam said.

'No more dramatic than the police arresting me because I knew David.' Nell took their food into the living room, where Adam topped up their wine and passed a glass to her. She sat down on the sofa, curling her feet under her and sipped her drink, deep in thought.

In the silence, they ate and drank, until Nell sat back, shaking her head. 'It's horrible wondering if someone you knew could have ... done that.'

Adam nodded.

'But I haven't seen him since I was a student,' Nell said. 'He may have changed a lot.' She shrugged. 'I mean, for one thing, it's incredible he's got a business going. I wouldn't have imagined he had the wherewithal to do it. But this is a large development. He must have got himself a good track record with other smaller projects ...'

Nell jumped up and retrieved her laptop from the kitchen. She refilled their wine glasses and settled back on the sofa, resuming her earlier search while Adam typed on his phone.

'I'm looking up his company via Anna Maddison's LinkedIn profile.' He stared at his screen, his face etched with concentration.

'I didn't expect you to help.' Nell didn't mean the words to slip out. She pressed her lips together.

Adam dragged his eyes from the screen. 'What?' He frowned. 'Of *course* I'm going to help. You may be Cookingdean's Most Wanted, but I'm your partner in crime. I'll help you clear your name. Or – you know – find the real murderer.' He gave a short laugh. 'You're going to do it anyway, so you need someone to keep you out of trouble. Didn't think I'd just leave you to it, did you?'

A smile spread across Nell's face. But Adam was already back to research.

'Nothing comes up about his company working on anything else,' he said. 'No schemes in the news, no project cases on the company website.'

Nell leaned forward, frowning. 'This huge development is his starter project?' She shook her head. 'How would he have enough money to get going? He'd need well over a million, plus a generous contingency. I remember what his idea of wealth was at uni. This scale of expense would be out of his league, surely.'

She thought for a moment, then said, 'I'll try Companies House. See what it says about the company and any investors.' She typed, then shook her head. 'Not much here, either. Looks like the company was only set up six months ago. No investors.'

Nell looked at Adam, her mind racing. 'Oh God. Of *course*. Sophie was the homeowner! If she owned an estate like Manor House Farm ...' She wanted to kick herself. *How have I not thought of this before?* 'What if his wife was the money ... What if ... What if ...'

Adam's eyes widened. 'He killed her to get his hands on it?'

Chapter 24

Nell opened the second bottle of wine and sloshed some into their glasses. 'So, we have one hypothesis. David killed his wife, Sophie, for her money and/or her property?'

'Or … thanks' – Adam took the offered glass – 'hypothesis two – she had an affair—'

'What, because divorce is so much harder than murder?' Nell countered.

'Not always straightforward, is it? People have secrets.' He sipped his wine.

Guilt stabbed Nell. She started to speak, but Adam continued.

'One of my mother's friend's nieces had an affair. A scandal amongst that particular group. She was in an arranged marriage; compatible on paper, at least, but no spark. Her husband had an affair, too, just more discreetly. Both families put pressure on them to stay together. Everyone thought they had the right to bail in with opinions and advice.' He shuddered. 'Horrible.'

Nell was stunned at the idea of arranged marriage. 'Is that an expectation for you?'

Adam laughed, settling into the sofa cushions. 'Nah, though Mum would tell you different. She likes to make suggestions. I go on my fair share of dates to keep her happy. I try to be charming, make the date a fun evening for whoever I'm meeting. But finding the person you have that spark with – well, it's a special, elusive thing, isn't it? I'm not sure my mum can pin down the person I have chemistry with! It's up to me to find them.'

The look he shot her – smouldery with a gleam of wicked – turned her insides molten. His arm stretched along the back of the sofa. 'I'm just saying, sometimes separating or divorce isn't easy. And it needn't be David playing away. What if Sophie was having an affair and David thought she was going to leave him?' Adam tilted his glass towards Nell. 'And sure, divorce is easier than murder. But it only leaves you with half the assets. At best. And Sophie may have had a prenup to limit what he could get even further. So, yes, there's hypothesis two.'

He glanced over to Nell's desk strewn with ongoing scientific experiments. 'So, if we'd usually gather data to test out a hypothesis, what can we dig up to investigate these two?'

'I don't see how we can find out any more than we already have about his finances, to be honest, so hypothesis one is a dead end. Could research Sophie? Anything online?'

They tapped their searches as if racing one another, Adam on his phone, Nell on her laptop.

The photo of Sophie flashed into Nell's mind. Sophie was twenty-six, surely she'd have an Instagram account, if nothing else? But searches – Sophie Crows, Sophie Crows Manor House Farm, Sophie Crows Royal Holloway University – all came up with nothing. Nell stared at her empty screen. Sophie had gone to as much trouble as she had to minimise her online presence. *Was Sophie just very private? Or had David been isolating her?*

An affair was a distinct possibility. He'd not wasted any time in making a move on Sophie Crows at the graduation ball, had he? David had seemed all about appearances, and struck her as the type to use people and move on.

What if Sophie had served her purpose? Nell sipped her wine as the idea evolved.

'I think you're onto something, Adam. I reckon David was having an affair. Sophie brought him the assets he needed for his business venture, and he was already moving on.'

'Yes … Yes, that could make sense.'

Nell leaped up and rummaged around her desk, knocking things, clumsy from the wine. With alcohol-induced triumph, she held up an object swirled with camo paint. 'And I can test our hypothesis with a bit of lightweight inductive eth-ethology: observe David in his natural habitat, see if his behaviour indicates or proves he's having an affair.' She put the camera on the table and flomped on the sofa. 'I can't exactly covertly track him, but I can set up a wildlife camera outside his front door. See if it captures anything.'

Adam stared at her. 'You're not serious. That's crazy. He'd recognise you—'

'Not if I was careful,' Nell protested.

'We.' Adam's correction was firm. 'If you're this determined to do something stupid, I'm doing it with you.'

Bank Holiday Monday 30th August – 8 a.m.

The purr woke Adam up. A head nudge on his arm stirred him to open his eyes, squinting in the light filtering through the curtains. The dry, stale taste of last night's wine lingered, pins-and-needles prickled in his arm, and Nell's hair tickled his nose.

She'd fallen asleep, almost mid-sentence, her head coming to rest on his shoulder, as they'd plotted how to find David. Watching her mis-typing on her laptop, he'd held his phone up, inched nearer, delighted when she'd curled up, and moved closer – but she'd had to, to see the screen.

Sleep had beaten seduction – but Nell had been exhausted and tipsy, and neither made it the right time to make a move. He'd just tucked the Aran-knit throw around her and resigned himself to losing the circulation in his arm. Even so, he never wanted to move. Her face, unguarded in sleep, was relaxed, softer. Beautiful.

A head nudge from Jezebel made Nell murmur. She squirmed into a languid stretch, then froze, eyes flying open. She stared at him and bit her lip. *Oh no. Was that regret?* Her hair was ruffled, sticking out around her ears. She looked like a cat who needed to be stroked.

'Morning.' Automatically he stretched, his arm tingling as blood returned.

She eyed him self-consciously, ignoring Jezebel's charm offensive: patting her arm with a paw, squinting her eyes lovingly and adding an adorable chirrup to her purrs. 'Oh my God, I'm so sorry. Have I made you stay like that all night?'

He shrugged, aiming for a hint of swagger. 'No point having pecs and biceps to die for if beautiful women can't fall asleep on them.'

'*Wo*men, huh?' Nell prodded his shoulder in deadpan assessment. 'If they're squishy enough to be pillows, you might want to up your gym game.'

He feigned offence with a shocked face and threw a cushion at her.

She dodged it with an impish smile and stood up. 'I better feed this one. Coffee?'

'Oh God, yes, please.' He got up, checking his phone. A stream of silent texts had loaded, all from his mother. Then he saw the time. 'Oh no. I'm running late for lunch with my folks.' He smoothed his rumpled T-shirt as he wandered to the utility room, where Nell was setting down Jezebel's food. 'Could I possibly grab a quick shower?'

Nell led Adam upstairs, running a quick mental inventory of her bathroom. She didn't *think* any laundry was lying around. Passing the cupboard, she grabbed a couple of her most luxurious towels and handed them to him. Opening the bathroom door, she was relieved to see it was immaculate.

Adam lingered in the doorway. 'Would you describe yourself as a *serious* ecologist?'

Her eyes narrowed. What was he getting at?

'You know, one who *seriously* wants to save the planet?'

She grinned, guessing his gambit and gestured at the huge limestone shower enclosure. 'There's not room in there for both of us *and* your biceps. And, anyway, you're supposed to be in a hurry.'

'Hey, I don't know what you're suggesting! I'm just proposing that we conserve water!'

Laughing, Nell shoved him into the bathroom and shut the door. She dashed to the kitchen to brew some coffee and nuke some croissants in the microwave. Digging a selection of jams from the cupboard, she set them on the table, along with plates and cutlery. As she poured the coffees, her phone buzzed. Percy was FaceTiming. Nell hastily stabbed the 'cancel call' button – but missed.

'Morning, gorgeous. How are things?' Percy asked.

'Can I call you back? I can't talk now,' Nell hissed into the phone, glancing upstairs.

'Why? What's going on?' At least Percy whispered as she leaned towards the screen. 'Hang on – two coffee cups? At half-eight in the morning?' At her squeal of delight, Nell hit the 'end call' button, puffing a relieved sigh as Adam's footsteps creaked on the stairs.

She put the croissants on a plate but she couldn't eat one. She couldn't shake off the lingering anxiety about the investigation – and now, her stomach fluttered with butterflies, delighted, excited at the definite shift between her and Adam. He joined her, holding eye contact as he took his coffee and they both sipped their drinks. Their gazes were magnetic, locked on one another. His lips twitched until finally *that smile* spread across his face. Nell couldn't suppress her beam. A buzz from Adam's phone broke the moment.

'That'll be Mum again. I better go.' He didn't move, didn't look away. 'Can I see you later?'

She shrugged, but her smile betrayed her. 'If I'm free.'

'Here's a tip. Don't get yourself arrested.'

Nell feigned a shocked face.

'OK, *especially* if you get arrested. I'll be your one phone call.' He drained his coffee and winked. 'I'd get you out of clink. We're partners in crime, remember?'

'If you're going on the run, you better steal a croissant.'

He took one with a grin and ran to his car. Reluctantly, she closed the door and opened the living-room curtains to watch Adam drive through the gate. He disappeared from sight and her attention turned to the plates, glasses, bottles and empty takeaway containers from last night.

As she put the wine bottles into the recycling bin, her guilt resurfaced. Adam had resolved to throw himself into danger with her, and she still hadn't told him about her background. It wasn't fair for someone to get involved without knowing exactly what they were taking on.

How the hell was she going to tell him?

Monday 30th August – 9 a.m.

James listened to Val's update, but his gaze strayed to Trent, glowering beside her.

Val summarised what most of the team already knew about Nell's arrest, Andrew Arden's closeness to Sophie and the lines of enquiry on Anna, Simon and David. The whole team knew she was going through the points for Trent's benefit; there was an itchiness about the officers, wanting to put precious Bank Holiday hours to better use.

James took up his part of the summary, trying to keep it brief as his colleagues shuffled papers, stretched and yawned. 'I've had emails back from Nell Ward's boss and a local bat expert who advised Nell about hibernating bats in the local area.' Holding up the printed pages, James said, 'If anyone wants to know everything about bats – where they hibernate, how important temperature and conditions are, roosts' legal protection – then feel free to read. But, in a nutshell, covering the gates back up was completely necessary.'

Trent pursed his lips. 'Does this mean you're striking Lady Eleanor off your list of suspects?'

James forced himself to look at Trent, and not at Val, who – despite rolling her eyes at his use of Nell's title rather than the name she'd requested – recognised the question as a tactical grenade.

'We still have questions around Dr Ward's activities,' James hedged. 'The badger pellets, for one …' He referred to the summary Val had just given. 'But, for now, we're focusing on other suspects.'

Trent glared at James, then said a grudging, 'Good.'

At Val's slight nod of discreet approval, James held back a gratified smile. Across the room, Ashley's eyes crinkled.

Changing topic, with a sly wink at James, Ed Baker spoke. 'I've been checking in with our call operators. After all the media interest and appeals for information, they're swamped. No doubt a load of saddos looking to fill a long weekend with drama. We've had' – he checked his notepad – 'twenty-one confessions. Someone check my maths, but I make that at least twenty hoaxes. Over a hundred witnesses believe they saw something important and fifty or so psychics have offered us spiritual insights. Yet they'll all need statements being taken—'

Trent cut off his complaint. 'Yes, yes. I've brought in more resources, so this won't add to your workload unless any of the officers find anything pertinent. The call operators will also screen calls more rigorously from now on, and they'll weed out the time-wasters. So no excuses of extra work distracting you from your enquiries.'

He looked at Val. 'I'll leave you to it. I'm away today but,' he said, his lips tightening, '*do* remember I'm at the other end of the phone if needed.' He swept out, letting the door slam.

A collective sigh of relief rippled round the team.

Val nodded. 'OK, last few points before we get going again. James?'

James walked to the map on the board, pointing. 'We know it's a long shot, but if Anna was able to get the Nye Hall CCTV footage faked, she could have easily got from Nye Hall to Manor House Farm, especially if she's a bit lively in her Porsche. We need to keep a track of where she's gone now. I'll follow up Andrew Arden's alibi today. I've asked tech to see if they can retrieve any messages which might have been deleted from Sophie's phone. They'll try to get back to me tomorrow. And I'll also try to meet Simon Mayhew. Get his first-hand account of his argument with David Stephenson.'

Ashley caught Val's eye. 'I had a bit of one-on-one time with David when I went to officially notify him of Marjorie Crows' death yesterday afternoon. I asked him how, in five years, he had not got around to meeting Sophie's only surviving relative? With his own family estranged or living abroad, I asked if this would've made him and Sophie closer to her grandmother.'

'And?'

'A load of excuses. Supporting his mother through his parents' messy divorce for a while. Then, Marjorie Crows' eyesight deteriorated, so she moved into Applewood … and Sophie didn't think that was the best time to introduce them. She wanted her grandmother to adapt. Then he and Sophie decided to elope, with David intending to join Sophie in her next visit to her grandmother so they could tell her about the wedding together. But, by then, David was working on the manor, absorbed with going to meetings, dealing with deadlines, talking to planners, getting quotes from contractors.'

Val arched an eyebrow. 'Did you ask how the plan changed from a modest renovation to a village masterplan?'

'Yes, he said the plan gradually became more and more ambitious. And when they realised the potential for a larger development, it was, in his words, a bit of a coup. But then, I caught him in a lie.'

The attention of the team snapped to her, the crackle of anticipation tangible.

James glanced around. 'Well, go on!'

'I finally got hold of David's solicitor. He confirmed that he didn't want Sophie's petition for divorce to just fall through David's letterbox without warning. He phoned – and he didn't leave a message, he actually spoke to David.'

'And what was David's reaction to the news?' James asked.

'Shell-shocked. Disbelief. Convinced there had been some kind of misunderstanding that he could put right.'

'When was this?' Val asked.

'Tuesday 24th August. But, yesterday, when I asked David outright if he knew about Sophie's plans to divorce, he denied it. Proper shocked face, stuttering, the works. Told me I'd got my facts wrong and shouldn't say things like that, I should show more respect.'

'Great.' Val brightened. 'So that's hit a nerve. We can use that.'

Hesha chewed her lip. 'Given how angry he got with Simon over adding costs to his scheme, how angry would he get once he knew Sophie planned to divorce him *and* sabotage his development?'

Chapter 25

Monday 30th August – 12 p.m.

Nell paced in her front room, wondering how to handle the conversational grenade. *'Oh, Adam, by the way, I'm an heiress of a huge estate. More wine?'* The background anxiety bubbled. If he knew about that, there was always the risk that something might come up to unearth the tape, despite the injunction. She felt sick.

But she was pretty sure she could trust Adam. He cared about her, and he wouldn't have gone into a crime scene for just anyone.

Nell chewed over their finds from that day, focusing on something she could make progress on. All she could glean from it was the route the murderer had taken and how they'd hidden their car. What if the police didn't know? How could she share it with them? Could she blame Zorro? Say she noticed it when she released him and had James and the guard to vouch for the fact there'd been no breach of the scene?

Hmm. In the dark, from the outside, where the damage wasn't visible. They weren't going to fall for that.

But an idea wormed in her brain. *I didn't find any signs of the killer in the woods. But what if the killer had taken signs of the wood into the house?*

Grabbing her phone, she scrolled through the pictures she'd taken during the bat inspection of the property for the close-up photos of the window frames. There were hundreds: all the weathering and damage offered numerous access points for roosting bats.

Opening each one in turn, she zoomed in, scanned the entire picture, drinking in as much detail of the room as she could. In some, her own reflection obscured the view. In others, the low, glinting evening light made seeing through the window impossible. It hadn't mattered at the time, she hadn't taken the pictures for the view inside the house.

The last picture was of the kitchen window frame. She dragged the enlarged picture, millimetre by millimetre, across her screen. The shoulder of her jacket was reflected back. It seemed to have a tiny red dot by the collar. She peered at the screen. Her jacket wasn't marked. The red dot was beside the doormat, in front of a door which, from its size, Nell guessed was a utility or boot room. Where, according to her Edwardian map, the tunnel connected to the house.

She stared at the dot. There was no doubt. It was one of the pellets she'd put in the bait for the badgers, before she'd found the tunnel, and about three hours before she'd taken this photo of the kitchen.

A chill settled around her. The killer had walked through the wood, picked up that pellet, then walked into the house, into the tunnel, finding Sophie, and …

At her desk, Nell drafted the email to Charles, then read it back, double-checking the timestamps of the relevant photos.

Photo 45 (timestamped 15.32) was taken immediately after I laid the bait mix containing distinctive red pellets, about 2mm in diameter.

After laying the bait, I moved on to survey the rest of the woodland and the tunnel, after which I went to the house to conduct the inspection.

Photo 288 (timestamped 18.44) of the kitchen window frame shows an example of the weathered wood, shrunk from the casing, creating a gap that bats could roost in. On looking through these photos again, I've seen that in the corner of the kitchen, beside the doormat, is a single red dot, which may well be a pellet from the bait mix …

She scanned the rest of the email and clicked send. Before she could even make a cup of tea, Charles phoned.

'Nell—'

'Hi, Charles. Have you read my email?' Nell asked. She dashed back to her computer.

He sighed. 'Yes, I have. And I'll need you to fill me in, please.'

'I reviewed my photos, and I found something which may be useful,' Nell said. 'Is the email clear enough?'

'Oh, perfectly.' Charles's voice had a slight edge to it. 'Did you return to the scene, Nell? Have you been poking about?'

'No comment.'

Charles groaned. 'I have to know, Nell. Even if it's not what I want to hear.'

'Yes, I went back,' Nell confessed. 'I walked along the lane to see if I noticed anything different. I found some torn traveller's joy. Which was significant …'

Charles listened to Nell's account and her theory about David's guilt. When she'd finished, he said, 'So you're hoping to direct the police to the idea that the murderer walked through the wood, having driven into it for a short distance. And that the killer was wearing boots with a deep enough tread for a sticky pellet to get stuck in it as they walked, and only dislodged by the doormat once they were inside the kitchen?'

'That's about it,' Nell said. 'And it's possible that more than one pellet stuck. They could check other places David may have been. His car, work, home—'

'Nell, it's not your business to go accusing others.'

'Sure, well – they don't have to limit it to David. It applies to any of their suspects.'

'The thing is, Nell, you're telling the police that you laid these pellets. And then you went to the house. The only print they have associated with the scene is your own boot print. They searched your house not yet forty-eight hours ago. Might they have found any other pellets?'

Nell glanced at the shelf which usually contained her tubs of pellets. They were missing. Her stomach dropped as she anticipated what Charles would say.

Charles spelled it out anyway. 'Might they, in fact, perceive this very helpful communication from you – which you've made only hours after your own arrest – not as help at all, but as a deflection from the potentially incriminating evidence you've just realised they'd have found during the search of your house?'

Nell swallowed. 'That's why I want to draw their attention to the photos. They already have them on a USB. They only have to look. And if the red dot in the photo is a pellet, it will give them a timeline of the murderer's movements. That's all I want to say.'

'I'll pass on the information,' Charles promised. 'But this isn't a game, Nell. Breaching a crime scene is an offence. You probably also realise that anything you find there and bring to the detectives' attention could well be rejected from the case because it risks compromising their due practice. You're still a person of interest. That's the lens the police will view you through for every piece of information you give them. If they have any cause to think you've planted information, they could also charge you with unlawful trespass and perverting the course of justice. You're *not* a helpful civilian, Nell. You're a *suspect*.'

Monday 30th August – 3 p.m.

'I can't believe you rushed back to join me,' Nell agonised. 'I did say in my text I'd go on my own.' She and Adam were parked opposite the Georgian building matching David's office address.

He laughed. 'Are you kidding? I'm not missing a stake-out.' His binoculars, like Nell's, were trained on the windows. 'All those buttock-numbing hours of sitting in hides, while the rare species you're seeking fails to appear – who knew it was just ideal training for this?'

Nell didn't know what to say. She wasn't used to having someone other than Percy to share things with. A warmth curled around her heart as she kept watch through her lenses, aware of every tiny shift and movement in Adam's body beside her.

Eventually, she spoke. 'I didn't mean to interrupt your family day. I just felt safer with you knowing where I was. Sharing my location. Just in case.' Nell's neck tingled with a flush of heat at the confession. She didn't like being vulnerable, she liked admitting it even less. But she was. And it was time to be truthful. She took a deep breath and turned to face him, searching for a way to casually mention her background.

'Well, I'd eaten,' Adam interrupted her without realising, looking through the lenses. 'Mum and Dad wanted me to give Aanya a pep talk. But she doesn't need one. More like Mum and Dad need to chill.' He sighed. 'Poor kid. She needs to move out, find a house share or go into halls … Hang on.' He sat up. 'Did you say he had a gold BMW? I think it's parked behind the building. I can just make out a wing.'

Nell raised her binoculars to view the rear of the property, focused the powerful lens. 'You're right! That's it!'

'Well, he's here, working, even though it's a Bank Holiday—'

'Or covering his tracks while Anna's out of the office,' Nell said.

'Let's see how much of a working day he'll put in,' Adam mused, glancing at his watch. 'It's half-three now.' He cranked his car seat back, stretched his legs and opened a packet of crisps to share.

He reached to turn the radio on, then stopped himself. 'Ah, I can't put any music on. As I found out on my dawn survey on Thursday, her battery's low. She keeps running down. I had to use a jump-start pack to get her going.'

'Oh, now you tell me.' Nell patted the Volvo's worn dash.

She hesitated. This might be the best chance she'd get to start the difficult explanation. 'Adam, I—'

'Is this him? Coming out of the office? Look.'

'Yes!' they both cried as he walked around the building, the BMW coming into view before driving away.

Adam's fingers curled around the key in the ignition, but Nell put her hand out to stop him. 'Wait, let him go past us first.'

David drove by. Then Adam turned the key. Nothing happened.

'Not now,' Nell groaned. 'Come on.'

Adam tried again, then a third time, and the engine spluttered into life.

Nell had been holding her breath. She exhaled in relief and laughed at the drama. 'Quick – follow that car!'

David headed towards the high street, parked and walked into the Chinese takeaway. There were no other parking spaces, so Adam pulled in at the bus stop, leaving the engine running, hoping no buses were scheduled for the next few minutes. As Nell looked around, the board outside the newsagents caught her attention.

SECOND MURDER IN CROWS CASE.

'Adam.' She pointed. 'Another murder?'

'Jesus.' He looked at Nell. 'OK, I think we should back off. This is dangerous, Nell.'

'Yeah, that's exactly why I *can't* back off. Second murders are always to cover tracks, aren't they? If that's what's happening then – you said it yourself – I'm on that list.'

'Which makes it bloody stupid to go running right into his crosshairs.'

'Which means I *have* to. I've got to get something on him – to show the police – before I run out of time.' Her thoughts flashed to Charles and his warning. But this wasn't a crime scene. They set up wildlife cameras all over the place to record birds and animals. It would simply be good fortune if they happened to catch anything else of note.

Adam raked his hair. 'I don't like this.'

'You don't have to. Just … look, there he is – drive!'

Adam didn't move. 'I'll only drive if you agree that I'll set the camera up. You stay in the car, out of sight. He won't recognise me if he sees me.'

'Fine. Just *go*!'

Adam followed southwards, keeping a few cars behind, then paused down the street, keeping David in view as he entered the Georgian house's ground-floor flat. Despite the brightness of the late-summer afternoon, he switched the light on and drew curtains across the large sash window.

'Have to be super quiet,' Nell said. 'The sash windows might not be double-glazed.'

'Yep. But good he's got the garden flat,' Adam said. 'Nice open lawn giving a good view of his front door and windows and a laurel hedgerow will be perfect to hide the camera in.' He appraised the area. 'It'll be easy to record anyone coming and going – in case your affair theory turns out to be right.'

'OK, he might be eating now. Let's go.' Nell braced herself.

Adam grabbed his backpack and checked Nell's camo-painted wildlife camera. He set the recording to be motion-triggered, adjusted the lighting setting, rested it inside the top of his bag, and nodded.

They both got out of the car.

'What are you doing?' Adam hissed at Nell as he pulled the bag onto his shoulder.

'Keeping watch.'

Adam sighed but had to move fast to keep up with her. Nell peered up and down the empty street, crept to the window and peeped through a gap in the curtains.

David was right in front of her! She jumped and adrenaline surged through her body. David sat down on the sofa, his back to her, thankfully.

Adam had dropped his bag as he searched the hedge for a branch strong enough to attach the camera to. Nell reached over to his backpack, grabbing the endoscope they used to search for bats inside cavities in buildings and trees. She sat with her back to the wall of the house so she could keep an eye on the street, and stretched the long camera cable straight up, bending the camera at a right angle, like a periscope. She stared at the camera's screen on the handle.

It gave her a clear view of David, shovelling noodles with a fork while he hunched over his laptop. Nell could see the screen showing what looked like emails, then documents, as he clicked the mousepad.

Nell glanced over at Adam, who lashed the camera to a sturdy branch, covering the door and path; hidden, yet not obscured by the shrubs in the borders.

She returned her focus to what David was doing. She'd let the cable drift and had to re-adjust. Now she saw that David had set his half-eaten dinner aside, and was leaning forward holding his head in his hands.

Nell held her breath. When David sat back, she instinctively shrank against the wall, but kept her eyes fixed on him, her heart thumping.

David pulled his laptop towards him. She could see the Google homepage as he typed, then a list of search results. He clicked. The website of the Pendlebury Regional Planning Conference appeared. He clicked on the list of delegates and studied the page intently. Nell could only read the title of the page. David sat forward and clicked a link.

Nell's eyes widened as the familiar 'News' page of EcoLogical's website appeared. David clicked in the area of the page listing Sylvia's social-media links.

Something suddenly made David collapse against the back of the sofa, dragging both hands through his hair. He clasped his hands behind his head and sat, motionless. *What had got him so riled?*

A touch on her shoulder made Nell jump. She nearly shrieked.

'God, sorry,' Adam whispered. 'I'm done. We can go.' He tugged at her.

'No … no we can't.' Nell's eyes were fixed on David, through the screen. 'Look. Something … something's happening …'

David was leaning forwards again, studying something on his laptop. He clicked the keyboard.

Nell frowned as Sylvia's Twitter feed appeared on David's laptop. He scrolled, halting at a picture that Nell recognised: the photo of Sylvia and Troy. Peering closer, David punched the arm of the sofa and leaped up, looking furious and swearing audibly. He stormed across the lounge, then paced back. Nell pulled the rigid cable down, and stared at Adam. After a few seconds, she risked sliding the camera up again.

David had returned to the laptop to continue scrolling through Sylvia's feed. He paused again at the picture of Bryniau Tawel farmhouse, then zoomed in to the name plate above the door and rubbed his head, before switching his screen to the Google homepage. He mistyped – bashing the keyboard – and Nell watched as the farmhouse website loaded to its homepage and some text she couldn't read. David highlighted some of it and then loaded Google Maps. A few seconds later, a blue route snaked across his screen. Pendlebury to the Brecon Beacons.

'What the …?' Nell murmured, as David rose and started pacing the room. 'He's talking to himself,' she whispered. Her body tensed as David slammed his laptop shut, then snatched it up.

'Oh God,' breathed Nell. 'Oh God, oh God, oh God …' She coiled up the cable and shoved it in the bag, her hands shaking.

'What is it?' Adam whispered.

'Sylvia. He's going after Sylvia …'

Chapter 26

Nell grabbed the bag and shoved Adam. '*Move.*'

They crouch-ran to the side of the house, flung themselves on their bellies and slid under the low branches to squeeze deep into the cover of foliage, glad of their practised hedge-crawling. Nell dragged the bag in, out of sight.

A second later, David burst out of the house, banging the door behind him. He was clutching a sports bag and looked ferocious, his face and neck flushed red. She held her breath, certain he could hear her. *Why* was he going after Sylvia?

David leaped into his car, started the engine and fixed his satnav to the windscreen. He punched in an address and roared off.

'Come on!' Nell scrabbled out of the hedge, ignoring the leaves and twigs clinging to her hair. She sprinted to the car, ripping her phone from her pocket. At the car, she searched for the number of Pendlebury Police Station and phoned, gesturing for Adam to unlock and start the car.

'Hi. I'm Nell Ward and I have some urgent information in connection to the Sophie Crows murder inquiry,' she said, breathlessly, as she slid into the passenger seat.

Beside her Adam was trying to start the car and failing, and she gestured frantically at him to keep trying.

'I have reason to believe that Sophie's husband David Stephenson murdered her, and I think he's now going to murder a friend of mine. Sylvia Shawcross.'

The car didn't start. Nell's gesture to Adam was frantic. He tried again … Again … Again.

'I … I think Sophie Crows was murdered by her husband, David, and I think he's going to murder my friend. She's … She's alone in a farmhouse in Wales.'

Adam popped the bonnet, raced to the boot and grabbed the

jump-start pack, then propped up the bonnet and disappeared behind it.

'No, I don't know why he … but you've got to trust me. She's in real danger.' She paused to listen. 'Yes, Sylvia's staying at a B&B called Bryniau Tawel in the Brecon Beacons …' Nell rattled off as much of the address as she could remember, then, 'No, David's *not* off on a mini-break, I promise you! Please, Sylvia's in trouble, can you send someone there?'

She ended the call, with no firm assurances that any police would be despatched to the farmhouse. She sagged against the seat.

Adam had got the engine to start and leaped into the driver's seat.

Nell tried Sylvia's number. Voicemail. 'Sylvia, it's Nell. This is going to sound crazy but I'm certain you're in danger. Please, as soon as you get this, leave the farmhouse and get to another hotel, or a friend. I'm serious. *Please.*'

She sent a hasty text and then an email. Then she remembered. Fear churned. 'Oh God. There's no mobile signal or Wi-Fi at the farmhouse.'

'Landline?'

It had been three years since the work trip to Bryniau Tawel, but Nell recalled the phone in the office – and Sylvia had mentioned a landline. She searched for the number, knowing it was unlikely Sylvia would answer.

'So are the police sending anyone?' Adam asked beside her.

'I don't think so. They said they'd "pass it on to the investigating team".'

Charles's voice echoed in her head and her heart sank. Even if some of the team were in, they wouldn't take any notice of information from her.

Inspiration struck – James had given her his card! She checked her pockets, then remembered she wore her leathers to give her statement. Had she put it in her jacket pocket? Or her bag? Or put it on her desk once she'd got home? She couldn't recall. *Great* … But then, she wasn't convinced James would believe her anyway … Depressing the sluggish accelerator, Adam drove off. 'If the police aren't going there, someone needs to.'

Relief flooded through Nell. 'OK, but not in this thing. It's too unreliable. It's a four-hour journey. We'll have to stop for petrol and we might not get going again. My place is forty minutes away but not much of a detour. Let's pick up my car.'

'Er, I think this is slightly faster than your little Smart car,' Adam rebutted.

'I'm not kidding. Just go to mine.' Nell brooked no disagreement as she finally found the landline number for the farmhouse. Adam muttered under his breath, but turned towards her house.

Nell groaned at the landline's recorded message. 'Thanks for calling Bryniau Tawel Farmhouse Bed and Breakfast. We're closed from August 30th until September 3rd. Please leave a message and we'll respond on our return.'

If Sylvia's parents checked their messages – assuming they didn't think it was a horrible hoax – might they contact a neighbour? Someone who could go over and persuade Sylvia to stay with them? Nell steadied her panicky breathing and tried to leave a clear, but urgent, message.

She kept the farmhouse webpage open, showing the address, and opened another page to search for the number of the farmhouse's local police station. She called. Another automated message announced the station was closed. On the advice of what to do in an emergency, Nell dialled 999.

When she was connected, Nell repeated the information she'd given Pendlebury Station. Her heart sank at the operator's response, and she ended the call.

'There's been a major incident in the local area. They'll send someone over as soon as they're free.' Nell shrugged, frustrated. 'Who knows when that will be?' She sank against the headrest.

'I hope this detour to your place will be worth it,' Adam said, clearly pained. They continued on, in tense silence.

After agonising minutes, Nell sent a text to Conor, then checked her phone as soon as it beeped. Opening another webpage on her phone, she studied it.

At Cookingdean, Adam stamped on the brakes for an elderly couple at the zebra crossing near The Mill. The car stalled, throwing Nell forward, her phone flying into the footwell.

'Sorry.' Adam turned the ignition. Nothing.

Nell leaped out of the car, grabbed the jump-start pack from the boot and opened the bonnet that Adam had popped. Behind her, the couple shuffled across the road.

'The pack's low,' Nell called.

'I've used it a few times. And I haven't charged it up recently.'

Nell tried, just in case. Nothing. 'It's dead.'

'Bloody bollocks!' Adam thumped the steering wheel. As Nell slammed the bonnet, he checked his phone. 'Twenty minutes for an Uber. That's what you get for living in the sticks.'

Nell fished her phone from the footwell. 'Let's push the car to the side of the road. My place is a mile that way. We can run it in eight minutes.'

Locking the car, Adam grabbed his backpack and followed Nell, already running, over the stile and along the narrow, chalk path. 'You realise,' Adam panted as they passed the church, 'your detour's costing us an hour. I know you're fast, but I don't see your Smart car cutting it.'

'I know.' Nell puffed, sprinting full pelt. Adam kept up with irritating ease. Conor was right. She needed practice. Reaching the field behind her house, she gave a final burst of speed into her lane. Gasping for breath, she punched in her gate's number, then the code for the garage.

Adam joined her as the triple garage door opened.

'Holy …!' He gaped at Nell. 'Who the hell *are* you?'

Oh yes, now's the time for that conversation … 'Professional carjacker.' Nell wished her dry delivery sounded cooler, but it was marred a bit by her wheezing.

She rummaged for a key, clicked a button, and the gullwing doors floated skywards. The sleek, matt-black Mercedes AMG SLS Black Series radiated menace.

Adam got in, squashing his bag into the footwell, following Nell's lead in reaching up for the handle to pull the door closed. When Nell started the engine, its resonant growl thundered around them. As he put on his seatbelt, Adam squinted past Nell's Smart car. 'Christ, is that a *superbike*?'

Ignoring the question, Nell handed him her phone and opened the car's hidden navigation system. 'You put the address in, I'll head to the motorway.'

Adam lurched backwards as Nell brushed the accelerator and they flew out of the garage. He managed to tap in the address as she sliced through lazy holiday traffic.

'If you open the app on my phone,' Nell said, 'it'll show you where the speed cameras are. Google Maps says it's four hours from David's to Sylvia's without speeding. I think that's how long it'll take David because I doubt he'll risk being pulled over. If we're an hour behind him, we'll need to average more than seventy miles per hour over the whole journey to reach Sylvia when David does. So, I'll have to hit about 120 on the motorway.'

She glanced at Adam, who was staring at her in disbelief.

'It's fine,' Nell joked. 'She's up to it – just warn me where the speed cameras are.'

She floored the accelerator and they hit the motorway at warp speed.

It was some time before either of them spoke. Adam seemed too shell-shocked, and Nell concentrated on the road, looking far ahead, anticipating drivers' actions. The traffic, for the moment at least, was light. Cars melted away before her as she dominated the fast lane.

'This never happens in the Volvo.' Adam eyed an Audi R8 deferring to the middle lane.

Nell smiled but kept focused.

Adam checked the phone. 'Speed camera, five miles ahead.'

Nell checked traffic and braked efficiently to reduce her speed in time, then stood on the gas. Adam craned his neck to watch the speedometer climb back up to 121.

'Did I ever tell you I get car sick?' he asked.

'No. Unlucky for you,' Nell deadpanned back. 'Just don't get it on my upholstery.'

'Ah – so this is yours! Not a carjacker after all,' Adam teased.

Nell didn't respond, concentrating as she accelerated past the next cluster of cars.

Adam checked the route. 'We're on here for another thirty minutes. Then an hour to Sylvia's on Welsh roads.'

'Thanks. We'll stop for petrol once we're in Wales. Can you find a station? On a roundabout or something, so we don't ruin our speed advantage.'

Adam tapped the nav screen. 'Yeah, in sixty miles. Got enough fuel to get there?'

'Just about.' She frowned. 'When we stop, would you queue to pay while I fill up? There's cash in the wallet in the glove compartment.'

Adam nodded and found the wallet.

Nell focused ahead. 'Oh God, look!'

Adam looked into the far distance. The low evening sun glinted off a gold BMW.

'Yes!' He fist-pumped. 'Oh, you marvel.'

'We still have to catch him. And he may have refuelled already . . .' Nell gritted her teeth and threaded through a throng of traffic. She veered out as someone cut in front of her, fighting to keep control at high speed, then swerved, undertook them in a wide arc and sped towards David's car.

She'd gained ground, but David didn't move from the fast lane. She checked behind her and undertook, crossing two lanes to give him a wide berth. Her heart pounded. What if he recognised them and swerved to cause an accident? She nearly laughed out loud at the absurd idea, but watched him like a hawk in case he made a stupid move as she passed him.

Her nerves melted and Adam exhaled heavily as they accelerated away from David and he became a speck in the rear-view mirror.

They hit the main roads into Wales as darkness fell. Adam pointed out the petrol station and Nell pulled in. Adam leaped out and ran to the shop as Nell filled the tank, willing on the rolling litres. She saw Adam grab some items, then charm his way to the front of the queue. She stretched her aching arms, rolled tense shoulders, stamped life into cramping legs. Cold sweat slithered down her back.

Adam ran back with a bag of food and drink. They sped off, rejoining the dual carriageway. Adam looked ahead and behind for David. There was no sign of him. 'No idea if we're in front of him or not now.' His worried tone echoed her concern.

'We'll just keep going.'

'I've got some supplies. You must be flagging a bit.' Adam offered a cereal bar. Nell nodded. He opened it and broke off bite-size sections to feed to her as she drove.

Nell sped down the carriageway but the winding mountain roads and minor routes were slower. It was agony. A traffic light stop was only welcome for the chance to gulp some water.

At last, they arrived at the narrow track to the farmhouse. The gullwing jarred over the cattle grids, ripping a tremoring, '*Bol-locks*', from Nell. She winced in mechanical sympathy, then floored the gas to roar up the hill.

Finally, they glimpsed the whitewashed stone of the farmhouse.

Nell spotted Sylvia's sporty Mazda in the corner as they turned into the drive.

Her relief turned to horror as her headlights panned across the driveway. 'Oh, Jesus. He's here.'

Chapter 27

Monday 30th August – 9 p.m.

Adam fumbled for the door release as Nell slammed on the brakes outside the farmhouse. He sprang out and raced to the front door. The porch light was on, and the light from the hall spilled out through the open doorway.

As he neared the door, Adam heard muffled panting. He could make out David kneeling with his back to him, a few paces inside the hallway. *Oh God* – Sylvia was lying on the floor, just past David. A superhuman burst of speed propelled Adam on.

David turned, scrabbled to his feet and lunged at the door to slam it before Adam could get in. Adam accelerated, shoulder braced, and rammed the door. It flew inwards, sending David staggering back. He tripped and fell on his back but held something out in front of him. With horror, Adam saw it was a knife.

Adam's momentum carried him in. Without stopping, he extended his running stride and kicked David's wrist, hard, thankful for his steel-toe-capped site boots. A sickening snap was followed by a sharp high wail from David as the knife flew across the hallway. David's wrist was bent backwards at an awkward angle, broken. He shrank into a foetal position as Adam loomed over him, then kicked him hard in the side, aiming for his kidneys.

Screaming, David rolled away, shielding his head with his arms, tucking his legs up to protect his groin. Seizing the advantage, Adam shoved David onto his face, grabbed his unbroken hand and yanked it high behind David's back and sat astride him, pinning his legs down.

Nell was behind him. 'Get my site bag!' Adam yelled.

Nell ran back to the car and retrieved Adam's bag.

'Rope,' Adam gasped.

Nell rummaged in the bag for the coiled cord they used for tree work, and handed it to Adam, then elbowed past him to get to Sylvia.

Adam crushed David to the floor as he shook the end of the rope free with one hand. David tried to move, trapped under Adam's weight. He moaned in desperation.

Holding one end of the rope in his mouth, Adam bound the other end around David's wrists with the expert precision of a climber. He tied two secure reef knots, strung the rope across over David's back and looped it around his ankles, crabbing his limbs together, stringing him up like a joint of meat. He yanked the rope to take out the slack, jerking David's arms and legs higher behind his back. David howled and raged on the floor, tugging at the bindings. Adam checked the knots would stay, tied another for good measure and guarded the furious captive.

Nell crouched, distraught, beside Sylvia, the floor flooded crimson with blood. She tore off her hoodie and wadded it against Sylvia's stomach, kneeling in her blood.

Adam turned as a low rumble of a motorbike was close, closer, then silenced with a squeal of brakes. He turned to Nell. She was focused on Sylvia, checking her airway, breathing and circulation.

'Nell,' he whispered in alarm.

A shadowy figure moved with silent purpose through the doorway. Both hands were held out in front of him, clasped around a handgun.

'Jesus. *Nell!*' Adam hissed, willing her to notice.

The gunman's movements were controlled, precise. He moved the gun with each turn of his head, checking right, left, above, down. As he came through the door, he pointed the gun at Adam. Without averting his gaze, he spoke in a commanding tone with an Irish lilt.

'Nell, fill me in.'

Nell had her cheek to Sylvia's mouth, looking along her chest. 'Adam has tied David up, he's the murderer. I need your help here, Conor.'

'What the …?' Adam stared at Nell, then took a step back as Conor approached.

Conor kept his gun on David as he leaned over and checked Adam's knots. A casual tug elicited a pained shriek from David.

'Nice work, keep an eye on him,' Conor said. He holstered his gun inside his jacket and stepped across to Sylvia, while Adam tried to not look flustered. *What the hell?*

Nell peeled back the blood-soaked hoodie to show Conor. 'Three stab wounds. Airway clear, breathing, weak pulse.'

Conor unzipped his leather jacket, revealing a stab vest, and ripped a first-aid kit from one of the pockets as he hunkered down, throwing it to Nell.

'Get my ID and gloves out.'

He repeated Nell's checks with military efficiency, then pulled on the gloves and examined the wounds.

'These two look superficial, but this one's deep. I think the knife twisted on entry.'

Adam craned his neck to see. The wound pooled with dark red blood at a rapid rate.

'OK, listen carefully,' Conor said to Nell. 'Call an ambulance. Give my name and ID number. Then,' he held his breath as he slid his finger deep into the wound and winced as he applied pressure, 'say the inferior vena cava has been lacerated and the patient is critical.'

With his other hand, he used Nell's hoodie to pad the blood and apply pressure to the wounded area, keeping his inserted finger still.

'Bleed-out time isn't long. Not as bad as an artery, but if I can't keep it shut, she's got minutes. Say there's room to land an air ambulance here. That's her only chance.'

Nell sprinted to the office's landline phone. When she returned, she grabbed two blankets from chairs next to Adam, who looked bewildered.

'Who is he?' Adam mouthed, gesturing at Conor.

'Conor's our chauffeur,' she whispered.

'*What?*' Adam stared as Nell hurried to Sylvia and arranged the blankets around her, tucking in her feet and wrapping one around her shoulders with gentle tenderness, careful not to nudge Conor.

'We need to keep you warm,' Nell murmured. 'Is that better?'

Sylvia's eyes fluttered. She mumbled.

Nell nodded at Conor. 'They're sending a chopper. And the police.'

Sylvia tried to speak. It took effort. 'I … I thought he was Troy,' she wheezed. 'He looks just like him. But he's not … He's not …'

Under Adam's weight, David shifted, twisting towards Sylvia. Adam hauled on the ropes until they bit into his wrists, and tied them tighter.

Nell cradled Sylvia's head, stroked hair back from her clammy, ghost-white face. Adam read fear in Nell's wide eyes and furrowed forehead but she wore a warm smile, murmuring words of comfort. 'How's that? Better? You're doing good. Medics will be here soon.'

The minutes drew out. Conor kept his finger firm and still. He continually checked Sylvia's vitals and talked to her to keep her conscious. Adam admired his stoic control. He must need to flex his fingers, or move, to relieve the pressure or cramp, yet his body was still as a rock. Only the sweat beading on his forehead indicated his exertion.

'It's hard to tell but it doesn't look like any internal organs have been injured,' Conor whispered. 'If that's the case, she's lucky.'

Conor raised his voice to speak to Sylvia. 'You've got the luck of the Irish, so you do. You'll be all right now. And help'll be here any second.'

They kept their tense vigil until the silence was broken with the whomphing of helicopter blades whirling low overhead. A searchlight flooded the driveway, field and doorway with brilliant white light.

'Ambulance is here, Sylvia,' Nell whispered. 'You're doing so well. Just hang on in there a bit longer. It's going to be all right.'

The helicopter hovered, then sank onto the lawn. The downdraught slammed the open door against the wall and ruffled the furnishings inside the house. As soon as it touched down, a team of three spilled out and ran in to attend to Sylvia.

One of the medics exchanged rapid medical terms with Conor and unwrapped a surgical clamp. With perfect timing, Conor withdrew his finger and the medic clamped Sylvia's vein. Another medic checked her vitals, while the third set out the stretcher. They hoisted Sylvia gently onto it, then carried her at a steady run back across the grass to the helicopter.

The remaining medic gestured at David.

'Perpetrator.' Conor gave the brusque answer to the unspoken question. 'Police are coming.'

The medic told them Sylvia would be at the local hospital but only immediate family would be admitted, then ran to join his colleagues.

The helicopter lifted off and Nell turned her face away from the powerful downdraught through the open doorway, making her T-shirt flutter. The bright light lurched around the landscape as the helicopter hovered and turned.

David squirmed and Adam pressed down harder until he groaned. Now Sylvia had gone, he could see how much of her blood had flooded the hall. *What if Sylvia didn't make it? What if they'd been one second later?* He felt a sharp satisfaction at David's whimper.

Glancing at Nell, Adam saw her shoulders tremble, one hand clamped over her mouth. *What was this sudden revelation all about? Who was this man, somewhere between a butler and a member of the SAS? And why, exactly, did Nell have him on speed dial?*

Chapter 28

As soon as the helicopter was out of sight, over the mountains, Nell turned to Adam, aching to hug him. And to finally tell him everything.

But Conor blocked her. He removed his bloody gloves and slipped his gun and holster into the nearest drawer, ahead of the police officers' arrival, then seized Nell by the arm and marched her into the kitchen.

Concern made his words direct, his accent more pronounced. 'You realise when the police turn up here, it's yours and Adam's word against that eejit's, don't you? And they could well arrest you again?'

Nell's stomach dropped. 'Oh, God, I hadn't thought of that,' she said. 'I did call Pendlebury Police. I told them Sylvia was in danger, that David Stephenson was heading here to kill her …' She trailed off, realising that might be exactly what a murderer might say, to divert suspicion. *Would James think that?*

Conor sighed. 'Right. Well, when the police get here, let me speak to them. My former rank, current role and ID will carry some weight, and it might simplify how they process the scene. Otherwise, you'll be looking for a roof tonight.'

Nell nodded. As an afterthought, she added, 'If you introduce me, would you do it informally, please?'

'I'll leave you to introduce yourself as you will. It's not for me to decide.'

'Police are here,' Adam called from the hallway.

Conor strode through to the hall and outside.

With a sudden burst of energy, David thrashed, trying to kick out at Adam. But Adam yanked the rope, crabbing David's limbs high up behind his back. He wailed, but lay still, furious, and impotent.

Nell turned the hall light on, flinching from the illuminated gore spread across the hall flagstones. She'd have talk to Adam later. As much as she wanted to explain about her identity, she wasn't going to do that in front of David, who'd just tried to murder her friend. She squashed the crowding emotions, and waited by the doorway as Conor greeted the two officers by their car. He showed them his ID and shook each officer's hand. Nell observed him talking to them both. The officers were listening and nodding. Nell took note of Conor's manner: unemotional and clear with the facts. She'd try to respond in the same way.

As they walked towards the house, Nell heard Conor describing Sylvia's condition and the hospital she was at. The first officer continued walking and talking, the second paused to make notes.

At the front door, Conor said, 'The assailant is in here. We've subdued him.'

The officers surveyed the scene, noting the blood on the floor and the footprints scurried through it by the ambulance crew.

They introduced themselves to Nell. Sergeant Quinn was tall, solid, dark haired and bearded. Constable Felix, lean with keen eyes, took notes while Quinn spoke.

'Dr Nell Ward,' she said, and gestured at Adam. 'This is Dr Adam Kashyap.'

Constable Felix took their details and carried on making notes, then photographed sections of the hallway. He noticed the knife and snapped on gloves to bag and label it, taking it out to the police car. When he returned, he held two plastic-wrapped parcels and gestured at Nell's blood-soaked jeans.

'I'll need to bag your clothes.' He turned to Adam. 'And yours, too. I'll need them now, so you can change into these suits.'

Nell took a suit first, and popped into the downstairs loo. The jeans clung wetly to her legs, and her knees and thighs were stained with Sylvia's blood. Blood on her jeans had been unpleasant. But Sylvia's blood on her skin somehow made the incident *real*. A ripple of horror made her body tremble. David was on the other side of this door. The same David she'd gone to her graduation ball with, who had just tried to kill her friend. And had killed Sophie. *Jesus*. She sat on the lid of the loo, forcing herself to breathe slowly. When her legs stopped shaking, she opened the door a crack, and passed the jeans, then her T-shirt, to Felix, and closed the door while she scrubbed her legs and climbed into the rustling plastic protective suit.

Outside, Adam had changed already and Constable Felix had labelled Nell's bags, along with Adam's now-bagged rope.

He bent over David. 'I see your wrist is broken. Have you got any other injuries?'

David shook his head.

'We can call an ambulance and wait, or we can take you to the hospital ourselves.'

'Take me to the hospital,' David muttered, studying the floor.

Constable Felix snapped a handcuff on David's unbroken hand and the other cuff on his own wrist and helped David to his feet and out to the car.

Sergeant Quinn went through the formalities with Nell and Adam. 'Usually, we would need you to vacate a crime scene and usually, we would take you in for questioning now. Major Kennedy's intervention means we can bypass those formalities.' Sergeant Quinn nodded at Conor, who stood like he was on parade, staring straight ahead. 'In this case, you can stay here, get a good night's sleep and we'll take your statements in the morning.'

Nell and Adam nodded.

'For now, please summarise what happened.' Quinn prepared his notepad.

Nell took a deep breath. 'I've been assisting Pendlebury Police Station with the murder inquiry of Sophie Crows ...' She paused, deciding full disclosure hadn't done her any favours lately. She gave a brief account of what she understood of Sophie's murder and recounted the evening. 'I saw David Stephenson looking through Sylvia's social media on his computer, and then looking up a route to get this farmhouse ...' She paused as Sergeant Quinn narrowed his eyes.

'You saw him?' said Sergeant Quinn.

'Yes, through the window of his flat,' she said. She knew how that must sound, but she carried on. 'I had a bad feeling that something was going to happen. So I called Pendlebury Station, the local police and 999. I wasn't convinced anyone would come.' She glanced at Adam. 'So we decided to come ourselves.'

Sergeant Quinn scribbled notes.

'By the time we got here, David had already stabbed Sylvia three times and she was bleeding heavily. Adam disarmed David, and tied him up, and then …' Nell looked at Conor. 'Conor … Major Kennedy arrived in time to apply some much-needed medical attention and, I hope, save Sylvia's life.'

Sergeant Quinn nodded, while Conor didn't avert his gaze from the far wall.

'We'll need to get SOCO out here to take records,' Quinn said. 'We'll photograph and tape up this hallway and David's car …' His enquiring look invited Nell to clarify.

'His is the BMW,' she said.

'Good. We'll do it now so these areas can't be disturbed while you stay here. To be honest, if you were going to tamper with the scene, you could have done it by now. No point in evicting you at night when you're far from home. And we respect Major Kennedy's assurances.'

Nell shot a grateful look at Conor. 'Sure, we'll use the kitchen door and leave this area alone.'

'An officer will join SOCO tomorrow morning,' Sergeant Quinn said. 'They'll take statements from you and Dr Kashyap. Major Kennedy, would you turn in a report via the proper channels? We won't need to see you in the morning if you can.'

Conor nodded. 'Yes.'

Sergeant Quinn took photos from every angle before closing and locking the front door and taping off the hall. 'Righto, thank you, all,' he called, as he left through the kitchen door, Conor going after him.

Nell and Adam hung back, watching as Sergeant Quinn put the bagged knife in the car boot, taped the BMW and, after concluding his discussion with Conor, got in the car and left.

Nell noticed Conor's bike – a black Triumph Speed Triple – on its stand, the helmet on the saddle.

Conor came back into the house. 'Are you all right?' he asked her.

'Yes.' Nell nodded, trying to ignore Adam's questioning look. 'I can't thank you enough for answering my text and coming out. I can't believe how quickly you got here.'

'Well …' A knowing smile flashed across Conor's face. 'I probably broke as many speed limits as you did.'

'We were just in time.' She sobered. 'You and Adam saved Sylvia's life.'

'Let's hope,' Conor said, and she saw how tired he looked. He'd want to get home soon.

'I'll make some tea, before you get going,' she said. 'And something to eat if I can find anything.' She put the kettle on and then found some bread, butter and a jar of Marmite. She knew Sylvia's parents wouldn't mind, under the circumstances. While Adam quietly sipped his tea, Conor downed his and devoured three slices of toast.

Nell knew Adam would want to stay and see Sylvia at hospital as soon as visitors would be allowed. Maybe tomorrow? In the meantime, they'd look after the smallholding until her parents returned.

Conor used the bathroom and then leaned over the police tape in the hallway to open the drawer and retrieve his gun and holster. He shrugged the holster on and wiped down the drawer before turning to Adam to shake his hand. 'You did good. That took guts,' he said. 'You seem a good lad, and if you're all right by Nell, then you're all right by me.'

His tone was light, but Adam's eyes narrowed. Conor just nodded before letting go of his hand and waving goodbye to Nell.

Indignation flared inside Adam as he watched Conor's bike rumble into the distance. He heard Nell washing up the crockery in the kitchen, but he couldn't join her. How could he make a pretence of having a conversation with her when it turned out he basically knew nothing about her?

Nausea mixing with the acid remains of adrenaline made his stomach burn. Restless, he paced into the drawing room. Relieved to see French windows, he unlocked them and headed out into the dark night.

Proper darkness, no light pollution from anywhere and only a faint moon, wrapped around him. *Nice to choose it, rather than be kept in the dark by someone keeping secrets.*

Running footsteps behind him invaded his silent peace. 'Adam? Are you OK?'

Obviously not.

'Adam?'

'No. No, Nell, I'm not OK.'

'Do you … do you want to talk?'

'No. I've come out here to be alone. So …'

'Oh. Sorry.'

He heard her take a hesitant step backwards.

He wished she was sorry. He knew that if he asked, if he just began the conversation, she'd explain. *But that wasn't the point, was it?* He pushed his hand through his hair. Hearing her walk away made his heart tighten.

After an agonising few seconds, he caught up with her. 'What was all this about tonight? Who the hell *are* you, Nell?'

As the light from the house hazed around her, she practically staggered back, as if he'd punched her in the heart. 'I'm sorry. Look, I know I've got a lot to explain. Can we sit down and talk?'

He'd known she had access to money. Her home and the way it was furnished – things that were clearly hers – oozed expense. But he imagined it would be explained by losing a relative and inheriting something. Or a lottery win. A house, he could understand, that would be a sensible investment. But supercars in the garage, and all this with Conor. It was other-level stuff.

He nodded and followed her into the drawing room, where she sat in the armchair, pulling her feet up under her. Adam sat down opposite her, a faded rug on the floor between them.

Nell took a deep breath, 'OK. Conor *is* officially my mum's chauffeur, but he is also her close protection officer. She's an MP working on a police reform bill, which attracts a lot of unwanted attention. She's had a lot of death threats, basically.'

Adam's head whirled. He hadn't expected that. But he didn't know what he *did* expect. He tried to listen and take in the alien words.

'My father insisted on her having protection. He's, um, the Earl of—'

'Hang on, your dad's an earl. So you're …?'

'A lady.' Nell winced. 'Sounds ridiculously outdated, doesn't it?'

Adam stared at her. He felt knocked sideways.

'But I should have told you Conor might turn up. I texted him, asking if he could help in case the situation here was dangerous. I didn't know if he'd make it. And it didn't occur to me he'd be armed, let alone point a gun at you, which is unbelievably naïve of me. I'm sorry. That must have been … well, traumatic.'

Adam couldn't begin to put into words how unimpressed he was at that. He clamped his mouth shut and stayed silent.

'Who else knows?' he asked eventually.

'About my background?' Nell shook her head. 'No one. Well, no one at work. Schoolfriends knew, but most of them were in the same boat. I've kept it private since I went to university.'

'Why?'

Nell's face flushed. 'A lot of reasons. But for work, the main reason is because I wanted to carve out a career that I'd earned. Not had handed to me on a plate because of my connections. I wanted to be able to take pride in my own achievements. And, also, to know any friendships I have are because people really like me for me –' she pressed a hand against her reddening cheek '– rather than what people think they can get out of me.'

Staring at the floor, Nell lowered her voice. 'When people know, they treat me differently. And I hate it. I'm sorry you think it means I've been dishonest about who I am. In all the ways that matter, I *have* been honest with you.' She looked at him. 'We … we …' She hesitated. 'How I feel about you is *real*, Adam.'

Adam stared at his hands, clasped in his lap. He wanted to believe her. But he couldn't. He'd known she was very private. He'd never have guessed she could lie so comprehensively. About everything. All the time. She wasn't who he thought she was – and it wasn't about her title, it was about her *character*.

'I'm honestly really sorry, Adam.'

He couldn't look at her. If she turned her wounded, wide-eyed expression on him he'd just want to gather her up, kiss the uncertainty away.

Eventually he shrugged. This was maybe his only chance to ask questions to understand her life. He didn't know what to say. The most trite question fell out of his mouth. 'So that's how come you have the fancy car? Because you're, what, landed gentry?'

Nell hid a grimace. He must have said something wrong. He didn't know anything about that world. He sat back in the chair, separating himself from it. From her.

She nodded. 'I suppose so. Dad's into classic cars. One of the ways the estate supports itself is through events, like the motor racing.'

'What's your estate?'

'Finchmere.'

Christ, it's a massive place. Hundreds of acres. Something about a rewilding scheme there that I'd love to … Argh! No! He gave a shrug. 'I've heard of it.' He looked at her again. She was a stranger. 'What's your actual title?'

Nell grimaced. 'Lady Eleanor Ward-Beaumont. Bit of a mouthful.'

Adam shook his head. 'I didn't even know your name was Eleanor.' He looked away.

'What did you think Nell was short for?'

'I didn't think it was short for anything,' he said. *I just thought you were Nell.*

A silence stretched between them but Adam's head filled with white noise. He got up, agitated, and paced to the fireplace. 'I don't get it. Why are you working as an ecologist and living in a semi-detached barn conversion? I mean, it's a bloody nice place and you've got all the tech, but why aren't you – I don't know,' he waved a dismissive hand, 'swanning around your mansion and going to balls?'

Nell rolled her eyes. 'Bloody hell, Adam. Thanks for that.'

'What?' Adam turned to look at her, surprised at the offence in her tone.

'That's such a cliché. Running an estate is hard work. Finchmere's been in the family for generations and one day it will be my responsibility to make my mark so I can pass it on. And there's so much to learn about. Understanding the ecology is an important part of managing the land, and one which matters to me. But even that's only a small part.'

Nell chewed her lip. 'Look, when my father inherited it, he was thirty-five and the place was a mess. The house was in disrepair, the roof leaked, there was damp in every room, and the staff costs were huge. Half the house was uninhabitable. He had to make some tough economies and set up events not only to make a living but earn enough to restore his home.' She looked at Adam. 'Have you got any idea how much repairs on a stately home cost?'

'Oh yes. I have three. Bloody nightmare.' His sarcastic reply was delivered in a fake posh voice. He folded his arms and leaned against the mantelpiece.

'No, think about it. We advise clients about things like that and talk to conservationists all the time at work. Seriously. The bills are huge. Crazy huge. And OK, it's all relative, but it still requires some way of making vast amounts of money. So the estate is the business. I have to run various parts of it but also need to think about how I can continue to grow it so it supports itself in the future.

'Dad started with track days. When he met Mum, she helped him expand it into a major annual event. Within about ten years, Fortnum & Mason supplied the hampers and Montagues ran auctions of rare classics. Mum likes to joke that she gave a new lease of life to a crusty old banger. *And* his classic Alfa.'

Adam didn't know how to respond to an anecdote of a family so different to what he'd imagined. What *had* he imagined? He stayed silent for a moment. 'OK, so why are you working as an ecologist? Why aren't you learning to look after old buildings or manage your estate?'

'Oh, I am. I've learned a lot from working with the conservators who've done repairs. But my project, where I see the estate growing, is in ecological sustainability. I'm working on some habitat creation schemes, rewilding, retrofitting sustainable technologies into older buildings, new business initiatives. It's a challenge, but it's important.'

Adam said nothing. He stared at her. In her eyes, was he and their colleagues and all their work just a side project? And once she'd wrung out enough knowledge, had she planned to return to her secret life? No – her real life.

It felt like gravity had stopped working.

Nell faltered. 'I … I suppose I have a bit of a chip on my shoulder.' She clasped her hands, squeezing her fingers together. 'When I was sixteen, Dad wanted me to get more involved in the day-to-day running of the estate. So I'd understand all the work involved, what it took, all the different elements.'

She took a deep breath. 'He'd arranged for me to shadow the new estate manager for two weeks. I was beyond excited. I'd trailed around after his predecessor from the time I could walk. To me, as a child, he was this ancient, wise, grandfather-figure. He seemed to belong in the wood. He had endless patience to wait in hides for badgers, teach me tree ID, search for tracks.' Nell glanced at Adam. 'I was captivated.'

Her gaze dropped to her lap. Her hands twisted. 'So, I went to meet the new manager, feeling excited, thinking I could share some of the things about the estate and, above all, learn. But, when I got to the door, I heard him complaining to a colleague about having to babysit some entitled, ignorant aristo. I hoped the colleague might say I'd be OK to work with. But he just joined in the general grumble.' Nell swallowed. 'Quite the wake-up call.'

Adam folded his arms. Now he was supposed to feel sorry for her? Poor little rich girl. He risked looking at her. She was crimson, mortified. This confession was a big deal.

'Did they know you'd overheard?' Adam asked.

Nell shook her head. 'I didn't want to make things uncomfortable. And I wanted to see how the manager really worked. If he'd known I'd heard him—'

'He'd have worried you'd use your position to get him fired. Or if there was any cause to complain about something, he'd blame it on you being vindictive.' Adam nodded.

She edged forward. 'And you saw Erin's reaction to Sophie's newspaper article. Entitled toff doesn't need to work, has everything fall into their laps. I mean, I sympathise with the view, I've met plenty of work-shy, entitled idiots. But I'm not like that.'

'You are a bit,' Adam ventured.

Nell's jaw dropped. 'What?'

'You say you want to earn your own way, but you've got a fancy place with all the gadgets, even ones you don't use. Jesus, Nell, you've got a supercar sitting out there in the drive and a superbike in your garage. Don't pretend those are all earned. On our salary? Come on.'

Nell looked stung. 'My issue isn't being independent of my home. I can't be. I'll run it one day. And I spend any spare moment working on it now. My issue is that I want to know my achievements are my own, and not have to deal with sycophants or detractors. I just want mutual respect with my colleagues. And *real* friends. In every way that matters, I want to be weighed for who I *am*, what I *do*. Not what I'm called.'

Adam raked his hand through his hair. *How has she made me feel like I'm the one in the wrong?* 'OK, I can't fault your work ethic. You never cut a corner. You take on all the tough jobs.' He looked at her. 'Is that what it's about then? Proving yourself?'

Nell's eyebrows rose. Adam sensed her hope rising with them.

'And why you use "doctor"?' Adam asked. 'A title you've earned not inherited?'

Nell gave a short laugh. 'Well, yes. At least I'm proud of that one. And with the job, it makes me feel like I've earned my stripes. Then, when I'm working on the estate, I—'

'Won't be dismissed as some lazy, titled, good-for-noth—'

'Yeah, all right,' Nell interrupted. 'Don't rub it in.' She gave a tentative smile.

Oh, it was so easy to fall into the teasing, their good-natured repartee, it made his heart ache. 'Doesn't leave much time for balls, then,' Adam conceded.

'Well, a few. We host a couple a year. Usually, they're fundraisers for some cause or other. The next one's in November.' Nell frowned for a moment. 'Oh, God!'

'What?'

'It's Mum's fundraiser for prison reform. With the home secretary, the chief constable and police officers from across the country.' She rolled her eyes. 'How well do you think it's going to go down that her daughter got arrested for murder?'

Adam didn't smile. He couldn't make light of her being in danger, however he might feel about her now. He fixed her with a gaze brimming with sadness. 'I can't believe I didn't know this about you. I thought we were ...' He couldn't say what he thought they were to each other, but he choked on the substitute word, 'Friends.'

Nell's gaze met his for a short, sharp moment. She looked as wounded as he felt. But he hadn't kept a whole secret life from her while making her believe they were growing closer, that they *had* something.

'If tonight hadn't turned out like this, would you ever have told me?'

She hesitated.

Adam waited the single second it would have taken her to say the 'Yes' he wanted to hear, then shook his head, squared his shoulders, and walked away.

Chapter 29

The next morning, as soon as it was light, Nell uncurled her stiff limbs from the awkward position on the sofa.

She hadn't followed Adam upstairs to sleep in one of the guest rooms; he needed space and she wouldn't invade it after she'd made such a mess of everything.

Besides, she'd thought they'd been growing closer. The fizzy flirtations they'd had just yesterday – *God, was it really just yesterday?* – seemed a lifetime ago. She'd been a fool to have read anything into that. Even after she'd told him absolutely everything – OK, nearly everything – he'd made it clear that, to him, they were only friends.

What had he really thought about me falling asleep on his shoulder? God, what if I had joined him in the shower? Has he only been flirting and getting involved in the case because I haven't fallen into his arms yet? Huh. He probably isn't used to that. Maybe I'm just some kind of weird challenge. God, how humiliating … Something twisted in her heart, the usual feeling of her guard coming up again, like a hermit crab scurrying into a new protective shell.

She'd spent a cold night on the sofa, under an inadequate throw, dozing fitfully.

Around midnight, guilt of another kind jerked Nell awake. A flash of Jezebel sitting, forlorn and hungry, at her food bowl at home. With no other option, Nell got up, forced through lack of signal to use the landline, and called Finchmere's estate manager. While Nell didn't live too far from her family estate, it was an imposition – his job description didn't strictly include being on call for pet duty. He agreed to use the spare keys that Nell had given her parents – on the proviso that they were to use them only in emergencies – to let himself into her house and feed Jezebel until she got back. But his tone was

232

pointedly clipped – an uncomfortable reminder of how she fell back on her privilege when she chose to. She winced.

The rest of the night had been fractured with sobbing silent salty tears until her face was raw, between fitful dozes full of nightmares: racing along dark roads, while knives sliced through the roof of the car, a rising doom of losing someone she cared about, only to wake in an icy grip of fear for Sylvia.

So far, she'd resisted the urge to call the hospital; her logical brain knew Sylvia needed urgent and lengthy attention and some recovery time, if an update was going to be meaningful.

By morning, Nell was wrung-out. She crept upstairs and into a guest room to use the shower. The hot water revived her aching muscles and she started to feel almost human. Her eyes were sore, her face blotchy from crying. She slathered on the moisturiser she found, and the redness subsided a little.

She still had no idea how she would fix things with Adam, and the icy clamp around her heart made her question if she even wanted to: Adam believed she'd betrayed his trust. As a 'friend'.

But he was right. He had been a good friend to her A *great* friend. But any protest she made now of how she'd wanted to tell him – had *tried* to tell him – would sound insincere, as if truth was an afterthought to her.

Forced to rummage in Sylvia's mother's dresser for something to wear, Nell struggled to find anything that fitted her very different shape. She settled on some lilac elasticated velour joggers but passed on the matching top, opting for a voluminous white T-shirt instead.

She heard Adam downstairs and braced herself. Another argument? Awkward silence? How had it all come crashing down like this?

The enticing aroma of a full English breakfast tempted her to the kitchen, where Adam tended bacon, sausages and eggs sizzling in a pan. Beans bubbled on the hob and toast popped up from the toaster. Nell hovered in the doorway, observing him as he cooked.

Somehow, Adam had managed to make baggy brown cords and a checked shirt look casually cool; sleeves rolled up, broad forearms flexing as he buttered toast and checked pans. As she moved in beside him to brew some coffee, she felt his eyes appraising her outfit.

'You raided the wardrobe, too, then. Feels a bit weird helping myself to someone else's clothes. And food.'

'They won't mind. I'll call the hospital, see if …'

Adam nodded, but didn't drag his attention from the cooking.

Nell hurried to the office. She phoned the hospital for an update on Sylvia. She had to sit down when the nurse informed her that an emergency procedure had been performed and Sylvia was stable. Beyond relieved, Nell left a brief message at EcoLogical's office to explain they wouldn't be at work.

She hesitated, then picked up the receiver again and dialled Charles Barrington's number.

'What laws have you broken now?' It sounded like he'd been munching toast.

'Could we drop the police complaint, Charles? I don't think it's necessary to pursue anymore.'

'Uh huh. What's going on, Nell?'

God. How did Charles always know?

'We caught David trying to kill Sylvia last night. The police have arrested him.'

Hearing Charles stifle a groan, she explained.

'Well, your wish is supposedly my command. I'll call Trent now so he can let the team know the complaint is dropped straight away. But Nell …'

'Yes?'

'I'm adding danger money to my fee. You're determined to run headlong into trouble, contrary to my very sage advice. And you said "we". So you've convinced someone else to get involved, too. I hope they have equally stellar legal representation so they're not left in the lurch?'

Nell squashed down the guilt. *Chances are, Adam won't be getting into trouble again on my account. And dropping the complaint was one less battle to fight, at least.* Nell hurried back to Adam, who was dishing up the food, and filled him in on Sylvia.

Adam paused, a serving spoon hovering in the air. 'What emergency procedure? Did they say?'

Nell checked her note. 'An exploratory laparotomy with ligation of the infrarenal inferior vena cava.' She looked up at him. 'David damaged the main vein in her torso. They basically had to tie it shut. It's a major op. High mortality rate. She's *seriously* lucky.'

Adam exhaled, his body sagged as if tension had been holding him up. He nodded, chin trembling, unable to speak.

'She had a fifty-fifty chance, apparently. If you hadn't managed to stop David …' She looked away, biting her lip.

'Wasn't just me,' Adam said. 'You're the one who worked out he was going after her. You drove like a demon to get us here. Your friend Conor dealt with the injury.' He stared at his plate. 'Does stable mean she's not getting worse, or actually recovering?'

Nell swallowed hard. 'Recovering, I think. They said she's doing amazingly well considering. She lost a lot of blood so she's had a transfusion overnight.'

'Can we visit?'

'Well, I had to pretend to be her sister to get any information.' Nell shrugged. 'They said only family could visit. She's still very weak. But her folks are away. We could take some flowers in, or some magazines, and try our luck?'

As Adam considered, Nell looked at him. She'd never seen him look so haggard. Even when they'd worked thirty-nine hours straight on the Audley building site, surveying and excluding bats from the building by night, dismantling buildings by day, writing reports at any available moment in between. His eyes were red, lacking their wicked spark, and so shadowed it looked like he'd been punched in both sockets.

Adam nodded. 'Have your breakfast while it's hot.'

His tone was kind, if guarded. Nell picked up her cutlery and started to eat.

Adam looked thoughtful as he chewed. 'I think the police might help us see Sylvia. They might want to question her, and we could help, if they think she needs moral support?'

'Worth a try,' Nell agreed. They ate in silence. She mopped up the last of her breakfast with her toast. 'Thanks for cooking.' She stood and put her plate in the dishwasher with the pans. Adam followed suit.

There was an awkward shuffle as they each tried to put their mug in the dishwasher at the same time, then both hung back to let the other go first, then both clashed again. Desperate for a break from the tangible tension, Nell spotted the chicken feed and recalled why

Sylvia was there in the first place. Filling a bucket with the grain, Nell walked out into the fresh, bracing air, following the sound of squawks to the enclosure.

She unclipped the coop's gate, closed it behind her, then opened the chicken roosts, collected five eggs and strewed the feed. The chickens pecked at the ground around her feet, clucking. The view across the valley was as stunning as she remembered. Rolling verdant hills, dotted with sheep, grew into craggy mountains on one side, cloaked by woodland on the other.

Nell had a sudden, deep ache in her heart. Gorgeous views were meant to be shared. But the one person she wanted beside her didn't want to know her. True, she should have told Adam about her background before now, but he didn't understand. She had to be so sure of someone before she did that. She'd thought she and Adam had a connection, and she'd just begun to trust it. But it turned out she'd been wrong about that. *Yet again.* Adam's moral high ground needled. Didn't he realise that this way he'd got to know who she really was, rather than who people perceived her to be? Didn't *he* trust *her* enough? A desolate black hole cracked open again, leeching any spark of hope.

She slammed the coop closed, along with her emotions. *I was right. I'm better off alone.*

Tuesday 31st August – 10 a.m.

A few hours later, Nell watched the last officer drive away.

The police had taken their statements, and SOCO had processed the scene and taken photographs, measurements and blood samples. The crime scene manager had stared at the crime scene, smudged with the footprints of paramedics, and made unhappy mumbles about compromised evidence. And, despite Nell's best efforts, the detectives steadfastly ignored any leading questions about visiting Sylvia in the hospital.

The hive of activity in the hall, it turned out, had been a welcome distraction. Now they'd gone, the unsettled silence between Nell and Adam became unbearable.

Restless, Nell jumped up. 'Come on, let's try to see Sylvia, even if we're there all day.'

Adam nodded. He pointed towards the kitchen. 'I made some sandwiches while you fed the chickens. Save us from the awful fate of vending machines.'

Nell smiled. Adam didn't.

The drive to the hospital was awkward. Nell's luxe supercar – a manifestation of all her wealth and privilege – made her hot with embarrassment. Adam didn't speak. Instead, he stared out of the window, avoiding conversation with her.

At the hospital, Nell approached the nurse on duty with a forced smile.

'Hi, I'm hoping Sylvia Shawcross is able to see visitors?'

'Are you family?' the nurse asked.

'Sister.' Nell blurted it out before she chickened out of the lie. *Did they have lists of family members for patients?* Sylvia didn't have a sister, but a nurse had accepted it when she'd phoned earlier, so maybe ...? 'I rang this morning for an update.'

The nurse nodded towards Sylvia's ward. 'Only for a few minutes, please. She's stable but she's not strong and needs rest. She already had to speak to police officers this morning. It's taken it out of her.'

Nell nodded, then darted a look at Adam, who sat down on a chair outside the ward doors and started flicking through a motorbike magazine. 'I'll be quick.' Nell hurried away before the nurse changed her mind.

Sylvia was propped up in bed, hooked into a beeping, blinking monitor and drip. The blue hospital gown made her pale face even more ghostly. Without her usual vivacious spirit, Sylvia looked shrunken and fragile.

Her clothes from last night were folded in a plastic bag, her phone within reach on the table. Her body was trembling. To her horror, Nell saw Sylvia was crying. Huge, wracking sobs made her whole body shake.

'Hi Sylvia,' Nell whispered. She took her hand gently. 'It's Nell. The nurse said you're stable and recovering. I'm so glad. You've done amazingly. Proper warrior queen.' She gave a bright, encouraging smile. 'How are you feeling?'

Sylvia turned her wan face towards Nell's voice. Her smile tremored. 'I'm a bit sluhh-gishh,' she drawled with effort. 'Spaaceey. S'all a drugs. Shorrry.'

237

Sylvia's face then crumpled, her mouth making a silent 'o'.

'What is it?' Nell crouched down to be at eye level with Sylvia.

Pointing to her phone, Sylvia managed a hoarse whisper. 'Troy.' The convulsing sobs returned.

Nell frowned. 'What?'

Sylvia gestured at the phone. 'Read it.'

Nell held out the phone so Sylvia could put in the code. A webpage of local news appeared: MAN BURNED TO DEATH IN CAR. Below the headline, was a handsome face. Pale eyes, blond hair. Troy.

A thirty-six-year-old man who was found dead in a car park in Pendlebury has been named by police. The body of Paul Dunn was found after firefighters put out his burning car late on Thursday 26th August. Mr Dunn was a personal trainer at HeavyWeight Gym in Pendlebury and an escort with Debonair, where he worked under the pseudonym, Troy Ambrose.

A Pendlebury Police spokesman said: 'Provisional post-mortem results indicate he had a head injury before the effects of the fire took hold. This injury is not consistent with any damage to the car, and this death is being treated as suspicious. If anyone can help the police with their enquiries, please contact Pendlebury Police.'

Nell looked at Sylvia in alarm. She'd worn herself out sobbing and now dozed. A sudden commotion outside made Nell flinch as the curtain swept open.

DS James Clark stopped talking to the duty nurse and stared at her. Nell did a double-take at seeing him again. Her stomach lurched.

The nurse held open the curtain. 'Only one visitor at a time, so I'll have to ask you to leave while the detective speaks to your sister.'

Oh God.

James started at the revelation that only-child Nell was sister to an attempted murder victim. Nell reached for the curtain, hoping he wouldn't say anything. At least, not in front of the nurse.

'Nell?'

Ugh. She turned. 'Yes, James?'

'I'm *so* glad to see you. Thanks for your call and quick-thinking last night. Your actions haven't only furthered our murder investigation, they've saved Ms Shawcross's life.' He arched an ironic eyebrow, but didn't drop her in it. 'Would you mind staying while I talk to her?'

Relieved that she wasn't in trouble for once, and appreciating his tact, Nell nodded.

The nurse left, closed the curtain behind her, muttering unhappily.

'And thank you. For dropping the complaint.'

'I can afford to be magnanimous now you know I'm not guilty.'

James nodded. Then his eyes dropped to the mauve joggers, his lips twitched. 'Only of crimes against fashion.'

'How superficial of you.' In spite of her heavy heart, Nell raised a smile.

He took a step towards her. 'Look, I need to apologise. For *that* line of questioning.'

She deflected the flash of embarrassment. 'What – that completely irrelevant, waste of time and resources while a dangerous murderer was on the loose?' Nell folded her arms. 'Good. You should be sorry.'

James shook his head. 'Where questions arose, I had to ask them, Nell. But I *am* sorry, it must have been traumatic for you.' His frank sincerity and earnest expression made it seem like he was the one who'd been hurt by digging up her past.

'Good thing I'm tough,' she said, with a half-smile. 'And I suppose you were only doing your job. Though, technically, I've done it for you …'

James nodded. 'Lucky we met, then,' he said. His eyes locked with hers. Feeling her cheeks heat up, she dropped her gaze.

Whatever spark there was between them, now was not the time. Not with everything with Adam so churned-up. And Sylvia was her main concern right now. Turning to her, Nell tucked the sheet gently around Sylvia's chin. A murmur made her pause, but Sylvia still dozed.

Glad to reset their conversation onto the safer ground of murder, Nell passed James Sylvia's phone. The screen had locked, so Nell searched on her own phone for the article and showed James. 'Sylvia showed me this. I assume you already know about the burned-out car? I think it's connected to Sophie's case somehow.'

James scanned the article. 'Yes, we're supporting the road team with it.'

Nell nodded. 'Well, Sylvia met him. Troy. Or Paul. At the planning conference in Pendlebury. It's odd, because the hotel was booked out for the event, and this guy wasn't a planner or a developer. So why would he be there?'

James raised his eyebrows. 'As an escort, presumably?'

'Yes, possibly. But if he was there in that capacity, how come he was available to meet Sylvia? They were together all night.'

'Maybe his original plans for the night didn't work out? Or … worked out very quickly …?'

'Yes, but *look* at him.' Nell took the phone and scrolled to the man's picture. 'He resembles David, doesn't he? When I was waiting for the ambulance last night, Sylvia said she thought David was Troy, and that's why she let him in. I'm not sure where that leads us.'

'*Us?*' James smiled.

Nell paused, then ploughed on. 'But it's too much of a coincidence that someone like Troy would be at a planning conference, and then end up dead the next day.'

'Yes, I agree. You could have something.' James nodded. He glanced at Sylvia. 'I'll phone the team while I wait for her to wake up.'

While James made the call, Nell stepped outside and relayed what had happened to a monosyllabic Adam, almost relieved when her phone beeped with a text. Nell checked it.

Percy: Free for a call, gorgeous? I'm worried about you. Miss you xx

She replied: Yes, love to chat later, not now, though xx

She pocketed her phone as Adam averted his eyes, a dejected expression across his face. As he checked his phone, it rang. He ended the call, glancing sheepishly at the nurse, but excused himself. 'Better go outside and take this. It's Mum.'

'Oh. Another date?'

'No. I've decided to travel to India earlier for Marla's wedding. She wants to know when I'll be flying out.'

Oh. Nell ached to ask the same question. But he'd tell her if he wanted her to know. And, if he didn't, it wasn't any of her business.

So why did every step he took down the corridor – away from her, without a backward glance – hurt so much?

Beside Sylvia's bed, James's phone call to Ashley was answered on the first ring.

Ashley's words rushed out. 'Great timing, James, I've just seen Mrs Lambert. She remembered what she meant to tell us. Before Marjorie Crows moved into Applewood, she had visits at Manor House Farm from a Dave Dixon, wanting to buy her home.'

James frowned. 'That's David Stephenson. How many times did he visit Mrs Crows?'

'Three, Mrs Lambert said. On the third visit, she gave him tea in the drawing room. A room which would have been full of photos of Sophie – the typical ones of her on horses but she said that there was also one of her at uni. We saw it in her room, James. Sophie was right beside the Royal Holloway Student Union sign. Would have been easy to search the letters. And, since his sister was at the same uni, there's every chance David recognised it straight away. Mrs Lambert said that when she, Sophie and Mrs Crows plotted to sabotage David's development, it was the first time Mrs Crows had the idea that Dave Dixon and David Stephenson were the same person.'

'I know he hadn't visited, but surely Sophie showed her photos? Of their wedding?'

'Well, that's the point. She had. But Mrs Crows' poor eyesight was the main reason she moved into Applewood, so David would have felt quite safe that when Sophie showed her grandmother any pictures, Mrs Crows wouldn't be able see well enough to make him out. But, on the day those women put their heads together to plot, she asked Sophie to play her wedding video. She hadn't seen it before.'

'Well, surely, if she couldn't see him in a photo, how would a vid … Ahhh …'

'Exactly. She couldn't *see* him. But she recognised his *voice*. Mrs Lambert had thought it odd she asked to watch it, especially under those circumstances. And Mrs Crows didn't react then or say anything in front of Sophie. She only told Mrs Lambert when she asked about it afterwards. And *that's* why she acted so quickly to change her will.'

James rested his forehead against his palm. 'So we have circumstantial evidence that David married Sophie to secure his ownership of Manor House Farm?'

'Yep. He had a stroke of luck seeing Sophie at the graduation ball. And he seized it with both hands, moving in on her immediately, becoming a boyfriend who was too busy to meet her grandmother, then marrying her when the opportunity arose with Mrs Crows moving to Applewood.'

James was silent as her words sank in.

Ashley gave him a moment to digest, then continued. 'And more news. Pendlebury Hotel have released the phone number called from David's room. The call was to an ex-pat, from the UK who moved to America a year ago. His name is Mark Dunn.'

James's attention spiked. 'What did you say his name was?'

'Mark Dunn.'

'Huh. I was calling you about a possible link with Sophie's case and the burned-out car in Pendlebury. They've identified the victim. A man called Paul Dunn.'

'I'm way ahead of you,' Ashley said. 'There's a link all right. Mark Dunn is Paul Dunn's brother. And Mark has never heard of David Stephenson.'

Glancing at Sylvia, James lowered his voice. 'And Paul was murdered. Just before Sophie was reported missing. So David used Paul and his resemblance as cover in the hotel? To give him an alibi? Hence the room service and the phone call?'

'Yes, but I doubt the call was part of the deal, given that Mark Dunn confirmed it was Paul. My guess is, David didn't endear himself to Paul, and perhaps a whopping call charge – that David could hardly refute – was his way of getting his own back?'

James's mind reeled. 'And *that's* why David tried to kill Sylvia – she'd met Paul, she was posting their pictures on social media, so someone was bound to realise …' He took a deep breath. 'So, if that breaks David's alibi, can we link him to the tunnel?'

'Kind of. Not as tightly as we'd like. Tech have recovered Sophie's deleted texts. Including one deleted from David, telling her that the planners needed photos of the tunnel to check its condition. But we can't *prove* David deleted it so he wouldn't be connected with luring Sophie into the tunnel.'

James leaned against the wall, suffering the usual frustration. 'The kicker is, even though Sylvia can testify that David tried to kill her, we need evidence to prove he also killed Paul, Sophie and Mrs Crows.'

'Everything we currently have is purely circumstantial. We might convict on it but there's a risk a jury could find reasonable doubt, even if the CPS approves it. And I can tell you now, you won't get anything less than iron-clad evidence past Trent.'

'Oh, fantastic.' He hung up, staring at his feet, noticing the grit he'd tracked on the shining floor, dislodged from the tread of his boots. A jab of memory bristled into inspiration.

He poked his head out through the curtain. 'Nell? I need to see you about some bats.'

Chapter 30

Four months later – Friday 22nd January – 10 a.m.

Adam had snuck into the back row of the High Court's gallery, and chosen a seat shielded by a pillar. He'd given his evidence yesterday. But he couldn't miss this.

Nell had the stand. 'I do solemnly, sincerely and truly declare and affirm that the evidence I shall give shall be the truth, the whole truth and nothing but the truth.'

Once the prosecuting barrister led Nell through her survey of the grounds, laying the badger bait, then surveying the tunnel and hearing the fateful thud before going on to do the bat survey of the house, he turned to the jury. 'The ecology quote drew David Stephenson's attention to the tunnel and a convenient timeframe within which he could both commit the murder and create an alibi. When his project manager, Anna Maddison, left work early, David Stephenson sent an email from Anna Maddison's computer to Sophie Crows, moving her meeting with Dr Ward by a crucial hour. He'd managed to make it look like Dr Ward had been copied in, simply by typing a comma rather than a full-stop in her email address. Then he deleted the 'delivery failed' message from Anna Maddison's inbox and deleted folders, and Sophie Crows was lured out there, alone.'

'Exhibit 42, ma'am.' The court clerk held up a printed email, the comma circled.

Adam saw Nell take a deep breath, glowering at David, her eyes burning with revulsion.

The prosecutor was on a roll. 'To make sure only Dr Ward was incriminated David Stephenson used the team photos in the ecology quote to identify Dr Kashyap, and follow him home, so he could slash his tyres on the day of the murder, whether Dr Kashyap went to Manor House Farm from the office or from his house. An opportunistic move to limit the people at the scene and prevent Dr Kashyap from arriving to Manor House Farm earlier than planned, and giving Dr Ward an alibi.'

'Exhibit 43, ma'am.' The court clerk held up the Bio page of the ecology quote.

Adam's heart lurched as Nell's face trembled and she bit her lip, hard. He hoped she didn't feel guilty over that. Or … did she still have feelings for him? *Four wasted months since I've seen her. What a bloody idiot.*

'And Dr Ward's past connection with David Stephenson, with its suggestion of motive, was an opportunity too good to pass up.'

'Exhibit 44, ma'am.' The court clerk held up the photo of Nell and David at the ball. Adam saw Nell turn away from the picture, her lip curling.

'Making Dr Ward perfect to frame. Or, if she wasn't found guilty, David Stephenson's next victim.'

Jesus. He'd said as much to Nell, but hearing it from a legal practitioner was different. Compared to her response to the other points, Nell looked calm. He could practically hear her saying, in full indignant-mode, *'The nerve!'*

The defence lawyer paced. 'You've just heard a lot of guesswork from my learned friend. But what we have to bear in mind, here, are a few pertinent *facts*. The first, is that David Stephenson is an old acquaintance of Dr Ward's. In fact, someone Dr Ward took as her date to her graduation ball. Where he left you for Sophie Crows. Isn't that right?'

'Well, yes, but—'

'Secondly, there's evidence of you entering the tunnel where Sophie Crows was killed. By your own admission, precisely at the time of her murder. Isn't that right?'

'Exhibit 45, ma'am.' The court clerk held up photos of Nell's boot print.

'Yes, but—'

'And, thirdly, after your arrest,' he half-turned to the jury, 'yes, *arrest* for this murder, your response was to derail the investigation with a complaint against police procedure and deflect it with ecological theories.'

In the box, Adam saw David fold his arms, smirking. Adam wanted to punch his smug face. He felt a flash of satisfaction when David unfolded his arms and carefully rotated the wrist his kick had broken, but the gratification was short-lived. He feared the jury would see a chink of doubt, and the case for Sophie's murder would fail.

The lawyer walked towards the jury. 'In a moment, you're going to hear about this investigation's reliance on ecological evidence, most of which was supplied by Dr Ward. Just bear in mind that David Stephenson isn't the only one who could be incriminated by that evidence, and that this, crucially, introduces an element of doubt into his guilt.'

The jury looked sober as most took notes, some appraising Nell. Adam prickled with fear again, as the lawyer addressed her.

'Your evidence is based on the pellets you used for the badger survey.'

'Yes. Because two of those red pellets were found during the police search.'

The court clerk held up photos. 'Exhibits 46 and 47, ma'am.'

Nell continued, 'You heard DS James Clark state earlier that one was found in the Manor House Farm's kitchen, the other in room 27 of Pendlebury Hotel. Those pellets are an ideal size to get stuck in the tread of a boot or shoe, and that's how the detectives believe the two pellets were transferred to their positions. Then they stuck in those positions due to how I used the pellets. They'd both been covered with honey – because I'd mixed them in the bait of Crunchy Nut and honey for badgers. It's a method cited on the UK government website as a standard way to survey badger territories.'

Adam checked the jury, glazing over as Nell quoted survey guidance. *Listen, you idiots!* He coughed. Loudly. A couple of jurors jumped.

'I laid those pellets at 3.32 p.m., and the red pellet in the kitchen appeared in a photo I later took of the house at 6.44 p.m. So, from the timing of my survey, I know for *certain* ...'

Nell stressed the word, leaning forward to look at the jury. Adam saw the jurors sit up, cued for a crucial point.

'... that someone must have walked through Manor House Farm's woodland, into the kitchen, towards the tunnel, around the time of the murder. And, afterwards, into room 27 at Pendlebury Hotel.' She paused. 'David Stephenson's room.'

The jury rippled as notes were taken and sidelong glances were shot between jurors.

Dismissed, Nell joined Sylvia a few rows in front of Adam. As Sylvia glanced round, he scooted back, hidden by the pillar, and stayed there.

'And we have another ecologist now. An independent expert witness.'

Adam resisted the urge to lean forward. This had been Nell's big inspiration in the hospital, when James came out from Sylvia's bay in the hospital and asked about the qPCR test she'd mentioned.

The expert witness ecologist took the stand, stated his name, credentials and oath. At the prosecution's invitation, he explained, 'I was given samples taken from boots belonging to David Stephenson, and from the footwell of an Audi TT belonging to Paul Dunn and asked to run tests for bat DNA. The fire damage in the car would have reduced the amount of material, but DNA can be quite resilient up to $1,000^{\circ}C$. It was more of an issue that the samples were small, especially to try to ascertain the mix of species present. So, to address that, I did a targeted quantitative polymerase chain reaction – qPCR – analysis, because that can check for multiple species in one sample, as several different bat species can roost together in hibernation sites, like the tunnel at Manor House Farm.'

'And did this indicate anything useful?'

'Yes, very good results, because the sticky patches on the boots, from the bait-marking honey, enabled a good transfer of DNA from site to boots to car. Both samples showed the same mix of DNA, proving the same combination of bat species were present in both samples, thus showing that David Stephenson's boots had been in the driver's footwell of Paul Dunn's car.'

'And did you compare these samples to the tunnel at Manor House Farm?'

'Yes. Not only did I get the same species data, it included two rare species of bats – grey long-eared bat and barbastelle – in all three samples, increasing the likelihood that the DNA on David's boot, which transferred to the car, had been picked up in the tunnel.'

The defence lawyer stood, pursing his lips. 'This all *sounds* like you'd have a limited chance to pick up DNA of rare species. But the local bat group confirmed that those same species hibernate in an ice house nearby. So David Stephenson could have picked this debris up on his shoes there. Or at any similar site.'

'Not so.'

The jury's heads snapped back to the ecologist as the judge invited him to explain.

'You're quite right to note there are rare species in lots of hibernation roosts, and that these roosts are monitored by bat experts. But, because of the sensitivity of the roost sites, they're usually highly secure and only licensed ecologists can access those places. The ice house you mentioned is locked and only accessed three times a year by the local bat group. Between December and March, *not* August, when Sophie Crows' murder occurred. And my samples also found irrefutable evidence that those boots had been in Manor House Farm's tunnel.'

Almost as one, the jury leaned forward.

'In all three samples, I found the DNA of a greater mouse-eared bat.'

Adam gaped. Peeping around the pillar he saw Nell's delighted beam and Sylvia's frown.

'This species is found in Europe but there are no records of this bat in the *entire country*. And, as you pointed out, the meticulous records of the local bat groups and Bat Conservation Trust means I can attest to this with absolute certainty. It's a *very* exciting find!'

The judge cleared her throat.

'Ah, yes, so, in conclusion the three samples gave me a *unique* mix of bat species DNA. Since nowhere else in the country has this DNA profile, I can be certain that the wearer of those boots, who then drove the Audi TT, had *definitely* been inside the tunnel at Manor House Farm.'

As several of the jury scribbled rapid notes, Adam wanted to cheer and hug Nell. It hurt that he couldn't share this triumph with her.

The summing-up was agony. As soon as the jury were dismissed and observers could leave, Adam stood and drew a deep breath. He hadn't seen Nell for four months while he'd been in India. Their brief time together in the office before he'd left had been tense. He'd given her space and waited for her to make the first move, but she'd made it clear she wasn't going to. His sister's wedding, catching up with family and conservation work had kept him busy, but hadn't been enough to stop him checking emails and texts obsessively.

And so much for her being private. When his curiosity finally got the better of him (which, OK, was at the airport – on the way *to* India) he'd come across Finchmere's Instagram account. There hadn't been anything of Nell on there, until her exhilarating race at the Autumn Finchmere Cup in September. But then she turned up wearing a stunning dress at a ball in November, and again, having fun at Christmas parties. So she must have overcome her reticence of being open about her background.

Unless … was he *supposed* to find these pictures? Was she trying to show him that she was being more open? He didn't know what to think. But he did feel guilty at giving her such a hard time about it. And, though he scoured social media, he never saw her with anyone who seemed special. *But then she'd never post about that. What if she* had *found someone?*

Now, staring at Nell's elated face while she chatted with Sylvia by the court's grand doorway, he wondered if the gap between them could ever be bridged. But, if nothing else, he could congratulate her on this evidence.

His heart pounded but, before he'd got halfway down the corridor, James walked over to Nell and enveloped her in a hug. Adam's heart jolted. It was the kind of hug he wanted to share with her. An intimate hug. *Are they a couple?* As a sick feeling churned, Adam watched James point to a coffee shop across the square, then gently steer Nell away, his hand on her lower back.

Friday 22nd January – 7 p.m.

As Nell got ready for the evening's ball, the ponderous courtroom seemed a world away. It had only been two hours since they'd left, stiff from a day sitting on the hard wooden pews. But now, in the luxury of Finchmere House, the orchestra's music filtered up the sweeping stairs, hinting at the elegance of the evening to come – as stark a contrast to bat excreta and murderous motives as Nell could imagine. *At least it's over now.*

Beside her, Sylvia admired her begowned self in Nell's mirror. The ruby A-line gave her scarred abdomen some room yet maintained a suitable Sylvia-level of glamour. 'Well, I must say, I look like I was born for this lifestyle. And look at you. Utterly divine.'

Nell smoothed her shimmering copper-and-verdigris silk gown. Her family had hosted hundreds of balls but tonight, for the first time, her stomach fluttered.

Sylvia glanced at her. 'You can't be nervous about a ball. Are you fretting about the trial?' She rested her hand on her stomach. 'I still want to ask James a few questions. I need … closure, I suppose. But I hope you're not reliving that horrible day in the tunnel. Or questioning your courage in your convictions.' She reached for Nell's hand. 'You need to know you can trust your own judgement, don't you?'

Nell couldn't reply. Too many unfortunate decisions answered that for her.

'Darling, people who make no mistakes can never learn anything.' She leaned closer, wafting musk, eyes dancing. 'And never have any *fun*.' She applied unnecessary lipstick and smiled, letting out a sigh. 'I owe my life to you trusting your instinct. So put that fear to bed. Life is precious, and it can be far too short. So seize it.'

Walking along the hall, Sylvia nudged her. 'Is Adam coming tonight?'

Nell shrugged. 'I don't know. Andrew Arden's the host. He sent invitations to everyone involved in the Crows' trial, as a thank you and to tap up Mother's contacts to support the horse sanctuary and his new venture. So Adam's included. But I don't know if he's coming. Going by his no-show at court today, I doubt it.'

'But … haven't you spoken to him?'

'Not since he went to India.'

Sylvia gaped. 'But he left in *September*. I knew things were frosty – the few times you were together in the office, it was so glacial it was like the planet's answer to climate change.'

Over the past four months, she'd checked and rechecked her emails for any contact. She'd even bitten the bullet and posted pictures of herself at events at Finchmere, being braver about sharing her background. Just in case … *Just in case of what? He's interested enough to look? Or comment? Or send a message? What an idiot.* She'd Googled him occasionally but found nothing. Missing Adam had made her restless, itchy. *Because our argument's unresolved? Or … more than that …? No – he'd done exactly what she was most afraid of: he'd used her background against her. There was no coming back from that.*

'Anyway, that's history.'

'Oh yes. I saw how interested James was in your, ahem, ecological theories. And I'm certain I detected a spark at his *debriefing* today, after court,' Sylvia chortled.

'I could say it was strictly in the name of duty,' Nell said, grinning. 'But there'd be no point.'

They'd had a coffee three months ago, when James asked for a recommendation for the ecological expert witness. The question and answer took five minutes and could have been dealt with over email or phone. But the next hour had flown as they'd chatted. They hadn't noticed Sylvia come in and have a latte, observing them, although Sylvia had given Nell her opinions about James's body language afterwards. They'd chatted until the café owner swept up and finally told them it was closing time. Sylvia's assessment hadn't been necessary. As they left the coffee shop, James had been quite honest.

'Nell, I think it's obvious that I like you.'

She hadn't been able to drag her eyes from his knowing, azure gaze. She felt a slow smile stretch across her face.

'Yeah, don't look at me like that!' James had shaken his head, stared across the street, then sighed and turned back to her. 'You know it means I can't see you. Not when we're preparing for a big court case, and when *you're* a key part of that case. But afterwards ...' He'd pressed a note into her hand – his personal number – and walked down the street. He turned to wave once, but backed into a lamppost, tripped and shook his head at ruining the moment, so didn't attempt it again.

This morning, she'd been fizzing with apprehension. But whether that was about seeing James, or the possibility of seeing Adam, or just sheer nerves at wanting to present her evidence on the stand well so the jury would make the right decision, she couldn't tell.

Reaching the stairs, Sylvia pursed her lips. 'We know James is coming tonight. What happens if Adam turns up, too?'

'I guess we'll have to wait and see.' Nell put on her game face: bright smile, shoulders back. And tried to ignore the butterflies in her stomach.

At least Sylvia's gasp as they descended the elegant staircase was gratifying. The hall, awash with soft glowing lights from elaborate chandeliers sparkling overhead, was milling with guests. Liveried waiting staff took invitations and coats from new arrivals, showed them to the ballroom and offered drinks and canapés.

Andrew and Liv Arden stood with Nell's mother Imelda. 'Thank you for all this,' Nell heard Andrew say. 'Hosting and making connections for us has got us off to a fantastic start. It feels like I'm fulfilling Sophie's wishes, putting a small bit right for her.' Beside him, Liv knocked her drink back and beckoned a waiter for a refill.

As Andrew turned to her, Nell felt agonised that she couldn't even glance around the room. 'I owe you a debt of thanks. Your evidence got justice for Sophie. And Paul, of course. But the Crows were ... a good family. I can't thank you enough.'

Nell nodded, but he continued. 'And thank you also for taking on the hibernation surveys of the tunnel, to monitor our newly-discovered rare bat.'

Hardly a chore, to survey such a rare species! She smiled. 'It's a pleasure, Andrew. Enjoy the evening, and don't let me monopolise you – you'll be in demand!'

Scanning the crowd, her butterflies clamoured. Nell braced as she and Sylvia walked towards the music. The ballroom buzzed with conversation and music. Dancing couples were swirls of jewel colours sweeping around the vast marble dancefloor to the orchestra's Viennese waltz. But no sign of James yet. Or Adam.

Sylvia nudged Nell's arm, pointing out Pendlebury's detectives and steered her over, catching the end of their conversation.

'... After the Police Reform Ball in November and tonight, I could get used to this.'

'Don't get ideas, Val,' Chief Constable Trent replied. 'As much as I'd like to celebrate you getting on the Strategic Command Course, we don't have the budget for a do like this.'

Nell and Sylvia greeted them but, as the orchestra began another waltz, Nell felt a tap on her arm. She turned. James held his hand out. 'Evening, Nell. May I have the honour?'

Chapter 31

Friday 22nd January – 7.30 p.m.

Adam turned into the long, avenued driveway to Finchmere House. After James had whisked Nell away at the courthouse, he'd been on the verge of changing his mind. But Nell must want to see him if she invited him. He missed their jokes, her company, her smile. *Her*.

I shouldn't have been so hard on her. But … is it too late? To put things right?

He followed the low gleaming lanterns bronzing the trunks of the bare copper beeches. Adam's stomach flipped at the thought of seeing her. The avenue turned to reveal the illuminated impressive, symmetrical Regency house. Adam whistled under his breath at the vast mansion, twinkling with inviting lights, set against the rolling downland. *Holy …* The landscape was obscured by darkness but – even in daylight – the view wouldn't take in all of Nell's estate. *What the hell am I doing?* His hand slid off the steering wheel and he blotted the clamminess on the fabric car seat so he didn't mark his tux.

He rallied. *I'm here now. Just go in and say hello.* Adam drove on, parked, showed his embossed, gilt-edged invitation at the door and made his way through the wide hallway. A huge room, bustling with guests, led through to the ballroom. He took a deep breath and walked in.

His stomach lurched. When Nell had described her background, the distance between them was theoretical. Now, he saw it. Felt it.

Across the dancefloor, a beautiful young woman in a sensational verdigris dress whirled under the glittering chandeliers. Nell. His heart thumped, his breath catching at the sight of her radiant smile. The room of dancers fell away, the music silenced. She mesmerised him.

As he watched, Adam saw Nell coaching her dance partner. *Oh, bloody hell. James. Of course it's James. He's treading all over her feet, and she's still beaming. I'm an idiot.*

He watched them linger together as the music stopped, his heart sinking.

Backing away, Adam hurried out to the hall, where Sylvia appeared from nowhere.

'Adam! How lovely—'

'Oh, Sylvia.' He shook his head. 'I was just going.'

As he walked on, Sylvia winced and held her stomach, stopping him in his tracks. 'You OK? Are you in pain?' he said, putting an arm around her and guiding her to a chair.

Sylvia drew a breath. 'I'll be fine. But … stay with me a minute, would you?'

Adam recognised a touch of theatrics in Sylvia's gesture, but he also saw her hand tremble. He took it, held it between both of his with tenderness. The past few gruelling days in court must have dredged up terrifying memories for her. 'Anything for you, Sylv.' He shot her a flirtatious, irreverent grin, knowing she'd appreciate the levity, relying on his protective concern being conveyed through his gentle squeeze of her hand.

A waiter brought Sylvia a glass of water and she took a sip, then fixed her eyes on him. A hint of a twinkle returned. 'Good, then the first thing you can do for me, is stay. Why on earth would you leave so early? You don't want to put that tux to waste, do you? Not when you look so ravishing.'

He managed a smile. 'Thanks, and thank you for the tux. It was incredible to get one made-to-measure.'

'You wear it well.' Sylvia smiled. 'Darling, you risked your own life to save mine. I can never repay you.' Now *she* squeezed *his* hand. 'So *I've* seen just how much courage you do have. Channel it, darling. Before it's too late.' She held out a hand and he helped her to her feet. Drawing his arm under hers, she leaned on it as she walked. 'Come along. Team talk time. We both have things to resolve tonight.'

To be heard over the music, James spoke into Nell's ear, his breath tickling warmth on her cheek. 'This place is amazing. I'd love a guided tour.'

She grinned. *He could just ask to go somewhere quieter. Or maybe he really did want to nerd out at the architecture.* Nell led him through throngs of guests, across the hall. 'In that case, you'll love this.' She opened the door to the library. 'This room's full of ancient history.'

Walking in, Nell did a double-take at Adam sitting by the fire with Sylvia. Adam immediately jumped to his feet, smoothing his jacket. He looked … *amazing*.

She wanted to bite back her unfortunate choice of words, and James's hand on her back felt like a betrayal of Adam. *It bloody shouldn't.*

Sylvia shot her a smile. 'Oh, good. Join us. I was hoping to speak to you, James. I hoped you might help me … draw a line under what happened.' She cradled her abdomen.

Glancing at Nell, James sat on the sofa. 'Of course.'

As Nell curled up beside him, Adam sat down, staring in her direction. But the shadows thrown by the flickering orange flames around the book-lined room meant Nell couldn't read his expression.

Sylvia took a deep breath, her theatrical nature unusually sombre. 'I … I need to know why David … *how* David …'

Nell knew Sylvia felt unable to attend Paul Dunn's part of the trial. Just as well. It had been gruesome. She hoped James would be gentle. He took Sylvia's hand. A good start.

'We all know David used Paul as a decoy, his alibi. When David briefly left the conference, the hotel CCTV showed him going out to the car park, then walking back in minutes later – but it was *Paul* walking in. When David returned, he used the back door to avoid CCTV, expecting Paul to leave that way, too.'

'But he didn't leave. He came to the bar and got chatting with me. And if he hadn't …' Sylvia's face crumpled. 'Did David kill him because I'd posted his photo?'

'No, Sylvia.' James's firm tone cut through her tremors. 'David hadn't seen them when he killed Paul. But Paul posed a risk because, once he heard about Sophie's murder, he could tell police at any time that David not only needed him *in* that room, but *obviously* there, ordering room service. It nearly worked. The busy waitress believed he was David, until we showed her pictures of both men and she changed her mind.'

'And while my poor Paul was there, providing a false alibi, David …' Sylvia shuddered.

'David used Paul's car – so his could stay in full view of the CCTV – to drive to Manor House Farm. David probably made sure Paul gave him the keys in the street, out of view of the cameras. David used a brick to attack Sophie, which we'd thought indicated it was spontaneous. But it was planned, so he didn't need to take or dispose of a weapon. He probably stashed a change of clothes at Manor House Farm, so he could change back and dump the ones he'd worn in one of the industrial bins at the Tesco on the dual carriageway – our ANPR cameras caught Paul's Audi there at 5.30 p.m. He got back, cleaned himself up and was seen in the bar at 8 p.m.'

'So how … how …?' Sylvia couldn't get the words out.

James took a deep breath, his brow furrowed. 'On the Thursday evening, before David reported Sophie missing – when he was supposedly desperately searching everywhere for her – Paul's phone has a record of a phone call from an unknown number. Probably David using a burner phone, arranging to meet Paul at the industrial estate, maybe on the pretext of more business. And there, Paul was killed by being knocked unconscious, and … his car set alight.'

Sylvia covered her mouth. Her shoulders shook as she held back tears. James let go of Sylvia's hand so Nell could gather her into a long hug and let her sob. Adam bowed his head.

'With Sophie killed and an alibi watertight, David knew the rest of his plan would fall into place. Because by that point, he'd already done what he needed to kill Marjorie Crows.'

Sylvia's shuddering breaths paused. She pulled away from Nell, frowning.

'He'd used Anna's computer to brand a polo shirt and baseball cap with A1 Alarm's logo, lifted from their website, to sign in – illegibly – at Applewood. Thinking he was a reputable technician, the receptionist gave him a master key and access to the office. He might have known from Sophie where the drugs were kept, but the key to the cabinet was in the drawer. He swapped Mrs Crows' high blood pressure pills, Hygroton, for low blood pressure midodrine, bought on the internet using Anna's computer – which was very well hidden and took our tech team a few searches to uncover – knowing it would cause a stroke and, very probably, her death.'

Sylvia gulped, and Nell guessed it was at David's cold premeditation. It was so brazen. Three people, all just collateral damage to him. Nell couldn't believe she had spent time with this guy, laughed at his jokes, danced with him. He was a monster.

'But we got the right result today.'

Nell's head snapped up. 'The verdict came in already?' She knew James had stayed at court, just in case, while she got back to help prepare for tonight. By the look on his face, he'd wanted to tell her when they were alone.

'Yes. David was found guilty of all three murders, plus your attempted murder, Sylvia, and given four life sentences. The judge set imprisonment for a whole-life term, meaning he'll never be considered for release.'

Wow. Nell felt a tidal wave of relief. She felt Adam's eyes on her, but James held her gaze with a steady smile, wanting to share his triumph with her. She smiled back, glad at the outcome.

'*Good.*' Sylvia dabbed her face with a tissue. Her tone was sharp enough to give Nell the excuse to look at her, then Adam. His gaze on her was fierce.

James nodded. 'And I have to give credit where it's due. Your statement made a huge difference, Sylvia. And there was no room for reasonable doubt, thanks to the bats. And your idea about the DNA evidence, Nell.'

'Never again, and I mean, *never*,' Sylvia pronounced, 'will I criticise your scatological interests. Those lovely little creatures made sure he didn't get away with anything.' She drew a breath. 'Shame you missed that today, Adam. The ecologist was great.'

'I thought *both* the ecologists were great,' Adam said.

Nell turned to him, puzzled. 'But ...?'

Sylvia's gaze flicked between Nell and Adam, then she held out her arm towards James. 'Goodness. I think I need a drink after all that.'

'Er, yes, of course.' James shot Nell an apologetic glance as Sylvia leaned on him and steered him towards the door.

Nell began to follow them, expecting Adam to walk with her, but he tugged her arm. 'Nell, can we talk?'

Oh, the butterflies in her stomach went berserk.

Adam raked his hair. It was already the unruly side of tamed. *More butterflies.* Nell noted the made-to-measure corded silk of Savile Row. *Wow. He's gone all-out ...*

'Thanks for showing up at court yesterday, Nell. You kept me going while that defence lawyer tried to make out I'd damaged my own car to incriminate you. As *if.* I've been beaming out good luck to you

257

all day. From behind that pillar at the back.' The surprise, and his sheepishness, made a short laugh escape from Nell's throat. 'I should have said hello. I should have got in touch sooner. The longer we didn't speak, the harder it was to make contact.'

Nell swallowed, her mouth dry. 'Yeah, I get that. Try finding a neat way to drop all this,' she gestured around the room, 'into everyday chitchat.' Sighing, she perched on the arm of the sofa. 'Look, I know you think I hid all this from you. It wasn't the case. I was on the brink of telling you so many times. But it's a bit of a conversational grenade.'

'I see that. And I'm sorry I gave you such a hard time. It was a shock.' He exhaled. 'I *do* understand about your background. I'm a hypocrite, really. I've been doing the same all my life.'

Nell stared at him. 'What do you mean?'

Adam patted his inside pocket and pulled out his invitation. He handed it to Nell.

She scanned it. Adam was crossed out and neat capital letters spelled out 'Aravindan'.

'Your name's Aravindan?'

'I was the only Indian kid in my class. My classmates struggled to pronounce my name. Even contractions still made me sound … different. I'd heard Adam being used in both cultures, so I said it was my nickname. It stuck.' He stared at his hands. 'Mum went on about me shunning my given name. Dad said it was sensible if it helped me fit in.' He shrugged. 'That's all you want, as a kid, isn't it? You don't think about anything else. So I could have been more understanding, because I get it. Different circumstances, sure, but boils down to the same thing. Wanting to be taken for who you are. No prejudice.'

He gave her *that* grin. 'I see from Instagram that you've been braver about your background. So—'

Nell gasped and he chuckled. 'Oh, come on, of *course* I've spent the whole time looking you up, wondering what you're doing …'

She laughed again. But she wasn't going to share the admission. He might be trying the irresistible flirting tactic. But she remembered what he said at the farmhouse. *Friends. Just friends.*

'So you've inspired me to go by my given name.' His face grew serious. 'Aravindan. Most of my family just call me Rav. What do you think?'

Nell nodded. 'I like it.'

His creased brow softened as his smile widened. 'Good.' He took a deep breath, 'Because I wan—'

The door opened with a cheerful James, calling, 'I've left Sylvia getting to know Conor, while he has his break. But I've brought along someone else.'

Nell's nod was automatic as she still stared at Adam – Rav. *What had he been about to say?* Rav sighed in frustration, but then a whirl of copper-and-emerald barrelled Nell into a hug.

'*Percy?*' Nell couldn't believe she'd made it. Even if her timing was terrible.

'Hey, don't spill my drink!' Percy held her glass away from her green gown, red curls tumbling to her waist, appraising the two of them with shrewd green eyes.

'So *you're* Percy? Oh God – it's *great* to meet you.' Rav's enthusiasm baffled Nell, until she recalled the text he'd seen in the hospital. The rueful glance he shot her over Percy's shoulder made Nell's heart contract.

James handed one of his two coupes of champagne to Nell, staying by her side.

'No need for introductions, Nell.' Percy's smile twitched. 'I mean, I've tracked down handsome James already. Even more handsome in the flesh.' Ignoring James's baffled but delighted face, she continued, 'And I've heard how well the case went. Congratulations, all.' She raised her glass.

'And you're Adam?' Percy guessed.

'Rav,' Nell said.

'Rav?' Percy turned to Nell and conveyed, '*yet another man?!*' with her eyes.

Nell felt her face flush. Percy was enjoying this too much. 'Well, yes, Rav is Adam. But he's using his given name now. Aravindan. Rav for short.' She hesitated. Given how upset Rav had been at her lack of disclosure about her background, should she introduce Percy formally, as Lady Persephone Doineann MacKenzie, daughter of the Marquess and Marchioness of Glencoille? No, Percy would wonder what the hell she was doing.

'What were you two doing hiding away in the library when it's supposed to be a party?' Percy blinked with faux innocence.

James shot Nell the look he had when she'd been a suspect, like he was trying to read her thoughts. *Good luck with that! Bloody Percy. She never could resist mischief.*

Percy downed her drink. 'What you need is a real party! If only you had a good excuse! Oh, no, wait – you *do*.' Percy flourished the left hand she'd been hiding. A vast emerald sparkled in the firelight. 'Say you'll come up to Scotland in March for my engagement party?'

'Percy! How could you not have told me? So Hamish finally proposed?'

'Pfff. Hamish is dead to me. He sodded off abroad and dropped all contact.' She side-eyed Rav, then shrugged. 'His loss. He had his chance. So now, I'm wedding Hawke MacAnstruther.'

Nell frowned. 'A whole new man I don't know anything about?'

'You've had enough on your plate. Let's just say, it's been a whirlwind romance.'

'But I haven't even *heard* of him, let alone met him.'

'You'll like him. He's funny, up for an adventure.' She gave an impish grin. 'Sexy as all hell. I'll make it easy for you to get to know him. I've planned a week of activities across the estate, as well as our celebration at Glencoille Castle. The party will be a bit … you know.' Percy nudged Nell's shoulder.

Nell did know. 'Parents' political guests, rather than friends. And you want back-up.'

'Exactly. Literally, anyone I can find who's under ninety who *can* come, *must* come. I know it has to be all grace and favour but I want some *fun*. So, James and Rav, you must promise to come, and you must promise to dance with me. If it takes two of you to get Nell into trouble, I want you both there. God knows, I've tried hard enough over the years.'

The men looked stunned at the impromptu invitation, especially when Percy added seriously, 'I'll send you formal invites so you can RSVP. It's March 13th.'

Less than two months away?

As James shot his wickedly knowing smile at Nell, Rav fixed her with an intense gaze, with that same hint of smoulder he'd had before she'd fallen asleep on him all those months ago.

Her butterflies took flight again.

'Feel free to bring a plus one,' Percy added to James and Rav. But her eyes slid to Nell and her mischievous smile twitched again. 'Or not.'

Acknowledgements

I am bowled over to have had the chance to write a book. And beyond delighted that the fantastic Katie Fulford (Agent Extraordinaire at Bell Lomax Moreton) used her magnificent matchmaking talents to enable me to join forces with the wonderful Hannah Smith, Emilie Marneur, Jane Snelgrove and Jennifer Porter at Embla Books. And, in turn, the amazing Hannah, for matching me with the most delightful editor ever, Emily Thomas. Thanks also to Jon Appleton (an eagle-eyed genius), the care and attention of Michelle Bullock, Robin Seavill, Laura Marlow and her amazing team for the audiobook magic and the artistic talents of Lisa Horton. I suspect it is a rare thing to find people who not only get what you're trying to do, but get it so well they can help you do it better – yet you've all made it look easy. It's been a total joy to work with you, and I can't think of a better team to help coax my manuscript from scruffy duckling to fully fledged *Anas platyrhynchos*. Thank you.

Writing a book is a weirdly personal endeavour which quickly has to become a very open one – or, at least, that was the case for me, as learning and improving was easiest (and often, most fun) through reading, writing, critiquing and listening to advice from my fellow writing group buddies: Erin, David, Mo, Venu, Sarah F, Brooke, Deb, Staci, Roxanne, Julie N, Kelly, Linell, Melee, Lisa, Raj, Cassy, Sarah, Julie, Annette, Jane B, Rachelle, Matt, Kirsten, Jennifer, Christiane, Julie, Erika, Carrie, Katy, Dan, Charisse, Grey, Heather, Al and Lou – I've learned something from all of you! Special thanks to Jane and Pam for your wise notes. And Tom Bromley, thank you for your editorial eye on the opening pages and advice that I've tried to carry through the book.

Julie S, thank you for taking me to court (not in *that* way) and introducing me to some incredible lawyers (hi, Scott), enthralling expert witnesses and impressive detectives who apply unbelievable skill and tenacity to extract often horrific information, while dealing with all the infuriating red tape that I've omitted. I know that my procedural elements have taken some liberties with timeframes, but I hope that I've conveyed the respect I have for those working in these roles. I was able to draw upon some invaluable expert detective insights from Graham Bartlett and Kate Bendelow and a plethora of other experts, like Brian Price, on Graham's brilliant detective courses, which never fail to fascinate and astound (any good bits are down to them, but the mistakes are all mine). I think I'm gradually learning the life lesson, never ask a detective for an anecdote.

Ecologists, on the other hand, are fair game for anecdotes a-plenty, as my various adventures with team mates attest. Thank you for the inspiration – stories of bodies in woods, forensic contacts, falling into ponds, and the importance of biscuits as currency – as well as the chance to learn from your expertise: Sabrina, Toni, Sasha, Wendy, Caroline, John, Jon, Jane, Huw, Matt, Tanith, Sofia, Vicky and many more.

Esther, Mark, Sabrina, Rachel, Jo, Matt and Lauren – as for most people, the Covid Years have been a dreadful challenge in one (or more) way or another. But it makes all the difference to have friends like you to share, mourn, support each other and laugh with. And my constant writing companion, Angel, thanks for occasionally not demanding fuss so I can – you know – actually type.

Mum – thank you for reading every single word. I know this is no Jack Reacher; I'm sorry there aren't more punch-ups. Even so, you've been brilliant fun to debate motives with. Dad – thanks for supplying Mum with gallons of tea while she read! 😋 I'm honoured you've also read this. The heartfelt encouragement from both of you has meant the world to me. I'm sorry I can't share this with grandparents and Aunty Glad, but there are elements of all of them all through this (you don't need to look far for a tough matriarch in our family!). Once a person is in your heart, they're in everything you do, aren't they?

And my brilliant husband, Ian – thank you, not only for reading every single word of every single draft (and there have been about a million), but for being persuaded to enact scenes and always being up for a good, gory plotting session over a (now traditional) Murder Brunch. Who knew what a deviously creative wicked mind you have! You've not only shared this adventure, you created the opportunity, you've been an unwavering support, and you've made every step of the journey the most fabulous fun. *And* your pull-up game beats Adam's hands down. 😊

And for anyone who's leafed through the pages, thank you for reading, and I hope you enjoyed it.

The Nature of Crime

You might be forgiven for thinking that the evidence that the Crows' case counts on is a little far-fetched – that there is only one record of a greater mouse-eared bat in the entire country. But this is completely true!

The greater mouse-eared bat, *Myotis myotis*, was officially declared extinct in the UK in 1990, but a solitary male has hibernated every year, in a tunnel in southern England since 2002 (with the exception of one other, spotted in 2001).

He was ringed before he was one year old and has been recorded annually (except in 2019 – missing; and 2020 – Covid) by the Sussex Bat Group, who, like every county's bat group, monitor their hibernation sites (by ecologists licensed to do so) and conduct various other surveys (again, licensed) through the year.

Despite those extensive surveys, we don't know where our single greater mouse-eared bat spends his summers. It's possible he migrates to and from France, and such frequent-flier miles may account for his impressively muscular shoulders under his lustrous, golden velvet fur. As bats go, he is a handsome chap, and I count myself lucky to have been one of the few who have come face to face with this lovely, golden-furred specimen! My huge debt of thanks for this honour is owed to the terrific county bat groups who lead surveys, help members of the public with bat-related issues, and who trained me in the various ways of the bat: Cath Laing, Martyn Phillis, Tony Hutson, Helen Yesugey and Sue Harris especially. My top tip for surveying hibernacula is to do so in ski gear, unless you want to get as frosty as the bats.

I also salute the tireless talents of the volunteers who run the two bat hospitals of Sussex: Amanda Miller, Sheila Wright and David King (and now-retired Jenny Clark MBE). Every county in the UK has at least one bat hospital, so any member of the public who finds an injured bat can find their local bat group online or call the Bat

Conservation Trust (https://www.bats.org.uk/) to help rescue their own Zorro. And please do. Most of our bat species are endangered through lack of habitat, injured by our beloved cat pets, and all bat species in the UK are protected. Bats depend on us. And the ones you may spot, circling in gardens, are probably eating mosquitoes before the mosquitoes chomp on you: a tiny common or soprano pipistrelle, weighing less than a pound coin, can munch 3,000 mozzies in one night, making them my personal heroes. (No one ever said ecologists have to like all the species.)

I should also clarify that badger bait used by ecologists (lacing food with inert pellets to establish a badger's territory) has nothing to do with illegal badger baiting. Badgers dig latrines along their borders so an ecologist can map the latrines and match the colour of the pellets that end up here, from the location of the bait, to see the extent of a badger's territory. But the illegal activity of catching and forcing badgers to fight dogs still happens in the countryside. As with bats, every county in the UK has a badger group (found on the Badger Trust website, https://www.badgertrust.org.uk/) who conduct badger surveys and also campaign to stop the various ways badgers are persecuted – which is why badgers are legally protected. Reporting sightings of badgers killed on the road, or crimes relating to setts, to the Badger Trust can help gather data to combat crimes. Badger groups are usually full of members who are as tenacious as the species they champion, so you can depend on any records provided being acted upon.

And finally, the clue that showed Nell how the murderer approached Manor House Farm was due to the humble dormouse. With the traveller's joy threading through the hazel trees being flayed, one poor dormouse would be missing an arboreal highway to scurry along. I remember being fascinated to learn that this mouse, named for its sleepiness and trademark pose of fluffy golden tail curled over a sleeping, snuffled-up face, lives up trees in the summer months and hibernates on the ground in winter. But I also have to admit that this fascination was relatively short-lived: after doing what felt like roughly a million voluntary surveys across four counties, including one in such a torrential downpour it destroyed a mobile phone under two layers of waterproofs, I am yet to see a dormouse in the fur. Plenty of meek wood mice, and plenty of the hardcore yellow-necked mice (the Mafia of mice-world, who bite first, ask questions later) – and indeed, plenty of *bites* later – still no dormice. That's ecology for you. But it is a reminder that this is another species which is protected because it's on the brink of extinction due to habitat loss – and that the only species who can do anything about that, is us.

Author Bio

After spending sixteen years as an ecologist, crawling through undergrowth and studying nocturnal habits of animals (and people), Dr Sarah Yarwood-Lovett naturally turned her mind to murder. She may have swapped badgers for bears when she emigrated from a quaint village in the South Downs to the wild mountains of the Pacific Northwest, but her books remain firmly rooted in the rolling downland she grew up in.

Forensically studying clues for animal activity has seen Sarah surveying sites all over the UK and around the world. She's re-discovered a British species thought to be extinct during her PhD, with her record held in London's Natural History Museum; debated that important question – do bats wee on their faces? – at school workshops; survived a hurricane on a coral atoll whilst scuba diving to conduct marine surveys; and given evidence as an expert witness.

Along the way, she's discovered a noose in an abandoned warehouse and had a survey de-railed by the bomb squad. Her unusual career has provided the perfect inspiration for a series of murder mysteries with an ecological twist – so, these days, Sarah's research includes consulting detectives, lawyers, judges and attending murder trials.

About Embla Books

Embla Books is a digital-first publisher of standout commercial adult fiction. Passionate about storytelling, the team at Embla publish books that will make you 'laugh, love, look over your shoulder and lose sleep'. Launched by Bonnier Books UK in 2021, the imprint is named after the first woman from the creation myth in Norse mythology, who was carved by the gods from a tree trunk found on the seashore – an image of the kind of creative work and crafting that writers do, and a symbol of how stories shape our lives.

Find out about some of our other books and stay in touch:

Twitter, Facebook, Instagram: @emblabooks
Newsletter: https://bit.ly/emblanewsletter